House of Glass

SUSAN FLETCHER

virago

VIRAGO

First published in Great Britain in 2018 by Virago Press
This paperback edition published in 2019 by Virago Press

1 3 5 7 9 10 8 6 4 2

A CIP catalogue record for this book
is available from the British Library.

ISBN 978-0-349-00767-0

Typeset in Bembo by M Rules
Printed and bound in Great Britain by
Clays Ltd, Elcograf S.p.A.

Papers used by Virago are from well-managed forests
and other responsible sources.

MIX
Paper from
responsible sources
FSC
www.fsc.org   FSC® C104740

Virago Press
An imprint of
Little, Brown Book Group
Carmelite House
50 Victoria Embankment
London EC4Y 0DZ

An Hachette UK Company
www.hachette.co.uk

www.virago.co.uk

Susan Fletcher was born in 1979 in Birmingham. She is the author of the bestselling *Eve Green* (winner of the Whitbread First Novel Award), *Oystercatchers*, *Witch Light* and *Let Me Tell You About A Man I Knew*.

'Brilliant characterisation, beautiful and mesmerising story: like entering a dream. I was spellbound and couldn't do anything else but keep reading' Jill Dawson

'A gorgeous, darkly gothic treat' Amanda Craig

'*House of Glass* may start as a ghost story but turns into something much more profound: a lyrical examination of how women carve lives out of a male-dominated society, even with a war looming that will change everyone. I was surprised and moved' Tracy Chevalier

'Magical and often extremely moving. A gem' *Daily Mail*

'Moody and atmospheric – and just as compelling [as Daphne du Maurier] ... Tense, thrilling and a true page-turner' *Image* magazine

'Fletcher's prose is dreamily sensual, full of the light and heat of an English summer, an eerie contrast to the shadows of the oncoming First World War ... *House of Glass* is a beautifully written, gloriously Gothic story of gardens, ghosts and old, uneasy grudges' Eithne Farry, *Sunday Express*

'With echoes of Daphne du Maurier, *House of Glass* is a mesmerising ghost story set in a dilapidated country house where things go bump in the night' *Good Housekeeping*

'A very satisfying read with a clever twist. I loved it' *Four Shires*

'As her heroine faces increasing dangers, Fletcher neatly changes the direction in which her story is heading. What seems initially a tale of the supernatural develops into something more' *Sunday Times*

For Olli

I

My structure is not quite right. By this, I mean my bones – the part on which the rest of me is stretched, stitched into place. I have marrow and cavities; I have the smooth, rounded ends which are cupped by other bones, and no part is missing. But my skeleton is frail. I creak with any transference of weight. In my childhood, I fractured so frequently – with small gestures, with the simple act of looking up – that doctors winced and shook their heads. She is imperfect, they said.

Its Latin name is too long to be said frequently or well. *Osteogenesis imperfecta.* Twenty-two letters which click in the mouth and which, at first, we tried slowly. My mother would whisper the name like a prayer or incantation. I, too, mouthed it privately. But this name was soon discarded and, in its place, it became *Clara's bones.* I heard it in hospital rooms and corridors, and this more accessible, intimate name implied that it was my complaint alone. That there was no other person in London or elsewhere whose ribs fractured on sneezing. Whose teeth might crack with a tap of a spoon.

These days, its grasp on me is less. I still have my curious shape. The whites of my eyes still retain their bluish tinge, as milk does, in a glass. Also, my skin is paler where it has stretched to accommodate a mended bone – a lifted rib, my indented clavicle – so I know I will never be truly free of this Latin name or its meaning. But I am, at least, fully grown. My bones have strengthened and settled themselves.

Yet as a child, I broke often. I lived in a world of doctors and splints, of tinctures which brought strange bone-dreams. Parts of me would swell; bruises would move over my body like storms or high tides – tender, and in every dark shade. The first break I can recall came in winter; I stood on the step, watching the snow, and what caused the audible crack in my arm was not the fall itself but the sudden grasp of my mother, lifting me up, hoping to prevent the fall. The instinct in her: *no, no!* But her act caused the snap in the humerus bone, and afterwards, she had her own pain. She rocked at my bedside, murmuring.

Later, a fractured jaw on Regent Street. Once, a stranger's elbow cracked my ribs and I exhaled very quickly, lowered myself to the ground as if punctured. In Trafalgar Square, my left shoulder dropped from its socket as I reached for a passing bird, and my scream sent every bird into the air so that I felt their downward draught. After this, the doctors were clear: I must have an indoors life. Until I was fully grown, I must be kept within my own four walls for my safety. And when my mother protested – *but she is a child!* – they spoke of the other, smaller bones in my neck. Vertebrae, and their implications. 'Do you understand, Mrs Waterfield? What might happen to your daughter?' They named the delicate part of my skull that could crack like an egg.

Ours became a house of cushioning. Of velvet and goose down, embroidered pillows, Persian rugs and silk. There was, too, a globe. A rocking horse that I could touch but not ride. And they'd bring home what they thought I might miss from the blustery world: fir cones and pigeon feathers, the scent of horses on my mother's red gloves which I'd inhale, eyes closed. Tales of how the river had looked at twilight. How the carol singers sang, despite the rain. When Mr Jamrah's menagerie acquired a bear, my mother lifted her arms and said, 'The bear was this high, Clara! This wide!'

Flowers in every room. Maps of distant countries on the walls. One autumn, I requested a real, physical offering of the leaves I'd read about in books – sycamore, beech, chestnut, oak – so my mother searched all the London parks. Daily she'd describe what she'd seen: the prettiest hat or the finest moustache, or a horse with a mark on its head like a star. She'd remark on chimney sweeps or fox-fur stoles, and if she'd not left the house that day, she'd offer her Indian stories, which made me feel travelled and wise. The corners of furniture were wrapped in cloth. Glassware was kept out of reach. For the sake of my teeth, Millicent – our maid – stewed fruit until it had no shape or flavour. She'd make softer gingerbread.

But above all, there were books. Books were my consolation. For if I could not walk into the bright, blowing world I could, at least, read of it; books, I was told, contained it all. So for my seventh birthday, the dining room was transformed into a library; a room of shelves and maps and tapestries, with a reading lamp with a fringed shade and a grand piano which I couldn't play for the sake of my fingers and wrists but my mother could, and she played it well. There was a chaise longue which was, at first, the colour of moss. But in time – as I read more, studied more maps – this deep, velvety green became the shade of hummingbirds' wings or Othello's envy or the gems which hid in equatorial soil. The green of a tiny jungle frog.

My mother, as governess. She had insisted she knew far more than enough to educate her only child – and didn't she? Chemicals and multiplication; constellations and verbs in French. And she knew, of course, the human skeleton; she'd learned every bone since my birth – its location and purpose, its Latin name. The sounds they made, on breaking. She'd list joints like continents.

We had books on the Arctic tundra. On seashells. On dinosaurs. How bees made honey. The Crimean War. We talked into the evening of the highest peaks on earth and the route of Magellan and the properties of mercury and the territories of owls and the name Pankhurst – *Do you hear me, Clara?* – and all the Greek gods and goddesses; later, their Roman names. Sometimes I would tap on Patrick's door so that he'd look up from his desk, lower his pen. 'What have you learned today?' And I'd inform him brightly: Saturn is the planet with rings. King Richard led the first Crusades. And he'd say, 'Goodness me!' – as if he had not known this.

Novels, too. Or my mother read them, at least. She had an appetite for them: Fielding and the Brontës and such huge translations of Russian books that they might break a bone on their own. But mostly I preferred what was true. I wanted facts, laid out by those who had clambered or swum or danced or had *done* what they had claimed to, not solely imagined it. For birthdays, I asked for almanacs. I liked calendars, for their form. And I have since wondered if this was compensation; if, since my own structure could not be trusted, I looked elsewhere for what could be fully depended upon: dictionaries, charts, miscellanies. The leathery, scented book on human anatomy gave me far more than bones: organs and capillaries, musculature and words such as ventricle. Botanical drawings. Encyclopaedias of birds.

*

4

My stepfather provided these. In the evenings, Patrick would return with books in his arms; he'd stamp the rain from his shoes in the hall, and I thought this act might shatter him for he was thin, angular. Patrick: so pale that he seemed bloodless; a shy, bespectacled man who spoke economically. He rarely smiled with his eyes. Nor did he read books very often, and he'd never left London. It seemed strange, therefore, that such a man should make a library for his wife's creaky daughter or buy a rocking horse. But perhaps he had sympathy, of a kind. For Patrick also knew the indoors life.

By day, he worked in a bank near Charing Cross; by night and at weekends, he'd spend his time in his study, a room of half-drawn curtains and mahogany wood, with a carriage clock that pinged on the hour. In there, he'd read newspapers. He'd smoke a pipe. On occasion, he'd play chess with my mother with the door ajar, so that I might watch them – a silent, slow enterprise in which they said very little; they'd only remark on the game itself or exchange a word or two on my bones. Yet they seemed contented with this – with their marriage, in which there were wide desert places. Sometimes Patrick played chess with his friend, instead – a cautious man with a scent of pomade. I could not observe their matches for he'd always close the door and the keyhole was too narrow to peep through. I'd loiter in the hallway instead, eyeing the trilby hat which hung there.

My mother – Charlotte – was a wholly different land. She was radiance and gestures and discovery. Also, she preferred the outdoors life, so that she'd often stand barefoot in our garden for no reason at all that I could tell. She was not tall but Charlotte had substance to her. She could fight, answer back; she'd march for women's rights and, on returning, would lay herself down on the green chaise longue with

5

a flush of rage or pride or exhaustion. She had, too, such strange, exotic stories of her childhood that I'd think of them for days afterwards: of the sorbets at Peliti's hotel, or night-flowering blooms which lost their scent at sunrise. Of the leopards that slept in trees with their four paws and tail hanging down.

A peculiar pairing, Millicent said, as she removed crusts for me. And how could I disagree with her? They were a moon and a sun in their differences. One retreated to a darkened room. The other preferred the early mornings, seemed made of light.

My small, wallpapered world. I was studious and cared for – and I could chirp like a bird, on good days. But I also possessed a dark temper. I might withdraw into my books for weeks, eat nothing; I could rail against my confinement as if it were the worst of cruelties. I'd try to open windows or throw books across the room – both acts that my mother would flash her eyes at. 'Your bones, Clara! Remember?' Once, I announced that my bones were, in fact, perfectly fine, that I no longer required a monitored life, and I dressed as if intending to walk into London; I pulled on Millicent's scarf and hat, requested my mother to let me pass, but she refused. She stood against the front door with her forefinger raised and a fiery expression. Reminded me of dislocations.

Petulant, Millicent called me – I heard her mutter the word to a chicken as she plucked it – and I'd not heard this before. In the dictionary I found its definition: *child-ishly sulky*. This was a new addition to my personal list of adjectives which I'd gathered and stored over the years: stubborn, indulged, unfortunate, rude. Sad. Demanding. *Poor little thing.* I was tired, too; an effect of my condition was a deep fatigue that would enter my bones like damp in the evenings. But I was also so tired of this way of living – of the long, monotonous days in which I knew wind only from how it sounded in the chimney breast, knew life only from the written word. My mother recognised this. She knew when I needed a careful embrace. And at night, as she moved the blankets around me, she'd speak of my adult days to come, in which I'd be strong, quick and unbruised. 'One day you will ride horses.'

Yet the breaks still came. All the cushions and reassurances could not prevent the occasional splintered tooth or the snap of a toe against furniture. Knees unbuckled themselves. I broke ribs with bad dreams or a single, huge sneeze in midwinter – and one afternoon, in my teens, I knocked my hip on the banister. There was a clear, audible crack; the pain was so fast and violent that my mouth filled with bitter water and the world was black, momentarily. A femoral break: it asked for three months of a thick, drugged sleep, of being strapped to a wooden board so that I lacked all dignity. I lost weight in this time. When able to, I'd cry – silently, facing the wall. The only consolation came from my mother's care and her best stories – of the country she'd lived in before me, where rain came on the hour. Where, in markets, men bartered with ice.

She had been born Charlotte Pugh. Daughter of a colonel in the British Army and his wife of proverbs and duty; a wife who had hated Calcutta. Hated the heat and the markets. Hated the smell of the harbour and the tiktiki lizards that ran across sideboards and left their droppings on plates. So every year, in the hotter months, they moved to Simla in the far north. Land of high tea and lawn tennis. Games of whist.

'You liked it there?'

A shrine to a monkey god on Jakku Hill. Stray dogs sleeping beneath their casuarina tree. 'Yes. I liked it there.'

'So why did you leave?'

She spoke of a mynah bird being struck with a stick and released, for having said an ungodly word – and in this way I sensed that Charlotte had been instructed to go. Why? She did not answer directly. She only said that she'd been too bold and black-feathered for her parents, who'd favoured faith, discipline; they could not forgive her – and what did it matter? 'I'm perfectly happy now.'

She smiled, yet I was not convinced by this. 'Could not forgive you for what?'

But my mother would not answer. She tended to my blankets; believing she'd heard Millicent calling she stood, left the room – and I looked at her chair, detecting the lie.

I asked again. I would not be dissuaded. On an airless night in late summer, as I lay on my wooden board and my mother read beside me with one leg tucked beneath her, I said, 'Was it my father's fault?'

She looked up from her poetry, penny-eyed.

'The reason they sent you away. For being black-feathered. Was it him?'

Charlotte seemed captured, stunned. She closed the book slowly, set it aside; for a while, she studied the opposite wall, and then she partly answered. 'I was nineteen, Clara. I was young, yet I thought that I was older than that; wiser – but I was not wiser. And afterwards, I boarded a boat called *Persia* and stood at the back. Watched as Calcutta grew smaller.'

She'd held the railing for hours, she said. She'd felt nauseous from far more than rough water. And I understood some of this tale, but not all. 'They sent you away because of me? Because I was growing inside you?'

'You? Oh no, not because of you. How could it have been you? You're my best thing, remember? No – I lacked a wedding ring.'

'Why did you lack it?'

'I did, that's all.'

'Who was he? My proper father?' Asked plainly, as if the question was small.

But the question was not small. It closed my mother suddenly, as a draught might close a door emphatically. She rose with the book in her hand. 'Your father,' she said, 'is Patrick. Your surname is Waterfield. Now, Clara, do you need more water?'

A new understanding, that night. It felt like a curious exchange: hill stations and frangipani and family – for what? For London. For an emphasis on grey. For a life with a man who rarely touched her, knew nothing of books or monsoons. And why had that exchange been made? For decency's sake, I supposed. A woman with child could not be alone; she'd needed to become a man's wife. A child, too, needed a father in its life. And I thought, no wonder she marches. No wonder she tells me that a person's strength does not, in fact, come from their bones.

As daylight came, I knew that my question had hurt her; I knew that I loved my mother too much to ever ask such a question again. And what did it matter anyway? I was a Waterfield. Patrick had tales of my first weeks of life – as a father should. So I would not ask again about the black-feathered bird or wedding rings. I dismissed *Persia*, rolling south.

As for the femoral fracture, it did not mend. Or rather, it mended in a fashion which disregarded measurements. My left leg shortened itself. I gained a rise and fall.

'Perhaps,' my mother offered, 'it will improve with walk-ing. With proper distances.' For there were no long journeys to be made in those wallpapered rooms.

The doctors agreed with her: it was time. And on a bright, cold Thursday morning in late October – three days after my eighteenth birthday – I was deemed strong enough, at last, to leave the house with her.

I woke early for it. My mother pinned my hair, dabbed a little rose water on my wrists and admired my reflection; she stood behind me in the hallway with her hands on my shoulders, and we looked so alike in that moment. 'Are you ready, Clara?'

I entered a world of leaf smells and pipe smoke, of the sound of geese overhead. Of bridges spanning the Thames and omni-buses and barrel organs and such air that it was like drinking cold water, over and over, and for a while, I forgot about my rise and fall. But then, I remembered. I caught my reflection in a shop window. And I walked deliberately, willing my limp to lessen or go. But it stayed. It would not leave me: a deep, rotational grind that meant I could not move quickly. My roll like seawater. I was my own pestle and mortar.

Cripple. This, too, entered my life that day. *Did you see that girl?* On hearing this, my mother tried to distract me with ornate iron railings and a poster for a circus act. But I heard and I did not forget it.

That evening, I said very little. My bones ached from walking. I was exhausted, coal-scented. But mostly, I was bereft; I could not bear the knowledge that I would limp all my life. I would be *cripple* for always, now; I'd never be as others were. And where was the *one day* that my mother had whispered of, to comfort me? In which I'd ride horses? I'd never ride horses.

*

I had to use a cane. Patrick bought it for me and, in its way, it was beautiful. Walnut wood with a silver tip. A round silver handle that pushed into my palm so that, at first, I'd bruise there. My cane made a small tapping sound on the ground as I went.

I told myself that I would not retreat into half-lit rooms. I would not hide from *cripple* or cry in the evenings – secretly, childishly – because no explorer or queen did that. Rather, I'd walk forwards. I'd see the art and streets and monuments that I'd heard of; I'd walk into London's maps. My mother came too. She stayed between me and the pavement's edge; she'd flash her eyes at those who came too near or moved too quickly and in wet weather, she'd summon a carriage so that I might not slip. But mostly, she named what we passed so that I might know it, understand it. A hansom cab. A hobble skirt. The Alhambra Theatre in Leicester Square. The violet-sellers and the Baptist preachers and the penny-pies being sold on street corners by boys who looked half my age and size. She explained, too, currency. Named every fruit in the marketplace. And in the National Gallery she led me to art in which the Magi kneeled or Venus reclined or in which Samson's hair was cut, so that books seemed tiny, insubstantial.

Afterwards, she took me for afternoon tea on the Strand. 'What did you think of the paintings, Clara?' The lace of the napkins was as delicate as breath; the cakes were topped with pink sugared roses. And as my mother poured the tea, I realised that beauty was in these perfections. It was in the intricate pattern on the teaspoons. It had been, too, in the flushed, naked Venus and every bared shoulder, in every plump thigh. Never mind what books had offered me: beauty was dark-haired and dark-mouthed; it was curved, in a way that I lacked entirely.

And as my mother used the sugar tongs, I realised that my bones were not my only strangeness. I seemed to be too thin. Too little – for I was less than my mother's height and she was known for being small. And I was too pale, by far: I had milk-coloured brows and eyelashes and hair which, once, my mother had compared to moonlight. I'd liked these stories, when younger. But now I wondered what part of me was worthy or acceptable. *Crippled, pale, petulant.* I stared at this realisation as my mother stirred her tea.

At night, in the bathroom, I studied the fingers that could not fully straighten; the smooth, vacated gums where molars had been. But, in the mirror, I also examined my translucency. My small, hard structure. The veins in my wrists seemed to match no other blue.

I was so absorbed in my appearance at this time that I failed to see the change in hers. Failed to see my mother's loss of weight, or her own, slower walking pace. But the seasons changed – and with them, I began to find my mother sleeping in chairs. On rising from them, she'd seem cautious; she'd reach for walls or furniture and these movements were new, did not suit her.

There was meaning in this. I understood that a woman who'd swum the width of Indian rivers should not have weakened so much that the piano lid required both hands. She should not fold at the waist for no reason. And in early September, with the swallows' departure, I walked with my mother to the nearest stretch of the Thames. Here, she offered words to me. Uterine. Fibrous. 'They say I have months, perhaps.' She smiled as if these words were acceptable; and, as if I accepted them, I nodded and looked across the water to where the trees were losing their green.

My mother did have months, but not many. Her hair

greyed; her cheeks hollowed themselves. Doctors closed their bags with care, as if for the last time. And I thought, but I am the one you come for. I am the imperfect one.

Patrick hovered on the landing. Millicent moved on the boundaries of sickness – changing linen, running baths. And I abandoned my new outdoors life for a chair by her bedside; it was my turn to soothe or offer water. In her final days, my mother turned to me and asked if I might read to her, from a book she had loved since her childhood. *Indian Tales*; a blue, clothbound, fraying book with a red ribbon marker and mildew stains. On its title page I found her name – *Miss Charlotte Pugh* – written in her teenaged hand. But I also found, in its pages, tales of a prince with jasmine-scented laughter, of tigers that spoke. Children grow into adults and adults, I realised, return to their childish state.

She faded, like cloth. She shrank as if in water.

Once, on turning, she smiled, so that I thought she was in London with me. But she said, 'The mango, Clara. It is too high in the tree.' And my mother, I knew, was not with me; she was in a land where white was the colour of mourning, where monkeys had learned the art of theft. And I thought, how will I navigate my life in her absence? She had been its heartbeat. She had been everything.

'I was born in a monsoon,' she said. 'Did I tell you?'

'Tell me again.' But she closed her eyes.

In the first, early hours of 1914, my mother winced and softened; I thought this was merely a dream moving through her so I soothed her, stroked her hand. But in that moment, she died.

Later, I joined Patrick in the garden. It was nearly dawn. The air was sharp; above us, we saw the first pinkish light of day. We stood by the pear tree without any words for a long time, looking up.

'You mustn't think,' he said, 'that I didn't love her.'

With this, he went indoors. Somewhere, Millicent prayed. I stood with my cane, watched the light change, so that rooftops and branches became clearer, and I considered the simple fact of her death. She had, for a time, been here. She'd been warm and scented. She'd played the piano, rallied for votes and she'd been able to whistle so loudly that horses responded. Where was she now?

I heard the city wake. Birds began to sing. I knew that the dictionaries and diagrams would tell me the truth: that her heart had stopped beating. That her lungs had stilled. She was dead and I would not see her again.

In the days that followed, I emptied the library of books. Millicent found me taking them down, filling boxes, running my hands over shelves to ensure that there were none left to be seen or read. She stood in the doorway, appalled. 'What are you doing?'

'We have no need for books now.' I had read them all, so why keep them? Why maintain a library at all? 'No one else reads in this house.' I gathered my mother's sheet music. Lifted maps from the walls.

Millicent stayed away from me that afternoon. She had endured two decades of various tempers from me but this was, she sensed, a new territory. She had glimpsed my grief and did not wish to go near it. On hearing Patrick's key in the door, she rushed to him. 'Clara is . . .' Furious. Quite mad, even.

After this, Patrick entered the library as if it contained a wild creature; he held his hat to his chest, looked at the shelves with unblinking eyes. 'What's happening, Clara?

What are you doing? Stop this – do you hear?' But such orders did not suit him; he was too thin and ill at ease with himself. He lacked all authority, and so I kept placing books in boxes. I dropped a cloth over the globe. Patrick, I'm sure, wished to stop me; they were his books, after all. But he could not grab my wrists, could not clutch my upper arms. He could only give orders, which I chose to ignore, and he backed away, closed the door.

Sometimes I'd stare at the piano keys. Find her indentations in chairs.

But mostly, I walked. I walked because there was nothing else to do; because I wanted to be away from the house, in which the cushions and bath taps and spoons still retained a sense of her. Where the stairs echoed with the sound of her rushing down. I wished to be away, too, from the grief of others which I could not bear. If I wasn't crying, why should they? Wasn't my loss far greater than theirs? Patrick would look out of windows. Millicent prayed as she wandered the house or wept into her floury hands.

So I walked – through parks, over bridges. I looked down the stairs in the warm, lit cavity of the Underground. I stood in the polished halls of department stores and galleries. I limped down alleyways so narrow that my hands brushed the brickwork on either side of me, emerged into squares. I passed cathedrals and fountains and monuments and rallies and arrests and market stalls and, one afternoon, I found a flight of dark, rotting steps that led down to the shoreline. I stood by the Thames at low tide. Its shores were slick with weed and decomposition; under bridges, men sat by fires. And I missed her so much, as I stood there. By the river, I longed for her singing voice or piano scales or explanations and I returned at dusk with a blackened hem, exhausted and shaking with cold.

Millicent threw her hands in the air. 'Look at the state of you!'

Patrick stepped forwards from his room like a ghost and asked, 'Where have you been? Where do you go? Clara, what were you thinking of?'

Hyde Park, I answered. Piccadilly. The shoreline.

'The shoreline? And what if you had fallen? What of the people there?'

'Which people?'

That night, we talked until twelve. Patrick suggested I knew very little of the world. That yes, I might be able to list the Plantagenet monarchs or explain refraction – but what of other matters? Such as crossing Oxford Street safely? 'Do you even know,' he demanded, 'how to board an omnibus? Or the art of polite conversation? The world, Clara, is a dangerous place.'

The art of polite conversation? I was incredulous at this, for how many people did Patrick see or converse with? Only his friend in the trilby hat who seemed just as mute. 'Are you,' I retorted, 'proficient in that?' Fast, stinging words which surprised me, but I was angry and lost and heartsore; I missed her too much to find words for it. I was inexpressibly tired, too, so I bade him goodnight, climbed the stairs stiffly and requested a bowl of warm water in which to bathe my feet, so that I heard *ungrateful* muttered in my wake.

But I knew Patrick was right. I could stand before portraits in galleries and recognise their subjects, yet I had no proper friends. I was poor at conversation. And no, I'd never boarded an omnibus. So on a blizzarding day, I took myself to Regent Street; I watched how others boarded and alighted one. I observed who they paid and how, and overheard the words they used. And then, clutching my cane, I boarded myself – and like this I came to know the interior of buses, the neat brass buttons of the conductors and the sense of human proximity which meant breath and warmth and varying smells. I cleared the steam from the window with my sleeve. Sometimes I drowsed with the movement of it.

Daily I took the bus. Patrick provided the money; I insisted it was a new, good education for me, and he could not challenge this. I learned which seats I favoured, how to pull the rope to request a stop; I discovered such boroughs as Finsbury and Lambeth and the observatory at Greenwich this way. And on a February morning, I stepped down from the bus in a place called Kew. This was a name I knew. For here, there were famous gardens, with rhododendron walks and glasshouses and pagodas. I'd read of them in books.

I entered through the gates of Kew Gardens on the twelfth day of February. My mother had been dead for forty-two days – she'd been in the ground for thirty-nine – and Kew was grey, desolate. Its grass was cropped by wintering geese; its lake had thickened with ice so that I asked myself, what is this? Why is this known, or written of? It seemed no different to other parks.

I decided to go home. But as I turned, I saw it: an extraordinary domed building of glass. A temple, or palace. I entered it and left February behind. England, too, was gone. For the Palm House at Kew contained canopies and ferns and damp wooden benches; palm leaves brushed my hair as I passed. Vines twisted on metalwork; condensation pooled on beams and, having pooled, dripped on my shoulders and the backs of my hands. A droplet hung so perfectly at the tip of a leaf that I stood by it, waiting. Small handwritten signs announced such words as *Indochina* or *frangipani*.

Now I wanted to be nowhere else. I was done with crowds and London's streets. Here was a new beginning. The betelnut's feathery leaves. The soursop and the kalabash tree. I'd move forwards to read their names. I'd wonder, too, how these plants might have looked in their homeland – if jewel-coloured birds had flown up to their branches, if they had offered shelter in rains that came without warning. And I began to write down what I liked of each plant: its brief, rare flowerings, or how, in its motherland, bats would sip from it. Their Latin names: *Crescentia cujete. Ficus benghalensis.*

Sometimes I'd drowse there; the heat and my own lasting fatigue meant I'd lower myself onto benches – and I was half sleeping, like this, when I met him. It was an overcast March afternoon. He stepped forwards. 'Excuse me?'

I rose quickly, awkwardly. I gestured with my cane, protecting myself, and the man stepped back, lifted his palms as if to show he meant no harm. He wore a cloth cap that had softened with heat; he was grey-haired, unshaven. 'Forgive me. I did not mean to startle you ... You come here often, I think?' He had seen me several times. Had simply thought to ask if I needed assistance, with my laboured walking and my stoop. Later, he'd confess to me that he'd thought I was a child.

Forbes. The foreman of the glasshouses – Temperate and Palm – with boots that creaked as I followed him. 'These plants,' he said, 'are like children to me.' In his wake, I saw how he praised the plants on either side of him. He'd speak of their history and purpose, list their characteristics. 'This cycad plant is a male ... see?' And when I demanded more

18

from him – brusquely, with appetite – he did not seem to object. Rather, he seemed pleased to speak freely: of how the banyan could outlive dynasties, how the brugmansia could cause hallucinations. There were, he said, seeds of trees which could drift across oceans like round, polished boats to find their new home. 'Whole oceans. They find new continents. And these seeds might have many years at sea in all weathers and yet survive. Is that not astounding?' Sea beans, he called them.

He'd press the aloe leaves to show their softness. Or he'd reach for the tendrils of jasmine, lower them to me in his cupped hand. 'Smell them, Miss Waterfield. That smell . . . '

'Where does it grow?'

'China. India. All parts of Asia.'

I had not gone to Kew for company. But here, I sensed an opportunity, firstly to converse politely as Patrick had wished for. (Forbes liked talking, after all: he preferred words to silence; if there were no words, he tended to hum.) Secondly, I wanted to learn beyond the page; to learn from a man whose botanical knowledge was, perhaps, worth twenty books. So I began to look for him. I'd seek his step-ladder or a movement in the high branches; I listened for any sound that was not water or air. And on finding him, I sought his knowledge – the truths of these plants, their habitats and their practical uses.

Forbes never asked me why I wished to know. He'd simply clear his throat and show me how to clean ferns, explain why the citrus trees needed magnesium, how the pelargoniums were prone to blight. How he'd light huge fires of tobacco plant in the Temperate House twice a year to fumigate the plants from mites and flies and all manner of bugs. 'And it works,' he said, 'although it does leave us all with a cough for a day or two.' Also, he loaned books to me. I'd carry them home on the bus – ancient volumes with thick, distorted pages in which the nature and requirements of plants were laid down as if they were heroes. The onyanga plant of the deserts of German south-west Africa, which consisted of merely two leaves and a root and could live without water for five years; hedysarum, which danced of its own accord; the baobab, which offered such strange and sparse foliage that it was said it had been turned upside down by a vengeful god.

'You were awake all night?' Patrick asked this, having seen my light.

'Yes. Reading.'

'Books? Which ones?' He was confused by this, for we had so few left in the house.

Linnaeus. White fly. How conversation was an exchange, of a kind. But also I learned about him: Edward Forbes. Whose thick, blackened hands were curiously adept at deadheading, or tying knots in string. Who'd push his tongue into his cheek in concentration. Forbes had his own phrases, too. He'd swap *yes* for *right you are*, and I understood that his accent was not the same as mine. By the banyan, I asked him. 'Where are you from?'

Scotland. I knew it on maps and had, long ago, read of uprisings. Of Presbyterians and snow. But I had not, until now, known the sound of a Scottish voice and I marvelled at its musicality. 'I'm from Auld Reekie,' he said, brushing his hands of soil. And as he explained this further, I thought, there is so much to know.

I had little to offer in return. I had no proper tales of my own. And Forbes – sensing this – never asked for them. Yet one afternoon, as he was pruning the plumbago on his stepladder, he asked, 'Miss Waterfield? May I ask if you have a mother who looks like you? Fair-haired and fine-featured? Also very small?' He'd seen her, he said. She'd come to Kew from time to time, pressed her ear against the mango's trunk.

I nodded. 'That was her.'

Was. He understood. He had already known, perhaps, that I carried a bereavement. Detected the hidden anger in me. He adjusted his cap. 'It never goes,' he said. 'You survive it – you do. But it is a different life to the one you had before.'

Later, too, he said, 'Tell me. What is next for you?'

We were standing outside the Temperate House. Late April, and the tulips were shining; we stood side by side, admiring them. Did he mean in the next half-hour? Or in the weeks to come? But then I understood: he was asking about the years ahead. And I felt weak at that. This was a question I'd never asked myself, and as I stared at the tulip bed, I saw my whole future as if written down. Patrick would find a husband for me. He'd locate a man of wealth and fine social standing; he'd offer a dowry to compensate for my bones and my stubborn nature and the unlikelihood of children. *A wife.* To take a new name. To be governed and grateful. To return to a life of wallpapered rooms, in which travelling was done through books.

At that, I dropped my cane.

Forbes retrieved it. 'Miss Waterfield?' He led me to a bench with a view of magnolias, and here my words rushed out of me. Suddenly, I wished to speak to him: of breaks and dislocations. Of opiate dreams and yellowish bruises. How *osteogenesis imperfecta* had always seemed too strange to say but sounded, now, botanical to me: a twisted, dark-flowering vine which lacked beauty and would never relinquish its grip.

I spoke of globes. Of wallpaper. Of how I'd had hopes of riding horses and dancing or jumping from a height. I spoke of Millicent's prayers for me; of her later, fervent prayers for my mother, who'd died in the first few hours of 1914 – and what good were prayers anyway? They'd served no purpose. I was still crooked; she was still dead. And I talked of the black shoreline. Of the omnibus and the galleries and the dark-haired beauties with wise shining eyes. How my mother's name should have stayed Pugh, as she'd wished it to, but she'd been ordered onto a boat and had married a man she never knew, and this seemed so unfair to me. A travesty. A waste of a life. 'Why can't we simply live as we'd like to? Why are there rules? And more for women?'

Forbes was still. Such words needed time to move through, I knew that. He pushed his tongue into his cheek, eyed the far distance, and we sat in silence for a time. 'Clara? May I call you that? I have something I'd like to show you.'

He stood, and I followed him.

It was a letter. A folded rectangle of perfect white. Handwritten, in such a slanting, decadent hand that I imagined the author had brought the words to his lips and blown. The letterhead was in gold.

'What is this?'

'A note from a gentleman. He wants to buy plants from Kew. To fill his own glasshouse in Gloucestershire with citrus trees and succulents. Such letters come, from time to time.'

A man called Mr Fox. And yes, in his letter, he was requesting all the finest plants – *a small, private paradise for my glasshouse*. But he was asking, too, for a person. For someone from Kew to travel with them, to lift these plants from their crates and establish a room of colour and scent and spectacle.

22

I wish it to be the talk of other country houses. And I looked up at Forbes, shook my head.

'I don't know enough,' I said.

'You do. There would be no propagation. No task that you have not already witnessed or read of. These are simple duties that would ask little of you.'

'Why not others? You?'

'Me? I have Mrs Forbes and I don't wish to leave her for a month, as Mr Fox requires. But you? The independent life that you seem to want? You will need money to have it, Clara. Look.' He showed me. The sum that was written down, underlined. 'For a month. That's all.'

I saw my own reflection in his eyes. I knew his hands were restless, closing and unclosing like weathered blooms. And I said, 'Who is dead, Mr Forbes?' For I knew that someone was.

'We buried a child of nineteen months old, one winter. It was many years ago now, but we buried a part of ourselves that day.'

He considered the tiled floor. And I understood that Forbes, too, had tried to lessen his loss with plumbago and citrus; he'd distracted himself with the intricate care of these plants. How old might his daughter have been, if she'd lived? I didn't ask. But I wondered if she might have been twenty. If, in her infancy, she'd been fair-haired.

'Clara, I thought you were a child when I saw you on that bench, but you rose as if wanting to fight me. You have a strength I've not seen in many men.'

He placed the letter in my hand, closed my fingers over it.

'The house is called Shadowbrook,' he said.

Did its name seem brighter for being in gold? Or for being seen in the afternoon light?

Later, Patrick blinked as if I'd spoken a new language. 'Gloucestershire?'

I'd be met at the train station, I told him. There would be maids and a housekeeper and fine accommodation. I'd arrive a few days before the plants, so that I might settle, regain my strength. 'I want to do this,' I said.

Patrick shifted his jaw. I wondered if he'd try to forbid me. But perhaps he knew better than to do so. Also, wasn't this an opportunity? For me to learn of the world, as he'd wished me to? I wondered, too, if he was thinking of a month without my compressed grief and indignance, without my muddied boots in the hall. His sigh, when it came, was extended. He removed his spectacles, closed his eyes and pinched the sides of his nose. 'Yes, Clara, if this is what it takes. I know you are not happy here.'

I expected triumph, I think. But the feeling that came was, in fact, sorrow. It rushed in, like water; it began to rise. And as Patrick replaced his spectacles, hooked them carefully over his ears, I remembered the Christmas morning when he had revealed the rocking horse – a brocaded scarlet cloth, pulled aside. I saw him returning with books in his arms. And I'd never thought to ask why he'd married Charlotte Pugh. It hadn't occurred to me to do so. Now, I could find no answer to it. What had he gained in doing so? A reduction of freedom, a strong-willed wife and twenty years of care and worry and expenditure for a child who was not truly his. A crooked child, too.

Later, Patrick offered to catch the train with me. He knocked on my bedroom door. 'I could be,' he suggested, 'a form of chaperone.' He could assist in such matters as locating the platform, carrying my trunk. And I was softer, at that moment; I saw his tiredness. I sensed my debt to him could not be repaid, and perhaps, therefore, I should say yes

24

to him; yes, come with me to the station at Cheltenham Spa. But my pregnant mother had travelled from Calcutta to London without company and survived it. The warriors and adventurers in books had not had their stepfather to open their doors. And I felt a need to travel alone, to start my independent life with no one to help or depend on – for how else might I rely on myself? Live without assistance? So I thanked him, shook my head.

The twentieth of June 1914. The day before midsummer. I washed my hair and pinned it. I packed clothes, my hairbrush, and I set three books into my trunk: an encyclopaedia of plants and a guide to human anatomy – my two most reliable factual books. I packed, too, *Indian Tales*.

Patrick placed my trunk in the carriage. He closed the door and looked through the carriage window. 'Promise me,' he said, 'that you will always use your cane. Clara?'

I promised. With that, he stepped back. He rapped twice on the carriage door with his knuckles to inform the driver to move away, and the horses strained. Patrick stayed still, moved out of sight.

Forbes showed his own concern. At Paddington, he turned the brim of his hat through his hands and spoke of the stations I'd pass through. I must not stand, he said, before the train had fully stopped. I must be careful of the distance between the platform and the door. 'Cheltenham Spa,' he reminded me. 'His name is Fox.'

I lowered the train window and looked back. As Forbes grew smaller on the platform, I understood that Latin names and measurements could not offer this exact moment. They could not give me the scent of a train compartment or how sunlight could lie down on the floor in a perfect geometrical shape. How nervousness and excitement were similar in the way they quickened the heart. Paddington grew smaller until it was out of sight.

As the train moved into countryside, I had a sudden wish to unpin my hair. To set it free. It felt like the appropriate act – uncustomary, new. So, one by one, I removed the pins.

All summer, I would wear my hair like this. In time, I would be known for my cane, for my forthright manner of speaking and for this heavy, milk-white hair that swung in my wake and caught on low branches. It would grow even lighter, from sunlight, so that I'd be told, in August, that I glowed at dusk and belonged with the moths in the white garden. He'd say my hair was like phosphorescence.

I did not know this yet, of course. Nor did I know how Gloucestershire looked or sounded. But I'd felt fearless on the dark Thames shoreline and I felt fearless now, on this train. For what could be worse than the loss of her? This fact was as true as Darwin's finches or the moon's phases: my mother was gone. And the forty-two fractures in my life did not matter; nor did the bluish whites of my eyes or the list of adjectives I'd made, or my height. What mattered was that I had nothing left to lose. So I looked forwards as we raced under bridges, emerged from tunnels into light.

II

The train arrived at Cheltenham Spa in the early evening. I did what Forbes had advised: I asked for assistance with my trunk, thanked the gentleman and, on the platform, stepped back from the slamming doors. The train gave a warm, gritty blast of steam as it pulled away so that I saw nothing, at first. But when the steam thinned, I noticed a lone figure at the far end of the platform, with a cigarette and a nonchalant air.

I chose to stay as I was: I could not carry my trunk and required him to help me. On recognising this, the man flicked the cigarette away. He lifted himself from the wall on which he'd been leaning and walked towards me with a slow, casual gait.

'Miss Waterfield?'

A moustache. The smell of tobacco. 'Yes. Good afternoon.'

'It's evening. Your train was late. I've been waiting for more than an hour.'

This was not the response I'd expected. I stiffened, and was briefly inclined to speak sharply to him. The train's lateness was not my fault, after all. But I supposed this would be unhelpful. 'I will need help with my trunk, please.'

'From me?'

'Yes. Or from someone else. I can't carry it.'

The man sighed heavily, glanced back down the platform. I thought he might refuse to help me, or walk away, but he stooped, lifted my trunk by one handle and dragged it away at a pace I could not match, so that when I reached his car – burgundy in colour – he was already seated, waiting for me. Drumming his fingers on the steering wheel.

'Ready?'

I nodded. Entered the car awkwardly, knocking my wrist, so that I winced, cupped it. He witnessed this yet did not comment. He only cleared his throat, told me to shut the door. As we drove, I thought, I have landed on a strange shore, of tobacco stains and impatience and, it seemed, worse manners than mine. And I'd never sat in a car before.

'Are you Mr Fox?'

'No.'

'Then you work for him?'

His jaw was hard and defined. 'Yes, from time to time.'

'A butler?'

He scoffed. 'Do I look like a butler? If he needs to be driven, I drive him. If he needs something brought to him, I might oblige.'

'That sounds like a butler.'

'Not,' he said, 'a butler. But you speak as if you've had staff of your own.'

I studied his profile. He was offended by me, somehow. And whilst I knew the train had caused him to wait for an hour, his resentment seemed deeper than that. Perhaps I'd been impolite. Or perhaps he disliked my appearance or gender or crooked bones or my unpinned hair. My lack of chaperone.

The hedgerows passed. In places the grass was so long

that it pattered against the side of the car. I might have stayed quiet. He did not wish to converse, I knew that. But nor did I wish to say nothing when there was so much to ask him, so much to learn. 'Are you from Gloucestershire?'

'London.'

'Where in London?'

'East.'

'East? I'm from Pimlico.'

He scoffed, dismissive.

'So why are you in Gloucestershire? If you are from London?'

'Why are *you*? Work. Money. Mr Fox asked me to.'

'You live at Shadowbrook?'

He gave a single, hard laugh. But he also tightened his grip on the steering wheel so that his knuckles whitened and his voice, when he answered, seemed softer. 'No. I would not live there.'

'Why not?'

He paused, glanced at a passing gateway. 'Others will tell you.'

'Others? But I'm asking you.'

His expression was one of disbelief at my tone, yet he still answered. 'There's been trouble at Shadowbrook.'

'What kind of trouble?'

I thought he might say more for he opened his mouth again. But then he snapped it shut and pressed his lips together for emphasis. 'No.'

I tried for other conversations. I gave the Latin for dog rose. I remarked on the car's interior and speed – and what kind of car was this? I thought compliments might help. But even so, he would not say more on this trouble. And a tiredness had entered him, so that he seemed distracted, elsewhere.

Evening deepened. I noticed how the headlights found moths, cartwheel tracks, signposts that pointed to Winchcombe and Stow and other foreign names. And at a crossroads, he reached into his jacket pocket, retrieved a gold wrapper and pushed its contents into his mouth: a hard, glassy confection that clacked against his teeth, so that I thought of my childhood of stewed fruit and crustless bread. Even now, I could never eat such a thing as this. When I asked for its name, he told me; I learned the word *butterscotch*. I listened to the pat-pat of long grass passing under the car; the word *trouble* was its own strange moth.

Eight in the evening. Trees and fields were darker but could still be seen. We rocked over uneven ground.

'There.'

With that, Shadowbrook was more than a name printed in gold. It was a house of pale stone. Clematis grew on its walls. Its courtyard was bordered with dark, leafy shrubs in which I could hear movement – roosting birds, or the scurrying of mice. Two storeys to it, no more. A small right-angled wing. On either side of its door there was a stone dog on a plinth with nasturtiums at its feet.

'The maids will carry your trunk for you.' With that, he turned.

'Not you? Will you not carry it? As you did before?'

'No. It's late.'

'Why does that matter?'

He said no more. He only returned to the car, turned the wheel so that its tyres crunched over the loose stones and moved away, through the gates and down the lane.

I listened as the car faded. Then I looked back at the house.

Later, I'd learn that this pale, honey-gold stone was not

Shadowbrook's alone. It was the stone of its landscape; I would find it in the flower beds, in the outer walls of the potting shed – and later, I'd find that all the buildings within the Cotswold hills were formed of this baked stone. Moot halls and bridges. Churches. Farmhouses and smaller homes. But I was not wise to this, at that moment. I thought this hue was only Shadowbrook's; a house formed of solidified dust and autumn leaves and old sun.

I stared at its walls. I studied the mossed roof tiles and the gold-coloured stone and the drainpipes in their rusting brackets, and I looked at its upper windows, which were open, with curtains half drawn.

Above it all, I saw a weathervane. It was silhouetted against the evening sky: a hare with its ears flat against itself, its limbs stretched fully, so that it did not touch the ground. A horizontal creature, between its compass points – a hare at its absolute fastest – and I was so taken with this weathervane that I did not notice, at first, the figure crossing the courtyard towards me. She carried a lantern, called my name.

'Miss Waterfield? Is it you?' She held up the lantern to see me better.

A small, inquisitive face. It peered at me; it seemed bright, unsure, and there was a youthfulness in this expression. Yet she was no longer young. Her hair was grey – a dark, metallic grey – and she wore it in a long, twisted plait that came over her shoulder and hung to her waist. Her hands had the texture of Millicent's hands. And with her smile, I saw the folds and creases that she'd acquired over fifty years or more.

'Welcome to Shadowbrook. We have been looking forward to your arrival. I hope very much that the journey was not too demanding. You have come such a long way to be with us, too. London! Gracious. You must be tired – and hungry. Are you? There is soup, if you will take some.'

'My trunk,' I said. 'I can't carry it. And the driver refused to bring it closer. I don't think he liked me, although frankly I didn't like him either. He was rude. We mostly drove in silence.'

Her smile never lessened. 'Oh, I'm sure he liked you. And I'm sorry if it wasn't the welcome you hoped for. Come inside, Miss Waterfield. Hollis,' she said, 'will bring it to your room. He has not yet retired for the night and would be perfectly happy to help. Leave the trunk and he'll find it. Come! You must eat and rest.'

She was Mrs Bale. Both young and old. She crossed the courtyard with small, rapid footsteps; she had a restlessness in her hands, so that she gestured constantly. 'This door is made of ancient oak; in spring, there are tulips all along this border, and I am so very fond of tulips that I'll take a stem or two indoors and . . . '

I could not keep pace. I swayed in her wake, rotated – and at the front door she paused, looked back with a frown as if surprised that I was not beside her. I saw her embarrassment then. She flushed on seeing my gait, and I wondered if she'd been told that the girl from Kew would be crippled and slow; I wondered, too, if she'd comment. But when I joined her, she only smiled brightly. 'This way.'

The hallway of Shadowbrook was lit by a single lamp. This was not enough for it: I saw the stairs and a grandfather clock, but the floor itself was hard to make out, and the wooden panelling on the lower half of each wall darkened the hallway further, so that it might have been midnight. I followed Mrs Bale down a corridor. I could barely see her as we went; my feet themselves were out of sight. Yet Mrs Bale seemed entirely unaware of this darkness as she pattered ahead, talking over her shoulder.

'You'll come to know the house very well, I'm sure. It isn't large. The kitchen, the dining room and the maids' quarters are all down at this end of the house. A bathroom and water closet, too. This door is the old library. And this' – she pushed a door so that it opened a little, but not enough to enter by – 'is the drawing room, which is a fine room to spend a little time in. Its French doors lead onto the terrace and the croquet lawn and it fills with afternoon light so that I wonder if it's not the loveliest of Shadowbrook's rooms, or of its downstairs rooms at least. Are you a reader, Miss Waterfield? It is an agreeable place to read a novel. If we had a gramophone, this is the room that would suit it, I think. Still, you need your supper, so let us carry on ... Will pea soup suit you? Maud made the bread this morning and I must say that she tends to burn it but today was a good day for her. This way, Miss Waterfield, and then I will show you to your room.'

I had no chance to reply. She spoke so quickly – her words poured out like water – yet she did not seem to mind my lack of response. Indeed, as we entered the kitchen, with its copper saucepans, patterned tiles and cracked sink, she simply carried on, regaling me with tales of market day in Stow, of the butcher in Chipping Campden whose boy brought the meat on his bicycle and rang his bell incessantly which he had no need to do. She ladled soup into a bowl, set it before me.

'And the gardens, Miss Waterfield. You are only here for a month, I know, but what a month you have chosen! The gardens are looking their best, I think. The roses are quite glorious. Did you know, we've had a robin nesting in the potting shed? Quite a foolish place to have chosen and I'm sure it's a perfect nuisance to the boys, but I confess I am rather pleased by it; I see the birds dipping in and out and I hear the chicks, too, as I'm washing the clothes. It's a good drying time. I can leave a sheet on the line and it's perfectly dry by the afternoon, but this is often the way, for we catch a breeze here for being on the hill as the whole village is. Well, the village's name will tell you this! Where else might Barcombe-on-the-Hill be? We have beech trees on one side of the garden and they protect us, yes, but the wind will always find its way. You might hear it at night. It can make the house sound like a boat on its mooring. Also, when the hayfields are cut, we can smell it on the breeze, and it is quite the most wonderful smell. Oh yes, Miss Waterfield. You've come to Shadowbrook at the most perfect time of year.'

She paused. 'Would you care for more soup?' She held up the ladle.

She was, I understood, expecting me to speak now. She wanted a response, at least. But I was exhausted. I could feel the throb of the growing bruise on my wrist; the pea soup was not warm, too thin – and I needed to rest.

Somewhere in the house, a clock struck nine.

'Mrs Bale, I'm tired. Where is my room, please?'

I'd tried to be polite. Even so, I saw a shadow pass over her – a brief alteration in her eyes which suggested disappointment. Yet her smile did not falter. She lowered the ladle. 'Of course, Miss Waterfield. This way.'

I expected to take the stairs. And she did, indeed, lead me back along the corridor to the hallway and the staircase. But we did not ascend. Rather, she ducked under the staircase; she moved past an umbrella stand and a single chair and turned to me. 'Here we are.'

A door in the wall, tucked in the corner. A downstairs room.

I turned to her. 'Mrs Bale, is this because of my bones? Did Mr Forbes tell you I needed care? I'm quite capable of stairs. I'm neither a child nor an invalid.'

She flinched, puckered her mouth. 'I'm aware of that, Miss Waterfield.' A clipped, fast response yet she quickly recovered herself. 'Your bones? No. This has always been a guest room. Well, I say that; I believe in the Pettigrews' day it was a morning room because it's east-facing, so that they might take their coffee in there, and there's a chance you will wake with the daylight, although the curtains are very thick in the hope of preventing that. But when Mr Fox bought Shadowbrook, he changed it. He thought it would make a fine sleeping quarters. The upstairs rooms are solely for his own use, so that this seemed an excellent choice to make. I hope you'll agree.'

With that, she pushed the door to reveal, firstly, a bedside lamp with an amber glow. In this glow, I saw a bed with a white coverlet. A table, on which there stood a blue water jug in a blue bowl. A towel. A single pale rose in a vase.

My trunk sat on the floor, waiting.

'Do you like it? You will have all you need, I hope. There is a wardrobe and a dressing table. The window opens if you wish it to.'

I saw the immaculate linen. I thought of the soup, which had been freshly made, waiting for me, and I understood that Mrs Bale had worked hard for my arrival. I felt the tang of shame in me. 'Thank you.'

For a moment, she only smiled. Then she bade me good-night, turned and walked into the hallway. I saw the door begin to close, so that I thought she had left me – but then she returned, stepping back into the room with purpose.

'Forgive me, Miss Waterfield. One last word, if I may. I spoke to you of the breezes here, didn't I? You mustn't

35

mind them. The house creaks sometimes, at night. It's an old house, and perhaps you're accustomed to old houses in London where the timbers are restless, although I'm sure such houses are cared for a little better than Shadowbrook has been. You know Mr Fox only bought the house last year? Before that, it was in a very sorry condition – it had been dreadfully neglected, with mice under the floors and leaves in the corners and most of the pipes had rusted through. And crows, he said, had been nesting in the library – crows! I never saw them but I saw what they chose to leave behind, and that took some cleaning, I can tell you. The whole place needed attention. But we cleaned it, scrubbed it, replaced most of the broken glass, and I think you'll agree that it is a very pleasant house and you might not know it had been empty. Even so, there is still a little work to be done here and there. So do please forgive any dust sheets or any damp on the walls ... These Gloucestershire winters. And I tell you this because I do not wish for you to be alarmed if a door closes on its own at night – there are draughts, you understand. And Mr Fox believes there is woodworm in the attic, which will be a future trouble.'

She paused. 'So yes. If there are any creaks tonight, or on any night ... Well, it is simply Shadowbrook's nature. You understand?'

I nodded.

'Well, goodnight again, Miss Waterfield.'

Her footsteps grew fainter as she walked away down the corridor.

I sat for a long time. I lowered myself onto a floral-printed chair and rested. I examined the bruise that was showing itself on my wrist. A stillness in the house.

I unpacked slowly that night. I noted these small acts of arrival: the unfolding of clothes, the placing of possessions, the opening and closing of drawers. *This is how it is done.* And there was reassurance in seeing my tortoiseshell comb on the dressing table. My three books by my bed.

London seemed a thousand miles away. It seemed to be a memory – a place that no longer truly existed; what existed was where I was now, at this moment. This room, at Shadowbrook; its embroidered cushion and curtains. Its single rose in its vase.

I combed my hair, listening. But the only creaks I heard that night were those of my traveller's bones as I climbed into bed and turned out the light.

A morning room – and it was. Despite the heavy curtains, I became aware of light early. I lay still, watched the room brighten. Saw the cracks in the plasterwork, the brownish bloom of damp in the corner.

I was slow to rise. Yet on drawing the curtains, sunlight rushed in; it flooded the room so that I raised my hand against it. My eyes took their time adjusting. Beyond the glass I saw a herb garden. It was square, bordered with brickwork; it had a sundial at its centre, and lavender and mint, and it had, too, a hush to it.

To be outside. I wanted this more than I wanted anything – not the interiors of cars or trains or any room – so I dressed, took my cane and opened my door. The grandfather clock struck six times as I did so. I tried the front door but found it to be locked. Last night, Mrs Bale had called the drawing room the finest room in the house; hadn't she said, too, that its French doors led to a croquet lawn?

I made my way down the corridor and entered a room of sofas and floor lamps and red curtains drawn back with gold tasselled cord. I saw a decanter of brandy on a side table, a bowl in which there were yellow roses spilling their petals onto the windowsill – and her. Mrs Bale, too, was there: upright in a wing-backed chair. Her hands were in her lap. She was looking out of the window, across a lawn. Her rope of hair.

'Mrs Bale?'

She turned as if I had seized her. Her hands broke apart and she gasped. 'Oh! Miss Waterfield. You quite startled me.' Briefly, she trembled; she placed her hand on her collarbone and breathed out. But then she rose, smoothing her skirts. 'Well, you move like a mouse, it seems! Perhaps it's because you're so small that there's no way of hearing you come and go, or it's because you must move slowly with your stick. And my goodness, look at your hair! What colour and thickness, Miss Waterfield! I thought to remark on it last night but I felt I'd talked enough when you had travelled so far. But isn't it quite a colour? And the fact that you wear it unpinned like that . . . It's unusual, I think. Or it's unusual here, at least. Is it the London style?'

She lost her smile quickly, came closer. 'Was it the light that woke you? We can find thicker curtains, I'm sure. Or I could ask Hollis to find some cloth to—'

'It wasn't the light. I often wake early.'

'Oh, so do I! Is the morning not the best part of the day? I was thinking that as I was sitting here. So quiet, is it not? Except for the birds, of course, who always have something to say for themselves! A little breakfast? The girls will not be preparing it for a while yet, being Sunday, but I can find you a pot of tea, perhaps, and . . .'

I followed her, trying to listen as she talked of her secrets for making tea – the hottest of water, a bone-china cup – and how she had never acquired the taste for coffee. But mostly, I watched her. My attention was on her mannerisms: how she fingered a silver cross that hung on a chain around her neck, how she blinked frequently. I also noticed her tiredness. The skin beneath her eyes had the grey-blue of gathered dust, so that I supposed she had not slept very well or had not slept at all.

Mrs Bale called the maids *the girls*, as if they were far younger than me. They were not far younger; one was sixteen and the other a year older. But even so, they were known as this, and both had a nervousness to them; they had quick eyes and hands, with a tendency to look at the floor when speaking. 'This, girls, is Miss Waterfield. From Kew – remember? She has come to establish the finest glasshouse in Gloucestershire and we must make her feel most welcome.'

With that, they bobbed and said nothing. I wondered what I was meant to do in return. I'd only known Millicent, and my relationship with her had moved between frozen and warm. She'd bobbed at no one; having known Patrick since he was small, she'd been regarded as a family member, so that her tempers and foibles had been endured as much as my own. There had been no curtseys from Millicent. How did one respond to maids on meeting them? I stood, waited. The girls eyed me, waiting too.

'I'm sure,' said Mrs Bale, 'that Miss Waterfield is very pleased to meet you.' And with that, she clapped her hands twice. At this, the girls divided themselves around the kitchen table and began slicing bread, breaking eggs into a bowl. I sipped my tea in its chipped cup and eyed the maids over its rim. They were not alike. Harriet, the elder girl, was tall, red-headed and slender, so that I had a clear sense of her bones as she worked: her wrists, the upper vertebrae.

Even her jaw was prominent; her skin seemed paler against it, as if pulled tightly across the bone. Yet she seemed strong, despite this. She moved deftly, precisely; I watched how she kneaded dough, folded packets of flour.

Maud, in contrast, was short. She was my height, perhaps; and, like me, she had a twist in her walk – not a limp, but a rounded manner of moving that accommodated her weight, for Maud was sturdy, compact. A daughter of cattle farmers, I'd learn later, and I could imagine this; Maud walking through wind and hard weather. Her bones were not prominent. Nor did she have Harriet's dexterity; she was heavy-handed, suspicious and took no pleasure in her work so that, as she beat the eggs, she studied me.

'Why do you carry a stick?'

'Manners, Maud! For heaven's sake!' Mrs Bale stamped her foot, appalled. But I lowered my teacup.

'Because I broke my leg two years ago and it mended poorly.'

'How did you break it?'

'I fell.'

'Old people fall and break their bones. You're not old. And your eyes are . . .'

This bold regard she gave me – from head to toe and back again – was not new. *Cripple* was unsaid, but I heard it, even so. I rose from my chair to meet Maud's height. In doing so, I hoped that she might see my eyes better. I wished to tell her the Latin name of my condition, to hook back my upper lip to reveal the hidden, empty gums, because I did not want inaccurate whispers. If she was to talk about me, let it be truthful and factually right.

I opened my mouth to say this but Mrs Bale stepped forwards, hands high. 'Enough, Maud! Gracious, did your mother not explain manners to you? I told you to be polite to her, child!' She turned. 'Miss Waterfield. I can only apologise for my overly familiar staff. Would you like to see the glasshouse? Where you'll be working?' And as if to reassure herself, she murmured, 'Yes, that's what we will do.'

The kitchen door took me between the stove and a sideboard of patterned plates and outside, into a courtyard. As soon as we'd moved into the sunshine, Mrs Bale began excusing the nature of the maids. They were, she said, local girls – Harriet came from Lower Barcombe, a mile away, Maud's family lived on the far side of Stow – and neither had worked in service before. Harriet was the better worker; she had tact and a very compliant nature, had been keen to learn the order in which to lay the spoons and how to fillet a trout and all manner of tasks that Maud, she said, had no wish to do.

'I rather despair with that one, I'm afraid. She is tardy, first and foremost – if Mr Fox asks for his afternoon tea at four, she will only start to boil the kettle as the clock chimes. But she is also terribly talkative. You are yet to see this, of course, as she offered the taciturn side to her nature just now – and a little insolence, I fear – but oh, she can talk when she chooses to! She gossips terribly, and seems quite incapable of working and talking at the same time so that I have, on occasion, left her with a duster and returned an hour later to find her still talking, with all the same cobwebs around her and the duster still folded. She comes from a family of talkers, though. I know them by sight and I confess I have crossed the road on seeing them.'

Mrs Bale gestured as she went. After ten steps, she turned back. 'Look at it,' she said. 'Don't you think Shadowbrook is a fine building? Simple, perhaps, and not large – I hope you weren't imagining Blenheim Palace, Miss Waterfield! But it's still very handsome, don't you think?'

I could not deny it. There may have been damp on my bedroom wall and dust beneath its furniture, but the exterior of the house betrayed none of the abandonment that Mrs Bale had spoken of the night before. Shadowbrook was simple, yes, but I felt I preferred it for being so: no columns or plasterwork; no Grecian maidens in alcoves, as I'd supposed there might be in London's finer houses. I liked what Shadowbrook lacked. I liked, too, what it seemed to have: the earthy cups of house martin nests; the iron drainpipes that ended in flowering pots. I liked how the western end – this end, where we were standing now – had a short, angled wing that was so covered in a twisted vine that its windows were partly shaded. *Wisteria floribunda*. This was my language: Latin names and botany.

'The wisteria grows well here.'

'Too well, some might say. The flowering season is over now, of course, but oh, when it blooms . . . This is our part of the house – the girls' and mine. That little window? Half hidden in leaves? That's my bedroom. You might think the wisteria makes the room rather dark, but I like the dappled light, and in April and May there's such a scent from the flowers that I will sometimes sleep with the window open to smell them all night. On the south side, you'll find our Rêve d'Or, a glorious rambling rose that is entering its finest time. It climbs right up the upper floor! It may be my favourite plant in the whole garden.'

I looked up. 'Mr Fox must have a good view of those roses. From his rooms.'

She also glanced at the first floor. 'Oh yes. He has a wonderful view, in general: over the gardens and fields and down to the village. I have wondered if he might see the Malvern Hills on a clear morning, although I've never asked him this; I am sure he can see the Broadway Tower, for all the high places in Gloucestershire and Warwickshire have a view of the Broadway Tower. Oh, they're a very fine suite of rooms.'

'Will I meet him today?'

'Mr Fox? Oh no, child. He's not at home currently. Indeed, he is often away.'

'But the windows are open.'

'He likes to leave them like that. As do I, for the breeze freshens the house and carries away the worst of the dust, although we need to be careful of birds coming in. This happened once with a pigeon and it was quite a story, I can tell you. I was gathering feathers for days!'

For a moment, we stayed very still. Two people looking up.

I thought to ask more. I sensed, in the silence, that she might have been expecting me to, or that she herself might have had more to say and yet lacked confidence. I felt she was wary of me. Yet we only stood.

'The glasshouse, Miss Waterfield? This way.'

My roll like a boat. My turning hip, as if held between hands and being forced into its unnatural movement. In my peculiar fashion, I followed her – past the old stables, a tool shed, a potting shed where the robin was nesting. These buildings spoke more clearly of neglect. Tiles were missing from the roofs; a clematis ran along the guttering of the tool shed and apple store and the branches came low, so that I imagined others would have to crouch to move beneath it. But there was, perhaps, charm in this – in the old wooden wheel propped against a wall, in the dandelions that grew by it.

Mrs Bale understood this, it seemed, for she said, 'Oh, it's peaceful enough now and it will stay so today, being

Sunday. But most days, by elevenses, there is clatter and voices and all sorts of noise and it isn't peaceful then. We have garden boys that work here. Eight, all in all – eight! With Hollis, of course, who has been working here for twice as many years as you've been living, I should think. He's the gardener here and he's excellent, and he knows the garden as well as anyone might, though there's far too much garden for one man to tend to. There's a step here, see?' We dropped down, passed under a holly tree. 'And I should tell you that if those boys say anything you don't care for, then tell Hollis. He's a kind man but he won't tolerate any smart language to a lady, and some of those boys need to be told very firmly because I sometimes wonder if they aren't being paid to dally and cause mischief rather than to rake the leaves or mow the lawn ... '

I knew what she alluded to. Knew they would see what Maud had seen: the limp and the strange eyes. And I thought to respond to this, to explain that I did not need protection from stares or rumour. But then I saw the glasshouse.

Mrs Bale came to my side. 'Quite a creation, is it not?'

This was no Palm House; it was no cathedral of glass in which the eyes looked up and up. But even so, it astonished me. My mouth opened as I stared; I crept towards it, trailing my cane – this perfected, reflecting structure of scrolled metalwork and glass. There was brickwork, too. Its back wall was made entirely of reddish, fox-coloured brick which must, I supposed, have been here long before the glasshouse had been. The wall was pockmarked in places. It had seen weather and hardship – and I wondered if fruit trees had grown against it, fanned out. Pear or plum.

Yet in all other ways, it was glass. A glass roof came down at an angle; the structure's two shorter sides, porch and frontage were all made of such clear, immaculate panes that I could barely see glass at all. 'This is new?'

'Oh yes. It is barely a month old, Miss Waterfield. We all thought at first that Mr Fox might build something rather plain by the drawing room – a little orangery, perhaps, through the French doors. But then he asked for the gooseberry bushes, which never gave fruit as far as I know – and who cares for a gooseberry anyway? They're such tart things, aren't they? – to be pulled up and the ground flattened and he wanted the old brick wall to be included. And so' – she sighed fondly – 'he built this.'

'Himself? Mr Fox built it himself?'

'Oh no. He paid men to do it. They came from Banbury and it was quite the excitement. The garden boys helped too, of course.'

It was all I could see. I could only look at this house of glass.

'It is unheated. But it is south-facing, and Mr Hollis tells me that the brickwork will retain the sun's heat so that most plants will survive perfectly well, even in the winter months. The front windows all open for ventilation. There are blinds – can you see them? – in case of very hot days. And you'll find all you need inside it; he has provided everything.' She paused. 'You like it, I hope?'

I nodded, wordless.

She laughed, as if relieved. 'I will tell Mr Fox. He will be delighted to know it, as he's really gone to such care.' And with that, she said she must prepare herself for church and ensure the maids were doing the same, and was she right in thinking that I was a little too tired from my journey to attend the service myself today?

'I don't go to church,' I told her.

She stopped as if ordered to. 'At all?'

'At all. I don't believe in God.'

Mrs Bale had a small physical reaction to this; she blinked rapidly and flinched. But then she collected herself, gave a single, pronounced nod and smiled as she took her leave of me, passing the holly bush and into the house.

It had no plants yet, of course. They were still at Kew, being lowered into crates and sealed ready for me. But even so, this was not an empty room. Inside, I found the thick, soft density of air that comes from trapped sunlight. Also, the smell of fresh paint. And I found furniture: high-backed bamboo chairs with cushions of an earthy hue; embroidered footstools; glass-topped tables and smaller wooden trestle ones; and at one side, a long iron bench with scrolled edges which I thumbed as I passed.

There were shelves, too, on the back wall; dozens of shelves and brackets and plinths and hollows, as well as wires on which vines could climb. Cradles were suspended from the glass roof, for hanging plants. And against the wall, Hollis had set down pots and containers of all shapes and sizes, waiting to be filled with earth from a braced wooden tub of such dark earth it looked unearthly. A metal trowel sat by it, to lift this earth. There was also a box – a tea chest in size, with a golden clasp – in which I found all the tools I could ever require. Countless trowels and forks and knives; a small saw; a hammer; gardening string. Propped against the brick wall I saw brooms and brushes. Low down, there were three watering cans of different shapes and sizes, beneath a metal tap. Mrs Bale was right: I lacked for nothing. It was perfectly done.

There was, too, a note. A square white envelope sat on the windowsill. It was addressed to *Miss Waterfield*, in handwriting I recognised.

Dear Miss Waterfield,

Welcome to Shadowbrook. I hope you approve of and enjoy your surroundings. I look forward to making your acquaintance in due course.

R. E. Fox

I lowered myself onto a wicker chair. The *x* was small and hard; yet the *F* of Fox was decorative, with a sweeping lower part to it, like a vine or a tail of some kind. And I thought, then, about him. Each wire was taut, measured. Each broom was spaced evenly against the brick wall. He was, I presumed, a man of accuracy. Of forethought and exact measurements. But he was also a man for whom plants and gardens took precedence. This was indisputable. For he'd bought a house in which the pipework shuddered with every turned tap, where crows had nested – and yet, rather than restore it properly, he'd spent money and time and attention on this: a glasshouse for palms and plumbago. Also, there were three workers within the house – a bright, sleepless housekeeper and two unsmiling maids – yet in the garden he had eight boys, and Hollis, who'd worked here for forty years.

In due course. I glanced up. The upper, open windows looked out over Gloucestershire. They had a view across the courtyard and outhouses to fields and woodlands beyond. A small breeze had found their curtains, for they moved in and out.

I thought: I wish she could see me. Here, with my hair unpinned. How far I was from the green chaise longue.

And I thought, too, of the hour. Today was a Sunday; they were all at church in their polished pews, not in the gardens. So I rose, adjusted my grasp of my cane and explored Shadowbrook's land.

*

The croquet lawn was the garden's starting place. Shadow-brook House – with its French doors and veranda, its urns of lavender – formed one end of it. But the lawn's other three sides were lined by hedges of beech and yew. And these hedges were huge, twice my height. In the weeks to come, I'd learn that their late-afternoon shadows would lie across the lawn with a mathematical precision. As for croquet itself, I saw no signs of it on my first day. But later, I'd note the garden boys' unruly, clattering version of the game; their mallets became weaponry, their rules became a battle cry, and balls would enter the undergrowth with a bright crack and a shedding of petals or a startled bird. It was a dangerous pastime for my bones. Furthermore, I'd sometimes find hoops pressed into the turf as I wandered; rusting hoops, distorted from years of use so that they seemed harmless enough. Yet to push a toe through such a thing would bring me down, I knew this. So I'd tug them up. Leave them on benches.

Arches had been cut into these walls of beech and yew. And each arch, I discovered, led to a different path, of brick or loose stones or longer, unmown grass; each path dropped away into the garden's depths. Such paths were the wander-er's dream. They'd lead into sun-baked corners or avenues, to benches or orchards or views. They'd find pools or com-post heaps. Beehives or rainwater barrels. Metal taps which defied their rust, so that, if turned, they shook into life.

There were, too, other, smaller gardens to find at Shadowbrook: as I wandered, I discovered grassy court-yards – square, private and bordered by four hedges, so that to enter was like entering a room. These gardens had their own nature. The white garden contained only white-flowering plants, or those with pale leaves: phlox, acanthus, dead nettle. The fuchsia garden brimmed with pinks. The bathing pool garden held, naturally, a bathing pool at its centre but it had, too, a portico whose walls were painted with Roman scenes, so that I felt watched in this garden and chose to move on from it. I preferred the lime bower. I preferred the red borders which within weeks would burn with colour: lobelia, dahlia, a rose so red that my hands would feel warmed by raising them to it. These borders were deep, fire-coloured. Standing there, I heard bees.

There is nowhere like this. I had seen nothing of the world but I felt sure of that. I fingered the metalwork of the gate which led to the beechwoods; I stood beneath the cedar of Lebanon, looked into the dark cavities of branches to where woodpigeons roosted and stared back. And I entered a courtyard of light to find topiary trees within it: four shapes of privet which had, once, been birds but were less birdlike now. Time had lengthened their feathers; wind and drought and English rain had hollowed them, yet they retained a sense of themselves. And I liked them for this, as I circled them. Imperfect, yet they had endured.

A tennis court. A dark, thatched tennis pavilion in which the furniture had rusted.

Beechwoods with a central pathway, like a nave.

An orchard, too, which seemed forgotten entirely, lost to long grass and buttercups, except for a narrow track. At its end, I found a rectangular mound of earth which suggested disturbance or burials. But there was no stone to mark the place.

And lastly, there was the kitchen garden. This formed, perhaps, a quarter of Shadowbrook's land: a flat, exposed plain on which there were bean frames of hazel, rhubarb forcers of terracotta and row after row of leafy tops which rustled in breezes. I would come to know this part well. Here, I would receive a handful of potatoes to carry to the house; here, I'd find the garden boys. But for now, there was only myself and the vegetables. Each crop announced itself with a small wooden stick on which I'd read such names as Scarlet Emperor, Black Beauty, British Queen, Globe. And whilst I was alone in it, there was evidence of recent human work. Footprints in the earth. Hoes propped against tool sheds. A spade, planted into the ground as a tree might be.

I had a curious sense of being watched; throughout the garden, I felt it. It was as though I had entered a part of it – the orchard, the lime bower – at the very moment that someone else had risen and left; I felt that any metal chair might retain that person's heat. It was an unsettling notion. I chastised myself for it – it was foolishness – yet I also looked down the lines of hedges. On the croquet lawn, I turned in a slow, complete circle to see it all.

Later, in the kitchen, I mentioned this to Mrs Bale. 'I felt watched in the gardens. Do you have that too?'

'Watched? No, child.'

I asked, too, when Mr Fox might be returning to Shadowbrook. 'Because I want to ask him about his gardens. How old are the beechwoods? Who painted the Roman faces? And—'

'Speak to Hollis.' She said this too quickly. But then she softened, retrieved her smile and repeated it in a brighter, nonchalant voice. 'Hollis – not Mr Fox. Hollis has been here for such a long time that he's the man to speak to. He's the man who knows.'

A quiet, uninhabited garden. Yet the following day, it altered: I woke to hear a low male whistling. On dressing, I discovered the gardens were brimming with noise. The garden boys: they arrived by nine every day except Sunday. And whilst I could not see them yet – in the vegetable garden, Harriet said; they always started there – I stood by the kitchen door with my teacup and listened. Names were thrown like balls. Orders were given and seemingly ignored and I heard a yell that suggested that a fist had been thrown, or something taken.

I partly wished to follow these sounds. To investigate. But I was also reluctant. It was not that I knew nothing of boys: knowing nothing of them – having never met one – was only more reason to venture forwards and watch them, introduce myself. Rather, I was wary of their physicality. I heard the clang of metal, spade against spade. One of the bright, laughing protestations was *get off me*, and on hearing it, I considered the bruise on my wrist which was finding new depths of blue. It seemed too soon to meet them.

I chose to find Hollis instead. The Shadowbrook gardener for four decades, who had carried my trunk to my room on my arrival without order or complaint. He'd had, it seemed, a lifetime in this place. And I looked, therefore, for a man who appeared to belong in these gardens: stooped from years of barrowing. Skin like bark. Hair with the hue and texture of a dandelion clock.

This was precisely him. I found Hollis beneath a magnolia tree. His movements announced him to me: there was a neat, rhythmical sound to his spade with, at times, a tuneless hum. And he worked slowly, with the care and exactitude that, I supposed, a head gardener would. Also, he seemed entirely absorbed in his task: he'd place his foot on the spade's uppermost edge, push his weight down so that it sank; having done this, remove his foot, bend his knees, alter his grasp on the handle and lift the spade as if the earth was sleeping and he had no wish to wake it. I thought, he has always done this. Around him, a robin bustled for worms.

'Are you Mr Hollis?'

He straightened. 'Ah! I'd heard you'd come. Yes, that's me, although I can't remember the last time my title was used. I've been plain Hollis all my life – to the neighbours, to friends. To my wife, even.' He planted the spade into the earth like a flag. 'I rather think you have a much finer name.'

'Do I?'

'Waterfield, isn't it? Yes, much finer. To my mind, that's a gardener's name.'

'I think it's too long.'

'Too long? Plants have far longer and are perfectly suited to them.' With this, he reached into his pocket and retrieved a handkerchief. He dabbed his nose with care. 'Well, Miss Waterfield. I hope you are settling in.'

'Yes. People seem kind enough. And these gardens are ...'

Hollis smiled. 'You like them? There's nowhere I love more. I took my first steps in the orchard, or so I've been told. Since then, I've seen saplings grow into huge trees. I remember my father planting these hedges, and look at them now. It feels like no time has passed at all, of course.' He folded the handkerchief, sniffed once.

'Your father gardened here too?'

'He did. He was the gardener for the Pettigrews for over fifty years, and *his* father had the job before him. My earliest memory is of watching my grandfather sweeping the leaves on the veranda. He died that same winter.'

I'd heard this name before. 'The Pettigrews. They lived here?'

'Yes, they did. For years. The last of the Pettigrews died in 1901, and since then ... Well, there was no proper ownership of the place until Mr Fox. You'll have heard.'

'Mrs Bale said the house had been abandoned.'

'Abandoned?' Hollis considered this. 'Too strong a word, I think. But I suspect you'll have already marked that Mrs Bale is fond of a tale. No, not quite abandoned. But neglected, certainly. A distant relative of the Pettigrews would come and go from time to time during those years – I met him, on occasion – but he never stayed for long. A week or two a year, maybe. He sold it to Mr Fox in the end. I hear you're from London?'

But I was confused by this. 'So the house was neglected in that time and yet the garden was not? That makes no sense.'

'Ah. When the last of the Pettigrews died, there was an understanding – a provision in the will – for a gardener to stay at Shadowbrook. Your expression, Miss Waterfield! Quite a thing, I know. The garden was always to be cared for, even if the house crumbled to dust. It suited me well, of course. Mind you, it has always been too large a garden for a single man. Even when my son helped me, we could not care for it all.' He paused. 'Albert's my boy. He works here too. You'll see him – tall.' He raised his hand above me to say *this tall*.

'Thirteen years of just you and Albert? In the garden?' I sifted this information. It seemed extraordinary – that a garden might be cared for whilst the house itself became a home for crows and dead leaves. 'Did no one see your efforts at all? It seems a waste.'

'Not a waste. We saw our efforts – Albert and I. We saw the bulbs come up in the spring. We maintained a vegetable patch.' Hollis seemed bemused. 'Mrs Bale told me you had a rather forthright manner to you. I think she was right.'

Forthright. I straightened a little. 'Why forthright? I like knowing things, that's all. I think it's a shame not to know what one can. Mr Fox bought the house after that?'

'He did. Employed the garden boys. Provided tools and paid us well.'

'He must love the gardens. Do you see him often?'

Hollis looked at his right hand. He opened and closed it slowly, as if the spadework had left a pain there. 'I should introduce you to Albert, Miss Waterfield. We think we've raised quite a fine, honest lad, his mother and I. We've an elder boy too, but he's married and lives in Moreton now so we don't see him often.'

An insufficient reply. Perhaps he had misheard me. But perhaps, too, it was an aversion, a step away from what I wished to know. By consequence, I came closer. 'Do you see him much? Mr Fox, I mean.'

'No. He's often away, you see.'

'And when will he come home?'

'I don't know. He rarely knows himself, I think.'

That single step nearer to him meant I could see more. The thin, plum-coloured veins by his nose. The spit that had gathered in the corners of his mouth. And I knew, too, that he could see me better – that at that moment, he was newly aware of my crooked collarbone and ghostly lashes. Of the moon-bluish whites of my eyes.

'The membrane,' I told him, 'is thinner. The capillaries and veins – the workings of the eye – can be seen through it, which causes the blueness. What have you heard about me, Hollis? Are they calling me crippled?' I was thinking, mostly, of the shorter maid.

He'd not expected this. He swallowed with embarrassment. 'Forgive me. I ... Crippled? No. No one has said that. Your gender, Miss Waterfield, is the surprise – we had been expecting a man from Kew. That has been the conversation, mostly – about how you came here unaccompanied and how you've acquired the knowledge you must have.

54

Your hair, too, has been mentioned, but how could it not have been? Untied like that?'

'What other things have you heard?'

'The garden boys are young, you understand. Wayward and talkative.'

'But what have you heard?'

He shifted his weight, unsure. 'That there was an accident with a carriage – that the wheel went over you, or the horse did. Of a malnourished childhood. The twins claim you were beaten by a cruel husband. I have berated them for all of these, Miss Waterfield, I assure you. But it's how it is . . . News moves quickly here.'

I felt flushed, unsettled. 'Will you tell them that I've never lacked nourishment? There has been no carriage or husband? It's a condition I've had since birth and it cannot be helped. Will you tell this to Mrs Bale, too?' For I knew she'd gossiped of it.

Hollis nodded. And I wondered how quickly this explanation would pass through the gardens or whether, like weeds, the rumours of malnourishment and violence would still find a way and choke the proper truth.

'And – may I ask? – is this not dangerous for you? You travel alone; it is commendable, Miss Waterfield, certainly. But are there not risks with your bones?'

I thought to defend myself, at first. To say that I was quite capable. Also, that a broken bone was far less painful than a parental loss and so I was quite unafraid of life. But his expression was a tender one; he'd asked with concern and did not deserve a sharp response. 'A few. I need to be careful of uneven ground. Wet paths. Croquet hoops.'

'Uneven ground? Ah. Then may I suggest you avoid the lower garden. Do you know it? It's half hidden by under-growth and so steep that we cannot take the wheelbarrows into it. I've fallen myself and won't walk there now. Its stream floods after rain.'

'And what of the orchard?'

'The orchard?'

'It's also uneven. There's a mound of earth in its far corner.'

'Yes. Well, I tend to leave the orchard be. Miss Waterfield?' He looked down at the flower bed, scratched his jaw. 'May I say something else? Please, don't be disheartened by the rumours. I shouldn't have told you about them but you asked so directly. There's no malice in them; the boys would not talk of what they weren't intrigued by. And you said *crippled*, but Miss Waterfield, aren't there plants that we strengthen with bamboo? They are no less lovely for it. So please, don't heed the idle talk from those who are bored or know no better.'

I had no reply to this. Only my mother had ever offered compliments. She'd called me radiant, once – said that my whitish colouring gave me my own form of light and I must not be shy of it. She'd also said that there was no human perfection; that if the flaw could not be seen physically, then the person carried it inside them, which made it far worse, and I'd believed this part, at least. But I'd never expected compliments from elsewhere. I felt partly suspicious of it.

'Well, Miss Waterfield, I have no wish to keep you from your business. And I fear I must return to the flower bed before it gets too late in the day.'

A farewell, yet I stayed. I studied him as he worked: the measured, dignified way of him; his acknowledgement of the robin and the quiet *up!* to himself as he strained to lift a loaded spade. 'Hollis?'

I asked him what a gooseberry was. Despite all my books, and for all the observation of Millicent boiling fruit to soften it, I'd never heard of such a thing before. At that, the gardener smiled. He leaned the spade against himself and used his weathered hands to explain their size and shape to me. Their hairy exterior. How they were veined, when held up to the light. And yes, they needed sugaring because they could be sharp little things. 'Mrs Hollis,' he said, 'makes a fine gooseberry jam.' Late May to midsummer was their harvesting time.

That night, we sat in the kitchen, the four of us. The meal was mutton, potatoes and a handful of peas that Harriet had shelled in the afternoon. The water jug was chipped. The napkins were pressed but carried old stains.

'I hear,' said Mrs Bale, 'that you met Hollis today. Near the red borders? Isn't he kindly? He's quite the gentleman. And oh, he works so hard . . . These gardens are Mr Fox's, of course, but they are the work of Hollis and his father before him, and *his* father – did he tell you? And aren't the gardens delightful?' She trilled of her favourite places within it: the bench near the rose walk; the beechwoods in autumn; the topiary trees which had been peacocks, once. She gestured as she spoke. The maids said nothing, looked at their food.

On returning to my bedroom, I noticed two things. Firstly, someone had entered it during the day. My books had been touched: *Indian Tales* and my anatomical guide had exchanged positions on the pile. But secondly, the rose, too, had altered. On my arrival, two nights before, it had been in bud. Now it had lost all its petals; its water had thickened and greyed, and this made no sense to me. Why might a bloom lose its petals so quickly? They had been plucked. Deliberately removed.

I carried it back to the kitchen. 'Did someone go into my room?' I asked.

Harriet was on her own. She lifted her hands from the sink, wide-eyed. 'I made your bed this morning, Miss Waterfield.' But no, she hadn't touched my books. As for the rose, she shook her head. 'It happens at Shadowbrook. Flowers last a day or so, that's all.'

'A day? Why only a day?'

'Mrs Bale likes to fill vases and jugs with flowers, and petals always drop very quickly. Within hours, sometimes. Once, she placed peonies in a jug in the hallway and within ten minutes every single stem was broken. She says it's the draughts. A draughty house.'

I might have contested this. I had not yet felt a draught here. Even so, how might a draught remove petals so quickly? Thicken water or snap peonies? But it was my hour of tiredness; I'd acquired bruises from exploring the garden and my joints, too, felt sore. So I bade her goodnight, left her.

I wrote to Patrick that night. I wished to tell him that I'd arrived safely, that my room was adequate and yes, I was using my cane. I signed, *In fondness, Clara*.

Afterwards, I could not sleep. I longed to, but my mind prevented it. I thought of my stepfather and the miles my letter needed to travel in order to reach his cool, pale hands. But I thought, too, of the lower garden. Of the strange fate of my single-stem rose.

Sleep came, in the end. But later, I stirred, roused by hearing the grandfather clock strike three times in the hall. I lifted my head from its pillow. And then I heard a creak. It was quiet, but enough for me to sit up fully. I held my breath in case it came again.

It did. A second creak. And a third and, later, a fourth. Was it pipework? The house's adjustment as the temperature fell? Or it was somebody walking above my head; a fox's weight, sniffing the air?

Four creaks and no more. I sank back down, into my nest of blankets and my body's own scent – and I dreamed strange dreams before daybreak: of petals that filled my cupped hands, spilled over. Those petals were the colour of bone; they had, too, a bone's powdery texture, and my mother moved on the dream's periphery. I could sense her, hear her padding feet, but I could not see her clearly, despite calling for her – both *Mama* and her given name.

III

Such bone dreams had frequented my London life. My fear of fractures, by day, would move into dreams in which my teeth rained into my hands; I'd see myself as piano keys on which unknown fingers played. But the opiate brought the darkest dream. In it, my bones would be taken from me; faceless men would dismantle me, removing ribs from my nose or my femur through my mouth like an ancient ritual to which I'd not consented. And with this, I would wake in need of water. Water, water. Feel across the dark bedroom for the glass on my nightstand.

But those dreams had reduced themselves, in time. I feared breaks and dislocations far less, and opium was gone from my life. Such dreams rarely came and none stayed with me on waking.

Yet this dream stayed. I thought of it as I dressed. I combed my hair, looked at my reflection and I thought, momentarily, that my mother had passed behind me; I thought I'd seen her rush across the glass. But there was only the wardrobe behind me.

I rose, opened the curtains. And there was rain, filling the ivy, pattering on the glass. On seeing it, I lifted the window to breathe the scent of a wet garden, reached out my hand – and my dream moved away.

*

Mrs Bale greeted me brightly – 'Ah! Here she is' – as if she had been waiting for me. I looked for the maids but she was alone, stirring the teapot.

'Good morning, Miss Waterfield, I am afraid you have woken to a rather grey day. I'd rather hoped that the fine weather would last, but it seems we must content ourselves with rain.'

With this, she poured tea and listed all the benefits of wet weather: that it would wash the windows, freshen the bathing pool which had greened a little, quicken the brook, and that every plant in the garden would be thankful of it. There'd be those in the village, of course, who'd grumble – Mrs Rudd with her sore joints, or the blacksmith in Lower Barcombe who disliked shoeing wet creatures. 'But there is no pleasing some people.'

I sipped as I listened to her, and tried to decipher if this was Mrs Bale's natural manner; if her musical voice and bustle had always been part of her. It was hard to know. But there was a small child within her still. She'd gesture with both hands, as if weighing the air; she rounded her eyes, smiled constantly. And such cheer and restlessness struck me, therefore, as either entirely natural and innate to her, or a deliberate act. I could not tell which. All I could be sure of was that, despite her babbling, she seemed no less tired. The inky-blue pouches of skin under her eyes were still there.

I held my teacup in both hands. 'I had hoped to see more of the garden today.'

'Oh you should! There is so much to explore; I keep telling the girls that. One could spend weeks moving through it and never see it all. It changes all the time, of course. Buds become flowers and flowers become berries. I am fond of the hydrangea bed. Have you found it? The hydrangea bed?'

'I'd also hoped to post a letter.'

'That's simple enough. Barcombe is half a mile away and Mr Jarvis's shop is perfectly good. He'll post the letter for you.' She began to sweep the table of crumbs with the side of her hand. 'It is an easy walk, Miss Waterfield. Take the lane downhill, past the Hollises' house and the rotten tree and the barley fields; you will be there in no time.'

'But I can't today. The rain.'

'There is a spare oilskin coat in the potting shed. I can't vouch for its cleanliness, I'm afraid, as the boys use it from time to time – and who knows what might be in its pockets – but if you wish to borrow it, then do, by all means.' Her permanent smile.

But it wasn't the rain itself that I minded. Wet clothes, after all, could dry. I was as wary of wet ground as I was of polished floors, or oil, or ice, and I explained this to her. Precarious places. 'Hollis says the lower garden is steep.'

'Oh, that's a dismal place. He's right; it's so steep-sided that I've always refused to go there. Also, it smells so dank, Miss Waterfield! It's full of hostas and snails. Wouldn't you think that a place of water would be light-filled? It's not at all. It's shadow and moss.'

With that, a memory seemed to come to Mrs Bale. She slowed as she dried her hands on a towel; she looked out at the rain – and I had her profile then. I had the short lashes, the softened jawline; I had the outline of her so clearly that I might have drawn around it, made a cameo of her and worn it as a brooch. Had Mrs Bale been beautiful? Was she still? She had the dark hair. The rounded dark eyes. Someone, at least, must have thought so, for her wedding ring caught the light as she set the towel down.

'And will I meet Mr Fox today? He's returned, I know. I heard him walking upstairs last night. Late – perhaps three o'clock, or four.'

At this, Mrs Bale turned. Momentarily, she seemed different: no smile or gestures. She only stared, searched my face as if my words might have a further meaning she couldn't be sure of. 'Mr Fox? No. He's not back yet.'

'He is. I heard footsteps.'

'No. I told you, Miss Waterfield: this is an old house and it creaks. Think nothing of it.'

'Draughts?'

She smiled her bright smile. 'Draughts. Precisely. I can ask Hollis to post the letter for you, if you'd like. Or one of the garden boys, for they all walk through Barcombe on their way home in the afternoons and there are one or two of them who might be capable of such a task.'

But I shook my head, mistrustful. They had been footsteps, I was sure of that. And I wanted to visit Barcombe-on-the-Hill, to learn how to post a letter myself.

I stayed indoors that day. I'd have loved to have used the oilskin coat – to have ventured out and witnessed the dimpling of the bathing pool or the lowering of branches. To have heard the dabbling of rain on the oilskin's hood, as my mother had described a day in London's rain. But I knew the likelihood of a fall. Knew that a broken limb would render me useless in creating a private paradise, as I'd been summoned to do.

I chose, therefore, to explore the house. I moved along the corridor, feeling the wood panelling, turning handles. Thirteen years of neglect? There were signs of this in every room. The drawing room was the brightest in colour and light; it felt used and cared for, yet it still had cobwebs between the furniture, damp in its corners and a hearth in which the last year's leaves had gathered and stayed. In the library, there were no books at all. There were only shelves where books might once have been in the Pettigrew age, but which now held dust and the frail, papery bodies of spiders that had died with their legs tucked up. There was a splintered desk with no chair. Also, a cracked window pane and such thick creepers on the exterior wall that the view from this room was lessened by blackish leaf and stem. How could a library have no books within it? Or be called a library at all?

Other rooms were no less bare. The dining room rug bore the indentations of where a table had been. On its mantelpiece, there was a porcelain jug of lavender stems so old that they'd lost their colour and held only the ghost of a scent. In the room they called the smoking room, the walls were yellowish; its ceiling rose had browned. And its view into a cedar tree darkened the room further, so that when I pulled the door behind me, I knew I would not return there.

I did not request to see the maids' room or Mrs Bale's. But otherwise I entered every downstairs room. And I felt that only four of them had any semblance of life within them: the kitchen, the drawing room, my own bedroom and the bathroom, with its blue and white tiles and peeling paint. It was used by all four of us, so that I'd find, sometimes, damp footprints in there. I picked rust-coloured strands of hair – Harriet's – out of the rose-scented soap.

But there was one further room. At first I'd thought it to be a cupboard: a panelled door facing my own, on the far side of the hall. But inside it, there was a bed. Also, a wide writing desk had been pushed into the window, so that a writer might find inspiration in the topiary trees and a holly bush. As I stood in its doorway, Maud passed me. She carried a mop, spoke bluntly. 'What are you looking for?'

'Nothing. Which room is this?'

She puckered her mouth. 'The billiards room – or it was. There was a billiards table in here when Mr Fox came. But the mice had gnawed the baize and there were stains upon it that Mrs Bale could not account for and would not try to clean. She said it looked like blood. So we burned it near the compost heap.' She shrugged, walked on.

I stayed, momentarily. A second guest room? So it seemed. It was larger than mine, and I wondered why I'd not been given this room instead. But mine, I felt, was better: I liked its position tucked under the stairs, how it received the morning sun. I had come to like my herbal scent and my view.

Pettigrew. I tried the name as I walked through the house. Had Shadowbrook always been theirs? I imagined the lives they'd had: card games and tapestries, fur-trimmed collars and long skirts that swept the floor with a shushing sound. In winter, a cinnamon smell. And children? I imagined them running in the long corridor, under the picture hooks which were, now, entirely bare. But once, surely, these hooks had borne the weight of portraits and landscapes and still lives of feathered game and fruit. I could see the outline of the paintings where they had been – the ghosts of them. And so, as it rained, I invented a family who placed a huge Christmas tree in the hall and gathered around it. Whose silverware shone by candlelight.

But I thought of Mrs Bale, too.

Yes, there was a childishness to her. An impishness, even – in her gesticulations, her breathy speech and in that smile that seemed pinned, stretched too wide. But there was also something darker. Within her, a shadow. And this shadow, I felt, was keeping her awake.

Draughts, she'd said. But those sounds above my head

had not been caused by any blowing air. What I had heard, in the night, was the slow, cautious transference of human weight. I was certain of that.

I looked up.

Dark stairs. A wooden banister rail that had been smoothed by years of hands.

I took hold of it, climbed up. A straight ascent to a landing on which there was a small rug. And here, I saw a painting. It surprised me: it was the only art I had seen in the house – a gold square in which a woman reclined on cloth. She was nude. Entirely bare. Her left arm draped over her upper thigh and, having angled her hips, a certainty modesty was spared. But the rest of her was fully exposed: flushed, rounded, fleshy with no suggestion of bone. She was, of course, dark-haired. Such luminous skin made her hair seem darker still, and beyond her, the world was nocturnal; she herself was lit by a single lantern's light, so that this painting spoke of shadows and secrets.

To my left, the corridor stretched away, unlit. It was the same as the corridor directly beneath it and yet, somehow, it seemed narrower.

He has a suite of rooms. I placed my hand on the handle of the nearest door, tried it – and it opened. But I walked into nothing. As with the library and the smoking room, it was empty of life. Or perhaps it was even emptier: no bookshelves with autumn leaves at their feet; no discoloration on the walls where, once, paintings had been. Outside, the sound of rain. Also, there was the soft bluish light that comes with rain, so that the room seemed stranger still, and on the floor, the dust was so thick and undisturbed that I had left footprints in it. My two feet, and the beady eye of my cane.

'What are you doing up here?'

Words like a slap. I turned, stung.

The girlishness was gone; no pinned smile. 'I told you. This is Mr Fox's floor.'

'Yes. But I did not think that meant I could not come here.'

'It means precisely that! It means that you have no reason or right to be prying as you are – opening doors, creeping like a ghoul! Come out of here at once.'

'I'm causing no damage.'

'Out. Out!'

I obeyed, but reluctantly. I took my time, twisting my hip. 'Why are there such empty rooms, Mrs Bale? No furniture. Not even trunks or boxes.'

She narrowed her eyes. 'And may I ask, in return, why you feel that is your concern? Downstairs now, please.'

'And the nude. Is there a story behind it, do you know? I was also wondering why she is the only painting in the whole of the house when there are so many empty hooks elsewhere—'

'Miss Waterfield.' She spoke as if she held a rock in her raised hand: a hard, clear warning.

I felt her eyes on me as I made my way down to the hall.

Impish? I did not think this now. Nor did I have any doubt that her bright smile was not to be trusted. Yes, she carried a shadow inside her. In the hallway, I turned to face her. 'You did not say that I could not venture there. You did not say it was forbidden, and yet you're reprimanding me.' Challenging, hard.

Her eyes flashed – with what? Anger? I couldn't tell. 'Well. Now you know the rules.'

That night, we ate our meal in silence which suggested that they all knew. That Maud and Harriet had been told of my wanderings, had heard more of my forthright nature.

The rain fell. Water glasses were lowered with care.

'The rain will make for a fine July, at least.' The house-keeper smiled, trying to be bright.

But I believed none of it. She could bring down a ruler on a schoolboy's hand. Could slap down a gavel in a court of law and place the square black cloth on her head. It was only later, as I was retiring to my bedroom, that I heard the patter-patter of Mrs Bale's feet behind me and she sang out my name in her old, pleasant, girlish voice. When I turned, she was smiling. She walked with her shoulders tipped for-wards, as if sheepish; her hands were pressed to her cheeks to hide a blush of shame. 'Oh, please forgive my manner with you earlier, Miss Waterfield. It was quite out of keep-ing and I fancy I startled you with it, for you gave me such a look! And rather a defiant air, too, if I may say so. Of course, I understand why. It is entirely my fault for having not made you fully aware of the rules of the house. And the only rule is that the first floor is Mr Fox's and his alone; it is quite forbidden to the rest of us. Even the maids aren't per-mitted to go there. So please do not think it's a rule against you only. He wishes to be undisturbed, you understand.'

'But you go there. You must. You open and close his windows.'

She reached for her plait, felt it with both hands. 'I do, yes. He permits me to do that. When he is at home I take his meals to him. Take his fresh laundry and a newspaper from time to time.'

'You said he has a suite of rooms.'

'Yes. His own bathroom and living quarters.'

'But that room is empty. It is so thick with dust that it can't have been used for years.'

'He has,' she said, retaining her smile, 'a suite on the south-facing side of the house. The north-facing rooms are not currently in use, as you saw. But in time, I am sure he will restore them and make them very special, as all of the house will be.'

She explained slowly yet I still didn't quite understand. 'So when Mr Fox is at Shadowbrook House, he has no need to leave the first floor? He can stay up there all the time?'

'Yes.'

'Why? Mrs Bale, why would he choose to do that?' It made no sense, and although I knew she was inwardly tired of my interrogation, I wanted to know, regardless of manners. 'Is something the matter with him? Is he a recluse?'

At this, she laughed. I felt offended by her laughter – a swift, tinkly peal that felt mocking, wrong. 'Oh, child! How can he be a recluse when he's away from home currently? No, he simply prefers peace and his own company when he's at Shadowbrook. And why shouldn't he? Hasn't he earned the right to do as he pleases? His quarters are perfectly comfortable, after all.'

I turned her answer over, not trusting it.

She waited. She expected, no doubt, a further question. When none came, she shifted her weight; she fingered the silver cross that she wore around her neck. 'I am his house-keeper, you see. I must take care of his house in the manner he desires, and to think of his wishes above all else. Can you understand that? But Miss Waterfield, in truth I was thinking of you too.'

'Of me?'

There was no smile now. She was serious, unblinking. 'Of your safety.'

'My safety? My bones? Mrs Bale, I am twenty years old and—'

'Not your bones!' She hissed this, said it quickly, and glanced back as if she might have been heard. 'I mean that it's not safe to be there! Not safe to walk on that upper corridor, not safe to be on those stairs.' She shook her head. 'I can't tell you more, or I can't tell you now, at least – and I don't know what you'd think of me if I did. You would think me to be quite mad, I'm sure, and rush back to London. But please believe me, Miss Waterfield, that it is best if you do not go there again. Only if he summons you.'

'If he summons me?'

'Yes. As he may, for I'm sure he'll wish to see you on his return. But only then, Miss Waterfield. In the meanwhile, please keep to the places where you are safe. The gardens, your glasshouse. Keep to the ground floor.'

I sat on my bed that night. I counted my new bruises and held my breath as I did so, listening for the single creak of a floorboard as if a foot was testing it.

Yet there was only the sound of the rain. So I climbed into bed and, for a time, I tried to read my anatomical guide. I mouthed the liver's function to myself, in need of facts; I wanted certainty. But within minutes, I'd pushed the book aside. Where was the sense in this? Mr Fox was choosing to make a small, narrowed life of his own, on his upper floor – yet look what he owned. Look at the gardens he had to explore – with peach-coloured roses and topiary trees. A circular bathing pool. Why buy such a house if he did not like gardens? And why build a glasshouse at all?

I was thinking of your safety. And *trouble*, too, returned to me; spoken of by the driver whose teeth could withstand the hard, repeated knocking of butterscotch.

I turned onto my side. Soon, the rain stopped. I heard an owl call twice, from the beechwoods, and something rustled outside in the leaves. But that was all.

*

The previous day's rain showed itself in hollow ground and on cobwebs and, in consequence, the herb garden seemed brighter for it. It was silver with light.

In the kitchen, Harriet was watching an egg as it boiled. She held a wooden spoon in the air, as if asking for order.

'Where is Mrs Bale?' It was after eight o'clock and I expected her to be here.

Harriet looked back. 'She is sleeping.'

'Sleeping? Still? Is she unwell?'

'I don't know. We knocked on her door and she said she needed more sleep. She doesn't tend to sleep well.'

'Does she have a fever?'

'No. I asked if we needed to send for Dr Warrimer but she said no, that a little sleep was all she needed. And Miss Waterfield?' Harriet delved into her apron, retrieved a folded square and proffered it. 'She asked me to give you this – for you're going to Barcombe, I think?'

I took it, read it. She'd written three items on it: *Eggs (a dozen). Flour. Tea.*

'We are low on tea leaves, you see, and we never know when Mr Fox will come back. He just comes, unannounced, and he likes his afternoon tea.' She looked back to the saucepan. 'It's a good shop. There is even a coffee grinder in there. Sometimes there are peppermint creams.'

'Have you met Mr Fox? Seen him?'

'No, I've not met him. Nor has Maud. It's always Mrs Bale who tends to him. There's a trestle table outside his door to which she'll take his trays.'

'And you don't think this is strange?'

The maid seemed cautious. 'Perhaps. But he only wants his privacy and he's so rarely here that it's hardly any trouble. He pays us well, Miss Waterfield.'

I looked down at the list. This strange, uneven

handwriting of Mrs Bale's. The *gs* in *eggs* were elongated, curled; the *o* in *flour* was as wide as the world. And yet I saw more than the ink. I saw the task ahead of me. I remembered my hours in snow, watching passengers alight from omnibuses and in this way I'd learned how to board a bus myself. But shops? I'd never entered one. 'Harriet? How do I do this?'

'Do what?' She looked up from the boiling egg.

'Buy them. How do I buy these things? Don't laugh at me.'

The maid lowered the spoon. She stepped back from the stove and faced me. 'There are whispers of you, Miss Waterfield. One is that you have lived your life like a queen with others caring for you. Is this true?'

Like a queen. Was that how it had been? Had I been regal, demanding? I'd ordered autumn leaves to be gathered. Thrown books that Patrick had bought because I'd wanted to be able to run or push onto the balls of my feet without fractures. 'I didn't stay inside by choice.'

For a moment, Harriet was expressionless. I felt that I'd handed these words to her and, now, she was turning them over in her hands, feeling their weight and curiousness. Then she set down the spoon; she dried her hands on her apron and came closer to me. 'Enter the shop. There will be a counter at the far end and Mr Jarvis will be there. He'll stare at you but don't mind that; he stares at everyone. And I don't think he'll care for your unpinned hair or your reason for being here because he has views on a woman's role in life. Just ask him for these things, on this list; hand the list to him, if you prefer. Tell him to put the cost of it all on Mr Fox's account.'

'What of my letter? The stamp?'

'The cost of that, too.' Harriet smiled. 'Miss Waterfield, I'm not laughing at you. But it's peculiar that you can travel unaccompanied and care for tropical plants and yet you don't know how to buy tea.' But she did not say this unkindly.

She retrieved the spoon, lifted the egg from the saucepan and, as she worked, she told me that I'd find the shop overlooking the village green, beyond the church and the mounting block, facing the ancient oak. That I might find I'd be followed a little, for Barcombe did not receive many new faces. 'Only in the autumn, when the farm gangs come. So you'll be noticed, talked of. But don't mind it.'

I felt gratitude, then. It wasn't a common feeling – although I'd felt it as Patrick had looked through the carriage window in London, nearly a week before. I'd felt it, too, in my mother's last hours. I'd thought, I've never thanked her – for every glass of water she'd brought to me, for each London view. I shook my mother away; I regarded, instead, the maid, who was placing a boiled egg in an eggcup: she was three years younger than me, with her large hands and freckled jawline, and yet she'd been the older one in regard to Jarvis's shop, and I could have thanked her verbally, at that moment. But I chose, instead, to find a pencil and add peppermint creams to the written list. Mr Fox could pay for those too.

The lane between Shadowbrook and the village of Barcombe-on-the-Hill was, at first, shaded by trees; it ran through beechwoods. On either side of me, I could see into their brambly depths. But the woods soon ended. After this, the lane entered daylight and moved between two hedgerows of nettle and dandelion and briar rose, of vetch and a white, cloudy flower whose name I didn't know. Above, there was a sky of thin clouds. Under my feet, the lane was hollowed from carts and weathering and so I was mindful, moved carefully.

A world away from Kew. A lifetime, it seemed, from a map on the wall and the carriage clock that ticked through the hours. I was walking between hedgerows that were far higher than me. I was passing new sights: a dead tree, wrapped in ivy; the smoothed, scooped earth where a creature had brushed under hedges at dusk. I passed, too, the Hollises' house. I knew it was theirs: the line of boots by its door seemed right for him. Also, in its garden, an apple tree trailed a long, fraying rope with a knot at its end: a swing which spoke of the sons he had raised. A childhood spent outdoors.

By a gateway, I paused. I shifted my spine from side to side, looked out. Barley, or I assumed it was. Mrs Bale had mentioned this. I looked across the wide, flat expanses of a gold-greenish crop through which a breeze was moving, and said the word, trying it. The barley was waist-high for me. I thought to reach forwards, to feel its feathered tip through the bars of the gates and, gently, I tried to – but I heard voices. Male voices were coming closer, ascending the lane. I knew whose voices they must be. It was a little before nine o'clock: the garden boys were making their way up from their homes in Barcombe and elsewhere for their day's work of digging and pruning. I recognised their exchanges, their light protestations and laughter, and I had an immediate choice: I could either retreat into the hedges to avoid being seen, or I could stand as I was, lift my jaw. I chose the latter – for despite their tales of malnourishment, they'd not truly seen me yet. They'd only glimpsed or heard stories. Also, I wished to see boys.

A black-haired boy saw me first. He was kicking a stone as he went; the stone came into the long grass near me so that he, too, came closer; on seeing me, he grasped the wrist of the nearest boy who in turn elbowed his friend, and like

this they looked up, one by one. They slowed. *Is that . . . ?*
And what I remembered, at that moment, was the geese that
had flown over London's bridges in formation with their
similarities and their small differences, and their soft, rum-
bling communication between themselves; how they had all
flown in the same direction. Eight boys stared at me. They,
too, murmured their private thoughts. And with only a few
feet between us, I knew they saw it all: the eyes, the fingers
that did not fully straighten, the milk-coloured lashes. I saw
it, too. Their prominent teeth and spectacles. Their early,
feathery hints of beards. A nose that needed a handkerchief.

'Good morning,' I said.

There was no immediate reply. But then the tallest boy
offered a good morning; he mumbled an order to the other
boys, so that their own small, clumsier greetings came. And
as they walked on, I noted the backward glances. The whispers and jokes exchanged between them.

News moves quickly here. So Hollis had said. I supposed
that if there were whispers of my appearance – true or
untrue – there must also be whispers of Mr Fox, passed over
teapots or the backs of horses. And if so, what might they
be? This man who kept to his suite of rooms. Who rarely
showed himself, it seemed. Did he carry a disfigurement, or
a broken heart? A history of espionage?

I readjusted my grasp on my cane, carried on.

A small iron sign in the hedgerow announced it: Barcombe-
on-the-Hill.

At its centre there was a village green – a rounded patch
of grass with a wooden bench and a noticeboard and an oak
tree of such age and girth that its lower, largest branches
were either propped with wood or had found the ground
of their own accord and rested there. One branch seemed

to have grown down into the earth before rising back out; another had been propped for so long that it had taken the prop into itself, grown round it, making it part of the living wood. An ancient tree. Loved, too, for the lowest bough was smooth, worn down. And I imagined the hands and bottoms of hardy pink children – Pettigrews, maybe – who had climbed on it, year after year.

Cottages of both brick and the honeyed Cotswold stone overlooked the village green. Some had thatched roofs. Others seemed bound by slate or ivy. Dogs scratched themselves on doorsteps, bicycles were propped against walls, and front gardens spilled with the last of the hollyhocks and nettlebeds. Yet there were, too, signs of wear. Thatch had thinned in places. Gates were splintered or off their hinges and anchored by weeds. And the women who watched me were already tired; they straightened from their mangles or brooms.

A church, half lost to yew trees. A drinking trough whose water was thickened with weed so that it did not seem like water at all yet a horse still drank, untethered; the horse belonged to no one, as far as I could see. A tavern, too: The Bull. It stood at the far end of the village, as the lane dropped down towards Lower Barcombe. A weathered, sun-faded sign of a bull in a yoke, with pointed horns.

The village shop was where Harriet said it would be. It was large, double-fronted, with a sign that read, *Drink Pepsi-Cola. Sold here!* Its frontage was black; *JARVIS'S* was announced in large gold lettering. And as I opened its door, a bell chimed; a clear, struck metallic chime announced my arrival. On closing the door, it chimed again.

I stood, assessed this place. A cool, quiet cave of luncheon tongue and aniseed balls. Newspapers. Pear's soap.

Mr Jarvis had heard the bell. He moved into view at the

end of the shop – deliberately, suspiciously. He had the most extravagant moustache I had ever seen: it was pure white, waxed at its tips so that I thought of the bull on the tavern sign. He wore his apron like a prize.

'Miss Waterfield?'

He observed my gait as I crossed the shop floor. When I was three feet from him, I proffered the list. 'I need these items. Please.'

He accepted it slowly. 'Anything else?'

'And may I post a letter with you?' I set it on the counter.

He examined the list. Peered at the envelope's address. 'You're from Kew, I hear. They sent you here?'

'Yes.'

'From the Gardens themselves?'

'Yes. From the Gardens.'

This, it seemed, troubled him. He sucked at his teeth, stepped out from behind his counter. 'You are arranging the flowers in the house, I assume? Filling vases?' He moved from shelf to shelf.

Mr Jarvis was a broad, heavy man. As he trod, I felt the floor move beneath me; I heard jars and metalwork tinkle on the shelves. 'Vases? No. Mr Fox wants a glasshouse and I am here to establish it for him.'

'You?' He looked between biscuit tins. 'How can you do that?'

'Because Kew have shown me how to.'

He raised an eyebrow, moved on. 'Mr Fox is paying you? You are being paid?'

'Yes. It's my job.'

'Yours? On your own?'

A hard, dark feeling rose in me. 'Yes, on my own.'

Mr Jarvis emerged with a brown bag of flour, set it down. Beside it, he placed a tin of tea leaves. 'I should not be surprised, I suppose. Not with the problems that women are causing these days.'

'Problems?'

'With their antics. Their marches. Give the vote to them? To women? They haven't the minds to know what to do with the vote. Most of them can't even write their own names. We'd be fools to think they could manage such ...' he paused, eyed the list, 'responsibility.' With that, he murmured *eggs* to himself and moved away again.

I had been warned that there were such sentiments in the world. Harriet, too, had alluded to Jarvis's views. But to hear them for the first time was an entirely different matter; to hear them said felt as much like an assault as if he'd physically touched me. In response, I felt my hand tighten over my cane. I wished to stab the floor with it; I had the sudden compulsion to knock at the newspaper stand by my side or run my hand over the counter so that everything on it would fall – and yet I knew this would not help matters. He'd only peer over his moustache, satisfied. Use it as proof.

'We can write our names.'

'You can, maybe, although I'm not sure how, with your crooked hand. But the women of Barcombe aren't the kind to have anatomy books by their beds, and they haven't the time or inclination to write at all. The vote? It's a bad idea and it won't come to pass. I'll post your letter for you. Will there be anything else?'

He stood back in front of me. He seemed even larger for having spoken this way, as if the words had inflated him. I could hear his breathing – the sound of his lungs under his apron and shirt – and I wished I had stronger bones, at that moment. Wished I had the right, clever words. 'We are equal,' I said. 'We should have the same rights as men, in all ways.'

A scoff from the shopkeeper. 'Equal? I don't think so. And at any rate, that talk hasn't been heard here for a long time.'

'Of votes for women?'

'Of equality. Of anyone being equal. You'll ask why, no doubt. Because of the house you are working in, Miss Waterfield. They thought they were the kings of their castle. That we were only their dogs to kick.'

I tensed. 'The Pettigrews?'

'Yes, the Pettigrews.' Mr Jarvis plucked the pencil from his ear, wrote in a notebook. 'No one cared for them. There isn't a single person in Barcombe who misses that family or protects their memory. That house lay empty for so long because no one would buy it. Their grave is untended because no one mourns. There are some in this village who will not even say the name itself – the name! – and that house, now? With its fancy gardens and hedges? It may have a new owner but that's still the Pettigrew house. That's still Pettigrew land. The air in its rooms will always be Pettigrew air.'

I left his shop with my groceries and a fast, angered heart. I'd hated his talk of votes. I'd hated the notion that I'd been called from Kew to place flowers in vases and no other reason. Also, I'd hated his slow, deliberate assessment of me as I'd crossed the room. I swiped my cane at a nettle patch, vowed to myself that I'd never set foot in Jarvis's shop again.

But the Pettigrews, too. The shopkeeper had spat the name, fixed his eyes in a wild form of anger. And in that moment, my image of the Pettigrew family – lace collars and silverware, impeccable manners – was gone. *We were only their dogs to kick.*

I entered the churchyard. It happened without intention;

I was absorbed with my thoughts, aware of my faster heart-beat, so that I passed through the wooden gate without meaning to and only understood where I was by the change in light. For it was darker, suddenly. Yew and chestnut trees grew on either side of me. I walked between gravestones, of every size and age. Some retained their sense of formality: straight and ordered, with only a little growth at their sides – of dandelions or thistles – and the names of their owners still visible despite the lichen and the years. But other stones had lost their dignity. They sprawled or had been broken. Some had tilted forwards, through human weight or time or bad weather; others were lost entirely beneath brambles or grass.

Untended, Mr Jarvis had said. Yet how might I know the Pettigrew grave when so many were fallen, or had been claimed by time? It was hard to know and harder still to move between these gravestones when the paths were so overgrown, when I had my cane and a brown paper bag of groceries, and the light, too, was so dappled and strange that I could not detect the proper edges of graves and the path itself seemed like water for how the shadows moved across it. I moved as if wading.

Their grave, he'd said – a grave of many, not one. So I searched for the larger plots. In doing so, I found, often, the same surnames: Bayley, Cartwright, Preedy, Rudd. I noted the papery bones of flowers that had been picked and left at the feet of the stones. I saw where boots had printed the grass.

Collier. Flint.

No Pettigrew.

But then – after half an hour, perhaps, or more – I found it. In the farthest corner of the churchyard, amongst bramble and nettle and briar, there was a monument; an ornate four-sided column of stone, with cherubs carved at the top, and in this way, it was grand. But it was entirely disowned. Ivy and bindweed grew round it; where stonework was exposed, much of it had been furred with moss or whitened by birds that had perched on the boughs overhead and opened themselves. There were no words to see. Yet I knew this gravestone must be theirs.

I stepped away from the path. I lowered the paper bag to the ground and, with my cane, began to flatten the nettles that grew at the gravestone's base. I pressed down the brambles; I reached to the ivy and pulled it away. And there it was: *PETTIGREW*. Carved into the stonework, greened with moss. A word like a face, staring out.

I parted the ivy a little more.

Here lie the sacred remains of THOMAS RUTLAND PET-TIGREW, born of this parish 5th June 1771, died 4th May 1852. Also, his wife, CATHERINE, died 12th January 1790. Also, his only son, MORTIMER PETTIGREW, born 12th January 1790 . . . I found other names amongst the brambles. *His sons FRANCIS (1838–1882) and HUGO (1840–1884). Blessed be their memory as they ascend into . . .*

I stepped back from the stone. *Also, his wife.* Catherine, I noticed, had died on the same day as Mortimer was born. A bloodied, fearful death for her. No other words and no maiden name.

Untended. It was. No powdering flowers. No footprints in the waist-high grass.

It will always be Pettigrew air.

I heard a sound behind me. It came from a twig giving way underfoot; a bright, hard *snap!* At first I thought there was no one there, that the figure I saw was, in fact, a statue – a neat stone effigy of an angled, slender man. He was holding a book against himself; he was half lit by the canopy's light and so perfectly still that I assumed he was part of a grave.

But then he moved. He retracted his foot; he adjusted his grasp of his book. And I saw his parted hair, of no discernible shade. I saw the glint of round spectacles; I also saw the eyes behind them – grey, fixed upon me as if I were just as strange and unexpected as him. I saw the white band at his throat.

Older than me but not by much.

'You're the vicar,' I said. He did not answer. This stirred my anger further: I knew he had heard me, so why did he not reply? 'I asked if you were the vicar.'

'Yes. Yes, I am. Forgive me. Yes. And you're from Kew Gardens, I think?'

'Yes. And the gentleman in the shop believes that women don't matter as much as men. If you're the vicar, you must agree. We're all spare ribs to you, I should think.'

Fast, unexpected words. I hadn't considered them; they rushed out – and yet even if I'd been able to stop them, I might not have chosen to. For my mother had never spoken well of the Church. Patrick had said nothing at all of it. And my own understanding had been that imperfect bodies were forms of godly punishment; that imperfect meant I was worth less somehow. I'd disliked this notion intensely. Also, I was not a spare rib.

The vicar looked down at his book. He did not answer straight away, or not audibly. His lips moved, as if trying words privately before offering them to me. 'Everyone is welcome here. Miss Waterfield, will you excuse me?' he said. 'I' – he lifted the book in his right hand – 'must see someone. A parishioner.' And he left, saying no more.

He hurried between the gravestones, passed under the yews, and I saw how quickly he strode, with his book pressed to his chest. There were two thoughts that came to me at that moment: firstly, that I'd started the day with thoughts of Shadowbrook's reclusive owner yet now the name Pettigrew intrigued me far more than Fox. It seemed to draw me, as the brighter light draws the moth, with this jungled grave and legacy; the Pettigrews mattered far more to me now. Secondly, the vicar knew my name. He'd called me Miss Waterfield, as the shopkeeper had done. And I supposed that Mrs Bale, with her silver cross and tattling nature, had offered my name and description to both of them, as well as a list of the books by my bed. Or the shorter maid had, perhaps: Maud, with her family of talkers. Either way, I understood that in Barcombe, secrets were hard to keep.

I gathered my brown paper bag and walked to Shadowbrook. And as I went, I considered my mother's mistrust of the Church. It had, I supposed, come from her childhood. I knew little about my grandmother except that she'd quoted the Old Testament; she'd hated the faithless, the faiths of others and Calcutta's monsoon heat. Also, Eugenia Pugh had sent her own daughter away for having made me – a sin, in God's eyes, so my mother herself had not cared for religion. In London, the only person I'd known who'd had faith at all had been Millicent. At any bad news, she'd draw the cross in the air with a floury finger and she would, at times, reassure my mother that she still prayed for Clara's bones in the hope of a cure. *One of His great miracles.* My mother would sometimes thank her curtly. But mostly she would not.

Charlotte Waterfield, née Pugh. We buried her in sanctified ground with a priest at her feet, speaking of shepherds and valleys of death. And I'd known – as Patrick had done, head bowed – that she wouldn't have wished to have been buried this way. In a January cemetery with sleet in the air.

Shadowbrook was glinting as I approached. Its southerly side was in full sun, and I could see the true expanse of the gold-coloured rose called Rêve d'Or. It was huge – thick, sprawled and glorious. It had grown up the drainpipe and fanned out; it clambered towards the first floor so that, in places, its tendrils were brushing the upper window panes and I wondered if their perfume might be detected in those upper rooms.

She'd have wanted that too, at her burial. Flowers that bore scent, and vibrancy. She'd have demanded jasmine or frangipani, and her instructions would have been for no mourning at all but to inhale and to walk forwards into the next day and the next without looking back. She'd have hoped for birdsong. She'd have preferred to be buried in hard, red earth which stained fingertips and retained paw-prints, the day's heat.

I had no wish to see others when I returned. I set the groceries down on the kitchen table, slipped back into the garden and, for the rest of the afternoon, I kept to its parts where the boys and Hollis were not: the beech avenue, the tunnel of limes which led to a single wrought-iron chair. Here I sat until it grew cool.

I might have sat there, under the limes, until it was dark. For the birds did not seem to mind me and would sing in the nearest branches or drop near my feet, looking for insects. But Jarvis had talked of the Pettigrew land, of some being fearful of the Pettigrew name, and I knew that as a child I'd have turned to books to learn more of them. I'd have run my finger down indexes, scanned footnotes. But there were no books at Shadowbrook. Here, the only source of knowledge seemed to be a man who turned the earth as if it had feelings, who had greeted the robin, so as the afternoon grew old, I rose from the chair and crossed the croquet lawn to the courtyard, where I hoped Hollis might be returning his buckets and hoes at the end of his working day.

He was not there. But I met him by the south-facing wall of the house; he was tying back a branch of roses that had fallen away with the weight of its blooms, or the previous rain.

'It's a good climber,' I said.

'It is, yes.' He knotted the string, stepped back and admired. 'Always has been. I planted it for that purpose, a long time ago now.'

I felt glad of him. Earth beneath his fingernails, a ball of gardening string in his pocket which trailed. He adjusted his cap to see me better.

'Has there been trouble here?'

His hand remained on the brim of his cap. 'Trouble?'

'Trouble. I was met at the station at Cheltenham Spa by a man who told me this house had known trouble. Mrs Bale seemed quite unlike herself when she found me on the first floor. And this afternoon, I met Mr Jarvis, who had no good words to say of the Pettigrews. He said they treated people like dogs. That the villagers were glad they were dead.'

He held his hands up, protesting. 'It's the garden I know about. The house ... I've barely entered it.'

'But you've been here all your life. A family of gardeners. You must have seen or heard something that could be called trouble. Or your father did, perhaps.'

At that, Hollis removed his cap. He ran a palm over his scalp three times before replacing it, and I knew he was thinking. He was sensing what he should tell me. 'Miss

Waterfield, do you remember how I said I berated the garden boys for having said such stories about you – untrue stories? It's because I don't like rumour very much. There are, I think, far better things to do with one's time.'

'Yes. But Mr Jarvis spat out the name Pettigrew.'

'Mr Jarvis is a man of temper. He has strong opinions and shares them too freely.'

'Are you saying he's wrong? I saw their grave, and it's neglected.'

Hollis exhaled. We stood with the Rêve d'Or above us; above us, too, were the open windows, the weathervane of the running hare that turned very slightly in a thin breeze. I watched this as he answered. 'My family has been at Shadowbrook for nearly a hundred years, that's true. But we've stayed to the gardens, Miss Waterfield. We are meant for the hedges and vegetable patch and this is what I know of – not the house. Even so, there are others who have known Shadowbrook – and the Pettigrew family – for longer still. The barley fields? Between here and Barcombe? That's Preedy land. The Preedys have farmed those fields for far more than a century now and he must know more tales than I do.'

'He?'

'Kit. He's the last of them.'

'So he'd know if there had been trouble here? He'd have heard or seen it?'

At that, Hollis looked at his pocket watch. He expressed his surprise at the hour and headed home, across the courtyard, trailing gardening string. And I knew he had not answered me as such. He'd only offered a farmer's name and left with a tap of his cap. But this in itself had been an answer. Yes, there had been trouble at Shadowbrook – although it was hard to believe at that moment: the roses were sweet-scented, a blackbird was singing its heart out from the top of the cedar tree and later, I found Mrs Bale humming to herself as she prepared a vase of dahlias.

'How was Barcombe?' she trilled. 'Thank you for the tea! And the eggs and flour, of course ... All perfect – as are these dahlias! Have you ever seen such a shade of pink? They are riotous in the farthest corner of the vegetable patch ... ' She looked rested, better.

But even so, the word *trouble* had worried Hollis, I knew that. That night, as I took a bath, I considered the bright, round-eyed expression that he had had on being asked, and I felt I'd seen it before. In Mrs Bale's girlishness. In the driver as he'd eyed Shadowbrook. In the vicar, even, standing under the yews with an outstretched foot, having startled me. I knew I had no real education in the detection of human feelings but I wondered, as I rose with care from the bathtub, if they'd been afraid. If fear looked like this in a person: a mouth of excuses, raised hands, and such bright eyes that I'd seen my reflection in them.

My body was discoloured, marked. I was, perhaps, more bruised than I had ever been: mauve and dark red and yellow in places. I examined the bruises one by one. I tried to remember the cause of each – a branch or a door frame, my own touch – and once, I might have minded such injuries. But now I saw those bruises as proof that I was living. I was no longer watching life from a London window, my hands on the glass; I was part of it.

IV

The plants arrived on my sixth day. A Friday, bright, and warm. I was washing my face in the basin when I heard a hurried knocking on the bathroom door. It did not stop – ten or twenty tiny raps – until I opened it. Harriet stood there, breathless. 'They've come.'

I came to know the garden boys that day – their names and natures. For the arrival of my plants drew them out. They abandoned their shears and hoes and wheelbarrows; they wished to see what curiosities had been sent from Kew Gardens – from London, which was a place they'd heard of but never been to. They elbowed each other as the truck lowered its sides; they called out as the crates appeared.

I stood with Harriet, watching. And as the boys skittered around the truck, she named them for me. Charlie Rudd was robust, sunburned; later, I'd learn that he only worked with vegetables for how much he would sneeze in the more flowered parts of the grounds – a sneeze like an engine, involving his sleeve. The Collier boy had missing teeth. The twins were the Mayhew boys, either arguing between themselves or side by side, as if glued. 'The only difference between them,' Harriet said, 'is that one has a birthmark on his forehead, but their fringes are so low, how might we ever see the mark?' They favoured the practical joke:

manure or a toad in a coat pocket. A cup of cold water balanced on a door.

As for Albert Hollis, he was like his father in his slow, considered movements. 'Do you see him, Miss Waterfield?' Harriet asked me. 'That one, there?' A thatch of hair and a slight stoop. A sideways smile, as if his mouth was being tugged by a string. And, being the eldest of the boys, he had a slight paternal air, calling out to others to join him. He said, 'See this!' The Collier boy kneeled by a crate, peeped through; a plumper boy with red-veined cheeks joined him, pushed his fingers through the wood. And the smallest of the garden boys – with grazed knees and a fringe that fell into his eyes – tried to carry a crate on his own and lost his balance, stumbled sideways. He mumbled, tried to right himself.

'How young is he?' I asked.

'Fred? He's fourteen. But he looks younger, doesn't he? His parents,' she whispered, 'aren't kind to him. His father has always been a drinker. Look to Fred's arms, when you can.'

Every crate was carried for me. The boys moved between the courtyard and the glasshouse; they leaned back as they walked, as if carrying barrels – puffing and straining – and they teased each other for weakness. Harriet returned to the kitchen. But I moved amongst the crates, inspecting their condition. As they passed me, in the arms of boys, I glimpsed foliage I knew: the verdant spikes of succulents; canna and pelargonium. A tree fern came without a crate at all; it was too large for such containment. Its roots and trunk were wrapped in hessian but its leaves were free, and the twins squabbled as they carried it between them.

Kew. This arrival – as if a family had come.

Mrs Bale joined me soundlessly. She came to my side, and

whilst she'd seemed brighter yesterday, I saw her tiredness again. Grey beneath the eyes. A woman without sleep.

'How are you, Mrs Bale?'

'Me? Very well, thank you. The other morning I had a foolish headache, that's all, from the sunshine, perhaps, for it's been a warm month. Oh, will you look at these boys! You can imagine how they were when the glasshouse was being built! So excitable that I feared one would break a pane of glass. It was quite a tense time, I can tell you. Hollis had to raise his voice on more than one occasion and he rarely does that, but it was mostly at those Mayhew boys who haven't had a day of discipline in their lives.'

'Practical jokes, Harriet said.'

'Oh yes. How they think of such tricks . . . '

'Mrs Bale, is there any further news on when he might return?'

'Who, child?' But she knew.

We watched Albert lift a crate with bended knees. He made a sound at the effort; his cheeks filled as he went.

'Oh, there'll be no warning. Mr Fox simply returns when he chooses to – he's a businessman, you see, and he can't be sure where his work will take him, which is why I asked you to buy a few groceries the other day as I must always make sure there's a hearty meal for him when he needs it.' She glanced at me. 'Did you like the village? They say the oak is eight hundred years old, which is older than my brain can conceive of, in all honesty. And the village green is such a lovely spot, don't you think? We sing carols there at Christmas, and on the August bank holiday we always have a fair there – the summer fair, we call it – with music and dancing, and we have a perfectly lovely time of it on those nights. Might you still be here for it, I wonder? In early August? And isn't it a fine shop? We're terribly lucky,

I think, for if it were to close, we'd have to travel another three miles to post any letters or buy groceries, which is frankly too far to be convenient . . . '

I opened my mouth to stop her. I wanted to ask about trouble. To ask how the vicar knew my name, how Mr Jarvis might have heard about my anatomical book – and what did she know of the Pettigrew tomb? Hidden by nettles and moss? For she must know plenty, I was sure of that. But she looked frail. Her complexion reminded me of dust. And my plants had travelled a long way to be with me; I wished to go to them now.

Agapanthus. Plumbago. The loquat, whose fruit had been written of in ancient Chinese poetry. Here was what I understood, in two dozen crates or more.

Hollis offered to help. He suggested that he prise off the lids of the crates himself, pull out the nails with his claw hammer – 'It would be no problem, Miss Waterfield' – and I knew he was thinking of my wrists and shoulders; how, surely, a hammer would be too much. But this was my task. It was my purpose and comfort; I'd been waiting to do this for six days now.

These gifts. Tiny ferns and huge ones; euphorbia, and a citrus tree which responded to its release by seeming to sigh, an expanding of itself. I loved the act of reaching into the crate, feeling the shape within it and taking hold. I loved the textures and coolness. And I thought, too, of Forbes's hands lowering these plants into these boxes a few days ago.

The plants were wrapped in brown paper or cloth. These parcels of root and stem were, in turn, tied with string, and on lifting each into the light, I saw the labels. Rectangular brown labels on which their names had been written: *Cobaea scandens (cup and saucer plant). Callistemon. Agave.*

Forbes had labelled every one of them. And on some he had written more than a name. *Be mindful of leaf fall* or *Wear gloves when handling* or *(Winter flowering variety)*. I read them one by one, and I wondered how long this had taken him: the labelling, the packing of plants and the knotting of string. I imagined him in his room at Kew. The precision of letters; every full stop or underlined word.

The last days of June and the first days of July were full and brightly coloured and I spent all my waking hours in the house of glass. I'd have breakfast, make my way across the courtyard to the room of trapped heat, and not return until dusk. Harriet would visit me, carrying trays of tea and sandwiches. Or she'd bring peppermint creams, without saying a word of how she'd found them amongst my brown paper bags of flour and tea, although we both knew. We ate side by side.

'And this is what you do?' she asked. 'Grow flowers like these?'

I listed their Latin names. The toxic qualities of brugmansia; how citrus trees needed magnesium for growth, and that there were seeds which travelled wide oceans called sea beans. 'The agave belongs in desert places. Its leaves contain water.'

She must have been interested by this because in the evenings, she asked for more. At the kitchen table, she'd ask a question gently, as if pressing a finger against me. 'Which has the loveliest scent, do you think?' So I'd tell Harriet and Maud and Mrs Bale of the night-scented jasmine, of the lush green jelly within the aloe, of the legend of the baobab tree being so beautiful that deities turned against it. They all asked to know more, one by one – wishing to hear about plants from other continents or climates as if, despite the

Rêve d'Or and the honeysuckled arches, they wished to be elsewhere.

Perhaps these tales awoke something in Mrs Bale. For two days later, I heard footsteps make their way to the glasshouse.

'Knock knock?'

Her long rope of hair was tied with a velvet ribbon; her silver cross shone against her chest. And on entering, her eyes moved from shelf to shelf, from crate to crate. She gazed at their abandoned lids, the sacks of earth, the enamel pots, the fronds of the giant ferns, and the palm which was already sitting free of its crate, unfolding itself. The height of the place. The light.

'Oh my . . . Look at it all!'

'It will look better when they've settled.'

She fingered the nearest leaf. 'What is this one?'

'*Streptosolen jamesonii.* Its flowers darken from orange to red.'

'That's its name? Why such long names?'

'Because they are scientific. Because their names provide us with both their family and an identifying aspect, such as their colour or growing place. The *Fuchsia boliviana* grows in South America.'

She raised her hands, inhaled. 'Oh! Which one is that?'

I pointed. 'It won't flower till the autumn but it will be scarlet when it does.'

There was sorrow in her smile. 'South America? I went to London once. Just once. When I was young I had a curiosity to go elsewhere. I'd peep through keyholes. But there is what we want and what we must do, and they are often not the same.'

This was a different Mrs Bale. She was still talkative yet

93

her tone was heavy and old. Also, since she'd found me upstairs, her skittishness had grown less; she moved more slowly, as if weighted, and I wondered if I had, now, the proper Mrs Bale. A woman of her late middle years. Wistful, regretful, tired in a way that was deeper than bones.

She lowered herself onto a wicker chair. 'I always thought Africa had a lovely sound to it. Mysterious and far away.'

'You could still travel.'

'Oh, Miss Waterfield.' She laughed. 'I admire your bold nature, I do. It's hardly becoming, of course, but I can't deny that there's something laudable in how you've come here alone, despite so much. But travel? How might I do that? With what? Nor do I mind saying that I lack the courage for it – particularly just now. The Balkan wars, recently, and the Irish troubles. And you heard of the prince?'

'The prince?'

'Or perhaps he was not a prince. An archduke? Or was he both? I quite forget where he might have been an archduke, but he's been shot, anyway – quite dead. His wife, too. It was in the morning papers. A foolish sort of business, for what does such an act achieve, except distress and vengeance? Still, at least it's far away from us.'

I wondered why she was here. She was giving no orders, making no announcements. She seemed to want nothing from me, and yet she was feeling the end of her plait and eyeing the fern. And I thought to prise her open, too. To lift out what was within her, dark-leaved and secret; to retrieve what I felt was stirring inside her and hold it to the light. I had no doubt she understood *trouble*.

'How are you sleeping, Mrs Bale?'

A faint smile. 'Oh ... Well, it's the housekeeper's curse, isn't it? So I've heard. Always something to think of. Always a day ahead to plan.'

94

'Did you sleep well before you became a housekeeper?'

'Oh yes. I'd sleep through the night, wake with the lark. My husband said I'd spend the whole night in the same position and not move once. A deep sleeper, then.'

'You're a widow?'

Her eyes looked ahead, through the glass. 'Yes. Widowed sixteen months ago. Married for thirty-four years before that, so that I can barely remember life before I knew him. Met him when I was Maud's age. At a sheep market, would you believe. No children. We tried but none came and perhaps that's a mercy.'

'A mercy?'

'I was more a nurse than a wife, in the end. How might I have cared for infants, too?'

'What was wrong with him?'

'Your bluntness, Miss Waterfield . . . On the night of your arrival, I thought you were merely tired and that you'd be a little more gracious in the morning. But I can't blame you for your manner, perhaps. Your bones must be hard to live with. We learn to cope, do we not? Ernest had tuberculosis.'

Yes, we cope. We carry the loss or waste or anger – and I had studied the lungs. I knew that tuberculosis killed slowly, could cause the spine to fold in on itself. That it bloodied the breath.

'Did you always live near Shadowbrook?'

She was expressionless for a moment – eyes open, yet not seeing what they looked at. She was in a memory, perhaps; she wished to explore every room of it before it slipped away from her. 'Not near. Or not in the village, at least. We lived in Chipping Campden which is where I grew up so I know it well. I spent my whole life there, until he died. Then I came here. My sister lives here – in the lone cottage near the humpbacked bridge, out on the Stow road. She is also widowed now, so we thought we might live together for a time. And then I heard that the man at Shadowbrook was seeking a housekeeper, so ... here I am. Oh, I still see Elspeth often. I meet her at church. Sometimes I'll walk up to her cottage and we'll take tea in her garden.' With that, Mrs Bale looked up. 'If we are speaking candidly, I'd like to ask you why you do not go to church, Miss Waterfield. You surprised me when you said this.'

How much should I tell her? This widow who had never travelled; who held the stem of her silver cross between her forefinger and thumb? Very little, I decided. 'Because I prefer what can be proven. I've always preferred that. Why might people accept something as real when there is, in fact, no proof for it? And I don't like the rules that come from churches which dictate who loves who, and how we should live. I was raised by people who thought the same.'

Perhaps this was too much for her. There was a physical response – she pressed one hand to her breastbone, the other to her lips – and I wondered if she'd grown paler. 'And yet your mother has passed on, I think?'

'How do you know this?' For I'd told no one. But then, I knew: Forbes. In the same neat handwriting in which he'd written *Avoid direct sunlight* and *Wear gloves when handling*, he'd informed Mr Fox of my mother's death. And I wished he hadn't done this. What purpose had it served, except to provide more pity and intrigue? To make me look weaker still? It had offered the garden boys more to speak of. The dead mother. The substandard bones.

'What of the soul, Miss Waterfield? Do you have no thoughts on it? On what follows our bodily life? You must have considered this.'

'My thoughts are that she is in a box in the ground. That there is no soul – because if there were, wouldn't we find it in anatomical drawings? Wouldn't it have been lifted out, as any organ or tissue can be?'

'Can breath be lifted out? And held?'

'No. But breath shows itself in the rise and fall of our chests. In our blowing out of a candle. In how I'm talking to you now. There's proof of breath.'

'There's proof of the soul, if one opens one's eyes.'

But I was done with speaking of this.

I returned to my plants. I thought Mrs Bale would leave me, offended, but she stayed. She considered the old brick wall beside her. She closed her eyes for a time and I noticed this, slowed in my work. *We learn to cope.* Perhaps the cross on her chain had been her sustenance. Perhaps the Bible had been, for her, the reassurance that maps and dictionaries and miscellanies had been for me – and I felt guilty, briefly. 'I met the vicar the other day. In the churchyard.'

She opened her eyes, lit up. 'You did? Reverend Dunn? Oh, I'm glad. He's a gentleman. So young, yet he is such a wise and informed and comforting presence that I might say his nature is twice as old. And his sermons . . . They are such an improvement on Reverend Stout's offerings. He was more interested in the seat by the fire in The Bull and his pipe than in any godly task. Why were you in the church-yard? If you have no faith?'

'To see the Pettigrew grave.'

Did a shadow pass over her, like a bird? 'Their grave? Why?'

'Because they owned Shadowbrook. Also, because Mr Jarvis told me that they are still hated in Barcombe, that their grave is untended because nobody minds that they're dead now. Who were they, Mrs Bale? And don't tell me to speak to Hollis; he changes the subject, makes excuses to leave me.'

'And you think I'll say more? That because I have a talk-ative nature I'd be happy to speak about her? About those dreadful men?'

'Her?'

Mrs Bale stilled. Her stare did not change; it was the look of someone who'd said too much and knew it. But gradu-ally she exhaled. Rubbed her brow with her fingertips. 'Yes. Her. The last of the Pettigrews was a woman, you see.'

'A woman? No. The last name on the gravestone was a man's.'

'Hugo? Yes, I know. Both brothers are buried there, Francis and Hugo, and I'd say that earth's too good for them. But they had a sister who outlived them all. She was ten years younger than the youngest son. Inherited this house.'

'She inherited it? Shadowbrook?' I lowered my trowel.

'You're pleased by this? No one within fifty miles of here was pleased, I can tell you.'

'Why not?' I cleaned my hands on my apron, came closer. 'Why was no one pleased?'

Mrs Bale considered her hands. Her fingers were laced together; her thumbs were uppermost, perfectly still. 'Because she didn't deserve it. Because most people say she was the worst of that wretched lot. There are plenty of tales of her brothers – rowdy, drunken, aggressive men who claimed whatever they wanted for themselves. Liked to shoot rabbits and leave them there, uneaten. But hers was a different darkness.'

'Different? In what way?'

She looked up sharply. 'Oh, I won't speak of it. What she did in Shadowbrook? What she performed? No. Not even you, Miss Waterfield, would wish to hear it. But I'll say this: that many think she was justly punished for her sins in the end. For she lost her mind in the last years of her life. She inherited this house and went mad promptly afterwards, so that she dismissed all her maids and cooks on a whim and the house became filthy and she only ate what she found in the gardens, which was grass and dead birds. Raw potatoes, pulled from the earth! Some say her teeth were green with herbs or some foul decay.' She sniffed, smoothed her skirts.

'Eating dead birds? From the ground? That's not true.'

'No? How do you know it's not? No sane person would do that, of course. But she was not sane by the end – do you understand? Her depravity undid her. And if Hollis does not wish to talk of the Pettigrews and walks away from you, I suspect it's because he saw this madness with his own eyes – how she walked unclothed in the garden or drank from the brook on all fours, like a beast.' A shiver. 'No more of this.'

She rose. She continued to smooth her skirts with her palms, as if the word Pettigrew still clung to them and she wished to remove every letter. She was flushed. Angered by it.

'How do you know all of this? You lived in Chipping Campden until two years ago.'

'Are you doubting me? Let me tell you, Miss Water-field, that news of her behaviour has travelled many miles beyond Barcombe-on-the-Hill! Oxford and Banbury know of Veronique. Say her name in Stratford-upon-Avon and someone will tell you to mind your language. Because yes, she's talked of. But it's always been done privately – in homes, you understand. Very few people will discuss her openly so that even you, with your bluntness, Miss Water-field, will not find many answers.'

Veronique.

I navigated my way through these words of hers. 'Would the man called Preedy know more? Talk to me about her?'

She was bright-eyed. 'Preedy? Kit Preedy? I suppose if anyone was to talk about her, it would be him. He has his own bad blood, after all, and he lives by different rules to us. But Miss Waterfield? I wouldn't ask. If I were you – here for a month, no longer, and quite oblivious to what has happened here over the years – I'd tend to your glasshouse, enjoy the gardens at their finest time of year and ask nothing more of the Pettigrews. And please – do not say her name inside the house.'

I supposed she meant well. As she prepared to leave me, she remarked on my hair's thickness; I understood the compliment was an offering, of some kind, an apology for having hissed *Pettigrew* and for having narrowed her eyes. She felt embarrassed, perhaps.

Yet in her wake, I knew that Mrs Bale had failed. Petulant – that adjective that Millicent had used to describe me, whilst plucking a hen – and stubborn, which had been muttered by my mother herself on occasion: both adjectives came to mind as I watched her go. For how could I ask nothing more? Ignore what I'd been told? It was an impossibility to me. It had been my mother's way – to push at a door which said *Keep Out*, to walk against a crowd for the sake of it. To not go to church if one didn't wish to.

That night, I did not sleep. I tried to, but my skeleton ached from the day's work and my mind was too full. I tried her name to myself, in the dark.

The patterned wallpaper of London seemed so far away. Yet I knew that I could have taken a pen at that moment and drawn its repetitive depiction of tied bows over and over. Had it been like this for her? Charlotte Pugh? Had she studied this same repeating pattern and wondered where India had gone? Nine months before, she had eyed the Himalayas at dawn; she had sat in a swing chair beside a rhododendron and pushed herself back and forth with a toe. And now she had a newborn daughter and a surname of six letters more than her own. These two versions of her.

No sleep for me at all. So I turned on the lantern by my bed. I sat up, settled myself and picked up my botanical book. Stamens and anthers.

I read. Somewhere, I heard an owl.

But I also heard a creak.

I lowered the book. What time was it? The grandfather clock in the hall wheezed into life and struck three times, answering me.

I waited.

A second creak came. Then, very gently, a third. And with this, there was no doubt: this was a person walking. This was someone above me. With a fourth creak, and a fifth, it became a person descending the stairs. They descended very slowly. They placed their weight on each step as if they wished to move unheard. To pass through the house without waking its sleepers.

A sixth creak. A pause.

I laid down my book, rose.

I did not take my cane. Rather, I lifted the bedside lamp. I held it high so that its glow went before me; it illuminated the floorboards, the skirting boards and the door. And at the door, I stood very still, waiting to hear more. Yet there was silence now. For a time, there was such a deep, absolute hush in the house that I thought, they have gone; they are no longer there. But then it came: a seventh creak, and much louder. It was louder because it was closer; this creak was so close that the floorboard beneath me – the board on which I stood, at that moment – adjusted itself. I felt it rise. A weight had been placed upon its far end.

Someone was standing outside my door.

I stayed perfectly still.

I listened. And I knew, with certainty, that they were listening too. I held my breath, knowing that they also held their breath. And I was also sure that their hand, like mine, was touching the door now; their ear was also resting against weathered wood, listening for me, and I knew that we sensed the other's presence.

In the hall, the clock ticked.

Tap-tap! A fingernail against my door – or against my ear, or so it seemed. The quick tapping a finger might make in investigation. A test.

I gasped, stepped back. Then more creaks in quick succession and the floorboard moved beneath me so that I knew that he – Mr Fox – was leaving me, that he had heard my gasp and detected me and was, therefore, stepping back from the door. I wanted to see him, to know what he looked like, so I reached down for the handle and opened the door and I walked out into the hallway, lifted the lamp and whispered, 'Hello?'

A rush of cooler air.

I inched forwards with my lamp. Its gold circumference of light caught the edges of panelled wood and the grandfather clock and I called out again: 'Mr Fox?' I looked down the corridor. Its far end remained in blackness. The lamplight only found a few yards of polished wall and, as I looked, I imagined a figure walking forwards, out of the darkness; I imagined him walking with purpose, coming towards me. And I called out, 'I know you're there.'

But no one moved or answered. Only one pair of eyes looked back at me. From the landing, she gazed down, with her velvet bed and her flushed bare skin. Her frame reflected the lantern's light. She has, I thought, watched him move past her. She has watched him knock – *tap-tap!* – on my door.

I wondered if this was a dream and I was, in fact, sleeping. But dreams, I knew, had no physicality. Dreams did not cause floorboards to shift underneath me, could not tap against varnished wood.

Back in my room, I took a blank piece of paper from my writing desk, folded it several times and pushed it under my door. I climbed back into bed, drew the sheets around me and watched the door's outline; I watched the handle, in case. But there were no more disturbances that night.

I stayed awake till morning; in those hours, I thought of that clear, unmistakable sense of company, of a human body being within inches of my own. And in the hallway, the air had been fragrant with more than dust or polish or wood. More than rose soap. There had been a sharper smell; not mint, as such, but mint was, perhaps, the closest scent to it.

In the morning, I found them in the kitchen. 'I heard him. Last night.'

'Heard who?'

'Mr Fox. I know he's back. I heard him walking down the stairs. He came into the hall and stood outside my room.'

The maids looked to Mrs Bale; the housekeeper, in turn, looked at me.

'Mr Fox,' she said, 'is not here.'

'He is. Why are you saying he's not? I heard him. He tapped twice on my door.'

At that, Mrs Bale made a sound – a sudden rushing of air, as if she had been opened. An unsealing of her, or dismantling. And she softened with this; she leaned against the kitchen table, dropped her shoulders as if she could no longer support them, and Harriet hurried to her, held her waist. 'Mrs Bale? Mrs Bale?'

They guided her to a kitchen chair. Her head lolled, as if her neck had broken; her hands, too, seemed too heavy for her wrists. I stepped back, appalled. 'Is she dying?'

'She isn't dying. She's fainted. Maud, get water. Sit down, Miss Waterfield. She needs space and air.'

I took the chair opposite them both and watched. Mrs Bale lowered her head to the table and rested there. Gradually her breathing steadied a little; the pallor that had washed over her features grew less. 'Mr Fox,' she said, with her eyes closed, 'is away. I told you this.'

I looked at the maids. I did not know if I should respond, but I did. 'This wasn't pipework. It wasn't draughts. It was a human.'

'He is away . . . '

'Then who else might it have been? Maud? Harriet?'

They shook their heads, unwilling. Maud pressed her lips together, eyed the corner of the room as if she hadn't heard me. Harriet's gaze met mine and it seemed to implore or warn me, and this told me I should keep asking. That here, in this room, I'd learn *trouble*'s meaning.

'Then who else is in the house? Someone must be. They are walking at night and hiding by day. Why won't you tell me?'

'I told you,' she said, looking up from her hands, 'not to ask . . . to let it be. I woke her.'

'Woke who?'

Harriet had her hand on Mrs Bale's shoulder: a pale, freckled hand against the grey blouse. She nodded, lowered herself, shook the shoulder very gently. 'Mrs Bale? Can you hear me? I think Miss Waterfield should know.'

*

In time, Mrs Bale sipped the water. Her hands were still unsteady. One hand held the glass; the other moved from her cross to her mouth to her length of hair to her collarbone, where it rested. 'You ask if there's someone else in this house. Yes is the answer. Yes, Miss Waterfield, a person – but they are not like we are.'

'In what way? Are they unwell?'

She smiled very faintly, as if I amused her. As if she were exhausted of this poor joke and pretence. She removed her hand. 'We never thought to speak a word of this to you. We hoped we might not have to. After all, you are only here for a handful of weeks; we hoped there might be no trouble during your time here, that it might pass without incident and so there would be no need to tell you what I am going to. It was also clear from your arrival that you are ... ' she paused, 'direct and scientific – and faithless, of course – so that we supposed you'd think we were all perfectly mad if we told you the truth. You might have returned to London, not wanting to stay in a house of fools. If so, the glasshouse would have stayed empty, and all his time and expense would have been wasted. Perhaps, in truth, we have also had moments where we've doubted what we have seen and heard, have doubted our own minds and by daylight have managed to convince ourselves that what happens at night is in our imaginations. And there can be many nights without any disturbance – without the walker, as we might call it – so that we could believe ourselves to be free of the trouble. Those are our reasons for having said nothing to you sooner. The girls,' she added, 'wanted to. This is not their fault.'

I said nothing. She was pouring words like water and I did not wish to stopper her.

'I was appointed in the autumn of last year, as you know.

I heard that Mr Fox was seeking a housekeeper. I was looking for work. The place was not in good repair, you know this – draughts, pails to catch the rainwater. Mice. And so in the early days I did not think very much of those night-time sounds; I thought it was a crow that had remained, or the house adjusting to human life again. But time passed, and I swept and polished. We plugged holes in the roof. The girls came, didn't you? And that's when I started to notice the trouble. It was pictures at first. You saw the empty hooks on the wall? You asked me about them – remember? There were pictures there to begin with. But each night, one would fall. The smaller ones would not wake us, so that I'd find them in the morning, smashed on the floor, and at first I thought it was those draughts again or a fault in the pictures themselves somehow. But then there were larger paintings that fell, and they woke us. We'd jump from our beds at the sounds. There was one painting—'

'Tell her about the boats, Mrs Bale.'

'I am, child. One painting, Miss Waterfield, of a sea with boats upon it, and a seashore – a fine thing, and huge; wider than my open arms – crashed down with such a sound that we all woke with it and rushed out. Even Mr Fox. You have not met him, I know, and so you do not know his countenance – but when he came downstairs later … well, he looked terribly pale. And what's more, the painting did not simply fall. It could not have simply fallen, for it was found ten or twelve feet from its hanging place. As if thrown. As if *thrown*!'

'Subsidence, perhaps? There can be small tremors of the earth's crust in any country.'

Mrs Bale laughed at this; bright, sudden laughter falling into a sigh. She set down the water glass. She brought that hand – fluttering, unsteady – to meet her other hand, which held her plait. 'You think that's all there is? Oh, there is more. All the paintings fell, yes. Flowers, too, would be stripped of their petals overnight, or I'd find their stems snapped neatly. And the walking ... Footsteps – the same that you heard last night – would move overhead. At first, I thought it was Mr Fox. But then these footsteps came when he was away from Shadowbrook; they'd descend the stairs very carefully. I'd hear them move along the corridor and in the early days, I felt brave enough to pull on my dressing gown and open the door to see who it was. But each time, there was no one there. Each time. And there would be knocking, too, on doors. Mine, and the girls'.'

'We heard it,' said Maud. 'Just two taps – very light, but we heard it.' With that, she took her rough, reddened forefinger and tapped the table twice. 'Like that.'

Mrs Bale watched my face. 'I see you have less to say now. Did you open your door too, and find nothing there? Only a sense of being watched, and a faint smell of herbs? I see your expression.'

I did not move.

'And there was the scratch. If you think we might all have been imagining such sounds, or that it was just a shift in the ground, I will show you my bedroom door. Because two nights before you arrived, Miss Waterfield, the footsteps came down the corridor to me. It was three o'clock – I know this because the grandfather clock had chimed, and she seems to favour that hour – and the footsteps stopped outside my door.' Mrs Bale leaned closer, laid her hand upon my wrist. 'She did not tap. I thought she would tap! Do you know what she did? She scratched my door. As if she had a knife, she carved a mark in my bedroom door. I heard the sound and I saw the door shake at the force of it.' Her eyes shone. 'This happened two nights before you came.'

'She? No. It must have been Mr Fox.'

'You think it's him? Do you? Carving up his own doors and throwing his own paintings onto the floor and smashing them? Why might he do that? Indeed, it is worse up there, on the first floor. He says that there was a knock upon his door one night. Not a tap – a *knock*, or thump, as if with a fist. You think this is his work? It is not his work.'

'Then why hasn't he gone to the police?'

'The police?' Mrs Bale straightened a little, widened her eyes. 'And say what to them?'

'That there is an intruder. That someone is entering this house at night and vandalising—'

She opened her arms, frustrated with me. 'But they aren't! No one is entering this house! There are no broken locks or forced entries. There are no secret passages or trapdoors at Shadowbrook, Miss Waterfield. And what might the policeman do, except look at us with the expression that you have now? As if we are as mad as she was? It is not an intruder.'

'It must be.'

'It's not!' she cried, irritated.

At this, Harriet's hand returned to the housekeeper's shoulder. Mrs Bale acknowledged it; she patted it, kept hold of it for a moment. 'I wish you to know that I consider myself a practical woman. I'm not minded to flights of fancy. I will be fifty-five next May and I've seen many things in my life, you understand, and I believe that most strange events are easily explained. But I have looked for every rational answer to this and found none. I know who is doing this.' She looked directly at me. 'And so do you.'

I held her gaze. 'You think it was the Pettigrew daughter? Veronique?'

At this, Maud cried out. 'Don't say her name! You aren't meant to say her name in the house!'

Mrs Bale stood. She reached for the girl's forearm and pulled it towards her, found her hand; she hushed Maud, urged her to be calm. Small, motherly words: *there, now; that's right.* And when this was done, she looked back to me with cool, glassy eyes that would not be swayed; she was not fluttering now. 'I told you that I don't care to speak of her. But the trouble, that you've heard of. From the driver, and elsewhere. It is her, Miss Waterfield. It is Veronique Pettigrew – despite her having died thirteen years ago. Despite it seeming so impossible to your bookish, practical brain. You have no faith; you think that when someone dies they are finished, and over; that every single part of them decays in a box, and nothing remains. But I tell you – she is still in this house.'

I left, crossed the courtyard, passed the tool shed and the washing tub and entered the glasshouse, shutting the door.

I sat on a bamboo chair. Held my cane with both hands, like a staff.

This was all I knew: that drifting seeds could cross wide oceans to find a new land on which to plant themselves and grow; that my bones were made poorly, and would always protest when I stretched or kneeled or tried to walk faster; that my mother had died in January; that newspapers talked of strikes and Home Rule and how women were not entitled to vote; that there were eight planets in the solar system and the Nile was the longest river and barn owls were white. And this, too: human life ends when the heart stops beating. Death comes when the body stills and grows cool. My anatomical guide – and histories, and science – had shown me this, proved it. And the other, intangible parts of a person? Character, memory, sentiments, voice; what happened to them with the body's demise? They belonged in the brain. They were caused by chemicals and electrical activity and so they too ended with death. No part of a human – except bones – remained.

Ghost. The word had not been said but we'd heard it even so. It had hung above the kitchen table; it had circled us, as Maud had performed her *tap-tap!* A thin, inconsequential, fictitious word. It had no place in diagrams.

I decided to occupy myself, so I filled the metal watering can. There was a fast, sonorous rush of water that rose in pitch, and I tried to think of plants. Yet I only wondered who was fooling Mrs Bale in such a devious, unkind way. For someone was. Someone was taking advantage of her frail, girlish nature. They were pressing their weight onto floorboards, snapping flowers, taking a knife to a door. And I wanted to know who, immediately. Mrs Bale's constitution could not, it seemed, endure this trickery for long.

Mrs Bale. She'd been afraid since my arrival – I saw this now. Every characteristic had been born of nervousness. That wide, stretched smile of hers reminded me of a butterfly pinned on velvet. Kept in a box.

I lowered the watering can. Dried my hands on a cloth.

She was in the courtyard. She was hunched over the washing tub, yet I could see that she had been crying. The sides of her face had reddened; her lashes were damp. On seeing me, she straightened, pressed the back of her hand to her nose.

'I said too much,' I told her. 'I did not mean to say too much.'

She nodded, dropped the sodden cloth back into the tub. 'I do not blame you for thinking as you do. I know how it sounds.' Defeated words.

'You said there was a scratch on your door?'

Their rooms – hers and the maids' small dormitory – were at the western end of Shadowbrook. It was a kink in the house's geography; this small wing of wisteria and smaller, higher windows. I had viewed it from the yard but had never entered it. She said, 'This way.'

It was a deep, purposeful scratch. Ten inches long or more. And it was not straight: it began high up, on the left side of the door; as it lengthened, it lowered and centred itself, as if the arm had grown tired of reaching so high. Then, near the handle, it began to rise again before ending. A reversed tick.

'I heard it being made. I was sitting up in bed, expecting a knocking, but she didn't knock. The door shook as she pressed down; I told you this.'

'Two nights before I came?'

'Two nights. On the Thursday. I'm sure you'll ask me why I didn't open the door, because you are brave, Miss Waterfield. But I have become too afraid to do it.'

I touched part of the mark with two fingertips. Beeswax would not be enough to mend it; the door would always be damaged, now. 'Was Mr Fox at home that night?'

Mrs Bale nodded. 'But he left the next day. Friday.'

'And he did not think to stay? After this had happened to you?'

'He considered it. But he had work, you see.'

I looked back to the door. 'What does he do? His work?'

A dismissal. 'He's spoken of it, but I can't remember.'

I disliked this answer. But I disliked, far more, that he had left her and the maids. Someone had entered the house, vandalised it and terrified the housekeeper – and yet he still went away and hadn't returned. Perhaps work mattered to him, yes. But surely his house and staff also mattered. 'Mrs Bale, who locks the house at night?'

'I do. I have the keys. The front door, the kitchen door and the French windows that lead onto the croquet lawn.'

'No other doors? No windows?'

'No other doors. And the windows all lock from inside; I check them frequently, and they are all quite secure. Many frames have swollen from years of rain and are permanently closed now, stuck in their casement; even the strongest of arms could not lift them up. Miss Waterfield, I know what you're thinking.'

'What of the upstairs windows? They are always open, day and night; you said Mr Fox prefers it. Surely they can be reached? And entered?'

'Not without a ladder and we'd hear such a thing, wouldn't we? And the drainpipes or roses couldn't bear a person's weight. Listen to me, please: this is not human work. You'd be wasting your time and efforts in thinking so. After all, why would someone do this? Where is the sense in these small, destructive acts? In the occasional tap in the dark? Intruders steal, Miss Waterfield; that's what they do, and nothing has been taken. Look at this house: what is there to take? A threadbare chair? A jug of dying blooms? Nor have they happened to leave anything behind: no footprints in the dust, no lost buttons or cigarette ends. And this, too, is a certainty: that if this was the work of a man, or two men, other men would know. This village talks! See how it has been with you? Your height and eyes and nature were all spoken of in The Bull within a day of your arrival. If someone had been entering Shadowbrook at night ... well, there would be stories. Someone would know.'

She said this without taking her eyes from me. I, in turn, could not look away or answer her. What reason might there be for entering the house if not to thieve? 'I see why you sleep poorly.'

'Oh, to have one night's rest. One full night's rest, without footsteps or the fear of them ...'

With this, we went outside. We drifted out into the afternoon where the daytime sounds seemed so bright, suddenly: a robin's song, the repetitive squeak of a barrow's wheel. Harmless, gentle sounds.

We found ourselves on the croquet lawn, looking up.

'Does the vicar know?'

'Matthew? Yes. He knows what is happening here. Reverend Stout before him showed no interest; he was here when it began, and would not touch the matter. He'd heard of Shadowbrook's history and refused to discuss it, you see. But then Matthew came in his place, and he has always listened; he has never doubted or mocked or judged me. He prays for my strength and safety, which I find comfort in. I'd like him to do more, Miss Waterfield. To speak to *her*, even ... ask her to leave in God's name and perform a ritual of some kind. But he says he does not have the authority for it; it's barely a year since he took his oaths. And this is not my house, of course.'

I looked up at the windows. 'What is he like? Mr Fox? Is he strange?'

'Not strange. If others say so, do not heed them; they have not met him to know.'

'But his absence, at least, is strange, is it not?'

'Not for a man with such responsibilities – in Oxford and elsewhere. You'll see, when you meet him. He's quite the gentleman.'

This was not, however, how I'd imagined a gentleman to be: a man who did not summon the police when his home was entered at night. Who abandoned his staff. Who chose to live upstairs, like a bat.

'When will I meet him?'

'When he returns.'
'When will that be?'
'Soon.'

I huddled deep in my bed that night. I lay on my side, looked at the wall. A day of ghosts. Of the sound of a filling watering can. A mark on a door. A painting, flung down.

If there were visitations of the dead, it was in memory; that night I conceded that much. For sometimes I could see my mother unfolding a map as if it were gilded, as she used to. I saw her face, briefly, in mine. But otherwise, I wished to prove them wrong. To wake them from this dreaming state. To look in the eyes of the person – real, warm, tangible – who'd knocked on my door and slipped into the shadows. For there were no ghosts. There was no Veronique.

V

I decided to go to the garden boys first. They would be, I felt, a fine starting place: their soft, shared babbling – of my malnourished childhood, of an accident with a carriage wheel – told me that they might have their own rumours. Intruders and foxes and Pettigrews; they might offer them to me if I asked. So I circumnavigated the vegetable patch that morning, walking along the lines of lettuce and radish and hazel canes in the hope that I might hear their conversations. But the boys quietened as I approached. Some straightened from their spadework, adjusted their caps to see me better. Others pretended I was not there at all.

Albert greeted me. 'Morning, miss. Can I help?'

He had the early softness of a beard. He offered a few small words on the weather, asked if I was enjoying my work at the glasshouse: such questions were, I felt, a conscious effort at being a man instead of a boy. I asked, in turn, about the strawberry season, and the netting to keep the birds away. And in time, I stepped closer and asked what he knew of the nocturnal trouble. 'Is there a particularly long ladder at Shadowbrook, Albert? One that might reach the first floor, say?' But he closed like a handclap. Scratched his upper arm, mumbled about the work to be done.

I also approached Maud. For I'd not forgotten Mrs Bale's

early summary of her – that she'd inherited a gossiping nature as well as dark hair and eyes. She was sluicing the courtyard, sweeping the water. 'I know you've not met Mr Fox,' I said, 'but what work does he do? And does he have any enemies who might wish to cause trouble?'

She set down the pail, looked disdainful. 'You're still thinking it's Mr Fox's work?'

'Not necessarily. But it's human, Maud, I'm sure of that.'

She shook her head. 'You and your books ... Thinking you know more than the rest of us.'

'Then what do you know of the Pettigrews that I don't? There must be plenty.'

But she resisted this. She went indoors, wordless – and it felt like everyone here had taken the same sealed vow; that a pact had been formed like a wall and I could not reach what I wanted to know. A team of them against me.

The swifts flew overhead. The broken cartwheel was propped against the tool shed. And the farmer lived differently, lived by different rules, or so the housekeeper had said. So I turned from the house without further thoughts, passed into the Preedy fields.

The barley grew in the wide, flat expanses of land to the south and west of Shadowbrook House. It was both greenish and straw-coloured. It was restless, too; even on the windless days there would still be movement within it. In gusts, the crop would flatten down suddenly, splay itself; I had never stood on a headland, but this rhythm and air made me think of open water.

There was a breeze that day. The beech trees had filled with air and as I walked, the barley brushed the sides of me. My hair snapped as if tethered.

I did not know where the Preedy farmhouse might be.

116

Nor did I know how far his land extended; it stretched further than I could see, moving down the hillside. A farmer, I assumed, would be on his land in the hours of daylight. But he could be performing any task on any part of it. Also, I had no description of him; I had no knowledge of his age or height or appearance. I had no real expectation of what a farmer might look like, or how he might dress. I could only walk his boundaries.

At the path's end, where it met a gateway that entered the back of the churchyard and a bank of bramble and yew, I turned right. I followed the line of the wall. There was no discernible path, now; the grass was high, undisturbed by humans. And I realised, too, that it hid dangers: foxes or badgers had hauled earth away to leave hollows and in places the wall had fallen entirely, so that stones were half hidden in the long grass. I thought of my bones as I went.

He saw me first. I was absorbed with my footfall and the undergrowth. He, in turn, must have heard my approach, or I had startled birds so that they'd flown out of nettlebeds with their scolding tone and this had been enough for him to pause in his work and watch me come closer. He must have been perfectly still – for it was his boots I saw. Their bleached, worn toes.

I looked up. And I thought, he is earth-coloured. This was my first thought: that he was the colour of the land around me; a dusty, sunburned man with dirt on his forehead and the backs of his hands. His braces hung down by his sides. His hair and beard were also earth-like – dark brown, with a reddish hue. He grasped a large discoloured stone; he held it against his body so that his torso was carrying some of its weight and for a moment he eyed me, indecision in him. But he chose to abandon his task, to drop the stone to the side of him. I felt its single, echoless thud.

The farmer. Not tall, as such. Not wide. But his stance made him seem larger.

'Are you Mr Preedy? I was given your name.'

He rubbed his beard and forehead with the inner part of his wrist. 'I'm sure. Who by? Mrs Bale? Singing my praises?'

He looked down. He was surrounded by stones. The wall to his left had spilled itself; weather or age or a deliberate act had caused part of it to fall, and now he continued his work as if I wasn't standing there. He crouched down, felt the boulders. He turned them over, one by one, feeling their edges and undersides. On tilting them, he revealed the paler grass beneath, the stone's indentation.

I did not know what else to say. I only saw how his shirt was too tight for his back. Also, his hair was too long; it brushed his collar, stuck to the sweat on his neck. I saw the prominence of veins in his forearms and temples – and I saw the scars, too: his hands and arms were covered in them. Puckered skin. White crescent moons.

'What do you want?'

No use in saying that I'd not been looking for him. This was private land. I had strayed from the path; skirting the Preedy land had been a deliberate choice, and what reasons might I have had for it? Other than to find him? 'I was told that you knew the Pettigrews. That your family knew them.'

At that, he looked up. Still crouching, he glanced across his fields, laid his forearms over his knees to form a still, balanced pose. I could never do that, I thought: rest my weight on the balls of my feet, look at the far distance and not fall. Yet this was a taut, familiar position for him. And I could also see his profile this way. He was forty or less. It was hard to know precisely, for here was a weathered, weary man who must have walked out in snow, squinted through storms or midsummer sun for his adult lifetime. The lines on his forehead were pronounced. Those that spread from the corners of his eyes were deep and permanent. And his beard was no affectation, as other beards might be; his seemed to be a necessity. It was unkempt, lacked symmetry; it was, I supposed, his own treeline. A shelter in all weathers. His sleeves were rolled past his elbows; his forearms were reddened with sun.

I had never seen someone like this, or expected to. Damaged, hard. Capable. Damp with sweat.

'Who told you this?'

The question was simple. He asked it quietly, still observing his land in windy weather, yet I sensed danger in it. I felt that the answer mattered to him, that I had walked into a dark territory and my reply might bring in a further darkness. But I could not be frightened. I had broken bones and lost my mother. 'Hollis. He said that your family have worked this land for generations. A hundred years or more. Is that true?'

At that, Kit stood. He rose in one movement – soundless, deft. 'Yes. And yes, we knew the Pettigrews. Why are you asking?'

'Because I want to know.'

Such boldness caught him. He looked at me directly for the first time, and noted, perhaps, all that he needed to in that handful of seconds: the white hair and eyelashes, the discoloured eyes. I saw a further scar on him – under an eye – and noted the first signs of grey by his temples. Like this, we each considered the other.

'What have you heard? Tell me.'

'That no one mourns them. That they treated people like dogs. The shopkeeper called them the kings in their castle.'

'Kings? That's generous. The Pettigrews thought they

119

had a right to everything. Thought the law did not apply to them. Like dogs? Worse than dogs. What else has been said?'

'They took what they wanted. Shot rabbits without eating them, although this doesn't strike me as enough to hate them as much as people do. Also, the daughter—'

'What's your name?'

This was unexpected. It felt intrusive, rude – although it was, of course, a reasonable request. And I thought, he doesn't know. Everyone else seemed to know my name but not this man. 'Clara Waterfield.'

'Miss Waterfield, you should be careful. Of rumour. It grows in this place as well as the weeds and I can tell you, too, that most aren't true.'

'I know that. There are rumours that I limp because I was underfed as a child, and that's nonsense. Even so, I want to hear what they say about the Pettigrews.'

He pushed at a stone with his boot. 'Well, you won't hear stories from me. I hate rumour. Hate that people choose to hear or tell it for amusement's sake. Won't listen to what's said in The Bull or the markets. Do those people have nothing better to think of? Talk of? And Pettigrew is an old name now. It's used up, done with, so what's the point in learning more? If you want amusement, Miss Waterfield, ask Jarvis. Ask any housewife in Stow and they'll give you lies, most likely, but at least you'll find your entertainment.'

He crouched again, seized a stone and lifted it. He grimaced with the weight; his fingers splayed to contain it and he took five pronounced steps towards the wall, set the stone down. I stared. His words had been brusque, emphatic. He'd been more dismissive of me than Maud or the shopkeeper or Mrs Bale and it angered me, quickened my heartbeat. This notion that I wanted entertainment.

120

That I was asking for boredom's sake. He positioned the stone, examined it. He scratched the back of his head with a hand that was dark with earth and his own bruises and there was a forcefulness in his gestures which suggested that he, too, was angry with this conversation.

'I'm not asking to be entertained. I have more than enough to occupy my time, thank you. I ask because someone is entering Shadowbrook at night. They are throwing pictures, knocking on doors at two or three in the morning. The housekeeper is terrified; she's lost weight in these past two weeks and isn't sleeping. She's convinced it is the ghost of Veronique Pettigrew. And this intruder? I think he wants her to believe this. I think he wants everyone to believe that Veronique is walking the house at night. He carved a V into a door, firstly. Also, there's a smell of herbs in his wake to echo the rumour that says she ate herbs until her teeth turned green, which I certainly don't believe. I say this man is simply carrying herbs with him, that's all. But the point is, Mr Preedy, that a trick is being played on us and I won't have it. So I'm trying to find out why. That's why I'm asking.'

The farmer looked at his wall. He stood with his hands by his sides, his back to me. Yet I knew that he was listening; I knew his thoughts were not on the stones.

Somewhere, a woodpigeon called.

He said, 'I don't listen to rumours but they've talked of ghosts for nearly a year now. The breaking of things.'

'There is no such thing as ghosts.'

He turned his head, so that I saw his profile again. A nose that had known its own damage; a brow which, from frowning, had permanently bunched itself. 'Nor do I bother with the rumours that you're outspoken and afraid of nothing. But they seem true, at least.'

Behind me, the barley filled with wind. It caught my skirt so that it flapped in a slow, clean rhythm. The farmer returned to the stones, selected a second one and lifted it with a hard breath out. I watched this impossible act. How he pushed this stone into place on the wall, stepped back.

I knew I'd disappeared for him. *Outspoken* – as much as I was crooked and strange and petulant. And he had told me nothing about the Pettigrews – as if he was like everyone else when in all other ways he did not seem to be. So I turned from him. I felt disappointed, frustrated and sore. And I felt alone, suddenly: I found myself wanting my books or the green chaise longue or my mother's hand on my forehead, as she used to when I'd wanted rest and could not find it.

I began to walk away. But he – Kit – called out. He did not say my name or raise his voice; he spoke as if I was still standing there – as if I'd not, in fact, disappeared – and when I looked back, he was watching me. He seemed softer. There was tiredness in him, or resignation; maybe he felt he'd spoken too briskly and that hidden in his stance there was an apology. 'If you want to know more, I'll tell you.'

'About the Pettigrews?'

'The Pettigrew men.'

'And Veronique? The daughter?'

'No. Only the men.'

I straightened, instinctively. Why not her? As if she wasn't worth speaking of? For being female? But I also knew that if there was a dark, beating heart in these rumours, it was hers; her name was, after all, the name that could not be spoken in Shadowbrook's rooms. That had not been carved on the Pettigrew tomb. And whilst this was not what I wanted – it was a compromise between us, the farmer and

I, and not enough – I nodded. For who else was willing to talk to me? And who else had seemed unaware of my cane? He hadn't even looked at it.

There were no other words between us. I walked back, thinking of how his scars had been of varying shades, from every stage of his life.

A meal of liver that night. I had never eaten liver before and I disliked it; the texture more than its flavour. I glanced at the maids as they ate. Yet Mrs Bale filled the silence with how she used to love liver as a child, that her mother had served it with thyme and shallots when shallots had been in season, and that dish had been quite a delicacy to her mind; also, that she'd always had a liking for luncheon tongue. This was, I knew, a distraction. She wished to hide the intruder with brightness, to smooth the carved V with her words.

'Ah!' she said, remembering. 'Miss Waterfield, a letter has come for you. I left it on your bed.'

The letter was from Patrick. I recognised his handwriting – small, measured, very black. And whilst it wasn't as comforting as the rocking horse or globe to me, it still spoke of the world that I'd known and been safe in. In it, I read of old, remembered things: the heat of the underground trains, the bridges, the blossom in Hyde Park, the specific sound of Millicent's shoes in the hallway. And I was, in truth, surprised by its beauty. My stepfather had not been a man of books – he'd read very little except *The Times* in his study, and had written even less. Yet here, he had set London down for me. On this paper I could find the echoed clopping of horses in rainy weather and my bedroom's view. I could see his moustache so that I might touch it.

Please be mindful, he wrote, *of your bones*. These were his last words to me before his tight, professional signature.

I missed it all, for a little while. But later, in my nightdress, I retrieved my pen and paper, sat at the desk with the open window and knew that I had so much to write – of the hydrangeas and the tennis court and the rooms of dust. How I'd run damp cloths along the loquat leaves unassisted. How his crooked stepdaughter whose knowledge of life had been limited to written accounts was now conversing with strangers. Making her own pots of tea.

Dear Patrick . . . I wrote until the clock chimed once – of the people I'd met, or some of them. How yes, I was minding my bones very much. How there was a portico with wise Roman faces.

I wrote nothing of the trouble in the house. Nor did I write of the day's education which was that there were different gradients of physical human strength. That the strongest of men were not necessarily the broadest or tallest. And later, in bed, I reached for my anatomical book, in which I reminded myself of musculature and ligaments. Bones, I knew, were either able or unable, and could not be changed. But the connective tissues and muscles had far more possibilities; they could alter their strength depending on one's daily tasks, on how one chose to live, and I mouthed *deltoid* and *extensor digitorum* as I turned the pages.

Bad blood. Mrs Bale's single description of Kit. There could be no such thing, just as no one could be physically heartless or could literally lose their mind. These were phrases, that was all. Yet I thumbed the heart's diagram even so. And I wondered what he had done to acquire this bad blood – if his physical strength had caused it, or his sharp way of speaking. Or maybe this was also a rumour that lacked any truth. A whispered lie.

Two in the morning. I did not think of intruders or Veronique or my mother. Nor did I think of Patrick's study with its carriage clock and its hush. Rather, I was aware of myself – of my skin's response to the nocturnal breeze and my own heart in its room. And I thought, too, of the others in this house or county, sleeping or trying to. With a leg exposed, or their hair fanned out. With their knees brought to their chest as a child might. Or – the luxury of the strong-boned – perhaps they slept on their front, with their body's weight on their cheekbone and ribs and knees and the palms of their hands, as they breathed in and out. Weight on the hinged part of the jaw, their weathered face.

VI

July brought in a deeper heat. There was strength in the sun by nine in the morning; within the first few days of the month, the grass of the tennis court radiated heat. The level of water – in the bathing pool and the rainwater barrel – grew less. And the garden boys changed, too. The heat reddened them. In it, their shirts darkened under their arms and they'd wet their hair with watering cans at one or two in the afternoon, so that their shirts stuck to their shoulders. Having done this, they'd rest in the shade. Sit with their backs to the potting shed. Smoke, eat and pass water between them.

As for my glasshouse, it magnified this heat so that I'd enter a thick, condensed atmosphere. It required effort to push through, like a wall. Kew's Palm House had been heated – pipework had run under its floors – but even so, this felt warmer to me. I'd unlock its windows sometimes; lower the bamboo blind to shield the more delicate plants from the overhead sun. And I watered far more so that in those first days of July, the plants saw their opportunity to grow taller and faster, to reach for the highest wires. The plumbago flowers were as open as hands. The brugmansia's scent could reach the potting shed. And I realised that Forbes had been right: this was an undemanding role. I would water the plants and deadhead them; I'd check the undersides of leaves for mites or decay. But otherwise, they cared for themselves and did not need me. By ten in the morning, I'd leave the glasshouse and only return when the shadows were long.

Mrs Bale disliked such heat. She felt it physically; she'd run her wrists under cold water and, when crossing the yard, would keep against the outbuildings for the little shade they afforded. Also, she spoke far less. Others – Hollis, or the butcher's boy who rang his bell in the lane – might have supposed this was the temperature's doing. Partly it was. But mostly it was her sleeplessness.

I mentioned this to Harriet. 'She's quiet.'

We were shelling peas. Or rather, I watched as Harriet did it, slitting the pods with her thumbnail and pushing the peas into an enamel bowl.

'I know. I found her praying yesterday – in the hallway, at the foot of the stairs. Also, she leaves for the church most days – when you're in the glasshouse, she hurries down there and spends an hour with the vicar, and I think it helps a little. But sometimes she cries; we've heard her.'

'She cries? Why?'

'You know why. She's tired. Afraid.'

I did not wish her to cry. Mrs Bale had been change-able, testing, and I felt neither of us could say that we liked the other very much – yet I did not wish her such distress. When I saw her one morning, selecting stems of Rêve d'Or with a paring knife, I asked her how she was finding the weather.

'The weather?' Surprised. Her cheeks were hollow; her eyes seemed larger than before, yet greyer, without reflec-tion. She looked at the yellow rose in her hand. 'It gets

127

worse. Since talking of her ... I feel she's with me constantly. I can't shut my eyes for thinking she'll come. I see her reflection in the night-time glass. Yesterday morning, I took a cool bath. Her shadow moved across the water's surface. I saw it.'

A fragmented way of speaking which was not usual for her. I also recognised that there was no use in reasoning. She was exhausted. Her hair was poorly plaited; she was pricking her thumbs on rose thorns and not even noticing because her mind was on the Pettigrew woman and not on the blooms.

'You said,' I asked softly, 'that her darkness was different to that of her brothers. Will you tell me how?'

But she hurried from me without answering. It was a pattering, uneven gait, and she misjudged the width of the door frame into the kitchen, so that she knocked her arm against it. I imagined the bruise that would follow in the coming days. The colours it would move through.

Birds drank from the bathing pool. And at the end of a long, airless afternoon, the garden boys set down their barrows. They carried their tools back to the shed – hoes, shears, spades – and trudged down the lane to their homes with their sunburn and fatigue. Having watched them do this, I sought the gardener.

He seemed pleased to see me. He was hanging the tools on the wall when I found him – one by one, with precision; there were implements of every age and size and purpose on rusting nails and wire.

'Tell me there's cooler weather to come, Miss Waterfield. Or that you've set a pot of tea outside the shed for me.'

'No. Sorry.'

He hooked a spade onto a nail. 'Ah, never mind.'

'How well do you know the garden boys?'

'Know them?'

'As individuals. How did they come to work here, for example? Did you choose them yourself? Had you known them before?'

He frowned at this. He came towards me, cleaning his hands on a cloth, and told me that he'd known Albert for eighteen years, of course. Teddy Collier, too, for he'd been Albert's friend since infancy. 'The others? Peter Bell, Charlie Rudd, the Mayhews, little Fred ... they were all just local lads in need of work. And I might not have known them very well beforehand, as such, but I've always known their families. Emily Rudd brought our eldest boy into the world. The Bells sell home-made jam at the roadside and we'll buy a jar from time to time and talk with them. That's happened for years. Why do you ask?'

'I was told they can be tricksters. The Mayhew twins?'

'They can play a prank or two, yes.'

'Would they think it a decent prank to enter Shadowbrook at night? Through the upper windows, perhaps? And pretend to be ghostly?'

'My boys? My lads? Oh, they like their mischief, of course. If a bicycle bell had been taken, or a spider placed on a laundered bed, then yes, I might look to the boys. But to carve a door like that? To cause such worry?' He shook his head.

'Can you be sure?'

'Yes, I can. Because they aren't cruel, Miss Waterfield. I could find many words for my boys, and not all complimentary, but I'd never call them cruel or unkind.' He dropped the cloth onto the worktop. 'Anyway, how might they reach the upper windows? They don't have wings.'

'But you must have ladders. You have such high hedges to keep in order. Where do you keep them?'

129

He was bemused, uncertain. 'Look above your head, Miss Waterfield. See it? That's our longest ladder, cobwebbed and splintery. I doubt it's been used this year, quite frankly. We have no need for it. The stepladders suffice for the hedges and the yellow rose is left to do as it pleases.'

He began to perform his last task of the day. He set a broom onto the ground and began to sweep the leaves, the feathers, the lengths of string and fallen earth into the courtyard. He hummed tunelessly.

'I heard she was mad, the Pettigrew woman. Mrs Bale said she used to walk unclothed through the garden and eat dead birds.'

He slowed, exhaled. 'Let's not darken such a bright day with these questions, Miss Waterfield. And don't heed every word Mrs Bale gives you: rumours can grow like weeds here, springing up and multiplying, so that the truth can be quite choked by them.'

Like weeds? 'Kit Preedy said that, too.'

'Kit? You've seen him?' Hollis looked up.

'A few days ago. I thought he might have answers for me.'

'And did he?'

'No. He said very little. I think he preferred the wall to my company. He seemed cross that I was standing there.'

'Cross?' Hollis returned the broom to its place. He retrieved a key from his pocket and I stepped out of the tool shed so that he could close its door for the evening. 'I doubt it was personal, Miss Waterfield. Kit has never been the talkative sort. I've known that boy all my life and I've never heard him sing to himself or tell stories to others. Perhaps he does prefer stone walls. But I can't fully blame him.' He tucked his key into his shirt pocket, tapped it twice.

'Why does he have bad blood?'

130

He paused. 'Mrs Bale again? Ah, well. I suppose there's no harm in talking of what is fact. And perhaps it's better you hear the truth than some flowery version stitched with lies. His father killed a man, Miss Waterfield. He died on the scaffold – thirty years ago now, it must be. Kit was seven or eight. His mother had already died in birthing him so he was raised by his uncle – but the loss changed him. And Bill Preedy's body wasn't released for a proper burial – he's in a pit somewhere, I suppose – so Kit's got no grave to stand by. That makes a difference, I think.' Hollis shook his head. 'There should have been sympathy for the boy. It wasn't his fault, after all. But mostly they know him to be a murderer's son, and that's enough. If there's a theft in these parts, you'll hear his name.'

'And does he thieve?'

'Kit? No. But he doesn't help himself by having a temper. A churlish, brawling nature that shows itself in The Bull sometimes.' Hollis shrugged. 'Men have lost teeth and pride to him.'

Teeth and pride. That explained the scars. That vertical line under his eye had not, perhaps, come from wire or blackthorn but a thrown glass or a sudden fist. And his resistance to rumours made better sense to me; all his life, he must have felt encircled. He'd heard *murderer's son* in his wake as I'd heard *crooked* or *such a shame*; no wonder he'd snapped his answers to me as if in dismissal. Talked of amusement as if it tasted sour. 'You know him well, Hollis?'

'As well as one can. He doesn't say much. But I knew his father far better. We were friends, Bill and I. He was a huge man, like a bear, and Kit would try to keep to his father's footprints by jumping from one to another ... '

Bad blood. Kit caused suspicion in Barcombe-on-the-Hill for having it. Yet Mrs Bale had not spoken suspiciously.

Her words had been spat; she'd seemed scornful of him, repulsed, so that I found myself asking, 'What else? There must be something else.'

'Something else?'

'How Mrs Bale talked of him. She doesn't care for him at all.'

'She's a God-fearing woman; I suppose she disapproves of how Kit chooses to live. Many do, I'm afraid.'

Even this felt strange. As we began to walk together – towards the lane, so that Hollis might go home – I felt that the facts did not quite meet each other; there was a missing piece, like a chip in porcelain. Yes, Kit fought sometimes. But didn't the garden boys? They'd also thrown punches – I'd seen this or detected the evidence on their jawlines or from their grazed knees – and yet Mrs Bale only spoke fondly of them.

'How does he choose to live?'

Hollis slowed. He breathed in sharply, removed his cap and looked at its interior as if it held the answer. 'When one gets older, one often says the wrong thing a little more frequently; I've noticed this in me. I shouldn't have said . . .' He sighed, in acceptance – and the pause that followed was so long that I wondered if he'd forgotten he'd started to answer, if his mind was fully absorbed in the cap. 'Kit knows women, you see.'

'Knows women? He is friends with them?'

He replaced the cap, looked at the ivy. 'More than friends. There's no need to say more to you, Miss Water-field. I think how someone chooses to live their life is entirely their own business. If it doesn't interfere with other people's choices, how can it matter to the rest of us? As I say, his father's death changed him.'

'He hasn't married?'

132

'Kit? No. Nor will he. I doubt he'd risk a proper friendship, let alone a wife. And speaking of wives ... mine will be waiting for me with a fresh teapot, if I'm lucky.'

We made our goodbyes. I could still hear Hollis's tuneless whistle – for my benefit, perhaps – as he moved down the lane, under the beeches and out of sight.

I stayed in the garden till dusk. I moved under trees, passed through archways. But also, I stood still for a long time, for the garden had new sounds at this hour. The closing of flowers, incrementally. The rustle of a creature making its way down the line of a hedge.

This was the time of day my mother had warned against, years before. The half-light, she explained, can change how things appear so that distances may seem less. Our eyes might detect movement when in fact there is none; a shadow might become a living shape. In short, I was more likely to fall at twilight. *Remember this, Clara.* But she'd loved it, too. It was an hour of potency. In India, this had been the time of the leopard's waking, in which jasmine smelled at its strongest. My mother would have walked barefoot across lawns that had been newly watered by staff, printed the cool floor of the house as she'd entered.

These thoughts of her, as I moved between the topiary trees. But I thought, too, of this new information that I'd been offered – dark, like an unknown bloom. A brawler? This had not surprised me. His arms had talked of such a history: scars as wide as my thumbnail, bruises of all the familiar shades, and I knew his nose had been broken. But this other fact? *He knows women.* This knowledge, I understood, had not come from books. He'd acquired it from life, from being in the presence of women, in the same way that he'd assessed the worth of those stones by his feet by touching them, turning them over. Some women must, therefore, also know men. And this world of shared knowledge was as vast and unexplored to me as a desert landscape. A place I'd never imagined.

I moved away from it. It had quickened my pulse so much that I'd felt unsteady and I thought, instead, of a smaller, younger version of him. He'd jumped from footprint to footprint in a ploughed field, in his father's wake; he'd tried to emulate him. And I understood this far better – for sometimes I'd find her suffragette sash with its lilac, green and silver colours, still warm from her, and slip it over myself in the hallway. I'd find her rose-water scent on it, a strand of her dark-blonde hair.

I did not have supper that night. I stayed in the garden until it was dark, thinking of London and loss. When the distant grandfather clock chimed ten times, I rose from the bench. I tapped my cane ahead of me, testing for croquet balls or uneven ground, and as I stepped onto the lawn, I found a sudden brightness. The upper floor of Shadowbrook was illuminated; every window on its southern side was lit. I saw table lamps and tapestries and a background of books – and I saw a man, silhouetted. He was standing, hands in pockets. Looking down at the croquet lawn.

For a moment, we both stayed very still. Surveyed the other, as animals do. It was Mr Fox who broke away. He moved from room to room, turning out the lamps that were not needed and drawing the curtains, one by one.

His arrival changed Mrs Bale. It did not mend her entirely but in the morning I found a kitchen of activity, of boiling pans and commands and steam on its windows, and whilst her complexion had not brightened, she seemed occupied.

She could not, I supposed, think of hauntings when there were five to cook for now. Could not move slowly when Mr Fox expected his breakfast to be delivered at seven thirty, with his softly poached egg and a pressed white linen napkin; and she did not seem to notice my entrance. She only muttered to herself that she'd not yet cut any flowers for him, so she hurried into the garden with scissors, returned with lavender. The maids sliced ham, toasted bread. They whisked a yellowish sauce in a pan, set his tray with polished cutlery and, two minutes before half past the hour, Mrs Bale carried the breakfast tray upstairs. She held it with ceremony, as if presenting a crown.

The maids, too, changed. They seemed alert, primed, aware that Mr Fox might make a request at any moment so that strands of hair which had, previously, been allowed to escape from their caps were fastened now. Harriet flitted from sink to stove to the cold store. And when they weren't in the kitchen, the maids would be in the courtyard, soaking and scrubbing his bed sheets, turning the mangle and hanging the linen on the line for the breeze to find. Later, they'd iron it.

In short, there was a new physicality – and I took myself away. I spent the day in the glasshouse. But despite my attempts at work – watering the citrus, rotating pots to find the most attractive side of each plant – I thought of Mr Fox: what he looked like, what he was doing at that precise moment. I looked up, frequently; I eyed the upper floor in the expectation that I might see him again, and in detail – his colouring or features, his clothes. This man who abandoned his staff.

'How long will he stay for?'

I asked this as Mrs Bale prepared his lunch. The maids were elsewhere. I leaned against the worktop as she rinsed carrots under the tap, chopped them brightly. 'We never know. He may leave tomorrow or he may stay for a week.'

'And does he know what's happened here? In his absence?'

The neat slapping sound of the knife on the chopping board. 'He knows there have been difficulties, yes. I told him last night. Said that she'd tapped on your door this time and he didn't like hearing that.'

'What will he do about it?'

'Do? I don't know, child.'

'And when will I meet him?'

'I can't answer that. Miss Waterfield, you must remember that his work can leave him very tired. I've told you this.'

I wasn't content with this answer. A gentleman, I told her, would see me immediately. After all, hadn't I come from London for this? Wasn't the house unsafe? Wasn't I working in the glasshouse at the height of the summer, at his request? These and other declarations I listed to her. But Mrs Bale merely murmured platitudes in a flat, grey-coloured voice.

She offered the vegetable peelings to me. 'Will you take these outside.'

I carried them to the compost heap which sweltered in the shade of the beechwoods. And as I returned, I looked up. This was a new angle from which to view the house. I could see the sideboard in the drawing room and the empty picture hooks. But I could see, too, into other rooms on the upper storey. Between the curtains, I saw bookshelves; I saw dark polished cabinets and a green-shaded lamp which stood in the corner. I could not believe that such a man – informed, businesslike, with so many books – might believe in ghosts as others seemed to. He'd be practical. And he might be tired from work, but didn't this mean his work was cerebral, of consequence? I resented him less at that moment. I realised what Mr Fox might be to me, which was a fellow pragmatist. A reader. An ally in this house of deception and dust.

That night I listened to the sounds of the first floor. His footsteps varied in pace and weight. Furniture was moved a little; a chair was pushed back or a table was lifted. There was, too, the occasional prolonged creak of a floorboard directly over my head, as if he was testing its structure.

The grandfather clock struck through the hours, and we slept.

But at three in the morning, I woke suddenly, alarmed; I grappled for the lamp.

And as I did so, I heard it: a huge, terrible scream. It rushed into my room like water. It was followed by a thud that caused the door to jump on its hinges and, too, a shattering of glass and I dropped out of my bed, found my slippers and lifted the lamp, then opened my door and hurried into the hallway.

'Mrs Bale?' For the scream had been hers. And now, in the half-darkness, I could hear other sounds from her – soft, small, repetitive. 'Mrs Bale?'

Her whimpers came from the foot of the stairs. By lamplight, I found her: folded, trembling. She was wearing her nightdress; her grey hair was fanned out on the floor and her knees were tucked up against her chest. A child's posture. A fist by her mouth.

I tried to lower myself to her but my bones were stiff from sleep and I'd forgotten to bring my cane and underfoot I felt the crunch of broken glass from her lamp so that I could not kneel. 'It's me, Mrs Bale. It's Clara. What happened? Are you hurt?'

She did not answer me. She merely moaned; stayed on her right side so that I could only see the left half of her face, her left arm, her left hip. I knew that I could not allow her to stay there. The glass itself was a danger to her. 'You need to move. Do you hear me?'

But when I touched her shoulder, she screamed. 'Oh! Don't touch me, don't touch my arm!'

'Can you sit, at least? Mrs Bale? Try.'

She wailed at the thought, but I insisted until she attempted it. She used her left arm and her hips to push her body upright, laid her head against the banister, and I saw she was drained of colour. Her skin seemed bloodless, loose. Her right arm remained tucked against her, with her wrist pressed to her collarbone: I recognised this pose instantly. 'You've hurt your right arm?'

She nodded, eyes closed.

She needed to be taken to her room. Yet I could not lift her or bear her weight; I could already feel my own bruises developing from the way I'd stumbled from my bed, and so I called out to the maids. I called – but they were already coming. They rushed down the corridor in their bare feet and cotton nightdresses, their hair streaming out, so that I thought of legends in which maidens rushed forwards, or angels did. Maud clasped her mouth with both hands.

'Harriet? Can you lift Mrs Bale? She's fallen and her right arm may be broken, so don't touch it. And be careful of the glass here.' But Harriet did not care for the glass. She kneeled, placed a hand on the housekeeper's shoulder and murmured something to her, so that Mrs Bale opened her eyes and whispered *yes*, and Harriet adjusted her stance, counted to three.

Suddenly, they were both standing. A single, fluttering cry came from Mrs Bale as she straightened; Harriet kept an arm around the older woman's waist and glanced back at me. 'To her room?'

Yes, to her room. We followed the glow of her bedside lamp. Entered a room which was scented with talc. The housekeeper lowered herself onto her bed with heavy, laboured breath. And as Harriet and Maud tended to her, I looked around the room. I had not seen it before. It was modest and neat, as she was. A lace coverlet lay on her bed, a wooden cross hung on the wall. I noted a pot of Pond's cream and a glass of water, half drunk. On her nightstand, a pair of reading glasses sat beside a novel that had a book-mark within it, and at her bedside, a wicker chair on which there was a cushion which had been embroidered with an unrecognisable flower. Real flowers, too, on the window-sill. Sweet peas that had withered, drooped. A cardigan hung on the back of the door.

The maids were small mothers to her. They murmured suggestions and reassurances. They tended to the pillows, offered to make tea, and yet they also looked across at me, wanting their own encouragement. No matter that Maud and I had a mutual distrust; now, she was frightened and needed comforting. And I, at least, knew broken bones.

'Maud? Fetch Mrs Bale a brandy. I've seen some in the drawing room on the sideboard. And Harriet, sweep the broken glass away in the hallway.'

In their wake, I came closer to the housekeeper. This empty, trembling woman whose wrist had not left the hollow of her throat. Whose lips were moving as if she was trying to speak. 'Open your eyes, Mrs Bale.'

She opened them. But her gaze only rested on me very briefly, as a moth might touch a window pane.

'What happened? Why were you on the stairs at this hour? It's three in the morning.'

She started to swallow rapidly and I thought that she might vomit; I knew that the pain of a splintered bone could cause that, the body responding with a sudden, violent expulsion. I thought to rise and hurry to the kitchen, find a bowl or cloth or warm water. But she did not vomit.

'You dismissed the soul – do you remember? You spoke of proof – that the soul could not be proved as breath could be, or an organ. Well, I wanted proof, too: I wanted to *see* her with my own eyes so that I could tell you that no, you're wrong to say there is no God. I wanted to *see* Veronique. And so when I heard her tonight – the same footsteps – I rose and walked out and climbed the stairs. I was afraid. But I was also tired of feeling like a fool. Tired of people thinking I'm frail and mistaken. And as I stood on the landing, I heard her footsteps.'

'Where were they?'

'In her room! *Her* room! The room that you entered on that day of rain. I could hear her, pacing up and down, so I opened the door. There was nothing there at first. Nothing! But then I turned back to face the corridor ... and there she was. *There she was!* Between me and the bedroom door, as if she had followed me into the room. And don't you dare tell me I was imagining it or that this was shrewd human work, because I *saw* her! I saw her in profile, first. And then she turned very slowly, like a machine or a ghastly child's toy – clockwork, or mechanical – until she was facing me with her green teeth, and I tell you this: I will never forget her eyes, for they were on fire with hatred for me. They were a lunatic's eyes – black and bright and furious – and I have never been so afraid in all my life; I have never feared for my life like that. I ran round her, ran into the corridor without looking back, but she followed me ... '

'How do you know that she followed you if you didn't look back?'

She grasped my nightdress in her fist. 'Because I felt her hands on me. I felt her! She pushed me! Why aren't you hearing me?'

'Pushed?'

'Oh!' She wailed, released her grip. 'I can't bear it. How can you be so certain? How can you doubt me, even now?'

She lay back, turned her face away from me and sobbed privately. Her crucifix heaved up and down; her right wrist remained near her throat, tucked up, and in her exhaustion and distress she seemed to forget I was sitting beside her, for she murmured words that I could not decipher – a prayer of some kind.

She was as pale as lace. As frail as an insect's wing, plucked free of its body.

I stayed with Mrs Bale. She tired quickly; the shock and pain had weakened her, and she needed to be roused to sip the brandy. 'Mrs Bale? Drink this?' She lifted her head from the pillow; Harriet held the glass to her lips.

The maids could do no more. I told them that we'd send for a doctor at first light, that any fracture could be mended; they remained moon-eyed but they did not contest this. They held hands, pattered back to their room, and I settled back into the wicker chair. I looked at the housekeeper's face for a time. This face which had been loved by a husband. Which had made vows at an altar and wept at his grave. And I looked at the paperback beside her; I saw the embroidered cushion and the wedding ring on her finger and her fanned dark-grey hair, which still held the mark of the ribbon that had tied it during the day. I assumed she was sleeping. But her eyes had opened and she was watching me.

'She was the worst of them. Did I tell you that?' Her

141

anger had gone. It had consumed her, like a blaze, and the woman who remained was softly spoken. Made of ash.

'Yes.'

'I did not want you to know. Also, I thought she might hear me ... but what does it matter? If she hears now? What more can she do?'

'Tell me.'

The housekeeper exhaled. 'She didn't gamble or shoot, like her brothers. Didn't leave the house. She was barely seen beyond Shadowbrook and yet she's the one they talk about ...'

'Why didn't she leave the house?'

'Haughty. Proud. I don't suppose she cared to see how others lived without pearls or fox furs. Had no wish to be offended by the sight of the poor. The villagers did not see her, but oh, the stories came. Stories of men. *Her* men. Any men. Lovers, one might call them. But they say that love played no part in it. They were acts of appetite. Wanton, depraved ... They had parties. *She* had parties, to which women were never invited. Men only, at her own request. And she'd ...' She turned to the wall. 'I don't need to say what she did. I refuse to. But she was devilish, Miss Water-field. She was a vile, ravenous creature who deserved the madness that came to her, and it was only her madness that stopped her from taking these men and ... She deserved that end. Sleeping in the woods like a rat.'

Mrs Bale glanced back, saw my expression.

'You'll want proof, I suppose. I doubt there's any now. If there are any men who performed such acts with her, they are old or a long time dead – or would not admit to it, at least. Yet everyone knows who she was. Those are the stories which travel furthest – wicked, godless stories. And she' – Mrs Bale looked at the ceiling, both afraid and challenging – 'she must hate that other women have come here. That we're walking through her house. And I think this, too: that she hates that I tend to Mr Fox. She wants him all to herself.'

At this, Mrs Bale closed her eyes. I thought she had only paused in her telling, but she seemed to physically drop into sleep, sink into the bedding. I stayed where I was, with the paperback and the talcum scent and the threadbare rug on her floor. With such words as *a ravenous creature*.

I could not stay. I needed air, my own rest, and so I carried the lantern into the hallway, passed the grandfather clock as it prepared to chime five times. On its fifth note, I slowed. The stairs were in front of me. They moved up into darkness yet I could see the gold picture frame. I could see a rounded, paler shape that was, I knew, the nude's upper thigh. I took hold of the banister. I ascended the stairs, and on the landing, I lifted the lamp to see her properly. Her rounded belly. Her casual, flushed hand that seemed to guide the eye. Her breasts of various pinks with shadows beneath them, denoting their weight. She looked back at me knowingly.

The upper corridor lay to my left. If I had felt differently, I might have opened the nearest door on the northern side and entered the dusty room, as Mrs Bale had done. I was not, of course, afraid of ghosts. But even so, I did not wish to open the door. Not at this hour, in which the house remained unsettled. In which the walls seemed to be holding their breath.

I looked to the southern doors. I thought of the bookcase behind them. I thought of the green lampshade and the cabinet and the map on the wall. In London, these things had formed a world in which I had known my position and worth, in which I had been comforted, and I wanted these things now. I wanted a room that had books with ribbon markers. To inhale that ancient scent of a page. So I walked to the nearest door and tried its handle. It was locked; locked, too, was the door after it, and the next, and the next. The last door on the southern side had a small trestle table beside it. I looked through the keyhole; I could detect a glow beyond it. I called out to him. Said his name.

He must, I thought, be awake. Surely he'd heard her scream. If so, why did he not hurry downstairs? If not, why might there be a light in his quarters at five in the morning? 'Mr Fox?' I tried the handle. 'Mr Fox? I know you're awake.' Yet the silence was absolute. Outside, the birds were starting to sing, and there was no use in calling for him.

I returned to the stairs. I descended carefully, aware of my tiredness and my thoughts and how much I needed my cane at that moment. I studied each step before reaching for it. And like this, I saw a silver flash. An eye-bright glint on a step.

Glass, I thought – a shard from the broken lamp which had not been gathered but needed to be. Or it was, perhaps, a coin. But I saw it was neither of these. I placed the lantern down on the stair, reached down and lifted a cool, round object that fitted in the palm of my hand.

Later, I held it to the light. It was a pendant. No chain to it; the chain was gone, but it was clearly a pendant. Silver, polished, perfectly round. Its front was curved and bore an engraving of a plant – leafy, with small flowers upon it. It had, too, a clasp, and when I pushed my nail against it, there was a small sound like a sigh. It opened like a small door – it was a locket – and inside there were two sides of red velvet. An interior no larger than the pad of my thumb. It stored nothing. No lock of hair or small note. No scent.

Mrs Bale's? She wore a silver cross on a chain, I knew that. But perhaps, sometimes, she also threaded this locket onto it. Exchanged the cross for ornamentation. Or she kept it in her pocket, maybe. Either way, she must have dropped it as she'd fallen that night.

This was the only answer. And I had accepted it, had reached to turn out my bedside light, when I chose to turn the pendant over. To look at the back of this bright silver eye.

It was flatter here. It had been designed to rest against a woman's collarbone, or a little lower. And there was more engraving, smaller, so that I raised it to see it better. Felt it with my fingertip.

I listed the possibilities. The engraving was a wishbone, perhaps. Or it was a delicate, airy depiction of wings, of a distant bird in flight. Or it was a strand of the flowering plant that had crept round to the back of the pendant; a tenacious vine. Or yes, it was a *V*, announcing its owner. And why should that be of concern for me? There were many other names that began with V. The late queen. Or *V* could mean verity or truthfulness. Venus, the goddess of love.

I placed the pendant in a drawer, closed it.

And I thought, oh, the game. The trick that was being played on us all. For if the intruder was wanting us to believe that Veronique was walking at night, wasn't this the finest way to do it? To place a pendant with her initial, bought at a market or stolen elsewhere, at the top of the stairs? To be found at first light?

I would not succumb. I would not, therefore, speak of the pendant to others. To do so would make it worse – this hysterical conviction in a form of afterlife. There was no such thing as that. I had seen the changes that came to a human

145

face in the seconds after death – the clouding of the eyes, the softened jaw. And I had begged my mother to open her eyes, to not leave me; I had pleaded with her to stay a little longer – just one hour longer – but she had left even so. And therefore, if I knew one thing with certainty regarding death, it was that it was absolute. It took everything and there was no coming back from it.

VII

I had not expected to sleep in the aftermath of this. Too much had been seen and heard; there was too much to think of. So I opened my curtains, lay on my bed and waited for the sun to rise higher. But then I heard the grandfather clock again, and though I imagined it would chime six times or seven, I counted ten – so yes, I had slept.

I did not think to dress. I crossed the room in my night-dress, grasped my cane and stumbled down the corridor with my knotted hair and unwashed face. Mrs Bale's door was ajar, so I knocked twice with my cane as a courtesy but did not wait for any answer. I entered her room saying, 'Mrs Bale, I—'

She was not alone. She was sitting on the edge of her bed, dressed, with plaited hair and a pinkish complexion and her right arm in a sling. But there was also a man. He sat in the wicker chair; he rose as I entered.

'Ah, good morning, Miss Waterfield,' Mrs Bale said. 'We were just discussing you, weren't we, Matthew?'

He was less pale than I remembered. Previously I'd seen him in the shade of yews; he was fully illuminated now. But in other ways, he was the same. His hair was still combed back to reveal his temples; he still wore the dark-rimmed round spectacles and the same clergyman's gown. The same collar.

He opened his mouth to speak. But then he glanced down, cleared his throat, shifted his weight from foot to foot – and I knew why. My appearance at that moment was all they were thinking of. I'd erupted into the room bare-foot in a white cotton nightdress with its uppermost buttons unfastened, so that my collarbone showed; my hair was wild and my limp was more pronounced from having not walked for five hours or so. I wondered if my face was marked from the pillow. If my bed's warmth was rising off me.

I could have left. But I rooted myself.

'Clara? Clara – may I call you that? At last?' Mrs Bale reached out her left, working hand. 'Come and stand beside me. It feels too wrong to call you Miss Waterfield now. I owe you such a debt.'

I moved closer but did not take her hand. 'I did not realise the hour. I was still sleeping.'

'Of course. You must have stayed with me until ... four o'clock? Five? You must be exhausted. Matthew, I have a cardigan behind the door. Might you pass it to her?'

I felt like an infant being cared for. So when the vicar offered the cardigan to me, holding it open, I seized it. I did not wish to be aided by him. I entered it by myself. Freed my hair from its collar.

'Clara. I've been telling Matthew all about your kindness. How you found me and nursed me – don't say you didn't! It *was* nursing. You brought calm and assistance; you offered company at a terrible hour and I can't thank you enough.'

I had not dreamt it all. The sling and her words were both proof of her fall. Yet I marvelled that this woman – talkative, bright, pleased to see me – was the same one who'd lifted a finger, five hours before, and said *don't you dare*. Five hours. She'd talked of debauchery.

'You'll see the doctor has been. He came at first light – Mr

Fox summoned him – and you're right, Clara. You thought it was broken, didn't you? I heard you say so. I have fractured my forearm.'

'Radius or ulna?'

'Oh child, I can't tell you that. But Dr Warrimer gave me something for the pain, so that it aches far less. And he has fastened my arm, as you can see. He says I must try to keep it very still which will be a perfect nuisance for I use my right arm for so much.'

'He did not think to take you elsewhere? To a hospital? A surgery?'

'What might they do at such places? That this sling and rest and stillness cannot? He's a good doctor and I trust him.'

'Mr Fox summoned him?'

'Didn't I tell you that she was all questions, Matthew? An inquisitor? I woke this morning to find him – Mr Fox – at the side of my bed, looking very concerned. It was a little before six, I think, although he said he'd been there for some time. He rang Dr Warrimer at seven and I was wearing this' – she meant the sling – 'by eight thirty. I consider myself very fortunate. I have been well cared for.'

I thought, he was awake. He must have been awake when I called for him, looked through his keyhole and saw his light. The wicker chair must have felt warm from me as he sat down in it. Yet why hadn't he answered the door to me? Or at least told me to leave him in peace? The vicar was leaning against the wall. 'Did Mr Fox summon you too?'

A slow answer, as if unsure of it. 'Yes. He rang me at eight or so. I came after the doctor.'

'I asked for Matthew to come. Because I have need of him, you understand. The doctor offers comfort to the physical body, Clara, but it's the priest who offers comfort to the soul and it is the soul where strength and happiness lie, and one's proper well-being. I had need of Matthew's company far more than I needed the sling.'

'Perhaps I shall leave you both—'

'Oh, heavens!' Mrs Bale's bright cry. 'Stay, Matthew! Stay a while longer. I was hoping you might walk with me to Willowbank, for I'm sure I'll be too weak on my own.'

My eyes returned to her. 'Where?'

At this, her expression changed. It moved through many shades – kindness, apology, determination. She smoothed her bedspread with her left hand, addressed it. 'I am leaving here, Clara. I wish to leave. I'm going to live with my sister now.'

'Leave? While you mend?'

'I will mend there, yes. But that's not why I'm leaving.' She softened. 'Child, you know why I won't stay. So does Matthew. So do the maids, who I have already spoken to on this matter. They understand perfectly. I will leave for Elspeth's shortly and I will stay there until the matter is done with. As long as it takes.'

'Six weeks for most bones. Maybe eight.'

'Stop pretending, Clara, that you don't know what I'm speaking of. I don't suppose you're any closer to believing me than you were five hours ago, but I know what I saw. I know I was pushed and I know whose hands they were. And I'm leaving because I can no longer bear it. I won't stay in this house with her.'

I looked across at the vicar but he studied the floor.

'I'll stay away for as long as it takes to get rid of Veronique. To remove her from Shadowbrook. I don't care how it's done. I only know that I'm tired of being afraid, tired of lack of sleep.'

She was resolute. But I had not believed her smile for

many weeks – pinned, false, a form of armour – and I did not believe it now. I felt she might cry at a single word. That if I blew gently against her she'd tremble. 'Mr Fox knows that you're leaving?'

'He does. I informed him this morning. He has been very understanding – how can he not be, when he's experienced Veronique himself? And what good might I be with a broken right arm? The maids will take over my duties. Harriet, at least, is able to cook.' Her smile could not have been wider. 'Matthew? Shall we? I'm ready to leave now.'

The vicar was watching me. He had, perhaps, his own private thoughts for this question seemed to startle him, bring him back. 'Yes, of course.'

They moved down the hall. Mrs Bale linked her left arm through the vicar's; he walked slowly, matching her pace. And I followed, barefoot, certain that I had more questions than this, that there was more I wanted to know and demand and yet I did not know what these questions might be.

They stepped into the courtyard. I could not follow onto the stones so I stopped, and the housekeeper turned back to me. 'Clara? Before I leave, I wish to apologise to you. I feel sorry for how I spoke to you that day – on the first floor, the day of rain. Can you see why I did now? You were in her room. And I was afraid for you, for what if she had pushed *you*, Clara? What if she had put her hands on your shoulder blades and pushed you down the stairs? You'd have shattered every bone, I shouldn't wonder. I always knew she'd be violent one day.' She paused. 'Also, it wasn't right for you to be in that room. What happened in there . . . I did not wish you to breathe the same air.'

There was nothing more to say to her.

Mrs Bale asked me to visit her – 'Will you? I'd like that.

151

The blue-doored cottage by the humpbacked bridge on the road to Stow. It has a rowan tree' – and I watched as they walked through Shadowbrook's gates, arm in arm.

A blackbird sang. A breeze shook the ivy, creaked the weathervane. I remembered that I was wearing my night-dress; I saw that the petals of the Rêve d'Or were almost transparent in such direct light.

The glasshouse was, for a time, my hiding place. For here, at least, there was common sense and supported explanations. Water and sunlight caused growth. Plants greened with chlorophyll. Petals would open with daylight and close in the evenings. And I liked finding Forbes's handwritten labels. *Do not overwater.*

What did I have, in my mind? An intruder who had grown violent. A housekeeper who was lucky to be living still – for her neck could have snapped in that fall. A house-owner who'd failed to answer his door as I'd knocked upon it at five in the morning. A vicar whose thoughts had seemed to be elsewhere. A farmer who'd walled him-self against others for years and knew the female form. And whilst Veronique Pettigrew was dead now – gone, not living – I understood that she'd been real. That in her lifetime she'd been disdainful of the villagers. Grandiose. Ungodly. Clinking with gemstones and ice in her glass. That she'd undressed men – or had asked them to undress before her.

I looked for Harriet, in the end. I feigned surprise – as if I'd merely happened upon her, scrubbing clothes in the courtyard with sweat on her forehead – but I had sought her company. I asked how she was.

She slowed, examined the soap in her hands. 'I'm not sure. Scared. Relieved, too, because Mrs Bale can rest properly now. She's close to her sister. They used to share the same rag doll as children and took it everywhere – to market, to school, to the bathtub. They'd walk with the doll between them, each holding a hand and singing to her.' A shrug. 'She told me that.'

'There'll be more work for you.'

'I suppose. Whilst Mr Fox is here, at least – although I don't mind the cooking, and there's so much in the garden to choose from just now. I promised Mrs Bale that I'd take the meal trays to him, leave them by his door. Said I'd look after you and Maud.'

With that, Harriet rose, straightened her skirt and began to haul the pail across the courtyard. She dragged it towards the mangle – rhythmically, using both hands and straining with the effort – and on seeing this, I imagined the hidden muscles in her; under her dress, there were sinews and joints. Tendons and ligaments.

'Harriet?'

She looked back.

'What have you heard of her? In life?'

'The Pettigrew woman? That she was selfish. Snooty. Didn't go to church.'

'That she stayed indoors. Did you hear that?'

'Yes. I've wondered if that's why she's still here; that she spent so much time in the house she refuses to leave it, even now.'

'And do you know how she passed the time? Indoors?'

Harriet regarded me steadily with her round pale-blue eyes. She searched my face for the same passing shadows that I sought in hers, and this expression told me that yes, she knew what I knew. She'd also heard of the parties and the men.

*

I stayed away from the vegetable patch that afternoon. Instead, I stepped down the five fanned steps into the bathing pool garden, skirted the pool and entered its portico. Instantly, it felt cool. A shaded place of plinths and urns. On three sides, it was open; the roof was supported by ornate classical columns which echoed the Roman forum or temples; but the fourth side was a wall. This wall was stuccoed, cracked – by design, perhaps. For it had been painted with classical scenes and references: Romans with wine, Romans reclining. Romans with their eyes on the bathing pool with quiet smiles, as if in approval. There was an older man with laurel leaves. Men with one hand to their chest. But there were women here, too: they offered platters of fruit, wine jugs; they served the men with shining eyes and dark coiled hair and gold bracelets; in one case, with a bare shoulder.

Glances were being cast between these figures, or so I imagined – between these sedate emperors and the bearers of fruit. And behind them, there was a single *trompe l'oeil*. I'd learned of these in books: a trick of the eye, a painting which plays with perspective so that it fools the observer. It looked like a single, narrow window, vertical, set into the wall and with views over a landscape of olive trees towards a distant Roman town; it looked so real that I felt I could reach into it. But it was flat, lacked dimension. I only touched a powdered wall.

I guessed the age of these scenes. Wondered which Pettigrew – Mortimer? His father before him? – had decided to decorate this wall with them, and who had swum under their black-eyed gaze. And I sensed tension in this wall, or expectation – as if, on my leaving the portico, the figures would move towards each other.

The vicar must have discovered me like this – thoughtful, my hand on the *trompe l'oeil*. I don't know how long he'd been standing there, at the top of the five steps. I only know that I stepped back, turned and found him standing within the archway of the yew hedge. No black gown; he only wore trousers and dark-grey shirtsleeves. But the white collar remained.

'I didn't mean to startle you,' he said.

'Why are you here? Is it Mrs Bale?'

'Yes. No. I . . . ' He shook his head. Moved his lips as if practising words. 'She's safely at her sister's, Miss Waterfield. She's being cared for. May I?'

He descended the steps, came closer. He had more to say; he stopped on the periphery of the portico, half shaded and half in light, and inhaled in preparation for it. But then he saw the Romans, and seemed to forget what he'd wished to tell me. He stared at the painted faces. I studied him, in return. This was the closest I'd been to him, so that I saw his eyes were grey, that his hair was of no distinct colour – it was neither fair nor brown – and his spectacles seemed tight against him, so that I supposed they might leave an indentation on the bridge of his nose or the side of his face. A rash on his neck – from a razor?

'I did not know these were here.' He meant the paintings.

'Why have you come?'

'To see how you might be.'

'How I might be?'

'We've barely met, I know. But Mrs Bale told me about your efforts to help her last night. I thought you might be shaken by it.'

'Shaken? No. Tired. Frustrated.'

'Frustrated?' He shifted his weight and in doing so, moved further into sunlight. A geometrical shape of shade fell on his left shoulder and the left part of his jaw, but otherwise, he was fully lit. 'With what?'

'With Mr Fox, firstly. He's here – he's in the house at this moment – but it seems we can only meet him when he wishes to be met. He did not show himself at all last night, yet he must have heard Mrs Bale's scream. And this talk of ghosts . . . as if they've all taken leave of their senses.'

I spoke like a child, perhaps. I could hear my petulance. I sounded harder than I felt, but he was a vicar; I did not care for what he represented.

'You think it's an intruder, Miss Waterfield?'

He seemed translucent in this light. I could see, with clarity, the textures of him. The part of his throat which moved when he swallowed; the pronounced bow of his upper lip; the vein in his temple. I thought I could detect his pulse in his jawline, too – a faint muscular flinch. And I remembered my anatomical book – specifically, the colourlessness of those human figures, their lack of identity. Without his white collar and spectacles, what distinguished him? Was it unfair to ask myself this? Perhaps his pallor was his distinction. But I realised, too, that I was a pale creature. That I was also able to trace the various shades of blue in my wrists and I had my own translucency. But whilst mine had been acquired at birth, I supposed he had gained his from the interior of churches, from bedsides. Standing beneath his canopy of yews.

'Yes. Or there is a problem with the pipework in the house, or the draughts. But it isn't Veronique Pettigrew. It is nonsensical to believe in ghosts.'

I knew this was provocative yet he said nothing. He merely looked back at the Roman wall with its *trompe l'oeil* – and this, too, frustrated me.

'Do you believe in them?'

'Me? I believe in souls. I believe there is part of us that cannot be seen but that is still real. That it is our most precious part. I believe it outlasts the physical death.'

'And these souls enter heaven or hell when we die?'

'Yes.'

'You believe this? Really?'

He smiled quickly, as if I'd embarrassed him. 'I do, yes. I'm a vicar, Miss Waterfield. There is a spirit within the Trinity; it is a fundamental belief that humans consist of more than flesh and bone.'

His words on souls seemed confident enough. Yet his delivery of them was not. His voice wavered, as if balancing; he moved his weight from foot to foot, looked down at his hands as if unconvinced by his own statement. Was he different in the pulpit? Did he become the fiery preacher who took the Bible's given word over sense and decency? Threatened damnation? Saw any disfigurement as a worthy punishment? Or maybe he quaked with his proverbs. Blushed at the sacrament.

'But there is no proof.'

'Belief exists because proof does not. Belief is about that – the risk, the step of faith in the absence of proof. One must trust one's own judgement.'

'And that's enough for you? What of books?'

'Books?'

'I do not mean the Bible.'

'I knew a man,' he said, clearing his throat. 'A vicar, more experienced than me. Every All Hallows' Eve, he'd hold communion in his church – for the lost souls, not the living. He'd stand at his altar, lift the bread to bless it and see, as he did this, the church filling up.'

'With ghosts? In pews?' I shook my head. 'Even if there were ghosts – which there aren't – wouldn't we see them constantly? Wouldn't we be seeing them now? The ghosts of Pettigrew bathers in the pool behind you? The ghost of a Pettigrew sitting in that chair?'

'Lost souls, Miss Waterfield. Lost. The souls of those who died violently, or with such grief or anger or sense of injustice that they have ... stayed. Been left behind, somehow. The vicar I mentioned? On All Hallows' Eve? He had books.'

'Was he looking for proof that night? Was it an experiment?'

'No, he wasn't looking for proof. He didn't need it, because he had faith, do you see? He believed absolutely in life after death. In the soul.'

I looked back towards the *trompe l'oeil*. My frustration was no less. But I felt tired, too, and a sudden heavy sorrow that made me want to sit down and sleep. Perhaps this sorrow had been near me all day; perhaps I'd carried it for many days and not wished to feel it. But I felt it now, in his company. With his white collar, with this talk of death and faith and churches. And I felt it with the sudden remembrance that there had been bathers in this pool once – wet-haired, warm, with their own veins in their wrists and their own thoughts on life after death – and where were they now?

'Miss Waterfield, why does it anger you? This idea?'

'Because I did go to church once, Mr Dunn. I was five. Neither of my parents had any faith of their own – they had their own reasons for that – and did what they wished on Sundays. But our housekeeper believed. And when I was diagnosed – *osteogenesis imperfecta*, which Millicent refused to say, incidentally; there were certain words she felt were curses – she decided that prayer was my only hope. She wanted to take me to her church; a whole congregation's prayers might strengthen my bones and cure me, she said. My mother was reluctant, of course. I think they argued on this. But I wanted to go – I'd never been inside a church and I was already stubborn at five – so I went. And do you know what happened, Mr Dunn? The vicar summoned me to his side. This was a large church – far larger than yours – and it was full. So I joined him by the altar and I thought to expect sympathy, I think; kindness, at least. But he talked of my previous sin. Announced that I deserved these bones. That each dislocated joint or fracture or bruise had been earned by my wicked ways, and did his congregation wish to be like me in the next life? To be poor and wretched? I was a warning. And yes, they should pray for me, but not for my body, because my body was my punishment and entirely deserved. They were to pray for my soul – that it was clean, or it would receive eternal damnation.' I turned, looked at him directly. 'I've not entered a church since then. Not cared for talk of souls since then.'

A wren sang in the hedge beside us; I heard, too, the distant garden boys, and I suddenly envied them. Their labours and friendships. Their homes which they returned to in the evenings. Their living mothers. Their ability to run.

'I cried so much that night that my mother feared I'd break a rib. But it led me to books. Books were inclusive. Books didn't offer cruelty. They showed me the liver and spleen and heart and brain in diagrams, but they never showed me a soul, tucked away. Nor did they ever speak of souls returning, except in fiction; in factual books, warriors died on their battlefields and stayed there. Birds came to peck at them. And if there were souls, Mr Dunn, my mother's soul would be here now, standing with us. She'd show herself to me – not because she was lost, as you say, but because she loved me and knew that I missed her.'

I knew I'd said too much. Felt something tighten in my throat so that speaking became hard.

Matthew removed his glasses at that. He closed his eyes, gave a single, hard exhalation. 'He said that to you? That vicar?'

'Yes.'

He moved his hand over his face as if trying to clean himself of my words; he replaced his spectacles, opened his eyes. And he looked at the Romans and the rusting furniture and the bathing pool behind him. 'He should not have said that to you. My God.'

I could not say more. In contrast, the vicar seemed as if he had so much to say that it caused a physical change in him; he was no longer still. He paced back and forth. He said *my God* to himself again.

He managed a few other words, in time. But they were small, incidental – a farewell, a remark on the weather. He left quickly, and I stayed by the *trompe l'oeil* with a hollow feeling which implied that this secret – of church when I was five – had occupied a physical space inside me, that it had had a tangible form. Secrets were not, of course, like that; they could not be identified in a human map any more than a soul could be. But I felt changed, for having spoken honestly.

A quiet afternoon. I wished to fill the hollowness with company so I went to the vegetable patch, where human life was. I accepted handfuls of earthy radishes from Albert; I stood at the ends of rows, watching the boys rummage and hoe with their damp underarms. Hollis stood beside me for a time. We discussed how the local soil was perfect for brassicas – cabbages, cauliflowers – and I felt grateful for this language of earth and fact.

But the vicar returned. It was late afternoon; the shadows were lengthening. I had gone back to the kitchen, was washing soil from leaves, when I heard a knock on the kitchen door.

He was breathless, as if he'd run here. 'Firstly, we are not all the same. We don't all think as he did, and I think that vicar should be ashamed of his words. But secondly, I want you to know that yes, I'm a vicar. I choose to be because I've had faith since I was small; it's what I believe in. But I'm also a man. I'm a man, Miss Waterfield, and sometimes I feel I cannot be both, that I must choose between one and the other, so that I choose to be the vicar because that is my calling; that's what is expected of me. I have duties. I cannot stop being a vicar at the end of a working day – and that is hard, sometimes. It is hard to act moderately, to hide the strong thoughts and feelings that a vicar should not show. But I am both these things. Can you understand that?

I stood, not understanding at all. I did not recognise him. I'd garnered a sense of this vicar's nature: mild-mannered, awkward. He fumbled with language, had a habit of pushing his spectacles up his nose with the back of his hand, and would often look down. Yet there was, too, this Matthew Dunn: a darker, breathless version who spoke with clarity, without embarrassment, and I could feel his heat rising from him. *I am also a man.* Said with defiance, as if claiming a throne.

Are you shaken? This, beneath the portico. And I'd said no.

But perhaps there are days when the fighters lay their armour down. We cannot carry all our burdens on our own, or without resting. And that night, I lay on my side; I brought my knees as close to my chest as I dared – and all I wanted was to hear my mother's voice again, or to have her enter the house in her raincoat, pooling water and speaking of what she'd seen on London's streets: the coalman's horse being washed clean, or a sudden river. I yearned for her.

But this did not last. It couldn't, for what good would it do? I strengthened myself, returned to the locket. *V*, which was found in such words as *bravery* and *agave* and *clavicle* and *love*. *Vases*, which held cloudy water. I listed such words until I found sleep, and did not dream of her.

VIII

I could have left Shadowbrook. Indeed, I would be asked this, in the months to come: why, after the violence that occurred that night – the fall, or push, of Mrs Bale – did I not choose to leave? To pack my trunk and walk away? After all, my purpose was done. The desired private jungle had established itself. And the adjectives used to describe me had grown so that I doubted I would be missed, if I went.

But I stayed. And it was hard to explain to those who asked why I had chosen to. Harriet, one evening, said, 'I'd go back, if I were you. Back to London.' We were eating early raspberries by the potting shed, watching the birds swoop in to roost. In response, I considered listing the precise measurements of every room in my childhood house to her, or how my mother used to whisper, *One day you will* . . . And these, perhaps, were the days she'd meant. So how could I go back there?

There were other reasons too. I had grown fond of the garden; I wanted to see the flowering of certain roses, to eat damsons and blackcurrants. I wished to see Barcombe's summer fair in early August, to watch the barley move through its phases. But mostly, I wished to stay because to leave now – without any explanation behind Mrs Bale's fall and the deep, determined lettering on her door;

without having met Mr Fox – would have been akin to leaving a library without having read an opening line. I'd always wonder.

Was this the education that Patrick had hoped for? Regarding people? My art of conversation had, it seemed, not fully improved. But I had met more people in three weeks than I had in my lifetime. Also, I'd become aware of bodies; of the breadth of a man's chest or how veins became more prominent when weight was carried. I'd compare Harriet's body, fully stretched to reach a saucepan or cobweb, to my diagrams. And who was this woman – long dead – who had lived so freely? With all the liberties of a man, and the complacency? I thought of her body as it had been in her lifetime – responsive and freckled, warm and creased – not as it was now.

The kitchen was empty. But the metal teapot remained on the stove, still warm to touch. So I made myself tea as if the kitchen was mine. I added milk, ate bread and jam.

There was a note on the kitchen table addressed to me.

Miss Waterfield,
  I'd be delighted if we could meet at last. Please knock on the very last door of the upper corridor at five o'clock. I look forward to making your acquaintance.
  Regards,
  R. E. Fox

I read the note three times. It was his handwriting, I knew that: ornate, ostentatious. The gold-embossed address was the same as before. And perhaps he was, in fact, a gentleman, for I sensed the cordial tone: *I'd be delighted if . . .* – as if inviting me to cocktails.

*

I was in two minds about how I should be. I thought perhaps to pin my hair, wear my best dress and arrive as the clock struck five. Yet I also felt a mild indignance at having been made to wait for so long, so that I considered climbing the stairs at ten past five or later with earth on my cheekbones and under my nails. To offer an air of indifference.

As it was, I knocked on his door – the last of the south-facing doors on the upper corridor, with the small trestle table outside it – at three minutes past the hour. Late, but not offensively so. And whilst my hands and face were clean, I wore my usual dress. My hair had been brushed but remained untied.

'Come in!'

I entered a room of light. It rushed in, such a force of sun that I lost my balance and raised my hand against it. I could see nothing but whiteness.

'Yes,' he said. 'I've been told it's a surprise, to walk from the corridor into this room. I chose these rooms for how the light finds them regardless of the time of day. Even in winter, they are bright. The north-facing ones are equally fine in size but they look towards the beech trees which means they lose daylight. This side is far better. Miss Waterfield? Please come in.'

I lowered my hand, stepped forwards.

He – Mr Fox – stood opposite me with his hands behind his back. He was, at first, a silhouette; he stood before the window – a huge rectangular window with a deep cushioned sill and decorative metalwork – so that his features themselves were unlit. I could not see his face at all.

'I owe you an apology, I think. It is over two weeks, I believe, since you came here. Nineteen days. All this time, and I have been unable to introduce myself to you – kept away by matters that were dull but necessary, I'm afraid. It was ungentlemanly and rude of me – you have travelled so far, after all – and I apologise for it, most sincerely.' He seemed to bow his head.

I could only stare. For as my eyes became used to the illuminated room, I saw his face a little better. And there was no disfigurement here; there was no damage to his face or any bodily abnormality that might give cause for him to hide upstairs. He bore the shape of a man – that was all. Shorter than most and notably slim in his frame, but in all other ways he was unremarkable. Greying hair, combed back. No beard or moustache

Mid fifties, perhaps. Neatly presented.

'You must think me a terrible host, having requested your assistance and not being here to greet you. It is no way to treat a lady.'

'Or anyone.'

A nod, accepting this. 'Or anyone. Quite. Old habits, I'm afraid. I fear I've been rather indulged in my life by those who either do not mind bad manners or who have bad manners themselves, and I've been quite absorbed in other matters recently.' He gestured to a chair. 'Come further in, won't you? We can't have you standing in doorways.'

I stepped forwards. This room did not seem to belong to Shadowbrook at all. Shadowbrook rooms tended to lack furniture. Here there seemed to be more pieces than in all the others together: a low velvet chair with gilded arms; a tall, polished bookshelf – the one I'd seen as I'd returned from the compost heap – on which there were dozens of books. I looked at their spines; he owned books on the Byzantine Empire and sculpture and birds of prey. I saw *On the Origin of Species* on its own shelf. And there were small trinkets amongst the books – a silver tankard, a pink-lipped shell, a stone in which I could see the fossil's impression.

A long, rectangular tapestry of a floral design hung on the far wall. A huge, rounded porcelain vase sat in a corner. Under my feet and cane I saw an embroidered rug of reds and browns and, on the nearest wall, were three botanical prints in oval gold frames: all poppies, in various stages of growth. Beneath these prints was a single shelf; on this, I saw living flowers – or flowers that had been living once. Sweet peas in a glass of thickened water; an act of Mrs Bale's before her fall. And yet despite these many distractions, it was the desk that my eyes came to rest on. I was most taken by it; a large mahogany desk that occupied, perhaps, a quarter of the room. Its sides were polished, reflecting the light; its surface was covered in a dark-green leather, held in place with brass fittings and studs. On it, there was a reading lamp, papers and an inkwell. An ink pen at rest.

He stood behind the desk. A flag, planted.

'It's not what you expected? My study?'

I wondered what I might say, or how it should be said. 'I've seen the bookcase from the lawn. I knew there were books and tapestries in here. And I know that you like to keep your curtains and windows open, even when you're not here.'

'I do, yes. I love the light. Love fresh air. I cannot abide a stale, sealed room – although I'm aware that some of the rooms at Shadowbrook are entirely that, currently. It will not always be the case.'

He regarded me. I could not see his eyes very clearly but I knew they were noting my deficiencies. The hair and the milk-coloured eyes. 'You love fresh air yet you are never in the gardens. You only stay indoors, Mr Fox.'

'This troubles you? I travel, Miss Waterfield, as you know. My work demands it, and it can become both tiring and so very tiresome that when I'm at home, yes, I prefer my own company and distractions. Rest. Books – I love books, as you see. I have both a telephone and a gramophone next door.'

'Can't you have your own company in the gardens? Read in the gardens? They are large enough. And the gardens are Shadowbrook's finest part – in this weather especially.'

'The gardens,' he said, 'will always be here. I can enjoy them at any time.'

'But you don't enjoy them. You're not seen in the gardens at all, so I wonder why you brought me here to establish a glasshouse when you have no interest.'

'I heard you weren't afraid of speaking your mind. That you weren't afraid at all, perhaps – and I commend that. The female voice is rising, it seems, and why not? Rest assured, Miss Waterfield: I am interested in the glasshouse. I have always had interest in plants, yet it is only now at Shadowbrook that I have the time – and, let us speak plainly, the money – to truly indulge that interest. I wanted the best glasshouse, so that I might enjoy plants and greenery in the very worst of the English weather. And I must say that I rather feel as if I'm under scrutiny. As if I'm defending myself to you which I have no need to do. I apologise for not having greeted you sooner. But my affairs remain my affairs, do they not?'

In reprimanding me, he had changed his stance. And like this, I saw that he wore an immaculately pressed shirt and a tweed waistcoat with a pocket watch – a watch that, in time, he'd consult before placing his hands behind his back again – and I knew that if Mrs Bale had spoken to me like this, I would have retorted. I'd have ignored her tone, asked more of her. With Mr Fox, I did not reply.

'Would you care for a drink, Miss Waterfield? Not tea, of course. Mrs Bale is not here to bring it, but even so, I feel we need something stronger.' He took a step towards his desk, opened a drawer. From it, he retrieved two glasses and a bottle of brandy; he set the glasses down on the desk and poured two measures. He took one himself; the other he left on the desk for me. 'I imagine that you think me to be not only a poor host but a cold-hearted employer, too. Indifferent to my staff by being away so frequently, and at such a time. Do you?'

'If we are talking plainly?'

'We are. I prefer that.'

'Yes. I don't understand how you can leave Shadowbrook so often when an intruder is entering it. All these acts of vandalism; Mrs Bale has been afraid since my arrival, and the maids too. And didn't you hear Mrs Bale's scream, two nights ago? You must have done, because you were awake at that hour; I saw your light and you knew to visit her at daybreak. But we needed you at three thirty, when it was still dark, not later.'

'I'm glad of your frankness. But Miss Waterfield, would you believe me if I told you that no, I did not hear her? That I sleep very poorly and that I take, sometimes, a light sedative? I'd had such a sedative that night. I heard nothing at all. And my light was not on, I can assure you of that. As for my morning visit, it will not surprise you to hear that Mrs Bale is very attentive. She knows my routines and knows to bring a pot of tea to my room very early; she leaves it outside for me. But I found no tea there that morning – her first such failure in the duration of her employment with me – and therefore I knew she must have been unwell.'

'So you looked for her.'

'Yes, I looked for her.' He rolled the brandy round the side of his glass. 'She told me about your care for her that night. Thank you for it. I have ensured that she has Dr

Warrimer's constant attention. Moreover, she will remain in full pay for as long as she needs to be. And the maids themselves are seeing an increase in their pay, for the extra work that will be required of them until Mrs Bale returns. It is the least I can do for them.'

'You think she will return?'

'I have,' he said, 'every intention of securing it. She's a fine housekeeper, and such things are hard to find.'

Mr Fox drained the glass. Having done this, he pushed it across his desk so that it spun on its base momentarily, and turned away from me to face the window. He placed both hands in his pockets and looked out into the distance – and I knew what he could see. The vegetable garden and the magnolia; the croquet lawn and the lime bower. I, in turn, could see him better. He was greying, yes, but Mr Fox's boyhood colouring had been a light red, a golden hue; not the dark rust red of Kit but a faded shade of it – the shade of a fox whose fur had grown old, been weathered and bleached by age and sun. He had a prominent nose. A looseness to his neck and jaw. Still looking out, he said, 'You think it's an intruder?'

'It must be,' I replied. 'It's the only feasible explanation.'

He surveyed his kingdom. 'Quite. It is a fanciful, damaged mind that believes in ghosts. There is no evidence for them yet people can devote their lives to the notion. They can believe a bird's shadow is a spectre and refuse to be told otherwise. I would often see this in my travelling days – stories that only an infant could have faith in, and yet the whole village would be quite convinced. It's strange how the human brain can grasp something so tightly that it won't let go. Do you think that?'

'Yes, Mr Fox. Yes, I think that.'

He glanced over his shoulder towards me. 'I thought it,

too. I wanted to buy this house. It was in disrepair, certainly, but I saw its potential and it suited me well, so I ignored the rumours about its previous owners. The past is the past, and ghosts don't exist. Mrs Bale, however, felt otherwise. She talked of hauntings from the start. The first painting dropped from its hook in October and she was already speaking of ghosts as she swept up the splinters. I suspect I was too firm with her; I told her that if there was an afterlife – and a capacity for the dead to return to us – wouldn't we be able to prove it by now? Scientists can do so much these days, after all. Flight, for example. Flight, Miss Waterfield! Can you think of anything more remarkable than getting metal craft into the air and keeping them there?'

'You still think this? That ghosts are an invention?'

His profile was so clearly defined by the light that I might have drawn it. And I thought, he is also tired. His eyes were distant and he repeated my question to himself under his breath. I waited for his answer. 'No. I don't think I do. You're surprised by that?'

'Yes. Because of the reasons you just told me.'

'I understand. But this, Miss Waterfield, is the truth of the matter: I have seen things here – heard things, too – that cannot be accounted for in any rational, calm, scientific way. I have tried to – believe me, I have. At first, I supposed it was the house's fault; warped wood or draughts or subsidence. Then the footsteps began. I requested new bolts for all the exterior doors; I checked every window, and on hearing footsteps in the corridor, I always came out to confront the intruder, but found nothing. You've heard the footsteps, I believe? There can be no denying them, no? But there has been more than that.'

'The mark on her door.'

'Yes. The tapping and trying of door handles. And how does one explain – in a reasonable, learned way – a hard, bold thumping on one's own door at three in the morning that rattles the glass in one's cabinets and causes paint to crumble and yet, on opening the door, one finds silence? An empty corridor? Or the unmistakable sound of someone entering the room and coming towards you, brushing the side of your bed?'

'This happened to you?'

'This happened to me, Miss Waterfield. I heard material – skirts – moving across the floor; there was no mistaking that sound. And I reached for the lamp very hastily – you can imagine – but there was no one there.'

'And had you taken your sedative?'

'You're saying I imagined this? I'd had my sedative, yes, but I hadn't lost my mind.'

I flushed yet I also felt cold. I could feel my pulse under my ribs, knocking. 'There are no ghosts.' But my voice was quieter.

Mr Fox shook his head, looked down at the window seat. 'All my life I've dismissed such talk. So it's hard for me to believe it now, to say that ghosts are possible. I feel embarrassed saying that much! I do not sound like myself. Like you, I have always preferred order and evidence. But I can assure you, too, that there was someone in my room that night. That she was female. She tugged on my bedlinen, Miss Waterfield; I felt it being pulled away from me very slowly. And there was no one there when I turned on the light. No sound of hasty retreat.'

'She pulled the sheets away from you?'

'Tried to, yes. Draughts do not do that. Mice or subsidence or thieves or rotting wood do not do that.'

We said nothing for a while. He seemed spent, regretful;

he exhaled through his nose, looked across his evening garden to the beeches and the barley. I turned to the bookcase beside me. I saw the red leather spines of books. I saw their age and use and discoloration; I saw, too, the tapestry and the seashell and the vase with its blue oriental birds and I still believed Mr Fox was rational. Knew he had an enquiring mind and would, therefore, not be easily fooled.

'But what you said remains true: there is no proof of ghosts. And wouldn't there be, by now? Mankind has existed for two hundred thousand years, Mr Fox.'

A weary, private half-smile. 'I know. I do. But I also know that once there were men who believed the world was flat. Who thought the earth was stationary and the moon and every other celestial entity orbited us; that we were the centre. A vanity, of course. But it was believed for centuries, even so. What if' – he glanced back – 'one day, in the future, there are men and women who marvel at the fact that at the start of the twentieth century, there were still people who did not believe in the human soul? Who thought there was only a corporeal life? What if those people in the future have their proof – that souls and ghosts are as real as you and I – and are amazed at how blind their ancestors were? At their closed minds and certainties? Their arrogance?

'The wisest man is the one who knows he knows nothing. And I do not consider myself wise but I recognise that I'd be a fool to discount all possibilities. That just because there is no proof now, at this moment, doesn't mean there may not be proof in the future. Tomorrow, or next year. In millennia.'

He turned back from the window. 'Miss Waterfield, to this end, I should tell you that I've invited someone to come to Shadowbrook to investigate this matter. He will come, and he will stay here in the house, and he will, I hope, uncover the truth of what's happening here. I hope he will solve the problem, so that Mrs Bale can come back and we can all sleep a little more soundly in our beds. In the meantime, I wish to ask three things of you, if I may. Firstly, I would like you to stay. I can see from here – and have heard from Mrs Bale – that the glasshouse is establishing itself beautifully, that I could not have asked for more from you. This might be enough to return you to London; certainly, the events of these past few days would send most people away. But without Mrs Bale, I fear the maids will be quite undone; they are young in both nature and age, and I believe they would be very grateful for your company. You are strong-minded and resilient, it seems, which are both assets in such uncertain times. I will, of course, continue to pay you. Indeed, I will increase your wage for the inconvenience and trouble.' He eyed me. 'Will you stay?'

I nodded.

'Thank you. The second request I have of you is that you assist the maids where you can. I realise this is not what you came here to do. I realise, too, that you are unaccustomed to housework. I do not suggest that such work is suitable for you; nor do I wish to imply that I feel the girls will not manage this house well enough without Mrs Bale. But, of course, this gentleman from London is coming. He will arrive soon, and his arrival will involve far more work for them and ... Well, Miss Waterfield, if you can offer them assistance I'd be most grateful. Whatever work you feel able or willing to do. I realise that certain tasks may be too physical for you.'

'What is your third request?'

With that, Mr Fox bent at the waist. He opened a drawer in the desk, retrieved a metal ring from it; on it, there were three keys. He laid them on the desk, stepped back. 'It was Mrs Bale's job to secure the house at night, in my absence. I have done it since she left. But I shall be leaving here again very soon, so I ask that you ensure the house is locked at night, and unlocked in the morning. It matters, of course. I no longer believe we have an intruder, Miss Waterfield, but the doors must still be checked and locked.'

'You're leaving again?'

His eyes remained on the keys. 'I know how it must seem. But I have urgent business to attend to near Oxford and I cannot postpone or alter it. Miss Waterfield, would it reassure you if I locked every upper room? If the upper floor was sealed off entirely? By which I mean both windows and doors? It will secure the house further, at least. And I shall give the maids a definite date on which to expect my return.'

I reached for the keys. 'Is he a priest? This man who is coming?'

'No,' said Mr Fox. 'He is from a society. The Society for Psychical Research, which, as I understand, makes no assumptions. It simply investigates – and, I trust, finds the truth.'

They were heavy keys. This was a curious, different feeling. Through his open window, I could hear the purring of a woodpigeon in the cedar branches. I saw the breeze which caught his curtains, flapped their sides, and I remembered the ancient maps of the world – a flat, discovered globe which boats could fall from. Womankind coming from that fictional rib.

'I was told that you lost your mother recently?'

'Yes. A tumour.'

'My condolences, Miss Waterfield. I mean that. Loss is a difficult thing which manifests itself in all parts of one's life. And regarding your condition, you must let me know if you need any help of your own. I rather suspect you'd be too

proud to accept it, but nevertheless, tell me. These are ...
well, strange days and nights.'

The conversation had tucked itself up for the evening.
I sensed there was nothing more to say, or to hear, so he
thanked me for my time and my efforts in the glasshouse;
also for my compliance in this situation. He wished me a
pleasant evening. 'I will depart in the morning. But I will
see you again, Miss Waterfield.'

I left. I went down the corridor, down the stairs and made
my way out into the garden, where the swallows were
skimming the bathing pool. Where there were all the old,
familiar, comforting signs of the day's work: a wheelbarrow
propped against the potting shed; a fork in the grass which
would, I knew, be damp with dew by morning. Tangible,
recognisable things. Also, a rusting croquet hoop which I
pulled from the lawn, laid to one side.

I could not decipher my feelings. Could not name them.
And if I tried, they felt contradictory – anxiety and relief; fear
and reassurance; less alone and more so. And I recognised,
too, that I'd felt softer in his room, as I sometimes felt in my
own room at night. That I had felt too tired to contest his
words. I believed Mr Fox: that was, perhaps, the truth of it. If
Mrs Bale had announced that her bed sheets had been tugged
by a ghost, I'd have despaired at her; I'd have risen from the
table and walked away. But with him? I didn't care for his
maleness. Didn't care that he was the owner of Shadowbrook.
But I cared for his apparent support of the female voice, his
talk of travel; for the wall of books whose spines were creased
or fraying from use. Darwin's book and, in the corner, a porcelain phrenological head. All those years of study.

The wise man knows he knows nothing. I wondered if I had
built my walls too high. And as I passed the orchard, I felt

relief more keenly. What answer did I have for the silver pendant? Which other human names began with V? My door had been tapped on. That upstairs room – with the deep dust and silence – had felt ominous, dense. Cut flowers drooped within hours.

I would try to be open-minded. Not a believer in ghosts – like him, I would not have recognised myself if I'd tried to be that – but supple, at least. Receptive. Less scornful of those who had such faith. Yes, I would aim for this.

A broth of summer vegetables that night. Moths knocked against the window pane as we ate it – Maud, Harriet and I.

'What is he like?' Harriet asked. This man whose linen they boiled and dried, whose meals they prepared. Who paid their wages.

I told them a little. Mr Fox was polite. Self-assured. Not tall. Perhaps he had once had reddish-gold hair, but it had greyed now. I gave my comparison of a fox that had aged, lost its pigmentation and shine, and I remembered how he'd stood between his desk and the window as if planted there. Like a spade set into a flower bed, to be returned to.

'What does he say about Mrs Bale? How will he bring her back?'

'A man is coming here.'

'Who? Who is coming?'

'A man from London. From a society that investigates activity like this.'

'A ghost hunter?' asked Maud.

'No, I don't think so. Not a vicar and not a policeman. He comes to find the answer, without agenda.'

Harriet lowered her spoon. 'When?'

'I don't know precisely. But I think he's coming soon.'

*

That night, I locked and bolted all the outer doors of the house – the kitchen door, the glass French windows in the drawing room and the heavy oak front door, which creaked as it closed. Pettigrew doors and Pettigrew keys. Three weeks earlier, this would have been a satisfying act; I'd have turned the key with conviction – thwarting the human intruder – and gone to bed. But a door is a shared entity; it leads between two worlds, so that if a bolt is drawn across it, it is both keeping the unwanted out and keeping it in. And, briefly, I saw this.

I set the locket on my bedside table and observed it from my bed. I did not touch it; I merely imagined it on its chain, resting against the flattened plain that lies between a woman's throat and her breasts. And in doing this, I thought of other bodies; I thought of all the bodies under clothes and how they must be different in their own, private ways. Blemishes and dryness. Old injuries. I thought of the vicar, at that moment. I saw Mrs Bale, too, and imagined her soft, resting body beneath a floral dressing gown, the bruises that must be blooming under her sling. I remembered the muscles in Harriet. Thought of the farmer, briefly – and I supposed there would be a differentiation in colour between the exposed, weathered working skin and his hidden kind. Sun-dark forearms and a stomach of milk.

These thoughts. That his blood was called bad for having such a father but also for his private acts. And had Veronique's acts been so different? She'd known men, yet she was called far worse for having done so. She was a devil. A depraved lunatic. Her name was whispered like a curse.

I thought of this, too: that there were empty picture hooks in this house. Mrs Bale had witnessed the destruction of every picture in the corridor and the seascape in the hall. But what of the nude upstairs? She remained in her gold frame. She had not been thrown down the stairs by any unseen hand. What could this mean? That she had been allowed to stay on the wall, with her bareness? With her coy smile and relaxed hand?

Instinctively, I chided myself for my answer. *There are no ghosts*; the old Clara's retort. But what if I humoured the others and said that yes, there were such things? And souls existed? If I took this mindset, my answer would be that, perhaps, Veronique had left this painting because it mirrored her life or a posture she'd assumed frequently. That it met with her approval – a hot-eyed, challenging woman with no wedding ring – and therefore it stayed, undamaged, on the wall.

Mid July. The lavender was humming with bees. I washed my hair that morning and after ten minutes in the glasshouse, it had dried completely. Hollis lowered the wheelbarrow to rest.

A baked day. But there was, too, a thin, occasional breeze; it moved through the barley as a single creature might. And I practised my questions to myself as I went – what I should ask, and how it should be done.

Kit's wall had been fully mended. I followed the line of it, under the last of the churchyard's yews, past a gate which had been secured with rope. Horses had been in this gateway. I could detect their scent; the hardening earth still held the shape of their hooves. Having passed this, I looked up, and wondered, briefly, if this was how I'd imagined farmhouses to be: roughened by weather, squat, with a yard of old carts and scrap metal and firewood and a rusting plough. A barn, in which I could see the yokes for the horses. Hay bales and tools.

And I saw him, too. Kit Preedy came out of the barn at

that moment, coiling rope from his raised hand down to his elbow and back. His attention was on this, so that he did not know I was watching him; he was entirely engaged in this single task. But then he looked up.

We did not greet the other. Kit finished gathering his rope, set it on a fence post and walked towards me. We met beside a water trough.

'Did you hear what happened at the house? Mrs Bale was pushed down the stairs.'

'Pushed?'

'So she says. And you said you'd tell me more about the Pettigrews.'

Kit felt his front teeth with his tongue, as if debating with himself. This lined face; this white scar like an early moon. He seemed lost, momentarily – not in the farmyard but elsewhere. Then he nodded. 'Come with me.'

We walked the boundaries of his land. He said he did this daily, to check the walls and trees, the crop itself. I understood this. And I understood, too, that Kit Preedy liked to keep moving. By the stone wall, he'd continued in his task, thumbed and lifted stones as I'd talked. Now? Even walking itself did not seem enough for him. He tugged at stalks of barley as he went; he touched walls, trees, gateposts as he passed them. His two horses dozed in the shade and, as we neared them, Kit gave a singular click of his tongue which was enough for them to raise their heads in expectation of more, yet he didn't stop. He strode on. I could not keep up with him.

I don't know if he noticed this. But on reaching higher ground, he stopped. There was a view here – across his land, across the roofs and church tower towards the far hills and woodland – and he stood with his hands at his sides, looked across. I reached him, breathless. 'Is this all yours? All of it?'

'Now it is. It was the Pettigrews' once. My great-grandfather leased it from them, as his son and grandson did. Forty-eight hectares for which they raised the price as it suited them. They hated my family and we hated them back.'

'Why?'

'Most disagreements are about money, women or land. We've not been saints – you'll have heard that – but the Pettigrews thought they owned people. That other lives didn't matter. You've seen their grave. *Blessed be their memory* ... Cherubs and doves?' He shook his head.

'Who was Mortimer?'

Kit pushed at a stone with his toe. 'He died before I was born. But I know he shot dogs for no reason. If his horse shied in the lane or threw him, he'd shoot it, replace it. My grandmother worked for him, for a time.'

'She did? Why – if he was like this?'

'Why do you think? Perhaps you can't imagine lacking money. She was a young widow with two small boys and two recent bad harvests, and Mortimer raised the rent that year. He was a widower. He hunted for pleasure – fox tails and birds' eggs ... My grandmother refused to stay. Left a month later.'

'And his sons?'

There was a circled part of Kit's beard, as if a thumb had been pressed into it and turned. Also, I saw that earth – or dust, lifted from the yard by his boots or a slight breeze – had settled into the lines by his eyes so that they seemed deeper. He reached over one shoulder, scratched there. 'Worse. They gambled, fought. Shot more than horses. A farm in Yabberton was burned to the ground in a fire that was started by Hugo Pettigrew and the couple died in it. Police blamed a spark from the hearth but others knew better. Said Hugo had shot them, lit a match. And the Pettigrews lined the pockets of policemen and innkeepers, so . . . '

'Why did he kill them?'

'Any small reason. A day of boredom. A joke. Maybe he wanted their land to rent to others at too high a price.'

Kit turned and walked on. I followed, wanting more. I knew that these had not been many words, but I wondered if they were like embers, so that if I breathed or asked more of him, they'd glow and increase. 'How did they die? The Pettigrews?'

Kit slowed, then. But it was in response to having seen something – animal tracks, or a flattening of barley where an animal had slept – and not to answer me. 'Mortimer died in his bed which was too kind a death.'

'And his sons?'

'One fell from his horse. The other was found in a ditch near The Black Swan in Stratford. A fight.'

'Did you meet them?'

'Never met them. One died before I was born; the other a few years after.' And with that, Kit set off in the same purposeful manner, so that I was left behind. To hurry would be to snap an ankle or bruise myself badly, and yet to ask him to stop would feel an embarrassment. So I called out her name. I shouted it, for I knew this would stop him.

'What of Veronique?'

His halt was abrupt, as if he'd been commanded. For a moment, he stayed perfectly still. Then he turned, walked back towards me. 'What do you already know about her? Because I'm not a gambling man, but I'd bet that you've heard something, and I can guess what.'

A challenge, or so it felt. He looked at me directly. And I wondered what to tell him; if I should declare that yes, I knew of her parties for men, her appetite and decadence, or if I should wade into it slowly as if it were water. He was studying me. His eyes moved between my own.

'That she preferred to stay indoors. She wasn't seen in the village very often. Did your grandmother see her?'

'She only worked there for a month. I told you this. And Veronique was a child at that time. Twelve, maybe.'

'Even so. Your grandmother must have seen her.'

Kit ran his inner wrist over his brow. I'd seen this act before; it was part of him, as much as farmland. When he dropped his arm back down, he looked across his barley and I knew he was wary of saying more.

'You know why I'm asking this,' I said. 'Someone is pretending to be her. And I'll be gone soon, Mr Preedy – back to London – so what does it matter?'

He plucked a stalk of barley and examined it as he prepared his answer. 'She'd keep to the edges of rooms. Or she'd leave a room as my grandmother entered it and would sit behind curtains or in dark corners. She played the piano. Had fair hair.'

'Fair hair?' The beech trees filled with wind suddenly; the barley flattened and rose, and Kit was also aware of this. He looked at the branches overhead and I wondered if he could tell the wind's direction from this, or the weather to come. If this sound was, to him, as carriage wheels had been to me in my childhood – familiar and yet still, on occasion, worth listening to, as if to remind oneself that it was a good sound. 'And you? Did you see her?'

'Twice, that's all. Both times from a distance. Once she was in an upper window, watching the harvest; that's an early memory, for me. Years later, I saw her in the garden. Her brothers were a long time dead and she died a year later.'

'How did she die?'

Kit shifted his jaw. 'My uncle found her. She was lying near the boundary wall in the grass. Not a mark on her. It was December.'

'She froze to death?'

'Or her brain stopped. Her heart.' A shrug.

Her brain. The organ of logic. Drinking on all fours like a cat, her tongue in the water. 'They say she went mad. Did she?'

'That word has different meanings. Most will say yes.'

'Would you say yes?'

Kit's patience was nearly gone. He threw aside the stalk of barley – an ending gesture – and glanced behind at the land that was waiting for him so that I knew he wished to leave me now. But his braces hung at his sides, the uppermost button on his shirt was missing – and I remembered Hollis's story of having seen Kit follow his father in a ploughed field. I didn't want him to leave me yet.

'No, I wouldn't say that.'

'I heard that she entertained men.'

Kit stilled. His stare darkened; he took one step towards me and I thought, this is how he might approach a horse, having spied its unsoundness. It is how he might challenge a man in The Bull who threatened him. I did not step back.

'Entertained?'

'Men. Yes. That she undressed for them and took her pleasures as if she were a man herself – freely, and without shame. She had parties for them, they say.'

He turned on his heel, began to leave. 'I've no interest in that talk.'

'Oh, surely you do.'

We both heard it. My insinuation. Those four words of mine – and their tone – said far more than all my other words. *Oh, surely you do ...* His own conquests were in them. His rumoured liaisons. And everything I'd imagined since Hollis had told me – *he knows women* – rushed out between us: his fast, perfunctory couplings with women he'd met in passing, in which no words were uttered except for requests or basic instructions. He had his own anatomical knowledge and it had not come from diagrams.

Kit almost laughed to himself. The field of barley had his attention so that when he spoke, he addressed it, not me. 'One day there'll be a story about me that's true – not partly true or a full lie. What have you heard? That I've lured half the women of Gloucestershire into my bed? Is that it?'

'Have you?'

'Have I? How you talk. How you ask questions as if you have every right to. Some. Some, is the answer. But I'll tell you this, Miss Waterfield: they've wanted to come. They have knocked on my door or asked me to knock on theirs – and where is the cruelty in that? The crime? And she was beautiful, by the way – Veronique. My grandmother called her a beautiful child, but I saw it too, when she stood in the window that autumn. By God. I've never seen anything more beautiful than her.'

He left, smacking the barley as he went. I watched him stride away, keeping to the periphery of his land and using his arms as propulsion as he passed between shadow and light. I thought, look back. But he did not look back.

She had been faceless till now. Air and rumour. Nothing substantial. On hearing her name, I'd tended to leave the conversation or roll my eyes at the prospect of souls.

But suddenly Veronique was real. She was, of course,

dead, and had been for thirteen years; but I returned from Kit with a sense that I could glimpse the person she'd been in life. Promiscuous? Yes. But she had, too, been private as a child. She'd been fair-haired and had played the piano. And these small offerings had been enough to give her identity, so that she seemed to have her own temperature now. Her own scent and want and expectations. If she'd placed her hand on the window pane, it would have left its mark.

And beautiful. I should have known that. For they had come to her, these men; one by one, they had climbed the stairs. Risking, perhaps, the wrath of her brothers – men who shot horses and set fire to farms – in order to see her, for a moment or two. Beauty. I had seen it in galleries. I'd seen it on omnibuses. I'd seen it in my mother, who, despite not being white-blonde as I was, had still been described as fair. And I saw Veronique at the window. Saw her coming down the stairs with a smile that spoke of knowledge or a wish to acquire more of it; a strong woman in every sense of the word. Her bones, I knew, had been perfectly made beneath her warm skin and velvet-trimmed dress.

A quiet house that night. Mr Fox was gone; the maids had retired to bed wordlessly. I could not sleep so I returned to my anatomical guide, turning to a page that in London I had not cared for; other diagrams – bones, brains, a dissection of the eye – had mattered more back then. But now, I wanted to see it. I whispered such new, tropical words as *ductus deferens. Pubic bone.* I traced shapes with my fingertips; I brought the page closer so that I might see the male organ better. Having done this, I studied the diagrams of the female part that it fitted, or so I understood.

Like this, I read until two in the morning. I imagined how these parts joined; how, having joined, they achieved their function. And later on, drowsing, I thought of Kit's question to me: *Where is the cruelty in that? The crime?* A simple, hard demand. I'd had no answer for him, in the barley. I'd felt like saying *none* – that there was, surely, no crime in the act that makes human life, and this was true; I could see none at all. Yet I knew the world felt differently. Knew that Veronique was hated for having lived like that. Knew that my mother had boarded the *Persia* when, in fact, she'd longed to stay.

I turned out the light. I thought of his sleeves, rolled up. Of where his shirt had darkened with sweat – on either side of his spine, under his arms, the small of his back. And I knew, too, that books only offered the official terms. For even as a child, I would stand before the map of India, learn its rivers and mountainous regions and the names of ancient capitals, and know that this was not enough; it was nothing compared to the country itself. I could not taste fruit from studying a sketch of it, cut in half. What use was only reading of acts and not doing them? Knowing the route of the Ganges was not the same as standing in it.

IX

I came into the kitchen and found Harriet there. She was holding a note, offered it to me.

Dear Harriet and Maud,

The gentleman from the Society for Psychical Research will be arriving on Thursday in the afternoon. I ask that you prepare the old billiards room for him. Also, please ensure that he has space to work, and that he is catered for to the highest standard. Remember you have Miss Waterfield to assist you.

I shall be returning on Saturday 1st August.

I leave the house, I know, in capable hands.

He signed with the flourish I recognised – an *F* like a vine.

Harriet frowned at the note. Psychical – a new, unexplored word. I explained its meaning to her: an adjective relating to human perceptions, and spirits, and the dead. And she, in turn, asked me if I knew how to press linen without burning either it or myself, for there was much to do before the gentleman's arrival, and when I said no, she smiled a little and beckoned me. Showed me where the pair of flat irons were kept, and the ironing stand.

Explained how to heat, and fold. 'Like this,' she told me. 'And this.'

With care, I ironed the linen for the bed in which the gentleman from London would sleep in two nights' time. The maids spent the following day in the billiards room: sweeping and polishing, cleaning the windows with vinegar, unpinning the curtains and carrying them into the yard to hang on the line and beat. They scrubbed the bathtub for hours. They ran towels through the mangle, dusted the shelves. I only observed most of these tasks – they were too hard for me to do – but there were other, less demanding jobs. I collected and peeled vegetables; Harriet asked, too, if I would gather flowers, fill vases and glassware for him. 'I know they don't last in this house. But Mrs Bale would want us to do it.'

It was a good task. The garden was luminous. The roses were at their finest; the peach and pale-pink versions in the long border were so heavy-headed that they spilled into the path; the Rêve d'Or had climbed the entire height of the south-facing wall. Near the bathing pool, the delphiniums were indigo. Violets bloomed at the base of the plinth of an urn. And in the vegetable garden, the blackcurrant frames creaked with the weight they carried. Hollis proffered a strawberry to me. 'Tell me,' he said, 'that isn't the finest taste in all England.' And I said that yes, it was.

The garden was a balm. I longed, suddenly, to fill the house with colour and fragrance – even if it meant that within hours, I might find broken stems or thick water. I ventured deep into borders, returned with more flowers than I could find vases for, so that I filled coffee pots and water jugs and flagons. Pushed ox-eye daisies into the old teapot with the cracked handle and spout.

189

As I did this, I thought of Mrs Bale. I cut the stalks, arranged them, and remembered her bustled welcome, how she'd sung about the garden to me. *What a month you have chosen!* And she loved hydrangeas, I knew that. She'd mentioned how much she admired their round, papery heads so I returned to the garden, collected more of them. They were the colour of talcum, with a greenish tinge; I held their heads as if holding glass and tied them together with string – a gift for her.

I remembered her instructions: the cottage on the Stow road. A humpbacked bridge. A blue-painted door. She had mentioned her sister's name to me, although I could not quite retrieve it. And I thought, she of the indoors flowers, who had left a single rose in my room to welcome me. Had she learned to speak this language in her married life? In her days of nursing her husband, had she found pleasure in filling milk jugs with buttercups, in slotting delphiniums into glass bottles? They felt like acts of self-care.

I thought too of marriage as I walked up the Stow road. Of the Bale marriage, specifically. How had they met? What qualities had she – Mrs Bale – possessed which had enticed her husband? Physically, I could see that she might have been enchanting in her youth. A small waist. Hips that, perhaps, he'd thought of cupping with both hands. Her plait of hair – not grey, but some other shade – would have swung in her wake. But there was, too, her nature – her sing-song announcements and girlishness; had she always been like this? Or had, in fact, that stretched, radiant smile developed within the marriage itself? Perhaps it had become a necessity.

Tuberculosis. I knew enough, from my books: a condition which corroded the respiratory system, folded the spine and bloodied the breath. The white death, it was called. And so, perhaps, after his diagnosis, Mrs Bale developed this talent that was so defiantly hers: to praise a dull morning or to marvel at the taste of a slice of buttered bread, to sing wordlessly to herself in her brightest tone as she performed her duties as a wife and nurse to him – emptying bowls, scrubbing handkerchiefs. Reducing the pain by fooling herself.

And Mr Bale? Perhaps she'd been drawn to him because of his kindness. His generosity or wit. Or perhaps her attraction to him had been a simpler affair; she'd liked him physically – how he'd danced in a village hall, or the ease with which he'd lifted an object over his head in a way that pronounced his musculature. A breadth of shoulder that strained his shirt. How he'd climbed a stile.

The cottage was easy to find. The humpbacked bridge had moss on its brickwork; Willowbank's door was a faded duck-egg blue with a brass knocker.

I leaned my cane against the door, knocked three times.

I waited. The door did not open, so I knocked a second time. And with that, I heard movement. A key turned in the lock; a bolt was drawn back and as the door opened, I heard a low, brushing sound as if something – warped wood, or a gathered rug – obstructed it. It opened partly but this was enough to see a little of her, for she peeped round it, wide-eyed.

'Yes?'

There was no doubting who she was. She had the same features as her sister. She, too, had lead-coloured hair, although hers was not plaited or over her shoulder. It was cut to her jawline. A fringe like a board.

'Good morning. I'm Clara Waterfield and—'

'I know who you are. You work at the house.' She held the door tightly.

'Yes. I have come to see Mrs Bale. I'd like to give her these' – I gestured with the flowers – 'from the garden and to see how she's mending.' I heard my politeness and felt proud of it.

But the sister puckered her mouth. 'She's sleeping.'

'Then perhaps I'll come back in an hour or so.'

'There's no need.'

'I'd like to see her.'

'But she, Miss Waterfield, would not like to see you.'

A tart, unexpected answer – and I thought, momentarily, that I had misheard. But her expression was defiant. She fixed her eyes on me and seeing this, I fixed my eyes back. What was this wall she'd built against me? I'd come with flowers and good intentions yet I'd been met with a half-opened door. I said, 'Let me in.'

'No. She wants nothing to do with you, or that place.'

'I don't believe you,' I said. 'She's frightened of it, I understand that. But she asked me to visit her. She gave me directions – the blue door, the Stow road. How else might I have known how to find you?'

'Someone else told you.'

'*She* told me. *She* did.'

This gatekeeper, whose mouth seemed to have been drawn shut by an invisible string. She wore slippers and her own silver cross; her knuckles had whitened from grasping the door, and I supposed that orders would not help me.

I smiled, instead. 'We miss her, you see. The maids and I miss her – will you tell her that? And would you give her the flowers, at least? She likes hydrangeas, I think.'

This was a better approach. Instantly, the sister seemed to grow smaller. A flush appeared on her cheeks; the puckered lips released themselves and her hand left the door frame, accepted the blooms. 'I'm sorry,' she whispered. 'I did not mean to be rude to you. What happened ... what has been happening at Shadowbrook; it has changed Eleanor, you understand. She was always the resilient one; she could endure – always! Oh, she endured. She was never ill or in poor spirits. But she is so much thinner than she used to be. She calls out at night, for she has terrible dreams, despite being here with me. Perhaps she asked you to visit her, yes, but that will have been her good manners, Miss Waterfield. In truth, she wants nothing from Shadowbrook. She won't see you, or anyone else – no company at all except my own – until the trouble is done.'

With that, she thanked me for my time and began to close the door. But I pushed my cane into the diminishing space, stopping her – and this startled her. 'Will you tell her this, at least? That a man is coming to Shadowbrook. I don't know his name, but he's coming to identify the trouble and banish it. And he might want to see her. Tell her this.'

The sister opened her mouth, unsure. 'When does he come?'

'Tomorrow – from London. Mr Fox has summoned him.'

'I'm certain she won't see him. She needs her rest, and no talk about that wretched house. But yes, I will tell her. Now, Miss Waterfield, will you remove your cane?'

I did as she wished. She closed the blue-painted door and I looked at it and felt physically sore, as if she had shaken me. Elspeth; her name came back to me then.

She wants nothing to do with you. I had not expected that. But I'd expected none of what had happened at Shadowbrook in these past few weeks. I hadn't expected to tend to a fracture that was not my own. I could never have guessed that I'd find myself thinking of our bodies beneath our clothes, with their flaws and warmth. Nor did I ever think I'd consider that a dead, buried person might, in fact, not be fully dead.

*

193

A restlessness in me, after this. I could not return to the house. Nor did I wish to move through the gardens or go to the shop or pass through the barley, and the glasshouse had no need of me.

Sixteen years had passed since Millicent – plump, floury-handed, with her tightly laced shoes – had taken me to church. Sixteen years; a generation of life. Yet I remembered the lectern in that London church had been a brass eagle; the hymns had been sung with such earnestness that I'd turned to watch the congregation and I had, I think, been nursing a broken rib that day so that the act of turning hurt me. So sixteen years felt, too, like an hour ago.

There had been no churches since. I'd cried in the aftermath. Despite being five, I'd known with certainty that I wouldn't go to a church again. Their ringing bells were to be turned from, and their clergymen were to be ignored; I'd follow my parents' example of dismissing bibles and viewing Christmas with a shrewd, superior eye.

Yet I stood before St Mary's church in Barcombe-on-the-Hill and imagined its interior. I had seen its exterior before; I'd entered its grounds, parted dock and bramble to read the name Pettigrew on a tomb. But I'd gone no further. Now the church itself was my focus. It was made of the familiar Cotswold stone, the colour of hayseeds. It was small and, despite being sheltered by yew trees, its edges had been softened by weather and age.

An owl, I'd heard, lived in its tower. The church clock told the wrong time.

Its entrance was under a pitched wooden roof at one side. Beside the door, I found a boot-scraper and a bowl of grassy water which was, I supposed, for dogs. And on the door itself was a handwritten sign, hanging by string from a nail: *Swallows nesting. Please do not close the door.* The door itself was propped open by a horseshoe, coppered with rust.

I entered soundlessly. I stepped down from a step which had been eroded by generations of feet. And I found gravestones in there, which I had not expected; bodies within the church's foundations. These stones formed most of the aisle: smooth, dark markers into which the names and dates of their owners had been engraved a century before, or more. On the walls, too, on either side of me, were memorial plaques. Most were very simple, engraved without embellishment, but there were, too, a few lavish creations with scrolling and angels. *Mr Carrington Bell, late of this parish. Mr John Bayley. Also his wife.*

Kneelers were embroidered. Hymn books were stacked at the end of each pew – fraying green fabric things. A wooden cross stood on the altar with a hewn version of the dying Christ. And whilst I'd known, of course, that Matthew Dunn might be nearby – writing a sermon or comforting a parishioner – I hadn't expected to find him sitting with his back to me. At first I thought he was at prayer. But his hands were not pressed together, as I'd heard hands should be; nor was his head bowed. Rather, he was looking into the rafters so I followed his gaze, above the wooden pulpit to the highest corner, where I saw the neat, muddied cup of the swallows' nest.

I am also a man.

His hair of no definable colour. His narrow shoulders.

'How long have they been here?' I asked.

I startled him; he'd considered himself to be alone so he turned awkwardly, half rising. On seeing me, his eyes widened. 'Miss Waterfield.'

'The swallows?'

'Three weeks, I think. Perhaps a little longer.'

'They arrived when I did, then.'

I wondered which Matthew was standing in front of me: the translucent, nervous vicar who might trip into a sentence and stumble through it, or the man who knew his words perfectly. His pose suggested the former – still half risen, grasping the pew.

'Can I speak with you?'

At Matthew's own suggestion, we moved back into the light. Perhaps he was mindful of the swallows in their nest. Perhaps he sensed I'd prefer it – grass, and light through canopies – to the silent church. So we circumnavigated the building, past lichen and brambles. 'I went to see Mrs Bale, to take hydrangeas to her. But her sister told me she won't see me. Won't see anyone. Yet you must have seen her, Mr Dunn. She said she needed you more than the doctor on the night she fell. Surely you've seen her?'

'Yes, I have.'

'And how is she? How is her arm? Her sister said she was having nightmares.'

At that, he adjusted his glasses in his own way – using the back of his hand to push them higher onto his nose. 'I don't know about the nightmares. I only know she's relieved to be at her sister's – to have rest.'

'What else did she tell you? Has she said more about what she saw on the first floor?'

'Miss Waterfield ...' He smiled cautiously, practised a word or two. 'I'm a vicar. People speak to me in confidence, of private matters. They speak to me because they know I will not pass it to others. It's part of my role.'

It was not the answer I wanted. Yet it was, too, an answer in itself. The vicar knew more than I did.

This dappled light of yews was, I supposed, like being underwater. It moved on the path, had a greenish quality.

I glanced across at Matthew – he walked with his hands clasped behind him, as an older man might – and I wondered, at that moment, if I'd ever offered an apology in my life. In my childhood, perhaps. I had memories of whispering *I'm sorry* to my mother – for any new bruise or suspected fracture. But the word, to me, was uncommon.

'I want to say sorry,' I said.

'Sorry? What for?'

'By the bathing pool – by the Roman faces – we talked of souls. Or rather, you talked of them and I said they were a ridiculous notion, that the soul couldn't be lifted from the body like an organ. I shouldn't have spoken like that.'

He seemed bemused. 'There's no need to apologise. Not everyone has faith, I know that, and the story you gave of the London church ... I hated that. I could not sleep that night for how much I hated it. I should apologise to you, perhaps.'

'You? It wasn't you who called me sinful.'

'Even so. You know I'm not the same as him? We might have the same collar, but otherwise ... '

We accepted the other's regret. In doing so, I minded him less. And as we turned along the southerly side of the church, where ivy was flourishing, I said, 'You mentioned a friend – a vicar, too – who held communion on All Hallows' Eve. Saw the lost souls fill the pews. Was this true?'

'Yes, quite true. I wasn't there, but he was, of course. And he's an honest man. He knew what he saw that night and I believed him. I believe him still.'

'And what did he see, exactly? Ghosts or souls. Are they still like people? Like the people they were in life?'

'I asked him this, too. I was young and I had not yet been ordained, so I wanted to know all of it. He said yes.

They appeared as if still living, in the clothes of their era. They were of human height and size, with human features. The only difference, he said, was that they were thinner in substance; he could see through them, to the far wall, and they'd pass through each other as if made of air.'

Once, I'd have dismissed this. Talked scientifically, mocked. But instead, I noted the vicar's earnestness. I saw how, briefly, he was no longer self-aware; he was speaking of what he believed in, gesturing carefully, and there was an articulateness to him.

'Have you seen this with your own eyes?'

'A ghost? Seen? No. But we can feel what we cannot see, of course. And I have felt many things – strange, palpable – that have suggested I've not been alone. A change in temperature; a sudden, absolute conviction that someone is standing beside me. I understand that this can be dismissed easily; the human mind is an extraordinary thing, which can persuade or imagine or—'

'I know I was adamant about an afterlife – or rather, that there's not one. I said there were no ghosts and that's still my inclination. But I met Mr Fox. He mentioned a loud, furious thumping on his door at night and when he opened it, there was an empty corridor; also, he said a female figure pulled his bedlinen away from him and that, on finding the light, there was nothing. He also spoke of being openminded. That the wise man knows there is so much we do not know. And who knows what proof we might find in the future? This is why I wished to apologise to you, Mr Dunn. I think I can be stubborn.'

'Matthew,' he said. 'Call me that.'

'These souls on All Hallows' Eve. Why were they there at all? Why weren't they . . . ' I shrugged, 'elsewhere? You spoke of them being lost.'

'This is what I've always understood. That their lives or deaths were lonely or unfair or ended in violence, and this stopped them from entering the next life; it kept them here. They say a priest's intervention can help in this, but not always.'

Lonely or unfair. There was nothing I knew of Veronique that implied she'd felt either in her life. She'd had her chosen company. Had lived in precisely the manner she'd wished to, regardless of social niceties and expectation – and hadn't her death been quietly done? In the garden, with her heart and brain slowing down? A frosty blue about her? These were my thoughts, passing under the yews.

'You seem troubled.'

'Not troubled.' But maybe I was. 'You'll have heard of how Veronique lived?'

His blush was immediate. It seemed to rise on his neck – a deep berry blush – so I knew that yes, he had heard.

'Mrs Bale told me that night. And I know how she feels about such behaviour; I know, too, what the Church says. Yet it seems terribly unfair to me, Mr Dunn. Veronique is hated more than her brothers and father, it seems, yet they killed a farmer and his wife, set fire to his farm; they bribed policemen and shot creatures for pleasure and performed, I'm sure, the same act with women ten thousand times over in the manner and place they chose. What people were they? Not good ones. Yet Veronique – who played the piano and shot nothing, as far as I know – is the one who's loathed. It's her name that's whispered, in case it's cursed. And it's her name – hers – that is missing from the Pettigrew tomb, as if she wasn't deserving of being acknowledged in her grave, when I see far more reason for having the names Hugo and Francis and Mortimer scratched out. They sound devilish, not her.'

I'd said more than I'd meant to. I'd said *the same act* and felt my own blush.

'Her name?' The vicar had slowed.

'Yes. I've studied the tomb, and her name's not there. If she haunts Shadowbrook, do you think that's why? The injustice of having no acknowledgement on the grave-stone itself?'

'But she isn't buried there. That's why her name's not on the tomb. Isn't she buried at Shadowbrook?'

Somewhere a bird sang its alarm. 'At Shadowbrook?'

'Yes. In the grounds. I heard she was.'

Matthew couldn't tell me more. He didn't know where Veronique was buried, or why – only that she had been laid to rest in Shadowbrook's earth, in unconsecrated ground. Yet as I walked back, I knew where she was; I knew abso-lutely, so that I wondered, how have I not realised this before? The long grass of the orchard, and the single path that led through it to a mound on which there were wild flowers. *I tend to leave it be*, Hollis had said.

He did not understand my frustration. It surprised him; he raised his palms as if protesting. 'Yes, she's buried here. In the orchard. Why are you so angry, Miss Waterfield?'

We were in the kitchen garden. Around us, the scores of raised beds. Radishes, spinach, the raspberry nets; the indentation of knees in the earth; spades planted, like announcements.

'Because you didn't tell me, Hollis. Why didn't you tell me?'

'Because I didn't think it mattered.'

'Didn't matter?'

'No – why should it matter when you were only staying a month? Also – since you are being so insistent – I'll tell you that I'd heard of your loss before you arrived. You'd lost your mother; this was in my mind, so that I didn't think you'd care to know that there was a grave within yards of the house. I did not think it would help you.'

We both caught our breath. The garden boys were near, and some watched us as they hoed or dug. But they were not, perhaps, close enough to have heard our exchange. The twins were examining a creature – a beetle or worm – that one held in cupped hands. Little Fred was brushing the earth from his bare knees. And I asked, 'Why is she here, Hollis? Why isn't she in the Pettigrew tomb in the churchyard?'

A small shrug. 'There was resistance to it, I know that. Her reputation ... There were parishioners who objected to having her buried in the same ground as their ancestors. Also, such an act would have required work – you've seen how overgrown that part of the graveyard is – and Reverend Stout was not keen on a difficult life. It seemed better to have her here.'

'You decided it?'

'I suggested it, that's all. There were no relatives, you understand – no Pettigrews left. No one to object to the notion of burying her in what was her own land, after all. And she was often in the orchard.'

'I thought you rarely saw her. That she stayed indoors.'

'And that's true; I rarely saw her. But I saw signs of her – books left on the arms of benches, or her discarded shoes. That sort of thing. I believe she used to sleep in the orchard, for there'd be flattened sections of grass. Sometimes a cushion.'

This seemed lovely to me. It seemed bright and strange and unexpected: to rest in long grass with books and a cushion. To remove your shoes and walk barefoot. This was madness? Or seen as such? To me, it sounded far from it.

I'd had such dreams as this in my childhood: to sleep under fruit trees. 'Was she mad, Hollis? Truthfully?'

He shook his head softly. 'I've no reason to think it. But people choose their beliefs, in the end. They believe what they want to. If she ever ate herbs, it wasn't in fistfuls. She'd pick the new mint leaves, at the stalk's tip. I know this because I'd find the mint like this, missing its greenest, uppermost growth. And I can't blame her. Fresh mint is a very fine thing, in a garden.'

'Kit,' I said, 'called her beautiful.'

Hollis considered my face. 'Yes, she was, although my sights of her were brief and not common. In her younger days, I might hear the piano and look up to the first floor and see her. Later, her hair reached her waist.'

'And you don't mind what she did here?'

I'd always known he was a good man. On our first meeting, I'd felt his decency – how he'd turned the earth as if it were sleeping, noted the robin at his side. And now he answered that such stories were never his business; that if we judged each other on rumour, what would be left? He returned to digging the vegetable patch, ignoring – as he'd always done, it seemed – the rumours of men. Hollis seemed disinterested in Veronique. But he had, also, arranged her burial under the apple trees; he'd allowed wild flowers to grow there, and this seemed a thoughtful act. Loving, involved – and not disinterested at all. An employee's duty did not, I supposed, tend to extend that far.

The trees were apple, pear and plum. Amongst them, the grass was deep, laced with buttercup and vetch.

Yes, this was her grave: a slight, rectangular banking of earth with four clear sides and, at its end, a small stone of no discernible shape. There was no engraving on it. Nor were there any offerings, other than those that nature had thought to leave. But it was Veronique's burial place. Here. On her own land – as it had been at the time of her death.

I gathered what I knew of her. She'd been a fair-haired child, motherless and the youngest of three; her brothers were ten years older than her so that she'd played alone, been self-contained. She had been, perhaps, indulged – the only daughter, with an imperious air – or she'd grown accustomed to her solitary life; a shy child, by consequence, leaving rooms as the servants entered, watching from windows. And whilst some said she was haughty, I wondered if she stayed indoors for other reasons; she must have known the family reputation, after all. If the Pettigrew name was hated by every village in Gloucestershire, why venture out at all? So she kept near her piano. Kept near her wardrobe of fine dresses and shoes, and her mirror. Money and beauty and books to read and a capable body; what else had she needed?

And the men? Had she had such parties? It no longer felt quite right to me. It seemed too strange and tawdry for the woman I saw in my mind – watching the harvest, playing Bach or Rachmaninov – to host such bold, unapologetic things. She had chosen a private way of life, surely. Later, she'd explored her garden, on her own and mostly out of sight. Parties of men? I didn't believe in them. Yet if she'd had no parties – if she had kept to her own quarters – how had she met those men at all?

I pondered this amongst the buttercups. And I decided, in the end, that she'd invited them individually. That a woman of learning and grace, as she had been, might have read of gentlemen in newspapers – musicians or explorers or poets – and written to them, asking them to come.

This seemed a far likelier tale. For what knowledge might be acquired from her brothers? From her brothers' friends, who wrestled each other? Why might she wish to know their drunken bodies, and join her own to them? She would have sought far better company. She'd have wished to hear accounts of the countries she'd read about but never seen; she'd have wished, perhaps, to debate politically – and those men must have been in awe of this radiant creature whom they had not expected to find in a house that was known for the shooting of horses, for drunkenness and too much wealth. Veronique, they'd breathe. An unimagined gift. And the heart of the rumour itself? That she unfastened her corsets for them? That still felt true, to me. She'd retained enough Pettigrew blood, perhaps, to consider herself above the rules.

Unmarried. There must have been proposals. Yet what need did Veronique Pettigrew have to be a wife? She watched her brothers drink. Knew the house would be hers one day. Knew she'd have her own fortune and secu-rity – and why leave Shadowbrook, in her later years? It was more than world enough with its seasons. And it had been her own.

I looked up into the leaves. I'd never been deserving of divine punishment; my mother had never been a disgrace to the name Pugh; and Veronique, I felt sure, had never lost her mind so that she ate birds, drank from streams. But rumours exist because we choose them. We believe what we want the truth to be – and so the Pettigrew daugh-ter had had parties of men, according to villagers who drank in The Bull. She had crawled on all fours on the croquet lawn.

My Veronique. I forged her in the orchard that evening. Dignified, resilient. A fine piano player. And her crime was solely that sometimes she'd stand before a man, reveal a bare shoulder so that he might touch it. Wordlessly reveal more.

These were my preoccupations. And I was so lost in Veronique that evening that I entirely forgot to expect a visitor. I did not notice a light in the old billiards room; I did not see his curtains, half drawn against the evening, or his travelling trunk in the hall.

X

There are trees in the Americas that grow to three thousand years in age and are so large that it might take fifty people to encircle a single trunk, arms out. *Sequoiadendron giganteum.* I might never see such a tree, but in my mind, their canopies are so high that to look up at them is to lose balance. Such trees would be like no other. They would lessen the trees I knew before.

George. Six letters. Two pairs of letters at either side and at its heart, there was a question: *or?* As if he were a choice. He was, at least, a contradiction. Either we had not imagined the man who would come – we'd had, after all, our other concerns – or we'd made assumptions: that a gentleman from a society would be white-bearded, fastidious, three times our age. Poor company, perhaps. Withdrawn from us. But George was none of these things.

He was, at first, a travelling trunk. I stepped out of my room to find it there by the wall, tucked tightly against it. Its metalled parts had rusted; a stain bloomed on its side, as if ink had soaked into the leather itself. And I saw the two weathered gold initials pressed into its handle. A trunk that had seen journeys. A man, therefore, who had.

This was in keeping with our assumption, perhaps. An

old, used trunk could surely only belong to a man of similar age and miles. But as I rinsed my hands in the bathroom, I heard his voice. Or rather, I heard the maids' voices, and they were not as they had been; they were quicker, a little higher in pitch. There seemed to be humour in how they spoke, and I wondered when I'd heard laughter at Shadowbrook. I decided I never had.

I turned off the tap, listened. The third voice came in. It was low and male; it seemed to have a pitch that carried vibration – a voice which one might feel in the ribs, if standing closer.

I grasped my cane, moved into the corridor.

On seeing me, Harriet smiled. 'Here she is. Miss Waterfield? This is Mr Lowe. From the Society of ... ' She winced, forgetting its full name.

'The Society for Psychical Research,' I said.

The man turned and looked at me.

He was the tallest man I'd ever seen. Instinctively, I thought of the beechwoods. We stared at each other.

He moved forwards, reached out his hand. 'Pleased to meet you, Miss Waterfield.'

I had not expected this. But I took his hand and, despite his size and structure, the handshake was light enough to tell me he'd noted my cane, the collarbone.

He was taller than me by nearly half my height again, and twice or three times as wide. A broad-shouldered man, hard-chested. Yet his strength seemed natural. It was not caused by any excess, or by years of physical work in fields; it was simply how he was made, and he seemed at complete ease with it. How he moved in the kitchen; how he opened his arms when he praised Harriet for the stew; how he rose to bring his plate to the sink, having eaten, and moved behind a chair to do so – turning himself, allowing for his size: these were movements of confidence but also movements that suggested he'd always been tall and wide.

It was trees, too, that he spoke of that evening. The countryside he'd seen through his train window – the greenery of Gloucestershire and Oxfordshire – had been, he said, quite different from the landscape of London, where the trees tended to have a little coal dust on them and were mostly encircled by railings. 'Except,' he said, 'in Kew. In Kew, one could believe one was in a deep forest.'

'Miss Waterfield is from Kew.'

'You are?' George had been drying his hands; he stopped, looked back at me. 'From the Gardens themselves?'

'Yes. Mr Fox wanted a glasshouse. He wanted the best plants; to have someone from Kew establish them. That's why I'm here.'

'Then you know the glasshouses there?'

'Of course.'

'I've been to Kew a few times – not often. But it's the Palm House I remember. I always felt as if I'd entered other countries by being there. I expected to glance up and find luminous frogs or a line of ants or a bird of paradise. And I'd stoop to pass under palm leaves – like a second Livingstone!'

I was wordless. But his words were enough to make me feel as if I was back there in the Palm House at Kew, with its banyan tree and betelnut palm. Condensation on the tips of leaves.

The maids looked at George, looked at me.

Maud spoke, in the end. She pushed a chair under the table so that she could be closer to him. 'And you're here to get rid of the ghost, Mr Lowe? Is that true?'

He did not correct her. And yet his tone was one of gentle correction. 'I'm here to find out the cause of the trouble you've had. To identify it, understand it. For it sounds as if you've had a very difficult time in these past few months. I'm sorry for that.'

'Will you stop it? The trouble?' This was Harriet. She turned from the sink, asked it directly. 'Will you make the house safe? Send her away?'

George had heard it – *her* – but did not comment on it. Nor did he offer promises that night. But his voice was firm, reassuring; he shared his gaze between the three of us, in turn. He could have created fables or spoken in tongues in the kitchen and I think we would have believed him; if he'd talked of other galaxies or five-headed monsters we would, perhaps, have nodded sagely. 'I will find the truth,' he said.

Formed, warm and capable. Articulate. Careful with the things he held. A man of symmetry, too, for at breakfast I watched him lift a plate from the table and felt that if I measured him, if I chose to wrap a measuring tape around his left arm or along his left jawline, his right side's measurements would match them. This man with his travelling trunk.

A strange, sudden alteration at Shadowbrook. The house felt different for having him here, even after one day. He made a physical difference, changing the light in rooms, bringing new footfalls to the corridor. But the atmosphere changed, too. The maids seemed to soften within days. They spoke more, not merely to him – for George arrived with news of war, Ireland, London matters, of the world beyond Shadowbrook, which caused them to ask questions frequently – but to each other, too. I'd hear them murmuring as they worked, in longer sentences and in a lighter tone. As for the garden boys, they gathered around George as if he was a new plant that had grown quite unexpectedly; they encircled him entirely, looking up, and as I watched this from the glasshouse, I knew that the rumours of him would gain pace now. They'd be carried down to Barcombe by these boys. Would be whispered in ears.

They welcomed him. But I was less sure. I began to spend more time in the glasshouse. There was no need to – the plants were caring for themselves by now. But I'd leave the breakfast table for it and spend hours checking for aphids or moving a damp cloth over leaves as I knew Forbes had done. All day I'd busy myself. And if I passed George in the corridor or by the tool shed, I'd answer politely, keep myself sealed. No more words than were necessary.

'Are you feeling unwell, Miss Waterfield?' Harriet spied the difference in me. I blamed the heat whilst in fact I'd sit in my bedroom at night and listen to the sounds of him: the opening and closing of wardrobe doors, a single cough. One morning – at six, or a little later – I heard the pipework shudder, so that I knew he was washing himself. I wondered how he managed this, for the bathtub was so small.

My excuse, however, was believed. For George arrived with more than a trunk; he came with a new, deeper heat which silenced the birds until late afternoon. The tennis court radiated warmth, so that to enter its pavilion was to find a dark, cool country; the bathing pool acquired a dark line on its inner wall, showing the old water's height. And the taps in the garden, if turned, vibrated under my hand yet produced very little, so that watering cans could not be filled. In the house, we drew the south-facing curtains against the heat of the day.

'You'll need a hat,' said Hollis. Two days after George's arrival, the gardener offered me a wide-brimmed straw hat – oversized, fraying at its brim. 'I don't need it,' he said cheerfully. 'And you'll burn if you're not careful. You'll be red, not white.'

I wasn't sure if I'd wear it but I took it, even so.

'Has he settled in?' Hollis asked.

'Who?' Which was, of course, a foolish answer: there were no other guests and no other men in the house. But it was enough of a reply to mean that Hollis did not ask me again.

So I retreated from George and others. Yet it was, perhaps, inevitable that he'd speak to me in the end. On his third morning, he came to the glasshouse. I did not hear him approach; this would, later, surprise me – that a man of such proportions could move with such little sound. I was picking the dead pelargonium blooms – gathering them one by one, dropping them in the tub at my side – and I only saw George when I turned. He was standing in the doorway with his hands in his pockets. He was sideways to me, considering the plumbago, which had strengthened against the warm south-facing brick wall.

'Better,' he said, 'than Kew.'

I dusted my hands of earth, suspicious of his tone. Was he mocking me?

But when he turned, his smile seemed simple. He considered me for a moment before saying, 'Miss Waterfield, may I speak with you?'

We moved across the lawn, George and I. He kept his hands in his pockets; he walked casually, with his eyes on the line of beeches or the sky or Shadowbrook, and yet I knew, too, that he walked this way because he had an awareness of my pace. He could have strode over the lawn. He might have crossed it in twelve paces or less. Yet instead, he'd pause to look back at the house; he'd consider a passing bird or the sun's positioning, and I knew why. He was allowing me to keep up.

'This place feels so far from London,' he said. 'Last night I heard an owl and it's been a long time since I heard an owl.' A glance. 'Have you always lived there?'

'In London? Yes. You?'

'Me?' He shook his head. 'I know London but I've not always lived there. I studied at Cambridge. I know Edinburgh, Paris.'

'I saw your trunk.'

'Ah, well. We take our friends with us, don't we? It's an old trunk. It's seen most of Europe.'

'Do you think there'll be a European war?'

'Perhaps. Every paperboy in London is shouting about it. Ultimatums, posturing ... But paperboys want to sell papers, of course.' He smiled. 'Nothing is certain yet.'

'Why do you want to speak to me, Mr Lowe? I don't know Shadowbrook. I've been here a month, that's all.'

'That,' he said, 'is precisely why. I'll speak to everyone, of course. It's why I'm here – to talk to every person at Shadowbrook about what's been happening here. And in truth, I'd usually speak to the homeowner first, or to the person who approached the society, but Mr Fox is away, I understand. So I've come to you.'

'Yes. But why me?'

'You arrived at Shadowbrook after the trouble started, I think. The incidents were already taking place. This means that you will be, perhaps, the most objective person. That these happenings can't be your doing. You are a good starting place.'

What I learned on our first day of speaking was that his hair had been this way since he was small: no natural order to it, and so stubborn in its curliness that no pomade or cream had ever been able to tame it. No cut, however severe, had prevented the curls returning or lessened their will. He had, he assured me, tried – particularly in his younger days. He'd wanted to look serious, learned; he felt that hair of springs and coils suggested otherwise. But, he said, very simply, he grew tired of that fight.

I also learned that yes, he knew his own measurements. When moving through doorways or under branches, he seemed to be aware instinctively when to bend his head and by how much; he had an immediate knowledge of where the Rêve d'Or grew low. Also, he could move between brambles by turning unconsciously and, in doing so, not touch a single thorn, move nothing – and he'd keep talking, too, as he went. I marvelled at this. Having this twist and turn in my walk made it harder to guess distances; nor could my body's movements be depended on. This struck me as being an animal's skill: to have a precise awareness of the space around you, and one's relationship to it. Cats and mice with their whiskers; bats with their unheard song.

'A problem I have,' he said, 'is that Mr Fox's letter did not say very much. He only said that there was something within Shadowbrook House that had been troubling its residents since the autumn. It has worsened, he said, and it can't continue. Nocturnal happenings.'

'There's been walking. Footsteps at two or three in the morning. Physical damage, too – doors and pictures. And the housekeeper was pushed twelve days ago; she fell down the stairs and broke her arm.'

He widened his eyes. 'Pushed?'

'Mrs Bale says so. She saw a ghostly figure in the seconds before it, and she was too scared to stay.'

'Which is why I am here.'

'Yes.'

With that, we came to an arch in a beech hedge. He gestured; the path was too narrow for us to pass through side by side, so I accepted his offer and moved ahead. George followed and as he straightened back up, he exclaimed, 'Where is this?'

'The white garden. They have such gardens here – small rooms, walled with hedges, and all with their own identity or purpose. Here there are white blooms, pale foliage . . . So what does your society do, precisely? Are you part of the Church, or do you hunt ghosts as others hunt hares or foxes?'

I heard my tone. It surprised me: it seemed provocative, defiant, invitational – which were sentiments I did not feel. Rather, I felt crooked and foolish. Partly I wanted to hide. Yet George did not seem to notice. 'No. Faith plays no part in what we do. Some members are religious, of course, but others are entirely faithless, and we all work together for the same intent.'

'What is the intent?'

'It is a misconception,' he said, 'that the Society for Psychical Research exists to prove there are ghosts; that we may see a movement in the fog on a winter's night or a shadow pass over a mirror and claim it to be a spectre instantly. I don't doubt that there have been some within the society's history who would have been too quick to believe in the supernatural, too keen to prove there's an afterlife, so that a chill in a room would be a ghost without question. But there's no room for such men now. Hunting ghosts like hares or foxes?' He smiled, shook his head. 'No, we don't hunt. The Society exists to investigate what cannot be explained by any reasonable or scientific means. That's it, very simply. We look for rational answers to irrational events.'

'So you're scientists?'

'We use scientific reasoning. But no, we are not scientists. The answers are not found in the use of strange instruments or incantations; no holy water. I won't be suspending weights or ringing bells, or whatever else is imagined of us. The answers are found in listening – or I think they are.'

'Listening? That's all?'

'You're surprised? The truth is, Miss Waterfield, that most of the cases I've attended or heard of have, in fact, been human acts. Deliberate human trickery – or the result of human flaws, at least. We are imperfect creatures, you understand. Poor memories. Inclinations. Misunderstandings. Damage. Hopes and dreams. Most phenomena can be accounted for this way. And I can only discover this by talking to those involved in the supposed haunting. Or rather, by letting them talk to me.'

'So most of your cases are human work? A joke or a misunderstanding?'

George smoothed back a curl from his face. 'Most, yes, but not all.'

I looked to the nearest plant – phlox, a little flower with its moonish glow at dusk – and wondered how much to offer him. Whether I should speak of Veronique yet; also, if there was any imperfection in George at all. So far, he might have been sculpted. He seemed so clean, immaculate.

'I've met Mr Fox,' I said. 'Only once, but it was enough to know that he's well read and pragmatic. He believed it was an intruder at first, as I did – human activity, as you say – because they have all been such physical acts. Requiring weight or strength.'

'Which acts?'

'The push. The throwing of paintings. Scratches on doors. He said someone pulled at the sheets on his bed.'

George listened, head to one side. 'Scratches? I've seen that before in my work – and on arms and faces. And yes, it's been deliberately done, most frequently by the person being scratched.'

'By themselves?' This seemed so peculiar but I supposed people could be. 'And what of ghosts? If such things exist, might they scratch?'

'I have a colleague who witnessed a scratch being made before his very eyes, on a woman's arm. She sat on a chair before him and as they spoke, three red, bloodied marks appeared on her skin as if fingernails were being drawn down her arm at that very moment. But no hand was near it. There was no one else there. I see your expression, but I have read the report on this. And why might I lie? I have nothing to gain from doing so. I do not get paid to find a ghost; only to find an answer.'

'What else?'

'What else?' He seemed quizzical, amused by me.

'What other events have you seen or heard of which had no human answer? I've felt floorboards shift underneath me. I've smelled herbs in the hallway. Has this happened to you?'

'Smells are not uncommon in poltergeist cases. A scent of lavender, say. Boot polish. I investigated a case in which the smell was of tobacco smoke; not the old, lingering smell but fresh, as if someone was smoking their pipe in the room with me. And there can be worse smells, too. Decay or vomit. Excrement.'

I held his gaze. I eyed the freckles over his nose, evenly distributed; I studied the light-brown eyes with their darker rim. I knew that he was testing me now. It was gently said; he was not seeking to cause distress or embarrassment and nor was there was any teasing in his stare. But even so, there was an experiment in it. I felt he was measuring my nature;

he was pressing, very carefully, at my constitution to see what I could endure or survive. He looked, perhaps, for a wrinkled nose. Shock or revulsion. A feminine swoon. I showed none of these things, felt calm. I had known hospitals, after all. Retched into my own hands with the pain of fractures too many times to account for.

We walked on. From the white garden into the yard with the maple tree; from here, we rounded the house to the garden of herbs. I saw my bedroom window; through it, my bed.

'How long have you done this? Investigating?'

'Since I graduated from Cambridge. Six years now. Nearly seven.'

'How many investigations?'

He answered without hesitation. 'This is my forty-seventh. My eighteenth on my own. You said that Mr Fox believed it was an intruder at first. He no longer thinks so?'

'He says he's open-minded. But yes, he's inclined to think it's a ghost, having found no sensible answer.'

A nod. 'He's right to speak of an open mind. It's the most important quality to have. Not courage or curiosity, although these matter – but impartiality. What of others? The maids, for example?'

'They are convinced it's a ghost. The garden boys too.'

'They are quite decided?'

'The maids are, certainly.'

'And you, Miss Waterfield? Who has come all the way from Kew?'

He asked this differently. It was softly done, intimate; there was a smile in his voice which I found, too, in his eyes and I felt he'd moved a little nearer me to ask it. I was still. No one had spoken to me like this before. I didn't know the tone's meaning; I could not even guess at it. And I wanted, instinctively, to turn from him, to walk back across the croquet lawn and into the house and to sit with its dust and damp walls. But I realised, too, that I wanted more. I wanted more stories of scratched arms and pipe smoke; of lavender scent and the movement of furniture. I wanted him to offer more investigations that had, in the end, no scientific answers for these were stranger and far more compelling than any fact I'd read in encyclopaedias. They made my heart quicken. So I did not step away. I held his gaze and assured him that I was also open-minded. That I was perfectly impartial.

He seemed glad of it. 'Miss Waterfield, might you be able to meet with me this evening? I'd like to speak a little more with you, to hear your account of the fall, at least. After supper, perhaps?'

'An interview?'

'Of sorts. If you are the one I'm most able to trust, I would like to begin with you.'

The floor lamp was lit; the French doors were open. I had dried my hands from the washing of dishes and removed my apron. Combed my hair.

As for George, he was wearing a different shirt to the one he'd worn at supper. Had a leather-bound book on his lap, pencils on the table, and he rose as I entered. 'Would you prefer the chair or the sofa?'

We sat with the table between us. And, having settled and propped my cane against the sofa, I looked up and acknowledged it. Beauty, in a person. It was as clear and real as the chair he sat on. As defined as the bowl of peach-coloured roses behind him whose petals were, I noticed, not dropping but retaining their proper shape. This face of his. It seemed perfect; it was symmetrical, unblemished with no discoloration. He had neat, deep brows and full lips. He was clean-shaven, yet I could see the alteration in skin colour where his beard, if he grew it, would start and end. He had traces of past smiles and frowns on him – light lines, and a dimple. Such lines might be called imperfections but in truth, they lessened nothing.

He readied himself. Sharpened a pencil, blew at its tip. He pulled his chair a little closer, opened a notebook and smoothed the page with his palm – and he had no awareness of himself in these acts. When he pushed his hand into his hair, the curls accommodated that hand; when he retracted his hand, the curls nodded and grew still.

He looked up. 'Miss Waterfield. Could you begin with how you came here? And then tell me what you have seen or heard yourself. I don't want what others have told you; their time will come. For now, I simply want your personal experience. Your telling of it.'

I offered what I knew. Firstly, the letter that came to Kew – the gold-embossed letterhead and its requests for succulents and citrus trees. Of my train from Paddington. Of the taciturn driver who'd smelled of smoke and butterscotch; his word *trouble*, which had been the proper start of it. And then I spoke of the housekeeper herself: talkative and tired in her features, with a smile so tight and permanent that I soon knew it was false. Also, how she'd spoken of draughts in the house. Of the long, dark abandonment of Shadowbrook in the years before Mr Fox's arrival, in which branches had pushed through window panes and mice had balled dust into corners, and nested; and how this abandonment was evident, still, from the blooming of damp and the warped window frames. And I told him, too, of the single rule of Shadowbrook, which was that the upper floor was out of bounds. It was Mr Fox's floor.

'The upper floor?'

'No one can climb the stairs unless summoned by Mr Fox himself. He locks all his rooms in his absence.'

'Why is this? Do you know? You said you'd met him.'

'He talked of privacy, that's all. He has a suite of rooms up there.'

'A suite?'

'A bathroom. A view across the gardens and fields.'

I spoke of his dinner trays. His frequent absence with work. How he seemed to favour fresh linen, for his bed sheets were scrubbed and ironed most days and how he took a sedative to help him sleep. I spoke of the measured transference of weight above my head, at night; the careful descent of the stairs, the quiet tap on my bedroom door and how, having opened it and stepped out, I'd seen no one at all and yet I'd felt watched. I mentioned the flowers that had, till now, died too soon in their vases. How Mrs Bale was terrified of the name Pettigrew. And I spoke of the fall itself, with her arm held against her collarbone and her huge single scream.

'The housekeeper – Mrs Bale – isn't here at Shadowbrook?'

'Not since she fell. She's with her sister in Barcombe and won't see anyone except the vicar. Not even you, or so I was told.'

He raised an eyebrow, half smiled. 'Not even me? And no Mr Fox ... Tell me, Miss Waterfield, who else should I speak to? Can you tell me their names?'

The maids. Hollis. The garden boys, one by one. I thought to mention Jarvis, too, for he'd have five thousand stories to tell. But then I stopped myself. 'There are so many rumours here, Mr Lowe. The whispers, the hushed remarks ... I don't know how many tales can be trusted.'

'Rumours? I'm interested in those. Oh, rumours are

powerful things, Miss Waterfield. People will often believe what they're told without questioning it, especially if it is a tale they want to be true. And so many rumours have a kernel of truth at the heart of them. What was the name you said just now? Of which the housekeeper is terrified?'

'Pettigrew.' I pronounced it carefully. 'The Pettigrews owned this house before Mr Fox. Owned it for generations and she was the last of them.'

'She?' He waited.

Briefly I wondered if she'd hear me. If, by saying her name, I might summon her, so that she would come downstairs later, place her hand on my bedroom door. Or was she already here, sitting beside me? Whispering *tell him my name* in my ear? So I told him. This man like a tree in which to shelter. 'She is buried in the orchard. Her name is Veronique.'

George wrote all of this down. I watched as he did so. The pencil's tip rarely left the paper; any tailed letter was elaborately done. And as I sat, one more name came to mind. Kit – his name, but also his colouring; how he'd clicked his tongue once and the horses had responded. Kit knew the most, I was sure of that. But I kept his name to myself. What use would there be in sharing it? He would refuse to speak of them. He'd walk away through his crops, away from George.

The scratch of George's nib. The knock of moths on the window pane.

The grandfather clock chimed nine times. 'Are there any more questions, Mr Lowe?'

He finished writing with a flourish, smiled. 'No. Or rather, no more about these nocturnal happenings. Miss Waterfield, I have a feeling we have met before. Do you feel that? I'm wondering if we passed each other in Kew.'

'No, I don't think so.'

But later, as I listened for creaks upstairs, I supposed that we might have done. That I might have passed through a door he'd held open for me and not noticed or remembered him. After all, I'd been lost in my grief for her. At Kew, I had not yet numbed myself so that all I saw was the backs of her hands as she turned pages, or her silhouette, and even a tree-tall, perfect man would have passed me by. He might, however, have seen me. I had been there constantly. And I'd have been a memorable sight – white-haired and crooked, sleeping on benches. Inhaling jasmine as if consolation was to be found in it.

The man from the Society for Psychical Research set his materials down in the old library, with its faint lavender scent and its broken pane. On the table he arranged his notebook and pencils, his pens and bottles of ink; on the shelves he placed his books on the human brain, on ancient doctrines and superstitions and paranormal histories. I paused in the doorway, watched this. He kept his back to me and therefore did not notice me, but I saw how the library might have been before its corners filled with dust. A room in use. Pages for turning.

It was here that George would bring us all, one by one. He announced this intention within days: that he wished to speak to every single person who worked at Shadowbrook. Moreover, he wished to talk to anyone in Barcombe – or beyond – who might have felt or seen any trouble directly. 'So please tell others to come here. If they have their own stories, I'd like to hear them.' A speech like a general, in front of the yellow rose.

This became George's routine: in the mornings, he'd open the window of the old library, set out his papers and ink on the splintery desk and wait for someone to come to him. And they would come. Maud was the first. She pinched her cheeks in the hallway before entering, spoke in a brighter voice than I'd known. After her, Hollis. He entered Shadowbrook as if entering a church, removing his cap and clutching it; also, he insisted on removing his boots at the kitchen door, so that he padded through in his socks, and I spied the holes and darned places. As for the boys, they were less mindful of this. The Mayhews drifted in, eyeing the possible sources of food – cake tins or the cold store. Peter Bell, when he came, brought the scent of the manure heap with him. Having decided to investigate the house a little, he pressed dung into the carpet in the drawing room, and Maud was incandescent. She chased him into the courtyard, her duster like a whip. 'Do *you* fancy scrubbing that?'

George always closed the door. Such conversations, he explained, had to be private; each person who came needed to know that their words were safe. And so, at lunchtime, he would open the door and emerge like a creature that had been sleeping; he'd stretch, rotate a shoulder blade and proceed to say nothing at all to us. Maud understood this. Even so, she'd approach him. 'What did Charlie Rudd tell you? Or Teddy? Or . . . ?' But this man of proportions and tact said nothing in response. He only remarked on the starched tablecloth. The delicious ham, laid on a blue plate.

As for the afternoons, they were too hot to stay indoors. He would roll up his shirtsleeves, lift his notebook and pencils, and walk out into the grounds. Sometimes he'd venture down to the village, returning with gifts for the maids – cold lemonade, or marshmallows – or with a question to ask regarding aspects of Barcombe. How old was the ancient oak? How many people used Jarvis's shop? 'And how,' he reasoned, laughing, 'might someone of my height ever pass through the door of The Bull? I've never seen a door so low.'

But mostly he preferred to stay nearby. To write up notes from the morning in a cool, shaded, intimate place. 'Where might you suggest, Miss Waterfield?' And I offered the places I knew: the tennis pavilion, with its low-slung furniture; the portico with its *trompe l'oeil*. One afternoon I found him in the potting shed amongst the croquet mallets and the rusted shears. He sat in a fraying deckchair, resting one heel on the windowsill – a slack, nonchalant pose. Yet it also suited him. This man for whom *trouble* was the mildest of words. I could not imagine him being alarmed, or afraid.

Of all the garden boys, there was only one who did not come. Fred Billings – the smallest, youngest boy – kept to the peripheries. Whilst others would follow George like a star, he kept to his work in the vegetable patch; he wiped his nose with his forearm and looked at the ground as George passed him. So one morning, as he ate buttered toast, George enquired as to whether we'd mind if he set out the croquet hoops. 'I'd like to speak to the reluctant one.'

I wondered who this was. 'Mrs Bale? Mr Fox?'

He smiled as he swallowed. 'Ah yes, they are reluctant too. But for now, I mean the small boy with the fringe. With the bruised arms. Would you mind if I set up the game, on the lawn?'

I wondered why he wished to do this. But later, as I entered the drawing room, I heard a crack like a broken bone in the garden and hurried to the French windows. Through the half-drawn curtains, I saw it: George was demonstrating the art of croquet to Fred – how to aim, the rules and the mallet's swing. He wore a pale-yellow shirt;

the child hopped from foot to foot in a way I'd never seen. And I thought, this man knows people.

George had walked out to meet the garden boy in his own territory; he'd sensed that Fred's answers would come far more naturally as they knocked balls through rusting hoops, with the woodpigeons calling, than at a desk in a half-dark room. And he sensed me, too, watching. For as he straightened from having struck a ball, we saw each other. There was a distance of lawn between us; he was too far away for me to read his expression. I only know that he looked at me for a longer moment than was required – what was there to see, except my oddities? – before turning his attention back to Fred and saying, 'Let's try this again.'

'It's hard to remember a time before he came here,' Harriet said. 'Don't you think? I feel he's been here far longer than . . . ' she paused, counted, 'six days.'

We were walking to Barcombe side by side. Harriet had groceries to buy; she'd knocked on the glasshouse door, asked if I wished to keep her company as she did so. It was a new request and I liked it.

It was early in the day. Even so, we kept to the shade. Our pace was slow and Harriet moved her hand against the flies, as if declining an offer. 'Of course, they'll be talking about him in the shop. Jarvis. They say women are worse for tattling, but he's the biggest talker of all.'

'About his job?' I could imagine that: fabrications of past investigations – headless horsemen and rattling chains – being murmured over the packets of soap flakes. How George had found blood on the walls at Shadowbrook.

'Probably. But I bet they'll be saying more about how he looks, don't you think? There was talk enough about you when you came; can you imagine what they must be saying

225

about him? His hair and face? The size of him? You know, George makes Maud blush just by walking past her. She's trying to curl her hair with twists of paper at night.'

'Blush?'

'Watch her the next time he's passing.'

There was a pause in the conversation yet I sensed Harriet had more to say, for she'd pressed her lips together; an expression of uncertainty.

'I suspect I blush when Albert walks by. Have you noticed?'

I frowned. I hadn't seen that at all. Yes, Albert might stand at the kitchen door sometimes and speak to her; I'd also seen them in conversation in shady places or corners, but I'd never seen any flushing in Harriet. They'd seemed like two people talking, no more.

'He loves me, you see.'

'Loves you? Albert?' I stopped.

Her smile was sudden, huge. 'He does. And I love him too. And we'd like to marry, but he would like to be more than a garden boy before he asks me – to be a proper gardener, like his father is. He also says he'll go to war, if there is one, so he'd be a soldier for a while and not a garden boy at all. He'd be so handsome in his uniform.'

Love? 'But you only talk of the vegetable patch or the weather.'

She laughed at this, walked on. 'Not always. In the evenings, we might meet in the beechwoods for a time, and then we don't talk about those things.'

I said no more to this. On reaching the shop, I announced that I'd stay outside, for I'd vowed never to enter Jarvis's shop again. I had no wish to be eyed up and down disapprovingly, or to hear his views on women or war or any other matter. So I stood in the shade of the ancient oak. From here, I observed the shop front: how people came and went. How they greeted each other. And I knew I ought to be glad that Harriet had confided in me. It must have meaning – that she liked me, or didn't mind me, at least. But I knew, too, how it was to stand in the beech-woods at the day's end; I imagined them together in its angled, silent golden half-light, speaking of love – or not speaking at all.

Did I feel pleased at this thought? For her? Partly. For I'd liked Harriet from our first meeting. I'd seen her pragmatism, her calm manner. Also, I liked her for her slight insouciance; how she'd close doors with her foot because it was quicker, or blow an insect from a lettuce leaf and carry on. Recently, she'd offered me a raspberry, held out like a thimble; no words, but with an insistence in her manner, as if to say, *go on*. I liked, too, how she was no dark-haired, rounded beauty; nor was she necessarily demure. Yet Albert loved her. Had talked of marriage. One does not need to be perfect, I thought.

Even so, I carried a weight as I stood by the oak. Others came and went. Women ushered their children into the shop before them; girls of my own age paused to converse. And I noted their competent bodies. Wondered if they knew the farmer or if he knew them. I thought of him as I stood.

Ten minutes later, Harriet returned with a brown paper bag in both arms. She shook her head and said, *that man . . .* And on the walk home, she offered the rumours of George that she'd heard from the shopkeeper: that he was a German spy or a secret prince. 'Or he intends to summon Veronique forwards with a seance and candles and strange markings . . . That he carries a crucifix to keep him safe. Have you seen him with a crucifix? I told Jarvis that was nonsense. Told him that the trouble seemed over already.'

'Over? Why is it over?'

Harriet shifted the weight of the bag. 'Because of how quiet it has been. Haven't you noticed? No walking at night, no tapping on doors ... Not since Mrs Bale left. And no one is talking about Veronique any more. See? I just named her, and even I didn't want to at the height of it.' And she talked of other things as we went – meals, the heat, the August fair which she hoped I would stay for – but I only half listened.

How far I'd come from the girl who required proof in every instance. Who had never cared for novels because such writers never wrote of what was true, or so I'd thought. That was the old Clara. The new one could not sleep. I sat upright, lit my lamp. And I moved through every downstairs room in the house, despite the hour; I moved from vase to vase, to every arrangement of flowers I'd brought indoors for his arrival. The ox-eye daisies in the teapot. The crimson dahlias in the glass bowl. Roses and old hydrangea heads. I circled each one, assessing them for thickened water or broken stems. But there was no damage to be found on them.

Back in my room, I stared at the wall. I did not want this trouble to be gone. I did not want George to discover that all of this was human work. I wanted ghosts, suddenly. And any small nocturnal sound – a mouse's scurry, the clock's wheeze, an adjustment of wood as the temperature cooled – made me think, it is Veronique. I wanted, now, the *tap-tap*.

I thought of my mother, too. Of hot, sleepless Indian nights in which she might hang a leg from the bed, swing it like a pendulum – full of thoughts, like me. Of how my grandparents might have cooled themselves by dipping their hands into cold water or fanning themselves. Others might have slept unclothed.

I've never seen anything more beautiful. At three in the morning, I retrieved her pendant from my bedside drawer and lay back on my bed. The V was her initial, I knew this; the locket's red velvet interior had once held her secrets – a petal or a lock of hair. I placed it against my own collarbone. I looked at the ceiling, aware of the locket's cool, singular weight near my throat – and I thought of education. Thought of how it might be to stand with Kit in the beechwoods or elsewhere. To have him say *Clara* as if the word mattered. Or simply to stand, facing the other, saying nothing at all.

XI

The dew had been burned off by nine. In the fields, the barley was ripe. It was golden, so dry that the feathered heads rattled as I passed through them; they caught and pulled strands of my hair. And as I approached the farmhouse, I heard water: a slow, unbroken, rhythmical sound. But there was no water here, or no moving water, at least. There were only the reducing levels of water in pails or rusting troughs.

I could not see Kit. I opened the gate, entered his farmyard and moved between the tools and production of his farming life, thinking to knock on the farmhouse door, or call out. But the rhythmic watery sound came from the barn. I approached it. I passed between a splintered cart and hayseeds and dung, and stopped in its doorway. Kit was sitting on a stool. Between his legs was a flattened stone; he moved blades against it, sharpening his shears and scythes – preparing for the harvest. A smooth, rounded action.

He looked up. No surprise in him. He regarded me without speaking, and if I could have named his expression, it might have been resignation or disappointment. He exhaled privately. He laid the blade down, wiped his hands on his cloth.

*

We settled against the fence on the northern side of the farmyard, in the shade of the barn. His horses were here, under an oak, flinching their muscles at flies. Kit watched them. He leaned forwards, resting his forearms on the fence and in doing this, his shirt slackened; it dropped forwards, creating a room in which his skin was paler, as I'd thought it would be. I saw the cleft that divided his chest. 'What do you want to know this time?'

I'd always come with questions previously. He'd assumed I'd come with more – and partly, I had. Also, I partly wished to ask nothing – to merely stand and look at the horses with him, or to sit in the barn and watch him work. But I would never admit this. 'More of her. There must be more. Anything.'

'Why?'

His hair had lightened. His beard had moved into a coppery hue and the grey at his temples was more prominent. His hair was longer, too, so that it curled near his collar and the backs of his ears. I said, 'Did you know that she's buried in the orchard? The locals didn't want her in the churchyard – polluting their sacred earth – and yet her brothers did far worse and are there in the Pettigrew tomb. It isn't fair or right.'

'What does it matter where she's buried? Or how? Dead is dead, Miss Waterfield.'

'You think this?'

'Don't you? I remember you said there were no ghosts. She's buried where she's buried. It makes no difference to her, at least.'

I remembered, then. His father had died on the scaffold. His body – Bill's? – had also been buried elsewhere; he'd been banished from the nettled green resting place of St Mary's in Barcombe-on-the-Hill, despite so many other

Preedys being there. So where was his father's body now? In no orchard, I was sure of that. There'd be no headstone for him. No flowers set down. And I was filled, suddenly, with a wish to move closer and ask more – not of Veronique, but of the farmer himself. Of this specific loss which he carried. Was he lonely? Did he have dreams in which his father was living and new again? Performing old tasks? So that, on waking, Kit believed momentarily that the death itself had been the dream and his father was, in fact, downstairs boiling the kettle or pulling on boots? I knew how this was. I had my own version.

'I've told you all I know,' he said.

'Will you tell me about her face, at least? You said she was beautiful.'

'I don't want to tell you about her face.'

The absoluteness of this. A statement which he meant – and it silenced me for a time, as a raised palm would have done: an order to stop. So I looked towards his horses, as he did. We observed the occasional stamp of a hoof, studied the cracks in the ground. And even though Kit seemed still, I knew he was not. I felt the heat and tension in him. There was unrest, and I supposed that he'd prefer to be doing anything other than standing here, talking to a crippled girl with a forthright nature. I saw his hands moving over themselves. Saw a redness on the knuckles of his right hand; on his left, there was a new mark which must have bled, when made, and I said, 'There's a man at Shadowbrook. Did you hear? From London.'

'Yes, I heard.'

'He's interviewing those who know tales of her, of the Pettigrews, which is most people, of course. He's spoken to the workers. He'll want to talk to others now – in Barcombe and further away.'

'I won't talk of her.'

'But you're talking to me.'

'And that's more than enough. I won't talk to him.'

An emphasis on *him*, as if the word was bitter-tasting. 'Why not?'

Kit scratched his beard. 'Those horses. See them? They're simple creatures. They learn and respond. I can plough with them all day and every furrow is as straight as the one before. That's habit. It's learned. But they have instinct, too. Know when rain is coming. Know my mood before I've crossed the yard. As a boy I had a dog, a good, hardworking dog who understood people before I'd said a word to them. Me?' He lifted himself from the fence, straightened. 'I've not left Gloucestershire. Never been in a library or studied at Cambridge but I can spot a lame horse from two hundred yards or a lame man from fifty, and I can tell who's made soundly and who is not. I've already met your man from the Society.'

'When?'

'Last night. In The Bull. He came in asking about the Pettigrews. And he might be seen as a gentleman at Shadowbrook, but I'll tell you this, Miss Waterfield: that's not how you talk in a country inn.'

'He asks questions. It's his job.'

'No. He talked far more than he listened. Drank too much.'

I did not believe this. George, who'd altered the house. Who'd assisted the maids in lifting what was heavy or high. I refused to believe it. 'No.'

'No? Fine. It makes no difference to me if you believe me or not. Mind him, that's all I'm saying to you.'

'Mind him?'

'My old dog would have growled, kept her distance.'

'I've been told to mind you, but I'm still here.'

At that, Kit almost smiled. He pushed a hand through his hair, clutched its roots so that he revealed his forehead with its lines and earth; for a moment, he stayed like this. Then he dropped his hand, looked at the fields. 'You shouldn't come to see me. Asking questions. I've too much to do, a harvest to ready for. But also, they'll talk if they aren't already – you know why – and I've got enough stories to carry the weight of.'

'I don't mind them talking.'

'No? Because you're young. You don't live here; you'll go back to London and leave these rumours and answers behind you. You don't understand, do you?' He eyed me, shook his head once. 'Damn it, Miss Waterfield. Keep away from me.'

On the London streets, it had been my appearance that they'd seen. Bones and colouring and peculiar eyes and smallness. These had been my London failings, I knew that. And had these same failings – old fractures, pale lashes – been enough to make him walk away, back to the scythes? To disinterest him? Kit knew women. Kit, by his own admission, had had women knock on his farmhouse door and yet he had no wish for my company. Had only seemed resentful of it. He'd strode over his land as if trying to lose a stray creature.

But my nature, too, was lacking. I listed all those adjectives which I had never fully minded till now: stubborn, temperamental. Demanding. Strange. I'd considered them strong, once; explorers and scientists and warriors would, surely, need such ways. Yet now they seemed an embarrassment. I asked too many questions, it seemed; I had been an irritant for him. And I wondered if these characteristics were more at fault than my skeleton; if they – not my bones – were my least beautiful part.

Beautiful. I supposed Veronique had been beautiful in every conceivable way – physically, yes, but also in her nature. For one by one, they'd come like pilgrims. Laid themselves down at the altar of her.

I returned to a garden of sound. Harriet was humming as she swept the yard. The croquet hoops and mallets had been left on the lawn, so that the garden boys were hitting balls haphazardly into borders and against brickwork. I watched this through an archway. Heard their clamour and whoops. Saw, too, how they lowered their mallets when George came into view with his easy, familiar gait and smile, and they hurried towards him with their news and requests: how tall *was* he, exactly? How fast could he run? If he had to choose between rugby and football, which would he pick? No questions of ghosts any more. And George laughed at being surrounded by them, raised his hands in defence.

A garden of light, of all kinds.

I could hardly stand it. I entered the house, tapped down its dark, cool corridor and climbed the stairs. Mr Fox had locked all the doors, I knew this. I could not enter Veronique's room. Yet I stood outside it, remembered the layer of dust that I'd stepped into. Remembered the view from her window which had taken in the beechwoods and the distant rooftops of the outskirts of Barcombe and the farthest edge of the Preedy land. And I longed to possess what she had; I wanted to absorb it – through the door handle, the corridor's air, the wood panelling that she must have passed a hundred times. I wanted to learn. To see her.

It was jealousy, perhaps. The tales. Later, I considered this: that the men whispered of her because of her beauty, but the stories of madness came from the women who resented far more than her freedom and wealth. This sour, lasting punishment. Call her insane. Work the truth over and over, as if it were dough, until it no longer resembled itself, so that Veronique hosted parties of men. Squatted in nettles. Drooled green.

The croquet game continued into the afternoon. Hollis announced the weather to be too much to work in; he ended their working day at two. So the boys played croquet or scooped armfuls of water from the bathing pool, soaked each other. Lolled in the shade like kings.

George could not be found. I tried the shaded, private places in which he'd worked before – the tennis pavilion, the portico, the potting shed. I knocked on both the library door and that of his bedroom. In the end, I asked Maud, and she eyed me with suspicion. 'The orchard,' she said.

He was standing squarely, as if on a plinth. Feet apart, hands in his pockets, so perfectly still that I knew he was deep in thought, that he might not hear me come alongside him. Hollis, I thought, must have told him about this secret, overgrown grave.

'Does it make a difference?' I asked.

He turned, smiled. 'A difference?'

'That she's buried in the grounds.'

An easy, welcoming face. He adjusted his stance to offer me more room. 'Perhaps. There was trouble in a terraced house in Kilburn once; we found a child's skeleton in the wall cavity – wrapped in cloth but bare otherwise – and we buried it respectfully, and after that ... peace. No more trouble.'

I must have responded to this – a tiny sound, or a movement.

'Forgive me ... that was too much. I should not have said it. It was merely in my head at that very moment and

I spoke without checking myself. I rarely talk of my work with others.' He shook his head. 'Perhaps it's the heat.'

Like a plant, he had responded to sunlight and the higher temperatures. There were more freckles on the bridge of his nose. Also, I saw a singular reddish mark on his jaw that spoke of sunburn to me; he'd held the same pose in direct light for too long, perhaps. I knew he would not tell me to leave him alone. He was too kind, too well-mannered. 'There's peace here too,' I said. 'Since you arrived, there have been no more disturbances in the house – nothing. You must wonder why you were summoned at all.'

'No. It's not uncommon for a place that's experienced activity like this to grow still with an arrival. I expected it.'

'You did? Why?

His brown eyes were edged with a far darker colour. 'If it's human work – deliberate, intended – they are wary. An investigator arrives; the tricksters fear exposure or recognise their game has gone too far. Sometimes they stop at that point. Other times, they see they have a larger audience and there is the new, alluring prospect of fooling a man from the Society. But they take their time, even so. A week or so of stillness.'

'And if it's not human work? If it's something else?'

'A natural phenomenon that's been misinterpreted? A new arrival can alter the temperature in a house. Or one more person using the taps may relieve the pressure within the pipework that was causing the noises, for example.'

'I don't mean that.'

George nodded once. He looked back towards the mound of earth. 'In those cases ... well, the moment of stillness rarely lasts. The activity returns; sometimes it increases.'

'Increases? You've seen this?'

'Yes.'

I wanted to ask more. To know how this activity – in some other house, another county – had grown and ended; how it had manifested itself. But George looked back to me. His gaze was direct, unembarrassed; he studied my face as if it were a book he was attempting to read, and this stopped me from speaking.

'Miss Waterfield,' he said. 'I talked of being open-minded. Would you say that you still are?'

A cautious half-smile from him. The wise detective. No, we had not met before, yet there was a familiarity in George which I felt grateful for. I might have known him for far longer than this handful of days.

'Why do you ask?'

'You moved through the house last night – examining flowers, I think? And in my company . . . it's always ghosts that you ask of, not practical matters. I sense a bias in you. I am not being critical, you understand; I'd only prefer you to be truthful.'

I nodded. 'Yes. I was biased, in the beginning: I was adamant that this trouble was a thief or a joke. But I met Mr Fox, who talked of being receptive to new ideas, and how a wise man knows nothing – and I realised he was right. And now I've found myself favouring this idea of ghosts, so that when I see flowers that have not died overnight or been deliberately destroyed, I feel disappointed – me! I don't recognise myself. I've changed, and I am embarrassed that I have. I can't imagine who I'll be when I return to London.'

'You're going back?'

'At some point, yes. Mr Fox will not always pay me.'

I felt breathless from having said so much. George, too, needed time. His hands remained in his pockets, but he looked up into the branches which he could have touched if he'd chosen to. Apples were forming above him. I saw, more clearly, the mark on his jaw.

'Would it help you to know that I was like you? That I favoured the notion of ghosts, by far? An afterlife: that was what I wanted. I wanted it so much that I joined the Society for Psychical Research because I thought I would find proof this way. I thought I would find all the answers – and comfort.'

'Comfort?'

He looked back. 'My mother died. I was young – eight. And after her death I moved through every room of grief: rage, denial, blame. I bit and swore. I retreated into myself. I'd either mock the notion of God or I'd drop to my knees in any church I came to, and pray. And then one day, I felt it. A vibration? Even now, I can't describe it well. But I felt it – *it*. An absolute conviction that I was not alone; moreover, that she was with me – my mother.

'It was a Thursday. It had been raining all morning; then it stopped very suddenly, so I went outside. I was standing in a passageway between two houses. There was no one else there, yet I felt watched. It was an intense, physical sensation. And there was no other explanation for it: no windows overlooked the passageway and there were no other people. My mother was with me, and not fully dead. And then, of course, I wondered why she had come to me – and in this passageway, of all places. Was she trying to reach me? If so, what did she wish to say? These thoughts.

'After that, I had a purpose. I wanted to investigate that feeling; I wanted to prove there was life after death, or to prove that a human had more than a physical form. So I read theology at Cambridge. There, I joined the Society. And within days of joining it, I met a good, wise man – dead himself now – who saw this hungry, reckless, furious

239

boy who wanted proof of an afterlife, and reasoned with him. Bought him a beer in a tavern that overlooked the river. Told him to have an open mind, always, because to venture forwards with the hope of finding a specific answer served no purpose at all. I had to have no bias, he said. No preconceptions if I wished to find answers. To have no private agenda. I owe him a lot, that man.'

'And have you managed that? Honestly?'

'I would be lying to you if I said that I did not still prefer the notion of a life after death to a black, absolute nothing. I think it's a human instinct: we do not like the thought of our existence ending – or that of our loved ones – like a candle, snuffed out, and so we prefer the other possibilities. Yes, I like the possibility of my mother still existing in some way. And in the early days I had to catch myself, chastise myself, for I needed to remain impartial in my work. I could not risk manipulating, consciously or unconsciously, what I saw or heard. I have learned impartiality now. I will never lie to myself or others. I'll ensure that the questions I ask are open, unguided. For there is enough deception in this world, Miss Waterfield – in a Soho medium, for example, or in a family who fabricate a poltergeist in order to find fame.' He shook his head. 'This work is about truth, if nothing else.'

All this, in the orchard. All these words and reassurances.

'You lost your mother too, I think? Hollis told me.'

'Yes.'

'How? Do you mind me asking this?'

'A tumour. She was thirty-nine.'

I wondered on vibrations. This had been his word and yet it felt a fitting one. I wondered if I had felt them myself: on the upper floor, or in the hallway when I held up the lantern and asked who was there. On the Thames shoreline on a dark afternoon in January, with grief in my throat like a stone. And did I feel it now? Standing beside him? With Veronique both at our feet and beside us, watching?

'I need your help,' he said. 'I have spoken to everyone except the housekeeper and Mr Fox. He is not here, I know that. But she? She's near. And I must speak to her, Clara; until I do, I cannot write my report or decide what's been happening here. Do you know where she is?'

'Her sister's. Yes.'

'Would you show me the place? Tomorrow, perhaps?'

'I doubt she'll see you.'

'I know. But the worst of these events – the push, the carved door – happened to her specifically. Would you accompany me?'

I nodded.

Mind him, Kit had said. But he was so broad and still that I felt I could rest in his shade; he spoke a language I understood, despite being so physically unlike me.

We drifted towards the house. Dusk. The shadows were long. I knew that the brickwork would feel warm to touch, that the bats would soon be dipping for insects. 'Can I ask you something, George? Did you go to The Bull last night?'

He slowed. 'Yes. You've heard that? Taverns can be useful places; people gather and talk. Tongues are often looser in them.'

'Did you meet the farmer there?'

'The farmer? There were several farmers.'

'Preedy. He farms the barley. Earth-coloured, reticent. He has a beard. Not tall, but he looks very strong.'

'Ah. Yes, I saw him. He didn't say much and left early. Clara, may I say something in return? It is hard for me, because I must be impartial, as you know, and have no preferences – and I've achieved that in forty-seven investigations. Yet with this one, it's harder. I know now what you want the answer to be. Mostly I never pay attention to what other people want – but with you?' He smiled. 'I want to find the answer that pleases you. Do you understand? And do you know why?'

I didn't reply properly for I had no reply to give. Also, this was the same low, intimate tone that he'd used once before and which I hadn't felt sure of. He looked at my hairline as he waited for my answer, as if my hairline and brows were worth remembering – and no, I did not understand him. I spoke of Harriet needing assistance and left quickly, made my way into the house. And I wondered when he and I had moved into calling each other by our first names – Clara and George, like old acquaintances – for we were doing this now.

We visited Mrs Bale on the hottest day so far. I met George on the veranda after breakfast. He was wearing a cream plaid shirt; he carried a leather bag over one shoulder and he watched as I came towards him. 'Ready?'

We walked past Hollis's cottage with its rope swing. Past the iron sign of Barcombe-on-the-Hill. George kept the slow, casual pace that I'd noted in him on our first walk; he matched my steps precisely, and if I slowed, he slowed also.

'I said too much to you yesterday. It was unprofessional. How I speak to you ... I ought to speak to everyone equally, and I don't suppose I have been. Also, I've not told that story – about my mother – for a very long time and you might not have wished to hear it.'

The reddish mark on his jaw was still there. But it seemed darker to me. And whilst he talked, I studied it. I glanced across, eyeing it in light and shade, and I realised that this was not sunburn. It was a bruise – plum-coloured, yellow-edged. I paused, feeling angry. 'Did he strike you in The Bull? Tell me.'

George stopped talking, turned. He knew who I meant. His hand went to his jaw as if trying to remind himself of the answer. 'It was nothing. An altercation which didn't last. He left afterwards.'

'Why did he strike you?'

He looked across the barley, unsure. 'He took exception, I think. He seemed protective – about the Pettigrews – and I can be persistent, I know that. It's part of my job, but sometimes . . . Well. The bruise looks worse than it feels, I promise.' A smile.

'Why didn't you tell me yesterday?'

'I saw no need. And I'm hardly proud of it, Clara. I'm a foot taller than him, perhaps, yet he still managed to leave this mark on me. A lucky shot, I'd call it.'

'You struck him back?'

'No, I did not.'

Mind him. I felt the words in my mouth. They pushed me into a dark, contemplative mood and George, sensing this, said no more, so that we walked in silence. We passed the wild roses and the greening water trough, and only by the ancient oak did we speak again. A sign was there: a rectangular piece of paper pinned to the bark: *Barcombe Summer Fair! Monday 3rd August.* Two days from now.

'Will you go to it, Clara?'

'I doubt it.'

But I was not thinking of the fair. Rather, I was thinking of Kit's words: that the Preedys hated the Pettigrews. That all arguments came from money, women or land. And yet he was so protective of them – or of her, at least – that he'd struck a man in a tavern. He'd fought a man of height and breadth and dignity. So what didn't I know? What was the secret of Veronique that I could sense but not touch or see? There was something.

We climbed the Stow road, came to the hump-backed bridge.

The garden at Willowbank had altered in the heat. Flowers had retreated. Leaves were discoloured with heat or curling on their stems. As we reached it, George exhaled and adjusted his shirt. 'Here?'

'Yes.'

He thanked me, walked down the path. I remained in the lane, watching.

He knocked five times on the door, stepped back. Within a moment or two, it opened in the same staccato manner that it had opened to me before, as if something was obstructing it or its wood had warped. Elspeth was wearing a brown cotton dress in this heat − floral, capped sleeves. She wore, too, her old expression of suspicion, grasping the side of the door. And whilst I could not hear George's words to her, I could see her response to them: her brow twitched; her eyes widened; she adjusted her grip on the door. She began, too, to shake her head. She did this resolutely, many times. She said *no* with such emphasis that I heard it from the lane − *no, absolutely not* − and she shut the door so hastily that it caused George to flinch, to lift his arms a little in bewilderment − a gesture to the blue door.

'What happened?'

He came back slowly, amazed. 'She told me to get away. Said that her sister would not speak to me today, or tomorrow − or any day.'

'Did you say who you were? From the Society?'

'Of course, but that didn't matter. She slammed the door. Did you see how she slammed the door?'

244

Incredulity in him. I had not seen it in him before; it showed itself in the deep, knotted frown and the shake of his head. But there was, also, something else: his eyes seemed harder. He shifted his jaw, considered the ground as if the ground was at fault. 'How,' he said, 'are we meant to know what happened at Shadowbrook if she won't talk? If she won't see me? She's the one who's *seen* this ghost. She is the one who fell . . . ' He looked back at the house, kept very still. 'I won't go back to London without an explanation for this. I've never failed – not once.'

At that, he turned. In six strides he had returned to the door and was banging upon it repeatedly, without slowing or lessening pitch. I could see the door shuddering on its hinges; I could see flakes of blue paint falling from it, and the sound seemed so sudden and intrusive that I felt Barcombe had been woken by it. He shouted, 'Open the door!'

As quickly as he'd started this, he stopped. He halted mid strike. His irritation and rage disappeared. He retracted his hand, came back to me with an embarrassed expression. He reached into his hair for a moment. 'I'm sorry. Clara, I'm sorry. It's . . . the frustration. Feeling so close to an answer. Wanting to find the truth . . . ' He dropped his hand, regarded me. His smile seemed meek, pleading. 'I have upset you.'

'No. I'm not upset.'

'You're pale. Clara, please . . . '

He became himself again. George like a tree. The man who'd advised Fred on the croquet rules, who'd spoken of bereavement as a poet might. He announced that he had, still, Mr Fox to speak to – and perhaps that would be enough to find an answer. He had, he said, talked to everyone else.

We reverted to politeness as we walked home. He spoke of the weather – of the need for a storm to clear the air, how little he was sleeping for the airlessness. And I wondered if the heat was partly to blame for I'd read of the difference to horses at full moon; how the winter months might cause a darkness to enter ourselves. Heat might try our tempers, perhaps. It might lessen our resolve or self-control. My mother had had stories of the days before monsoon season – the gathered heat, the arguments in markets. How birds panted, open-beaked. Marriages faltered and goats were slaughtered poorly. And as we passed Jarvis's shop, I saw his newspaper board with its headline – it spoke of the approach of war – and I had no words to say. I had no trust to give. I felt too tired to speak or think. I only wanted certainty. A quiet sleep.

We separated after this. George wished to enter the shop, buy a newspaper; I, in turn, longed for a cool, private space in which I could rest. I returned to Shadowbrook and was greeted by the extraordinary bleached white of bedlinen on the washing line. The upper windows were open; through the still curtains, I could see the hanging tapestry and the reading lamp and a movement in keeping with Mr Fox rising from his desk. My first thought, instinctively, was relief. He was back – with his rational thought and his books and his structured days; wouldn't we find an answer now? Also, I thought how hot and airless his south-facing rooms must be after two weeks of having been shuttered and closed. But I supposed that if there was any breeze, it would find him there.

XII

The fair was spoken of that evening. It was Saturday night and the calmer, restored George mentioned it to the maids as we ate. Had there been such a fair before? What might it entail? What was the reason for it?

'Every August bank holiday,' Maud said. 'It's tradition in Barcombe. And all the villagers come.' There'd be dancing and music. A roasting pig. It would last, she said, until midnight or later, and I saw how she glanced up through her fringe at him. 'You'll come?'

'Yes, I hope to come.'

I had no wish to attend the fair. Never mind the physicality of such an event; what reason was there to dance, or sing? War was coming. The newspapers declared it; the garden boys murmured of it as they ate their sandwiches at noon. I knew, too, how it would be. I could not dance. I would not know many people.

Perhaps I had always been different and alone. But I was, now, feeling it more keenly. The rumours of Kit had proved right, it seemed: bad blood, with a tendency to brawl. He only wished to know women who had the perfect feminine form. As for George, he worked in the library with the door ajar, remarked on the teapot that Maud carried to him – yet

I could not forget his temper at Willowbank. The way he'd banged upon the blue-painted door.

There was no one to trust or to speak to. Harriet was finding tasks to perform in the vegetable patch, talking to Albert as he drank water; the vicar remained the vicar, a man of the cloth who had two natures – *I am also a man* – so that I had no wish to find him. As for the garden boys, I did not know them. Saying Veronique's name brought no change at all.

Since there was no housekeeper now, I climbed the stairs at eleven in the morning, made my way down the corridor and tapped on Mr Fox's door. 'Can I talk to you, Mr Fox? It's Miss Waterfield.' I wished to speak of anything. The theory of evolution. Empires. Tapestries. The elegance of his handwriting. But he did not respond or open the door.

Only Hollis remained. I watched him for a while before he saw me. He soaked his handkerchief at the tap in the yard, wrung it out; he returned to the tool shed, settled into his deckchair and laid the handkerchief over his brow with his eyes closed – yet he still sensed me standing there. He opened one eye. 'Ah. Come and sit by an old, tired man.'

I lowered myself onto an upturned crate. Around me, his tools: hoes, trowels, hazel rods, flowerpots and pliers, hammers and nails. An old teacup. A pair of boots whose soles were peeling away.

'It can't last,' he said. 'Everything is wilting. We need a mighty downpour – thundercracks and flashes – and I think it's coming. Can you feel the weight in the air? Smell the rain?'

I looked at him. Eyes closed, with his wet handkerchief. Hands on either side of him. His chin disappeared into his neck's softness and I imagined him sleeping like this. A lifetime of rest in this position.

'Miss Waterfield? Two minutes in my company, and you've not said a word. I can only think you're unwell.'

'Hollis, will you talk to me?'

'Of what?'

'Of her. I know you don't like to and I know you didn't see much. But you've worked here so long . . . Anything.'

He detected my sorrow, perhaps. Or he, too, was so affected by the hot weather that he had no strength to resist my request. He was settled, tired. And with his eyes still closed, he relented. 'This was her weather. Perhaps all weathers were hers because in those later years she was always in the garden, even in rain or high winds. But she'd prefer the summer months. In June and July she'd carry food outside. I'd find books on the arms of benches, as you know. Wet footprints by the bathing pool.'

'What else?'

'What else? Let me think. She'd bring flowers into the house – peonies, most often. Roses. Every Friday morning I'd find my wages wrapped in brown paper and string on my desk in the tool shed – every Friday, without fail – and there'd be a note too, sometimes. Gratitude. She'd tell me how fine the foxgloves were that year, or how delicious the latest blackcurrants had been – those things. She was fond of the topiary trees – the peacocks? She was always grateful for those and would tell me so. And sometimes I'd find a gift of some kind – a feather, or the first plum of the season. I've been thinking of her lately. I know there's been all this talk of her walking in the house, and Mr Lowe has been asking about her as you have been. Your hair, Miss Waterfield, is how she wore hers – unpinned and very long. Have I told you that? Later, it greyed, but she still wore it untied.'

'Was Kit in love with her?'

Hollis opened his eyes. 'Kit? She was thirty years older than him, or more.'

'Then his father loved her, perhaps? Bill. Perhaps he visited Veronique in her room, and . . . '

Hollis removed the damp cloth, tried to sit up. 'Visited . . . ? Oh no, no. Bill hardly saw her. She hardly saw anyone – although she grieved his death when it came, I know that. Many of us grieved him. Bill was a good man, despite what they say.'

'This,' I said, 'makes no sense to me. I thought the families hated each other.' Why might a Preedy be mourned by a Pettigrew?

'Bill hated her brothers, yes. And look at his death on the scaffold: wasn't that proof of how much he loathed them? Or how much he loathed the younger one, at least.'

This was too much. How was it proof? Hollis's words were so fast that I felt as if I was catching water, and I shook my head, blinked rapidly. 'I don't understand you.'

In that moment, Hollis realised that he'd said more than he'd meant to. Or that there was a distance in my understanding that he had not thought to bridge. But there was no stepping back from it. No form of disguise. He wiped his mouth with the back of his hand, very slowly, preparing himself. 'Bill Preedy was hanged for killing a Pettigrew. For killing Hugo, the younger son. I thought you knew this?'

I hadn't known.

He exhaled, shook his head. 'A fight in Stratford-upon-Avon. One punch from Bill. It was enough to snap Hugo's neck and Bill's own neck was snapped soon after. The judge, I suspect, knew the Pettigrews. The manner of his death is what Bill is known for, but it shouldn't be; he was a strong, honest man. And who doesn't make mistakes? We all do.'

I stared. 'Kit never said this.'

'No. Why might he? He hasn't said a word about his loss since the day it happened. That boy ... he thinks that ignoring a feeling will make it lessen, but I doubt it has. He's sealed himself up against every emotion since, it seems, and that's no way to live. Preedy ... that's a name to be proud of. I've told him this, many times, but he won't listen. There's never been bad blood in their veins.'

In my London life, having woken from an opiate sleep to find it was not yet morning, I'd watch the stars. There was little else to be done: I'd be drowsy, too nauseous for books. My mother would sometimes sleep in the chair beside me, and I'd wake her if I was in pain or afraid or thirsty. But mostly I'd look through the curtains at London's version of stars and imagine gathering them. Picking them one by one. And, having picked the brightest stars, I'd form my own ball of bright, extraordinary light which might outshine the moon itself.

These small, shining facts about Veronique. Her brown paper parcels for Hollis. Her enjoyment of plums and the topiary trees. I received them from Hollis and pressed them into the previous knowledge of her – the older stars – so that Veronique became brighter still. But I thought of the Preedys too. I'd known so little of them; now, I thought of vertebrae. I thought of the single punch in Stratford-upon-Avon – one temperamental, drunken act which meant that Bill Preedy's neck was cracked on a rope and his body dropped in an unmarked grave near the Birmingham scaffold. One decision made and his life had ended. One quick act and Kit's life had changed. And I thought, it takes nothing. A second or less.

The farmer made more sense to me now. Trusting

251

nothing. Moving quickly. Saying no more than was needed and seeking no friendships except for those with his horses and a childhood dog. Perhaps this change to his character had come slowly, in the days after Bill's death; or perhaps he'd made a hard, deliberate decision that took a moment or two. Perhaps, on hearing the news, he vowed not to smile or care for others; a conscious choice in the mind of a boy who would not see his father again. I recognised this. But there was, too, a part of it – a single star – that made no sense. For, very simply, wouldn't he loathe them all? If a Pettigrew's death had in turn caused his father's own, he'd find no beauty in Veronique. He'd nod at any dark tales of her, or add to them. And he would not strike a stranger in The Bull for having spoken against her, leaving a bruise on his jawline. If anyone hated the Pettigrews, it would be Kit.

I spent the day in the places I knew she had been. The bathing pool. The iron chair under the limes with its view of the lower garden. George found me here. He looked unsteady, tired.

'I've been looking for you, Clara. I searched the garden and the glasshouse; I've been down in the village, asking if they'd seen you.'

'I've been in the tool shed with Hollis. Why?'

'Mr Fox.'

'You've spoken to him?'

A tight, dissatisfied smile. Frustrated. 'No, I've not. That's what I want to tell you. He will not see me; or rather, he left a note in the kitchen in which he says he wishes to rest before we meet. To rest? I could understand this if he required an hour, or half a day. But I must wait till the weekend, Clara – the weekend. It's Sunday. I have six days to wait?'

His voice was steady, not raised. The brief, furious George of the day before – striking the door – had gone. Yet he was not the same. I could feel the energy in him; I saw him clench and unclench his hands.

'Six days ... which suggests, surely, that this does not matter to him. This talk of ghosts.'

'It matters to him. I know it does.'

'Does it? Then why won't he meet me today, or tomorrow? The last two people I need to speak to – the two most important, it seems – are, as it stands, refusing to meet me. Is a game being played, Clara? I wonder if I shouldn't pack my trunk this afternoon and catch the train and begin a new investigation, in London or elsewhere.'

I held his stare. 'You'd be willing to leave without having solved this? Without finding proof, or an answer? You promised the maids.'

He stared at the ground for a time. Then he looked up into the limes, saw the sunlight through their leaves. Whilst noticing this, he answered. It was a softer, private voice. 'I think I have an answer.'

I thought I had misheard him. 'An answer? You have proof of Veronique?'

He rubbed his eyelids, exhaled. He had an air of defeat to him and when he looked back at me, I saw sorrow, briefly. Regret in this wise, symmetrical face. 'It is an answer, Clara, yes. But it's not the one I hoped to find.'

We walked for a time, stopped near the glasshouse, for it had filled itself. Blooms had opened too far, folded back on themselves. Vines had pushed their way through the vents, climbed into the open. Pollen had smeared the glass.

'When I met you, we discussed my job, didn't we? And we talked of what the findings could be: a natural, explainable occurrence, such as a change in temperature or a rusting of pipes; a human trick, deliberately done; or something without scientific explanation – ghosts, in short. Three outcomes. We talked of that. Clara, what if I told you that I believe it was none of those things? That there is a fourth possibility?'

I dismissed this. 'What else is there?'

'Misconception. Longing. Human work, yes, but without malicious intent. Accidental human work, in effect. Do you remember our first walk through the gardens? I told you – in the white garden, I believe it was – of human flaws, of humans being such imperfect, fallible creatures. Oh, we are. I've seen it elsewhere. We can forget or misinterpret. We can be so ill that we believe we see what is in fact a product of our fever – a hallucination, a dream. We can want something with such intensity that we can convince ourselves it is happening or has happened.'

'No.'

'Listen to me. I have not met Eleanor Bale, of course – but I have learned about her from you and others. A widow of sixteen months or so. Who married at eighteen years old – thirty-four years of marriage, I was told – which means that her entire adult life was spent as his wife. She was his nurse too, I think? Tuberculosis? That's a wretched disease both to have and to witness. I can't know what her married life was like. But I have looked in her room. In it, I found a romantic novel with the corners of pages folded where there's the most impassioned talk of love. I saw the wooden crucifix, which tells me she already believes in souls, and in life after death. And does she like to talk? An imagination: you said this yourself. A dramatic nature. A gossiper.'

'Are you saying that she imagined what happened here?

That's nonsense. She didn't. I heard the footsteps too. The mark on her door is no hallucination.'

'No, I'm not saying that she imagined it.' He paused.

'*She* did this? All of it? Oh, you're wrong.'

'I know how it sounds. But I've seen this before: a need for comfort. People see what they want to see. For is there a greater desolation in this life than losing who we love? A greater longing than to have them come back? You and I both understand that. Sometimes people are fully aware of their actions: they are perfectly lucid and aware of their deceit. But other times, they aren't aware at all. Mrs Bale? I'm saying that she *was* the footsteps, that those footsteps you heard were hers. That those picture frames broke because she chose to throw them. I'm saying that she carved the V into her door of her own volition because she is desperate to believe that her husband is not gone, that she is not alone. An undead Veronique – or any ghost – would suggest this to her. And Clara, I am certain that she performed these acts in a half-dreaming state, that it's only now, away from Shadowbrook, that she can truly understand what she's done. Which is why she won't see me. Why she won't see you.'

'No. Because when I heard the tapping on my door, I opened it immediately and there was no one there. I'd have seen her.'

'She knows the house, does she not? Its shadows and weaknesses? And she is quick, you say, in her movements. Maybe she crouched down by the hatstand. Or pressed herself into an alcove. Or she understood the sight lines of the corridor so well that she was, in fact, still there and you simply didn't see her. How well did you search the hallway that night? Be honest.'

'Very well,' I snapped. But I felt a deep, awful turning in my belly; an unease which came from knowing that I had not perhaps searched very well that night. I had not checked every corner. 'And what of her arm? Are you suggesting she broke it deliberately?'

'No, I'm saying that she probably didn't break it at all. She only thought she had. Just as she only thought she'd seen a ghost upstairs. You understand that she didn't choose to fool you? That it wasn't a deliberate trick? But the human brain is a curious organ. And her distress would have been entirely real to her. Her sleeplessness and her longing for peace.'

'There,' I said, pointing a finger, 'is the flaw in your logic. For if she was longing for peace, why invent a concept that terrified her? Why cause her own trouble?'

'Veronique might have frightened her, yes. But a part of her was finding peace from it, too, for a ghost would mean an afterlife. Clara, I think she's a little like you.'

'She is nothing like me.'

'But you and she both want there to be a ghost at Shadowbrook, and for the same reason. Can't you see?'

I felt I lacked my body. As if all my organs had instantaneously been removed, so that I was made of air and had no substance. This sensation translated to my face, perhaps. For George came closer, laid his hand on my forearm. 'Listen. Look at me, Clara. This does not mean there's nothing else. It doesn't mean there's no soul. And I'm not saying that our mothers haven't taken some other form or that there's no residue of their bodily life. Do you hear me? I'm not saying that. Only that here, in Shadowbrook, I think it was all Mrs Bale's own work.'

'You haven't,' I said, 'even seen her. You haven't heard her version of it. Or Mr Fox's.' I paused, unable to catch my breath.

He came closer, spoke very quietly. 'This is what I believe has been happening here.'

'No.' I stepped back. 'I know this isn't true.'

'How do you know?'

'Because Mrs Bale is no fool. A widow, yes, and she might read romance novels and show her emotions – but she's not deluded. You didn't see her fear. That was real. And what of the doctor who wrapped her arm in a sling that morning? Surely he'd have noticed if it had been fine, and not broken? And Mr Fox, too. Let me tell you that he is a learned, rational man who had applied every scientific explanation to these events at Shadowbrook, and yet none has been enough. By his own admission, they have not given an answer. His blankets were pulled from his bed! I told you this. Who could imagine such a thing, and believe it?'

'You said he took a light sedative. An opiate of some kind? Clara, I looked for the truth and I think I've found it.'

'You haven't found it.'

His expression was new. It was, partly, tender; his head was tilted very slightly and he gave a faint, sorrowing smile. But there was a studiousness too. He looked at different parts of me: my collarbone, the discoloration of my eyes. He looked at my brow and, briefly, my mouth – and I protested again that he hadn't found the truth; this was not the answer. You are, I told him, wrong. But now I heard the weakness to my voice. He also heard it and came nearer, hushing me softly as it I was a child. He laid his hand on the side of my face. 'Clara . . . ' he said. But I stepped back – outraged, tearful, afraid – and stumbled into the depths of the garden whilst George called my name, asking me to come back.

Rain in the air. And I was two Claras. Firstly, I was furious. Unprepared to believe a single word of George's answer:

it was uninformed, foolish. It was wrong – and this Clara muttered this to herself as she hurried.

But the second Clara had heard *longing* and could not be rid of it. It was the emotion I knew more than any other: to want something and to carry this want like a physical object – a stone or a coin. For I'd spent eighteen years wanting to venture outside into the blustery, bright, complicated world of landscape and museums and people. I'd wanted to replace the structure of me with something better – bones that served their function. And the pain? I'd begged for it to stop, at times. Reached out with both hands for the tincture or for my mother, as children do.

And since her death, I'd not stopped longing for her. None of my efforts had lessened how much I missed her. And whilst I'd tried to hide or contain that longing, it was so hard to do when I thought of her constantly. So much named my loss. A rose's shade matched the Empire's pink on the globe that she used to spin for me; in the potting shed, a shaft of dusty light reminded me of how she'd move her hand through such shafts in evening rooms. And I longed for her face all the time. I longed for it now, with the first drop of rain on the back of my hand in the garden that I'd used for comfort. I could imagine her – holding out a palm to check that yes, she had felt rain; she had not been mistaken.

A single low rumble of thunder moved from west to east. There was ten seconds, perhaps, of the rain strengthening, in which the garden either closed in on itself or opened in preparation. And then the downpour was absolute. It was force and draught and saturation. I had been dry; now, my hair stuck against my cheeks, and my dress, as I walked, made its own slapping sound.

I should not have been here, with grass like a polished floor and a loss of visibility and the cane slipping under my weight. Yet I did not want to go indoors. I wanted to be *in* it: this purpled, trembling garden which, momentarily, would be struck with light. I wanted my own monsoon. To be clean of the loss and uncertainty and permanent tiredness. And as I stood on the croquet lawn and looked back at the house, I thought: show yourself. I wanted to see her – just once, and briefly. Now was the time for her to appear; more than ever, it was now. So I stared at an upstairs window and with each lightning flash, I asked that I'd suddenly see Veronique's ghost in the window, formed and undeniable.

I imagined her perfectly. But I knew that imagining her was not enough. I knew that a dream faded on waking. And as it rained, I heard the old London Clara. The scientific, certain girl with her own library stepped forwards and spoke clearly. I heard her through the downpour and the thunder's roll. Show him the proof, she ordered. Go inside.

I returned to the house in my wet, clapping dress. Printed the floor of the drawing room.

The grandfather clock was striking eight times as I opened my bedside drawer. The locket stared back at me like a silver eye – bright, perfect, with a weight and shape that felt right in my hand and a V like a wing or a mark of approval. Didn't it have to be hers? Veronique's? No wedding ring inside it and no lock of a child's hair. A pendant that had been hers alone, as her life had been.

The herb garden was, briefly, illuminated.

I banged on George's door with my cane. He opened it very quickly, as if he'd been standing behind it. His expression was, firstly, one of surprise; he opened his mouth to greet me. But then he looked down. Saw my dress wrapped around me like a second skin. Me, pooling water.

'You've been outside all this time? In this? Clara, what the hell—'

I held out my closed fist. At first, he didn't look at it. He only noted my darkened hem, how I sniffed to remove a drip of rainwater. 'Look,' I said, hard, commanding him. He frowned, glanced down. Slowly he cupped his hands beneath my fist so that I could loosen my grasp, allow the locket to fall to him.

'What is it?' He kept his hands close to his body, as if the gift might leap or take flight. And on opening them, he stilled. Said nothing.

'It's a locket. Silver. I found it on the night of the accident. I went upstairs afterwards and it was on the staircase. Look at the back. *V.* See it?'

George took a single step back. He seemed to lose his balance, rested against the door frame.

'Does this change your answer? George, it's hers. Veronique was there.'

With that, lightning came again. It flashed three times in quick succession; three brief, illuminated moments in which I saw us perfectly. He was cupping the locket in both hands; it seemed as if he'd struck a match and was protecting the flame from draughts or my breath, and I asked again: *Does this change your answer?*

His eyes were as round as the locket itself, and as bright. Yes, he said.

XIII

The storm lasted all night. The thunder, at its loudest, rattled the handles of furniture and shifted the windows in their casements – and I did not sleep. I thought of the storms my mother must have seen in her homeland. I thought of George in his own room, awake, with the silver pendant.

In the morning, the house was still. I lifted my soaked dress from the floor, carried it into the courtyard and laid it out to dry. Even the birds seemed quiet. The roses hung away from the wall; leaves shone. The air smelled of damp and greenery, and I stood for a long time.

In the end, Harriet appeared – but she too did this sound-lessly. She stepped into the courtyard with one hand shielding her eyes against the reflecting light and she did not see me at all at first. No apron. She was in a dress I hadn't seen before – green, with petticoats. Also her hair was untied so that I saw its true colour, how it curled at its ends, and with this I remembered the day. 'Harriet?'

She came closer. 'Did you sleep at all? I didn't. The noise of it! Albert says a tree was struck on the Moreton road and caught fire. There'll be flooding, I'm sure. Look at these roses.'

The Rêve d'Or had pulled away from the house in places. Its heavier blooms had lost their petals, but I looked beyond the roses to the upper floor. His windows were closed. The shutters were drawn against the daylight. 'Where's Mr Fox?'

'Gone. He must have left before dawn – whilst it was still raining, perhaps – for I found a note on the trestle table when I took his morning tea to him.'

'Gone? What did the note say?'

'That he had urgent business to attend to.' She shrugged.

'On a bank holiday? And he's only just arrived here.' Shadowbrook, I thought, was barely his home at all. Mr Fox was an insect that brushed against its windows before leaving again; his company was transient – and George, I knew, would be frustrated to learn this. He'd been told to wait six days, and now? 'What of the others?'

'Maud left at first light. I think the storm scared her and she wanted to be with her family, although she wouldn't admit this. Mr Lowe has gone too.'

'George has gone?' I stared back at her. All of them had lifted themselves up, opened their wings and flown away? 'When?'

'Ten minutes ago, maybe. I don't think he'd slept either. He looked very pale, rather strange, in fact, and he said he'd be away all day. That he had telephone calls to make to his society. Something has come to light; those were his exact words. He called it unprecedented but he wouldn't say any more to me. What has he found? Do you know?'

I shook my head. 'He'll be away all day?'

'He said he'd be back by the evening, for the fair. Miss Waterfield? I can stay here tonight if you'd like me to. I was going to stay with my family but I can come back.'

'Stay?' I frowned, confused by this.

'With Maud and Mr Fox elsewhere, it will be just you and Mr Lowe here tonight. People will talk, you know that. If you'd like me to stay, I will.'

A chaperone. Three years younger than me. Freckled and prepared. Yet I supposed she'd prefer, by far, to be dancing with Albert tonight; to be watching him over the fire as he, in turn, watched her. 'No need,' I told her. 'They'll talk anyway.'

She took leave of me. And with the holiday, I knew no one else would come. The house would stay empty. The garden would stay still.

The night's rain had caught in hollows, in lupin leaves. Cobwebs were so bright that I might wear them. The water level in the bathing pool had risen by several inches; everything dripped, and if I stood still, I could hear rushing water. I followed this sound, looked down into the lower garden; its stream had swelled over, covered the hostas and ferns, and was parting round stones and joining again. A drinking world. And in this way, it felt cleaner.

Yet there was no denying the losses that the storm had caused: broken stems, the splaying of bushes. Petals lay discarded under flowerless plants. And the barley, too: I looked over the wall and saw that it had suffered. It was disordered, darker in colour. In parts it had been flattened entirely as if something had wandered into it and I wondered what this meant for the farmer, if he'd already walked his boundaries at daybreak and seen the damage. If so, I knew he'd have crouched to feel the barley, to assess his financial loss by its weight or texture. Having stood, he'd have kicked a stone or slashed the side of his hand through the remaining crop in frustration. I wanted to find him then. I wanted to walk through the soaked longer grass that bordered his land, find him and tell him that his father was not, in fact, fully dead. That a grave only held the bones, and not what truly mattered.

But I could not see him. *Keep away from me.* There was no fighting against such a command. And despite the world's newness and deep, damp fragrance and the proof of Veronique, I felt a terrible ache.

The churchyard had mostly escaped the storm. Its yew trees had sheltered it; their branches dripped, so that I passed under curtains of raindrops as I entered. I was not sure, at first, why I'd come; I had no intention of standing beside the Pettigrew grave or of entering the church itself. But I found myself walking around the building with purpose until I came to a line of smaller, roughly hewn gravestones, all of which bore the name Preedy. No brambles. There were dandelions and ivy, but not of such thickness that they obscured the lettering. Here they were. Preedys from centuries before: Nathaniel Preedy had been born in 1643; Rose Preedy had lived for two years and nine months; Emily Preedy, née Bliss, had died in her twenties, thirty-seven years ago, so I knew I had found Kit's own mother, and I felt like greeting her softly. There was a grave, too, which spoke of a married couple who must have been Kit's uncle and aunt for their deaths had been at the century's end, which suited my knowledge of him. And I thought, these are his people. The ones who made and raised him. Or these are their bones, at least.

I wondered if he ever came here. There were the indentations of boots in the earth; there was an absence of moss on the gravestones, as if someone had picked it away – and this was, perhaps, his doing.

'Miss Waterfield?'

I turned too quickly. I thought *Kit* and stumbled, and the vicar's eyes widened; he stepped forwards.

'I startled you. Are you hurt?'

'Not hurt.' Matthew, too, had not slept; this was immediately

264

clear. The skin beneath his eyes had the appearance of having been plucked and held; he was slow in every movement he made.

'Did you hear the storm? The village green looks very different. The bunting has been brought down by it and there's been a little flooding; the earth's too hard to absorb the rain entirely. But I trust it will be gone by this evening; it would be hard to dance a jig in water.' But he saw, then, my expression. 'Has something happened?'

I answered simply. 'She isn't fully dead.'

Briefly, he bit his lower lip. Then he released it, cleared his throat. 'Do you mean Veronique?'

'Yes. She's not dead. She's at Shadowbrook. She walks, still.'

'Walks?'

'Not lately. But she's still there, Matthew. Her ghost is in the house.'

I tried to smile. For this was, surely, good news to him: I had become a believer. I'd moved into believing what he had spoken of by the portico once – of souls, and continuation. And, therefore, I expected him to smile back; I thought he might raise his brows a little or laugh. But instead, he made an unexpected sound. He removed his spectacles, placed his left hand over his eyes and inhaled very quickly, as if surfacing. He seemed unsteady. 'God help me,' he said.

'Are you unwell?'

'Unwell? Perhaps I am. Or perhaps I have been.' He removed his hand, replaced his spectacles. 'I have asked myself many, many times what is right. The right thing; what is the right thing to do? And I have had two answers. I have moved between them so that I wake and think that I have decided: *this* answer. But then I see you, Clara, or I hear rumours of Shadowbrook, and I doubt myself, lean towards

265

the other answer. I told you I would not share the confessions of others, didn't I? I still can't. But I am going to tell you this, at least: go to Mrs Bale. Knock on her door.'

This seemed like madness. 'Why?'

'Because I'm asking you to.'

I adjusted my stance. 'She won't see me; you know that. Nor would she see George.'

'Go back. Knock again. Demand to be seen. Tell Elspeth ...'

'Tell Elspeth what? She won't let me in.'

Matthew pressed his hands together. He clutched them, as if in prayer, raised them to his mouth, and he held this posture for enough time for me to sense that something was coming that mattered; that his following words would have significance. He lowered his hands. 'I want you to know,' he said, 'that what I'm about to tell you doesn't alter what you have come to believe. There are souls, I have no doubt of this; there is a life beyond this one, and yes, we are far more than bones. But I fear it will change your views on me, whatever they are presently. Her arm is not broken and never was.'

'It was. How she whimpered and held the break against her. The doctor came.'

'She pretended. And there was no doctor. Eleanor tied the sling herself.'

'Is it because she's heartbroken? Grieving her husband still?'

'Heartbroken? No. Clara, I can't tell you more. But she can, and she must. By God, she must. I won't do this any more.'

The rain had pulled the rose away from the front of Willowbank so that I had to bend to pass underneath it. On the ground, a thousand petals; brown and pink.

Elspeth answered as she had done before; sharply, with the door as protection. 'She slept poorly with the storm. She won't see you.' Her hand grasped the door so hard that her fingertips had blanched with the effort.

'I know her arm is not broken.'

Her eyes rounded childishly. She adjusted her grasp. And she parted her lips to speak, but the voice that came was not hers; it was a voice I'd heard before; a voice which had had, in the past, a tendency to pour out words like water, to fill a room with her tales and thoughts. 'Elspeth . . . ' it said, coaxing her.

The door widened, and Mrs Bale came to her sister's side. I might not have recognised her if we had met elsewhere, for she seemed so much older. There was a greyness to her – her skin was matt, unreflective – and yet she wore clothes that seemed brighter and which I could not have imagined her wearing in Shadowbrook House: a cream blouse with pearl-seed buttons; a green skirt with a polka-dot print. On her feet she wore slippers – pink, with bows. And her hair, too, had altered. It was no longer plaited. It was loose, and it fell over both shoulders. No sling.

'Hello, Clara,' she said. 'I knew this would happen. I didn't know when, of course, but you are too smart to have never guessed it.' She laid her right hand on her sister's left shoulder. 'Let her come in.'

The room was homely. Crocheted blankets were folded over the arms of chairs; cushions held the impressions of heads, or lower backs. On the shelves there were ornaments – of bone china, or glass, or lace – and it felt like a feminine, secret place, so that I could imagine her here. Reading, in the evenings. Missing her husband so much that it hurt her.

Mrs Bale offered me a chair. She sat herself down opposite me, crossed her ankles.

Next door, a kettle's sound.

'How did you know about my arm? I thought you suspected that night, in fact. You, the queen of fractures. When I first saw your cane and learned of your condition, I wondered how on earth I might convince you; I wondered if I should try for something else – a sprain, or a physical cut that I might perform on myself. But it had to be a break; it had to be enough to send me away from there. You don't understand, of course. How could you? It was important that you couldn't, that you'd be fooled – as you were for a time, at least.'

I stared, speechless. Elspeth set down a tray. She did this with precision: the teapot, two cups on saucers, milk. She returned with two slices of buttered fruit loaf and, having set them down, left without words. Eleanor watched her go.

'Elspeth is younger by seven years. As children, that difference in age felt like an ocean to me. She was a baby; she was always too young to be played with, and too slow, and I had no wish to care for her. I wanted to be rid of her, in truth. Now, I'd be lost without her. And in these past two weeks, she has been like a mother to me.' She lifted the teapot, poured. 'She's a widow too. There was a farming accident near Moreton ten years ago this autumn and he bled to death. Can you imagine? Harvesting. He set off to work that morning whistling, with his lunch in his coat pocket; by evening he was in the undertaker's in a box, empty of blood and seeming half his size. Of course, the real difference is that Elspeth loved him. The shock nearly took her away. She mourned her husband and mourns him still. He was a good man.'

I flinched. 'But your husband was a good man. You're still grieving.'

She looked up. 'Was he? Am I? What has made you think this? If there are stories of his goodness in Barcombe, I've not heard them. And if I had heard any, I'd have corrected them promptly, for whilst my husband was not a bad man, Clara, I can't tell you honestly that he was good. If I've mourned at all, it has been for the life I lost when I married him. I've mourned the life I might have had if I'd been stronger, defiant and had married elsewhere or not married at all. I still wonder, you know, the other path I might have wandered down ... You saw that, I think, when I talked of Africa with you, and foreign places. But never mind; I know you haven't come to hear about my old daydreams.'

She offered me a cup of tea with a firm, confident hand. 'I want you to know that I have taken no pleasure in a single part of this. Before I tell you more, I wish to state that very clearly. It's true that I've not been sleeping.'

I watched her. How she stirred her tea, tapped the cup twice with the spoon.

'How much do you know about love, Clara? I mean of romantic love. I have heard rumours about you, of course. Even here at Willowbank, the whispers find me. I've heard the change in Matthew's voice when he speaks of you. Heavens, I saw his blush when you entered my room that morning – in your nightdress, child! – so I've been aware of his interest, at least. I heard, too, that the London gentleman made claims in The Bull a few nights ago that were not, in fact, too gentlemanly. Yet' – she sipped her tea – 'these are the feelings of others. What of *your* heart, Miss Waterfield? Have you loved?

'Of course, you are twenty years old. Even if you were to claim that yes, you knew love absolutely, I wouldn't believe you. I do not mean that cruelly, you understand. Love has merely not acquired its proper weight or meaning at your age. You cannot understand it fully – or feel it fully – until there has been loss and disappointment and more broken things than bones alone. You can't know what it was like to be in that marriage. Ernest never struck me. For that, I suppose I am lucky; I know of other wives who, even now, claim they are perfectly fine but we all know better and see their stiff movements. But there was no love, Clara, none. We married ... oh, who knows why. For propriety's sake, perhaps. Because I'd been called a plain child and I wanted to prove that I could still be desired. But I wasn't desired. And whatever his reasons for marrying me, they weren't affection.

'It was a dull marriage. It had a single, established routine which lasted for three decades, in which I starched his collars and swept his hearth and plucked hens for roasting and he, in return, either worked or smoked his pipe in his chair. Those were his two occupations. No word of thanks, either. But then, of course, he began to have the symptoms: a cough that would not lessen; fiery sweats at night, even in winter with a frost on the ground. He grew thinner, too, so that his cheeks dropped inwards. And only *then*' – she raised a finger – 'did he want my company. *Then* he wanted my help. To speak to me.' She paused, sipped her tea.

'Why did you stay? If you weren't happy?' But I knew.

'Money. Decency. What might I have done if I'd left him? How might I have lived or been treated by others? So I stayed. And I was dutiful in his illness. I nursed him. Prayed. I sat by his bedside with my embroidery when he feared death would take him; he had a notion, I think, that my presence might be enough to keep it away in the same way I'd kept away mice or silence – although it wasn't, of course. In his last hours, he looked so small and afraid. No longer the broad, muttering man, but an infant. And I felt, briefly, tenderness. I held his hand. I offered words from the Bible – *Even though I walk in the shadow of the valley of death, I will fear no evil, for You are with me* – and I dabbed his brow with a damp cloth. All I craved, then, was an apology. Or an acknowledgement between us that our marriage had not been a good one for either of us – distant, and hollow – because that in itself would have felt like intimacy; it would have felt honest, just for a second or two. But Ernest's last words were of complaint. And at his graveside, I thought of the thirty-four years of my life that I'd given him. Of the thirty-four years I had wasted on a man who wasn't bad, as such, but I rather think he'd have preferred a dog for company.' She paused, looked at the wall. 'Thirty-four ... That's not far from two of your lifetimes, child. Still. I could not change it. It was done.'

'And then you came to Shadowbrook.'

She corrected me. 'To Willowbank. And within a few months, yes, I began to work at Shadowbrook – for a man who was considerate, polite, grateful for each small task that I performed and each meal I made. He complimented my soups. He said he'd assumed I was far younger than my age. And he asked a little about myself, from time to time. Which season did I prefer? What were my views on our King? And let me tell you, Clara, that it was like rain after hot desert weather. It was ... ' She shrugged. 'It was more than I can explain to you. How can I expect you to understand what it is like to be old and tired and plain, only for a gentleman to ask me if I like roses? Or to request a tale from my childhood? He was a cool drink. He was a new view. And the gratitude I had ... I would have done whatever he asked of me. I'd have reached for the moon and stars. I lied because he asked me to.'

This was a world away from what I had believed of her. Servitude in her marriage? Yes, I had expected that; the duty of provision, the demure agreements and wifely lack of complaint were not surprises to me. But the emptiness. The cave in which nothing echoed. I had not expected this. I'd thought she'd been a happy wife.

'So you love him. Mr Fox.'

Mrs Bale lowered her teacup. 'Yes. I love him.'

'And he asked you to lie?'

'He did. There was never a ghost at Shadowbrook, you see.'

'You're wrong. There was a ghost. There *is*. She is Veronique.'

'Oh, child. She lived, Clara; she was real in that sense. She and her brothers and all the wretched Pettigrews were perfectly real – oh yes. But a ghost?' She shook her head. 'That was our doing. And we must have done it well to have convinced you, of all people! He wished for a ghost – for a poltergeist, one that the whole county might hear and talk of – and he asked if I might assist in the creation of it. I did, of course. We made our plans and took our time. I began my whispers at church – of a broken picture frame or a curious creaking at night. I asked others about Veronique and allowed them to have their own quiet thoughts. There was no hurrying this stage; it had to be carefully done for the rumour to take seed. For it to grow.'

She eyed me. 'I thought you'd guess, of course. You arrived with such boldness, such an enquiring mind – all those questions! And you announced with such fire and certainty that there were no ghosts, that this was human work. Well, we hadn't imagined such a creature as you, that's for certain. I felt sure you'd ruin our plan within days.'

'The footsteps were yours.'

'Yes, they were mine. I'd stay awake until two or three in the morning, creep out. Certain parts of the staircase make no sound at all when trodden on; others creak like a ship in a storm and so I could walk up and down those stairs as I chose to – either heard or unheard. Whichever was required. As for the flowers in the vases, I snapped them myself. Added milk to their water. It's a neat trick and works well, I think.'

She spoke so casually. She said these words like they didn't matter, when they meant everything. I felt towers collapsing, water washing the ground away from under me, and here she was, with her floral teapot and dainty slippers. 'And what of the maids? Did they know?'

With this, Mrs Bale looked down. She brushed an invisible mark from her skirt. 'They knew nothing of it. They still don't. The girls came to Shadowbrook in the early days. Plates had already fallen from shelves in empty rooms by then – or supposedly, of course; door handles had been tried by an invisible hand. They were part of the plan without knowing it. Harriet is an excellent maid and we are lucky to have her; she was hired because of her good work. But Maud? You've seen. She is reluctant and inattentive, but she is also dramatic and comes from a family who need gossip as others need air to live. And so Mr Fox hired her. What better than a maid for whom a dropped vase is a catastrophe? Or for whom a marked door is the end of the world? She was quick to believe that the house was haunted; she told her family of this, and they in turn ... Well, Maud did my job for me in that respect. She can't sweep properly or boil an egg, but she has proved perfectly adept at telling tales of the trouble at Shadowbrook.'

I tightened my grasp on my cane. 'You carved your own door? Really?'

'Yes. With the vegetable knife. Quietly, of course, for I did not wish the girls to hear. Then in the morning I said, oh, have you seen? Did you hear? And I feigned my distress and they believed it entirely.'

'How could you do that to them? Deceive them like that? Thou shalt not lie, surely. Aren't there a hundred Bible verses which talk of being kind to one's neighbours and strangers? Don't you know how frightened the maids have been? You speak as if you are proud of this when you should not be proud. You should be terribly ashamed; you should be on your knees!'

At that, Eleanor rose. She moved across to the window with a fast, decisive rustle of skirts. 'There she is, the superior Clara. I'm not proud. Deceiving the village? Oh, I could lie to them without pricking my conscience. I only gave them what they all wished for; they scratch the ground looking for stories as hens seek grain in the dust. But to lie to the maids? And to you, Clara? No matter that you can speak sharply; I can see – we can all see, I suspect – that you speak in this fashion to compensate for your bones and losses, and I'm sorry that you've endured what you have. I admire your bravery. Your decision to live as you do, unmarried. So no, I'm not proud of having lied to you and the maids. Not at all.'

Here she was. Fifty-four years old, in her pale-pink slippers. And yet these slippers were the only part of her that seemed girlish now. She talked boldly, with emphasis. And she talked of love as if she knew it all and as if love excused her actions – yet where was he? Where was the man she loved? He was not sitting here beside her. There could be, I knew, inequality in sentiment.

A carriage clock pinged the hour. Four o'clock.

'Why?'

'Why?' She looked at me.

'Yes. Why do it? For love, you said. But why did Mr Fox ask you at all? What was the purpose of making a ghost?'

Mrs Bale did not answer for a while. She returned from the window, lowered herself back down in the chair. We had not eaten the fruit loaf; a single bead of milk hung on the lip of the patterned milk jug. And far away – beyond the blue door and the humpbacked bridge – I heard the first sounds of music coming from the village green that told me the fair was beginning. At last she said, very simply, 'I don't know.'

'Nonsense. You must.'

'I do not, although I don't blame you for being suspicious of this. I know how it must sound, and I've shown that I'm capable of a lie, that's true. But Mr Fox has never told me. I asked him once. Last autumn, I asked him in the beech-woods; I turned to face him and asked what we were lying for. Why we wanted to create the myth of a ghost.'

'And he gave no answer?'

'He said he would not tell me. That it was a very private matter, that it would be far better for me if I simply did not know. Trust me, Ellie, he said. And I did. But he did make one promise to me that day. He promised that there was no malice in it; that any unkindness or distress that might be caused by the lie would be redeemed by its outcome.'

'Its outcome?'

'I don't know,' she said, 'what its outcome will be.'

She sat quietly. She sniffed once; for a time, she kneaded the palm of her hand. And as she did so, I considered her wedding ring – so embedded into her flesh that all the soap in the world might not remove it. A ring that did not speak of love but of decades of carrying bowls of warm water and ironing clothes and other, unacknowledged wifely duties. One day I might feel sympathy for her. But I did not feel it yet.

Fox. Like cool water, she said. A man whose favoured stance was with his heels together, hands behind his back. Brisk and efficient, always – and, it seemed, a talented fraud. For on meeting him, I'd thought him to be the first decent, rational person; I'd noted *On the Origin of Species*.

'Who else knows? That you and he are liars?'

She straightened herself, disliking my tone. 'Matthew. Yes. I know you must marvel at the cross I wear now. Yet I have lost count of the times that Matthew – kind man – has sat in the chair you are now sitting in, leaning forwards as I've confessed to him. The patience of him! For my confessions have all been the same, you see: that I am lying, and might he absolve me? Might God forgive me?'

'And does he absolve you? Matthew?'

'How can he? When I tell him that, despite my guilt, I have every intention of continuing to lie. It's troubled him greatly, I know that. He has counselled me to speak the truth at last, since it's only by speaking honestly that I can be truly forgiven by God. But I have not been ready to do that. Until now, that is.'

I understood it then. My realisation rushed in like water: Matthew's nervousness, his dual nature. His stillness on finding me by the Pettigrew tomb was because he knew that this girl – crippled and knee-high in brambles – was being lied to. Fooled from the start by the Shadowbrook pair. And yet what could he do? Without breaking his confessional code? *I am also a man.*

I looked out of the window. Through trees, I could see farmland; but I could see, too, how Matthew had stood in Mrs Bale's room that morning, leaning against the wall, fixing his eyes on the ground. His silence. His blush. His frustration in knowing that the arm was not, in fact, broken. And why hadn't he told me? What might have followed if he had? I felt furious, foolish. *Are you shaken?* he'd asked me. Hiding his guilt in false concern.

'There is,' she said, 'one more thing I should tell you. Perhaps it is not my news to tell, but I think it may matter. I'm speaking candidly now. Clara, I told you that I applied to work at Shadowbrook House, didn't I? That isn't quite true. He came to me. He wrote to me on gold-headed paper and asked if I might work for him. Me – old and tired. There are far better housekeepers, of course. Younger ones. Yet he chose me. Do you know why?'

I had no wish to guess. Refused to look at her.

'He'd heard of Ernest, my husband. He'd bought Shadowbrook and heard of a man who'd died the previous winter, and he wished to know more. How long had my husband been ill for? Had I cared for him on my own? Had I also had blood in my spittle or any manner of cough? Those questions. Do you see? I think you do; your expression has darkened further. I was not only Mr Fox's housekeeper, just as I was far more than a wife. I am neither young nor beautiful, I cannot reach the higher cobwebs and I cook simple food – but I know how to nurse.'

'Mr Fox has tuberculosis.'

'Yes, he does. It is advanced, too – he is not, I'm afraid, a well man. It is why his windows have been open so much; it's why he does not come downstairs and why he has been adamant that no one should venture to the upper floor unless there is a need to. And you thought he was rude, didn't you? Heartless, on the night I fell?' She shook her head. 'He's not like that. He's very aware of what he carries inside him, and how it might pass from lung to lung.'

'And you? What of your lungs?'

'If there is proof of God, in my eyes, it comes in the fact that I breathed the same air as my husband for all that time and yet I have not coughed once. Is that not divine intervention? A reward, perhaps, for the service I gave?' She looked down at her cross, fingered it. 'Mr Fox heard of this. Supposed that I was either resistant to the disease or I had it already and it lay dormant, as it can do. And I knew, of course, what he needed. So yes, he chose me.'

'You took the meals to him.'

'Yes.'

'And the bedlinen. There is always linen being boiled or pressed.'

'The night fevers, Clara. The sweat can be so much that it takes all my strength to carry those sheets downstairs before the maids wake.'

'And the maids have not guessed? When they're out in the yard, scrubbing his linen for the tenth time?'

A shrug. 'He is particular about his bedding. No more than that.'

So many lies. A garden of them, in bud for so long, but now these lies were riotous and entwined and I hated them. 'I trusted him. I believed him when he mentioned his bed sheets being pulled away, and everything else. Do you know where he's gone, Mrs Bale? Because a man with tuberculosis can't have urgent business to attend to.'

'There is a sanatorium on the Oxfordshire border. One of the very best. He bought Shadowbrook to be near it.'

'And he is there now?'

'Yes. If he's not at Shadowbrook, it's the only place he could be.'

Mrs Bale left me for a while. She rose, carried the tray back into the kitchen and I heard her speak to her sister in a soft, familiar tone. In her absence, I noted the room. The crocheted blanket. The small framed watercolour of a wood with bluebells in it. A porcelain figurine.

I could have broken this figurine with my anger. Swept the trinkets from their shelves. But I also could have cried. I could have entered the kitchen and begged her: *tell me you're wrong.* But I chose to rise, to walk through into the afternoon light where I found the two sisters standing near the sink.

'Why Veronique?' I asked. 'Why didn't you choose one of the brothers to emulate? Or make Mortimer the ghost, with his gun and his appetite?'

This question seemed strange to Eleanor. 'Because of how she lived. Because she is buried where she is. And because it's such women – those who break rules and act disgracefully – that we do not forget.'

We regarded one another as challengers might.

I told her I would not forgive her for this deceit, ever. And I left the house, walked down the lane.

I followed the music – over the humpbacked bridge and down. It was not quite dusk, but the fire was already burning. There were lanterns edging the village green. And there were more people than I'd ever seen in Barcombe before: a group of fiddlers played; a bearded man I'd seen once outside The Bull, chewing tobacco, struck a drum with his hands, and there was dancing and cider and clapping in time and laughter and everyone was brighter, on one side, with firelight.

Nothing felt the same. The landscape seemed tilted; I felt a need to reach for anchored things – a fence post or stone wall – and there was not enough air in my lungs so that I paused by the sign which said Barcombe-on-the-Hill and bent at the waist, breathed in. To have been lied to. To have been fooled so emphatically.

I wished to tell George all of this. Also, for him to sit beside me and speak of the silver locket which was still, surely, a form of proof. No ghost at all? But Veronique's locket remained; I moved through the crowds, looking for him. I moved between people as I'd move between trees, my palms raised but not touching them. Some people stepped aside to let me past; others remained rooted, looked down. And I heard the old words. *Cripple. That's her.*

Matthew was there, his spectacles reflecting the fire's glow – and momentarily I thought to go to him. But he, too, had been part of the lie. I neither trusted nor liked him for it. And as for Harriet – kind, oblivious Harriet, who'd thought to chaperone me and had offered raspberries and who was, at that moment, talking to Albert near the ancient oak – what could I tell her? How? She was twisting a strand of her hair as she spoke. Albert, in turn, was transfixed by her.

Kit, I knew, was not there. I did not look for him. If he'd been at the fair I'd have known it; I'd have detected the man on the edges of the firelight, unable to stay still for long. Scratching his beard or pushing the earth with his heel, as if testing it. Why might he come to a celebration? He celebrated nothing, felt nothing. He'd walled up his own grief and loss and he was, surely, elsewhere, hearing these sounds from a distance. In female company.

XIV

I looked for George in the garden. The light was less by now; the sun had dipped beyond the hedges and the shadows were longer. I called but he did not reply.

Nor could I find him in the house. I looked in every downstairs room. I knocked on his door; having received no answer, I tried the handle and walked into his room in case he'd been sleeping and had not heard me. But the room was still. An immaculate bed. A desk on which his instruments – ink, blotting paper, notebooks, a knife for sharpening pencils, a pile of books with cracked, tired spines – were laid out.

An empty house. And I felt furious in it – at Mrs Bale's performance that night – *Don't touch my arm!* – and at every single lie that had preceded and followed it. I was furious at her false, bright girlishness. At her trembling hands, which had been manufactured. I loathed the deliberateness of it. But also, I was furious at him: the king of this cobwebbed castle. The conductor of the orchestra. The engineer. He was the man who'd decided that forging a rumour – gathering all the parts that a lie requires and igniting it – was an acceptable task, and not unkind. It had not been acceptable. It had not been kind.

I'd stood in that room and considered the literature on

his shelves and his rationale and his elegant, precise manner of speaking, and I'd believed him. I'd been swayed by his argument. Had he practised his words beforehand? Had he heard, from Mrs Bale, that I was practically-minded and godless and would, therefore, need persuasion? Oh, a fine performance from him. And whilst all of this angered me, my anger doubled when I considered his other secret. His rank, discoloured lungs. That still-warm linen which the maids must have scrubbed and bleached and ironed and hung out in the yard dutifully whilst breathing the remnants of him. And what of this handful of days since Mrs Bale had gone? When it had become Harriet's task to carry the tray to the first floor and leave it outside his door? What of the teacups she'd brought back down? She'd breathed that air in that corridor. And I resented that deeply. Harriet did not deserve such risk. Neither of the maids deserved to work for a man who dealt in lies and disease.

Coward. That was the word. And I spat it out like a pip.

A creak.

The house was empty. Yet above me, I'd heard a single human tread. I did not think of Veronique. I thought of him – Mr Fox – creeping like a strangling vine in his quarters, and I wanted to pour my rage on him. To upend it like a pail of black water. So I made for the staircase, seized the banister and climbed to the first floor, passing the reclining nude and heading down the corridor with my scalding words in my mouth. But there was a change here. This corridor was always in darkness. Yet its far end was partly lit; a geometric shape of evening light fell against the panelled wall so I knew his door was open.

No key had been used. I saw paler, splintered wood. The door frame had been broken; the door held a deep indentation – more splintering – as if something had been thrown against it. A chair or a shoulder.

I entered cautiously. I expected his study to be in disarray or damaged. But it was precisely as I remembered it to have been three weeks before. Shells and botanical prints. The boxed window with its cushioned seat. It seemed entirely unchanged, save for the door in its right-hand wall. For this door was also open. It, too, had been forced.

I entered a room that was three times the size of his study. It was as large as the drawing room beneath it, or larger. A room of curious light. Its windows were wide, receiving the last of the sunlight, and yet it seemed darker than previous rooms. For what it contained was dark-coloured: walnut bureaux, ebony desks, shelves of polished wood that reached the ceiling and spanned the width of the room. Every wall was covered in books. There were thousands of fraying fabric spines, of books on top of other books, of books in columns from ceiling to floor. And where there weren't books, there were cabinets. Huge cabinets of glass and sandalwood held objects that I'd never seen, never imagined: an ivory drinking cup; painted silk of crimson and gold; a clay pipe with a blackened tip. Two dice made of yellowing bone. A single rose that had powdered, and browned. Tiny carved figures in sea-green stone. A vast shell with a pinkish interior that would take two hands to lift to the mouth or the ear.

I moved round the room's perimeter. Pots that smelled of spices. A ship in a bottle. A gnarled grey circular stand for umbrellas and walking canes which had, I saw, the semblance of a creature's foot. An elephant? I did not touch it.

A sketch of a woman's back.

A deck of cards. A feather-tipped fan.

As I turned, I saw that I was being watched. A pair of

eyes were on me: yellow and fixed. Also, a mouth, cavernous, toothy, with a pink, stiffened tongue and blackish gums. A tiger sprawled on the floor. Its body was entirely gone; it consisted of its head and its fur, fanned out. And I thought, surely a tiger is orange and black? Like fire? This tiger's fur seemed bleached by age and wear; it had greyed, so only its head retained any semblance of the creature it had been in life. Glass eyes. Raging. The captured final expression of it: murderous at its moment of death.

Plunder. These treasures were precisely that: exotic, unpleasant, tinged with a sense of violence or loss. How could this be Shadowbrook? The house of empty spaces whose rooms tended to contain dust and nothing more? It was a hall of curiosities. It was, too, a room of inexcusable waste: all these remnants of lives. The tiger and the elephant. The beast that left its parched bone to be whittled into a mouthpiece. The sea crustaceans which had lost their homes. The framed display of moths. The ivory figurines. A speckled egg.

Voyages. Continents.

At that moment, eight bright, clear chimes rang out; tiny, as if from the smallest of clocks. And as if I were a clockwork child, I responded to them. I moved towards a curtain that hung on the far wall, for the chimes had come from beyond it.

I pulled the curtain aside.

A small, plain room. His bedroom. Unlike the museum, it felt clean and light. It lacked ornament. It seemed quite ordinary: on the floor was a pair of tweed slippers; the linen was ironed, and white. There was a commode in one corner with a porcelain washstand. And I knew, too, that this room was directly over my own. It had the same shape; its view was of the herbal bed.

Eight o'clock. The villagers of Barcombe were dancing near the ancient oak, laughing with friends. And I stood in a room of sickness.

'Clara?'

I hadn't heard him. I stumbled back into the museum and saw George. He stood near a cabinet of weaponry. And he seemed hot and real and breathless in this room of skinned creatures. 'I have so much to tell you,' I said.

'You're pale. And you're shaking.' He tugged a chair – leather stretched thinly over black wood – and gestured to it.

I came forwards. 'The door.'

'The door is my fault, my doing. I broke it because I wanted to enter.'

'You've seen this place? Been here? When?'

'An hour or so ago. Listen, I'll tell you why – but you must sit first.' He took my cane from me as I sat down; he set it against the wall, near the elephant's foot.

George himself did not sit. He seemed too roused, too restless. Rather, he paced the room, ducked beneath a narwhal's tusk and as he did this, I noted his unsteadiness. He'd always walked slowly before, statesmanlike. But now he moved as if exhausted or preoccupied; as he turned by the huge wooden globe, he partly tripped.

'Won't you sit too?'

But he shook his head.

'George, I've seen Mrs Bale. She's been lying. She tapped on doors and plucked petals from flowers and she never broke her arm. She meant it. It was deliberately done.'

'Did she say why?'

'Love. Mr Fox asked her to lie and so she did.'

He exhaled. 'Yes. I know this too. Her marriage was nothing, so that when she came here, she thought he was wonderful . . . a charming man.'

'How do you know?'

He stopped pacing. 'I met Mr Fox last night.'

'Last night? When? I saw you last night. I knocked on your door.'

'You did. In your wet clothes with your wet hair – I remember. You gave me the locket. And afterwards, I could not sleep so I came to see him.' His speaking, too, seemed tired. His language was less distinct – soft, as if he longed to drowse. His eyelids seemed heavy.

'What time was this?'

'Late. Midnight. I was angry. Insulted at being made to wait for six days to speak to him – six: I told you this. And so I knocked on his door and he opened it like a little boy, peeping. Yet he wore a purple dressing gown. Silk, with the finest gold trim.' He paused by the window, looked out. 'They invented the ghost of Veronique.'

'Why? Why did they lie like this? Mrs Bale didn't say.'

George lessened the light in the room by standing there, half filling the window, casting his own shadow over cabinets and the tiger-skin rug. 'To summon a member of the Society.'

'*Your* society? For psychical research?'

'It sounds simple, doesn't it? Maybe it was. But there's more. Mr Fox didn't just want any member, oh no. He wanted a specific person' – he struggled with *specific*, wiped his chin – 'to come to Shadowbrook. He wanted that person to travel to Gloucestershire and stay in his house and eat his food . . . investigate these ghostly matters.'

'What's wrong with you, George?'

'Wrong? Nothing's *wrong*. I may have been to The Bull but I won't have you looking down from your throne at me. I *have* drunk but I'm not *drunk* – there's a difference.' He raised a finger, emphasising this. 'He wanted me to come here – *me*.'

I stiffened in my chair. 'Why?'

'Clara,' he said. 'Oh, Clara, Clara, Clara . . . ' like a gentle reprimand or a nursery rhyme. And I feared the tone. It implied danger, or that I'd been the only foolish one. 'Imagine loving a thing. Not a person; I do not mean a person. I mean an inanimate object, something very small. It might not be beautiful; it might not be of any real financial worth. But to you, it's precious. To you, it matters very much. And imagine, now, that it disappears' – he snatched the air, demonstrating this – 'so you miss it and look for it but cannot find it.'

'What precious thing?'

'You grow. You live elsewhere. You find other precious things and distractions and you accept that you will not see this object again. But you do not forget it, Clara – no. You do not stop missing it *here*.' He punched his chest. 'And then' – he leaned closer – 'one night, there is a knock on the door. And this old, familiar treasure which you thought you'd never see again is offered to you. Returned. You think you are dreaming at first. You wish to embrace this tiny, soaking part-angel who has found it – part-angel, part-devil for how much she's entered your brain and blood.'

I frowned at this, seeking meaning.

'The locket was my mother's. She wore it. I knew what it was as soon as you passed it to me.'

'Your mother's?'

'Would you believe that I was fair-haired as a child? Very fair. People would touch me in case it brought good fortune. But by my fourth birthday I'd darkened. My hair has always curled.'

'She died when you were eight. You said this. How can it be her locket?'

He waved my question away like a fly. 'She had curls

too. She was so tall she'd stoop in crowds, and she'd lift this locket over her head and swing it like a pendulum when I couldn't sleep.'

'Your mother was Veronique?'

He laughed. 'What? That sluttish, grubby Pettigrew? No, of course not. My mother was Violet – see? *V.* The locket is engraved with violets, and yes, she died when I was eight, and I saw it happen; it happened in front of me and I could not stop it.' His expression was scornful, dark-eyed. 'And you know who my father is.'

There had been days after Charlotte's death in which I'd wanted to open my body up – to crack it in two, like a shell, to make a cave for her. I had had dreams of this nature. In my old bone dreams, I'd hollow myself for her – removing organs and muscle, sweeping the dust – in case she might return to me. She was a bird in these dreams but no bird that I'd ever seen. She was orange-feathered. She sang her own tune. She would dip under my ribs; perch in the branches of my curved bones – and I might believe these dreams so entirely that, on waking, I'd feel bereft. They were, on their own, too much to bear. So I sealed myself up. Pressed my loss into the depths of myself and found distractions in bus rides and long botanical names.

Yet George still seemed cracked in two. He wiped his nose on the back of his hand. Lumbered towards a cabinet – heavy, purposeful steps – and laid a hand on its glass. 'The man lacked empathy. I remember that as a child; he could not imagine the feelings of others. Could not climb into another's mind or circumstance and understand it. Selfish. A selfish, self-serving man. He left when I was seven. Seven, which is old enough to remember it all. Old enough to feel it keenly, with adult feelings, but I don't think he knew or minded. I don't think he ever paused to think of pain or legacy. He said he wanted more than this. That was his phrasing. *More than this.*'

'Mr Fox is your father?'

'Ah, she understands! That's not his actual name, of course. But yes.' George leaned back against the wall with a single heavy thud. He crossed his arms, looked at me. 'Twenty-one years later, he wants to see his son again. And he does not simply *write* to me, with pen and paper, as any reasonable person would. Why might he do that? Be straightforward and decent? No empathy, remember, although he must have known enough about feelings to rec-ognise that I might not have cared for such a letter. Would not have answered. Would have set it alight or torn it up.' He looked down at the carpet. Studied the elephant's foot.

'The ghost was the lure?'

'The ghost' – he raised a forefinger for emphasis – 'was the lure. The worm for the fish. The meat for the fly.'

'And you knew this from the locket?'

'Not at first. You knocked on my door in wet clothes, gave it to me – and afterwards I sat in my room ... You must understand, little wide-eyed Clara, that I had last seen this locket on her collarbone, two decades before. It had rested here' – he indicated – 'on this plain of skin or on the lace that covered it. And yet here it was, in a crumbling house in Gloucestershire. So I climbed the stairs to meet the owner, who'd told me to wait six days.'

'You knew who he was?'

'No. But then I saw him – peering round the door in this fanciful purple dressing gown, like a sheikh or a retiring king or God knows – and I knew. He was older, of course. Thinner. I pushed him back into his office and he threw up his hands and talked of illness; he cowered, in fact. I might have pitied him once. But anger can fill you and stay, and there he was, in a dressing gown that would have cost more than I'd earn in six months or twelve.'

'What happened?'

'You didn't hear? Oh, I shouted. I cursed him. I said what I'd wanted to say for twenty-one years, what I'd practised in mirrors. I thought you might hear but the thunder kept on and the rain kept on . . . ' He licked his lips. 'What weather. Wasn't it? It didn't feel English to me. When a sky empties like its belly's been slit, that's Indian rain. Monsoon season. And I said this to him as we stood in this room with all these fucking trophies; I said, isn't it appropriate? Like old times?'

He paused, caught his breath. But he also watched me – hard-eyed, expectant; there was a part-smile, as if satisfied. He witnessed the effect of his words on me. He watched my expression as the meaning of *monsoon* rose in me like floodwater.

Tell me about . . . And she used to. Pawprints by the river. Cheroot cigarettes and the games of lawn tennis in which they'd break for mint water. Dust storms. The weight of a goldmohur coin. How she'd seen a cobra once.

As for monsoons, she'd known them in her Calcutta days. The earth could boil underfoot; ditches would rise with the clay-coloured water and spill over. And she'd loved those hours of rain: the draught and the hammering; its precision, so that clocks could be set by its daily arrival; how shelter was found in the smallest of places – an overhang, or a leaf. In its wake, the land steamed. Water evaporated from the backs of cows. Birds would drink from guttering.

I saw her in this museum of loss. Saw her exactly, sitting on the green chaise longue with one ankle beneath her.

'Clara . . . ?' Coaxing me back. 'Have you worked it out? Or shall I keep talking?'

'You lived in India.'

'Yes. But there's more.'

George lifted himself away from the wall. He paced as he talked, tripping over the tiger, grasping the backs of chairs. 'A dying man, a man of wealth and empire and superiority, buys an English house in which to spend the last, wheezing months of his life – and having got there, he thinks of his son. His boy he walked out on two decades before. Who perhaps – and at last – he feels affection for, or whose abandonment has not been easy to forget – although I doubt he'd have used the word *regret*. And this man is dying, of course, so he wishes to make amends. To meet his maker with a clear conscience – ha!

'But first he needs to *find* his son, who's a man now and may no longer have the same name. So he hires a detective of some kind to seek out the truth – and he finds the son is alive! And in England! What marvellous news for our silk-wearing king. The boy, too, has done well for himself. He has studied at Cambridge; he has friendships and appetite and physical strength and the attention of women and above all, he is passionate about the notion of life after death. He investigates occurrences, writes papers on the human brain. This son who for a long time, Clara, longed to find proof of the human soul.

'So how might this selfish dying man lure his son to Gloucestershire? To the wretched house he only bought to be near his favoured sanatorium? Well, he can't simply tell the truth. If he did, his son would either come with knives and rage and bitterness, or he would not come at all. No, this man must conjure a lie. He must trick his child into coming here. And what might work better than ghosts, since it's ghosts his son has an interest in? How easy it is to fabricate one, for his house has its own histories. There are already stories of a scandalous woman whose bones are buried in the grounds. Mr Fox charms a lonely housekeeper to lie on his behalf. To weep and worry and whisper into ears and as she does this, he writes to the Society for Psychical Research: *We hear there's a gentleman who works for you called Lowe . . .* Are you with me so far?'

One nod.

'On to the gardens, Clara. *Your* gardens, with their topiary and orchard and bathing pool and foxgloves and plant after plant. The dying man himself does not particularly care for gardens. He's disinterested; he's never set foot on the croquet lawn and is unbothered by trees. And yet – yet! – he announces that he'd like a glasshouse at Shadowbrook. An Eden! A jungle that might be the talk of the county! He orders one to be made, luxurious, expensive – and why does he do this, Clara? When his lungs cannot stand humid places and he is, frankly, bored by most flowers? Why does he write to Kew Gardens not only for the plants to grow inside this glasshouse but for someone – *someone* – to come with those plants to establish them? Mr Fox has Hollis, after all. It could be argued he doesn't need further assistance. And yet he asks for you. For *you*, Clara. Why?'

'You're drunk.'

'Ha! So you think I'm lying? Let me ask you this: did you see the letter from Shadowbrook? Sent to Kew?'

'Yes. I saw it. And it did not mention me by name. It only asked for assistance – from anyone. You're drunk and you're wrong.' I stood.

'Oh, I'm not wrong. There'll have been a second letter that you did not see, I promise you that – in which Mr Fox named you. You specifically. He'll have offered money to the man who'd send you to Shadowbrook. Who managed to convince you.'

'That's a lie.'

'Is it? Oh, I can't prove it, and I know how much you like proof. But Mr Fox wanted to find you, Clara. His detective tracked you down in London and followed you, noted your habits and tendencies; he identified what you love most of all. Which was the glasshouses at Kew, I assume. A knowledge of tropical botany ... Oh, the irony in that! That you spent your time with the plants he'd have walked past with his wife and son in Delhi and elsewhere! Who knows if he saw it this way. But he ordered his own glasshouse for you.'

George paused. 'Do you need me to say why? Surely not ... A glasshouse and a rumoured ghost – well, yours was the pricier lure.'

I had no wish to stay. I needed air and felt my way between the furniture; I skirted the tiger, moved into the study and through the splintered door. Somewhere behind me he was saying my name as if in appeasement – 'Clara ... ?' – but there was warning in it. And I would not stop. I wished to be outside, away from him, and it was only as I stepped down through the French doors and onto the veranda that I realised I was lacking my cane; it remained upstairs, near the elephant's foot.

A deep twilight now. A mauve garden with shadows. It was the hour in which distances were hard to measure, in which colours were less distinct. I could hear the fair. It was half a mile and a universe away. The villagers clapped their hands to a tune I partly recognised but could not name, and I wished to be there with them. Or I wished to be in any place where George could not find me: in the portico or the potting shed or under the cedar or the bower of limes. I hurried as much as I could. Held onto branches as I descended the steps.

I did not hear him follow me but I knew he must have done. I stood between the topiary trees, clutching their tail feathers for balance and navigation, and listened for footsteps. But I only heard applause. I heard something winged in the trees. Then George was suddenly beside me, so close that I could hear the moisture in his mouth as he spoke and I could smell The Bull's interior and tobacco on his breath.

'Clara. You can't run from this. We need to talk, you and I.'

'No we don't.' I stepped back. I circled the peacock, keeping one hand against it.

'No? You don't have questions for me? You always have questions. You start every sentence with *how*, or *why*. Ask what you want to.'

'I have no questions. My father is Patrick Waterfield.'

'Who? He's not, and you know that. Emerson. Rex Emerson. That's the name you need – and it's quite a name, isn't it? He was always proud of it. *Rex*. Felt it suited him. But I knew this name, of course; if I'd seen it stamped on a letterhead, I'd have recognised it and not come, and that was not what he wanted. So he chose a new identity. Fox. I haven't asked why, although he probably thinks it's a noble creature when it is, in fact, a scavenger. An opportunist. Sly. Are we to walk round this bush all night, Clara?'

'Leave me alone.'

I let go of the peacock and walked away. Moved between hedges. I passed beneath the cedar, entered the white garden with my hands held out in front of me, as a sleepwalker might, and George remained so close to me that I could feel his breath on the top of my head.

'Let me tell you this: no, he didn't care for any trees or flowers, except one. I don't mean violets. He can't have loved violets, after all. I mean the single plant from which he made his fortune. Don't you wish to hear? The reclining nude, Clara.'

I came against the plinth of a Grecian urn. It was a sudden meeting – the stone against my ribs – yet I took hold of it. 'What of it?'

'Look closer. Not *at* her, as such – although she wants you to look at her, doesn't she? Those eyes. No, look at the bed. At what lies beside it – pipes and bowls. At the low lighting. And if you look through the window behind her, you won't see an English scene.' He brought his mouth to my ear. 'Poppies. Do you understand?'

Did I? What did I know of that small red bloom? Enough. Those childhood slumbers. Those dreams from which I'd wake calling out for water. And I remembered the botanical prints in his study, poppies in oval frames.

'I want you to listen to me, Clara. There is no good in that man. Don't think he's a poor widower. Don't think that because he's got encyclopaedias and poetry on his shelves he has morals or decency, because books do not mean wisdom. And don't think I've lost my mind and that I'm telling you lies, because why would I do that? That man? Clara, he's a philandering opium dealer who fucked someone else – Charlotte, wasn't it? – and left his wife and child and got rich from poppy seeds grown by poor starved farmers in the hills above Simla who had to walk to find water and died young whilst he considered himself a king and lived like one. And two decades later he coughed up blood, changed his name and moved to a house in Gloucestershire, as if the gentle English rain might wash his sins away like some laughable baptism. A croquet lawn and an orchard. A liar at every damnable turn. That's my father – and yours too, Miss Waterfield. Or Miss Emerson, to use your proper name.'

I let go of the plinth, gasping, yet it was George who collapsed. He had not, perhaps, seen the urn. Or the half-light and drunkenness had caused him to miscalculate a step. But he tripped, clutched air and foliage, and I made my way towards the croquet lawn. He'd follow me, I knew this. I heard him curse behind me, heard the effort of standing back up, and I hurried whilst I was free of him. I sought any dark place. And as I moved into the space between the beechwoods and the tennis court, I heard the difference in his voice: the scorn and mocking had given way to a wild, snarling, animal hate. 'God damn you, Clara! Do you think you can run?'

I grasped ivy and trellises. I felt my way along lines of hedges, crept into the cavity of a holly bush and waited until he'd passed me. And despite being unable to see me, he continued to shout across the gardens: 'Do you know how she died? My mother? Not tuberculosis. Not a tumour, like yours. The railway station in Delhi, Clara! Eighteen ninety-five, nearly two years after he'd left us, two years in which she'd grown thinner and distant and had sold all that we had – bone china, silver, every piece of jewellery except for her locket – for food. But she'd lost hope, too, and every form of self-care. So on the fourteenth of April, she let go of my hand and stepped in front of a train, and I didn't notice her letting go. I was a child. Are you listening to me, Clara? I'd been watching the drongo birds move between baskets of fruit, and I only knew she'd gone when I heard the brakes and saw cloth I recognised – yellow with a white spotted pattern – rising into the wheels of the train. And what does a boy do after that? He goes to England, of course. Lives with a cousin on his mother's side and takes their surname. Reads. Explores. Attends seances. Hungers for vengeance.'

All this as he staggered through the garden. He shouted or muttered it; he pronounced it through cupped hands or wailed it to himself privately. *I was only a child ...* Several times he came near me. But only having spoken of vengeance did he stop directly beside the holly bush and cease talking, and I knew I'd been found. 'I can see you ... ' sung like a nursery rhyme.

I rushed out; I fought through holly and I hissed and spat – 'Get away!' – but he lunged towards me, seized my wrist with such ferocity that I knew the bruise would be black and a month long in healing, and it hurt instantly. 'Nothing to say, Clara? Nothing to say sorry for?'

'Sorry? Why? This wasn't my fault.'

'Not your fault?' He came so close that I could feel his breath on me; his eyes were brilliant, fixed. 'Oh, it was. Or your mother's, at least.'

He tightened his grip. I saw his jaw clench with the effort of it; his eyes narrow. I could hear the distant music and laughter and my own laboured breathing, but I also heard a single, audible crack. Like glass or ice. I knew the sound.

He heard it too. And we both felt it: a neat readjustment of bone inside me. A giving way in my wrist. Then a new sound entered the garden: a frail, tremulous, animal wail which rose in volume. It was a wordless howl which, without changing pitch, became worded, so that I pleaded *let go please let go my wrist you are breaking my wrist let go.* But George did not let go. Rather, he pulled me closer; he twisted my wrist with deliberate intent so that I heard a second, deeper crack that was grittier, fragmented. A crunch of bone.

The pain was enormous. I was blinded by it. I bellowed,

felt my tongue stiffen and my mouth fill with sour-tasting liquid so that I vomited – noisily, repeatedly – onto myself and onto the hand which grasped me and only with that did George let go.

I stumbled into the dark. Grazed myself on brickwork, tore my skirt on thorns. *Find somewhere to hide.* But I could think of nowhere. No single place would be enough. It was people I needed – it was an army, another, human company; it was my mother, who might stand herself between George and me like a living wall with her flashing eyes and say *don't you dare*. But my mother and the fair were a thousand miles away. So I went to the only peopled place I knew. I went to the portico, brushing against hedges, using my unbroken arm to fumble along the lengths of walls and round the circular bathing pool and in the twilight, I reached the wise eyes of the old painted faces who had seen far more than this.

I thought, I'll find a chair. I'll haul it towards the wall, crouch behind it; I'll hide between the chair and the Romans and they will be my guards. But the chair struck a second chair as I did this. Their two metal frames made a single bright chime. And I looked up, appalled – for George, I knew, would have heard. And there he was – framed by an archway, standing on the croquet lawn with his arms by his sides and his chest rising and falling; he saw me in return. A smile appeared on his face. And with that, I knew I could not run or fight or hide elsewhere, and the *trompe l'oeil* could offer nothing as the Romans themselves could not. I could only stay as I was, crouching. Murmur *no, Mama, no* as he began to run.

He came with long, heavy strides, his weight forwards. He came with his eyes fixed on me, as any hunting creature would run. Then for a moment, he seemed to fly. He seemed to leave the ground, birdlike: he was horizontal, expansive, with no part of him touching the stonework or the grass. And there was, in this second, a silence. No cursing or footsteps.

He fell onto the steps. The impact was dull, echoless; I saw the single, bounced action of his head striking the ground, and no groan followed. There was no sound at all except for a high, metallic, rotational sound – like a coin falling on its side – and I knew what it was. Knew that a rusting croquet hoop might seem too small to trip a man of such height and breadth.

I waited until I knew he would not stand back up.

I could not make it to the house. I had nothing left in me. The fractures had consumed me, as a furnace does.

I dropped down. Kneeled, with my forehead on the ground. It was a posture of prayer or supplication; it was a sleeping position in other countries, and I closed my eyes but did not sleep. I had half-dreams – of a tiger's last moment, near water, of red dust on the soles of my mother's feet – and a voice was saying my name insistently. 'Clara? Clara, can you hear me?'

I opened my eyes and I did not believe what I saw. The beard. Those lines by his eyes. The voice, it seemed, was Kit's – but how could this be him? Kit was elsewhere. He was mending walls or lifting his shirt over his head in his bedroom or drinking. He was walking away from me with a dampness in the small of his back having said *keep away from me*, with the yard on either side of him. *No*, I said. But it *was* Kit. His palms and left cheek were pressed to the grass. His mouth was saying, 'Clara?' His eyes were trying to find my own.

*

I saw the shirt he wore – blue, with the sleeves rolled up. I saw the loose threads and the buttons that he'd not fastened. And I saw how he watched without blinking as I tried to right myself, as he must have observed animals or the stages of grain.

'You need a doctor.'

'No.'

'Then you should go inside.'

'No.'

He did not contest this. He did not touch me. He only watched as I positioned myself, as I wiped my mouth with my forearm and folded over my broken wrist, speaking to it. I settled, and Kit studied the garden's near-darkness. He listened for any human sound – a voice or footfall. 'Where is he?'

'By the bathing pool.'

Kit rose. He walked across the lawn, passed into the archway and dropped out of sight, and I cradled my arm without taking my eyes away from the place where he had been. I knew what he'd find. Knew that, on his return – when I'd see him again, when he'd appear and walk back across the croquet lawn – my life would divide itself into two parts: before George's death, and after. Two Claras, in this way. But there were so many pairs of me now. My life had divided itself when my bones had been called imperfect; when I came to Shadowbrook; when my mother said *fibrous* on a bridge over the Thames. When I'd heard the name Emerson. When I'd walked along a boundary wall with no preconception of what this farmer might look like; later, a different Clara walked back through his fields.

These things. I tasted sour. In the distance, people still danced by a fire, and I wished to close my eyes and sleep. To be able to wake from this.

In time, Kit returned. He crouched down, gave the news of George's death as if death was small to him. I knew it was not small. Yet Kit reported it without shock or sentiment. Said that George was cooling. No pulse in his wrist or throat. 'What happened tonight?'

My words fluttered. They came in no proper order; I was too faint with pain, too tired to arrange them. A silver locket, bones, a sanatorium. A Delhi train. How a man called Patrick Waterfield married a pregnant girl. I spoke of opium. Explained that George had, for a moment, been suspended in the air like a tree's branches and that when he had landed, a croquet hoop had sung its bright song. My wrist. How there was no ghost at all. The proof of her had gone.

Mr Fox, I said, was not Mr Fox. I spoke of fathers.

Kit stayed very still, listening. Having understood enough, he looked away. And at that moment, a breeze came up; it moved through the garden, finding his blue shirt and my hair, and it filled the hedges so that they shuddered. Kit inhaled. Ran his palm over his beard. 'He was in The Bull today. Before that, The King's Arms in Stow.'

'You saw him?'

'Others did. Argued with him. Clara, he did this to your arm?'

It had doubled in size. And I was breathing as I used to in London with fractures – too fast, shallowly. I whimpered, nodded once.

He studied his palm, opened and closed it.

Kit crossed the lawn and veranda, passed through the French doors and entered the empty house. One by one, I saw lamps go on. I saw him moving through the rooms and I wondered if I'd ever imagined this: Kit, away from his labour, performing small, ordinary, human tasks that did not require muscle or any proper thought – running a bath or washing clothes. Boiling a pan of water.

We moved into the drawing room. I lowered myself onto the sofa and in the lamplight, we could see the change in my wrist more clearly: it had darkened, twisted. The skin itself seemed to pulsate; it had stretched so much that it looked as if it might split. Kit kneeled before me, studying it. He asked me to move my arm slightly. He in turn angled his head to see the discoloration and form – and I remembered old doctors who'd stared like this. How they'd shaken their heads at me.

He brought water, a blanket that I'd not seen before. He sat on the opposite chair.

'Let me tell you what happened here tonight.'

'I told you.'

'I know. He was drunk and he tripped on a croquet hoop – I know. But they won't believe you.'

'Who won't?'

'Everyone. The villagers, the police. They won't believe you because of what you've gained with George's death. What you've become.'

'Gained?'

Kit glanced up. 'This house. This land. If he is your father – Mr Fox – you're the sole heir to Shadowbrook now. And you think they won't find a story in that? Won't find a rumour? The truth won't be enough to protect you, Clara, you know this. Let me tell you what happened here.'

He was right. Moths tapped against the window panes and as I watched them, I thought of the rumours that found their way over fields and into houses. Of tales that rolled across flagstone floors and stopped against boots, so that people paused, lifted them up. Never mind my size. Never mind my imperfections. It would seem a convenient fall to them – I had, they'd say, so much to gain from George's death, after all – and so they'd change the truth, in The Bull and elsewhere. Talk of the stone I'd picked from the borders. One hard, unexpected blow to the tenderest part of his skull.

Yes, I saw. The girl from Kew. They'd say, I never trusted her.

So in the drawing room that night, we developed our own truth. This is what happened, Kit said. George came to Shadowbrook at dusk and fell. He'd been in the lower garden. He'd been navigating the moss and floodwater – for a reason we'd never know. He had, too, been drinking all day – others would testify that yes, they'd seen him – so that his balance and footing were poor. Easy to fall in such a place and state. And the cause of death would be readily known, for his temple would show the clear, bloodied place of impact. (Does it, I asked? Show the place? And I knew from his silence that it did.) An unfortunate act, that's all. In the morning, the girl with the cane walked outside, and whilst she didn't enter the lower garden because of its steep sides and slick stones, she could see it from the lime bower. Could see George, laid out like a twisted star. And she hurried to him, called for assistance. But this girl – Clara, tiny, imperfect – also fell on the wet surface. Broke her wrist in the fall.

'The lower garden? Why?'

'Because you don't go there. Never have.'

'But he's by the bathing pool.'

'I'll move him. Take him down to the stream. This will work, Clara.'

I believed him. This man of few words who, in the fields, had removed the sweat from his brow with a single sweep of his inner wrist, like the hand of a clock face. I studied him at that moment. I saw how he leaned forwards with his elbows resting on his knees; how he turned his hands over, examining the scars and the marks on his knuckles – and I knew they'd talk of him too. Of his propensity for violence. Of the bad blood in his veins. I knew that others had seen him strike George in The Bull – others, perhaps, had pulled them apart – and what had this punch become since then? A battle with knives? A war between them?

'You aren't safe either,' I said.

Always, a noose waiting for him. He knew this too, glanced up. 'I started that fight, not him. And they saw me leaving the fair tonight. Knew that I was coming here.'

For a while, we sat quietly. Kit laid a hand over his mouth in contemplation. He tapped his forefinger against his jaw, thinking, and I wondered if his father had done this – a gesture Kit had inherited unknowingly, or had copied from him. I wondered how many women had seen it performed.

It was, I knew, my turn. Kit had formed a story – a lie – to keep me safe; I would create my own truth for him to shelter in, far better than stone walls or trees. I thought of Veronique. I thought of her legacy. How these tales of her – lawless, shameless, unclothed – were the strongest and most enduring. What else would be believed of Kit? Beyond violence?

'We'll tell them,' I said, 'that you stayed here.'

'Stayed?'

I offered this to him: that yes, Kit had left the summer fair to come to Shadowbrook. He'd come because tonight – for the first time since the fair-haired girl with the cane had arrived – the house had been empty. The maids, the housekeeper, the owner and even this new, tall London guest had all been elsewhere – dancing, or with family. Or drinking, it seemed, in The Bull. The only resident that night had been me: the girl from Kew with the demanding nature. And wasn't this a tendency of Kit's? To knock on the doors of women at night? To undress them, or watch as they undressed before him? They said if you asked him to list the women he'd known in this way, he'd run out of names.

Kit stared, as if disbelieving.

'You stayed here all night,' I said. 'With me. I'll tell them this.'

Our words – his and mine – as protection of the other. It seemed so simple to me. An exchange of breath, that was all. Yet it was right, perfect – for what else might we offer in defence of ourselves? What else would they accept as the truth?

But Kit shook his head, shocked. 'You don't know what you're saying.'

'Yes, I do. I do. Tell me that it wouldn't work, Kit. Tell me they wouldn't believe it.'

But I knew he could not tell me this. For oh, they would believe this version. They – the villagers of Barcombe and Moreton and Stow and beyond – would rush to this tale as if it glinted; they'd love to believe that Kit Preedy had come to me, for one purpose. That I'd stepped out of my dress with defiance. That I'd revealed my scars and deformities to the solitary man with dark-coloured blood. *Can you imagine . . . ?* A scandalous act. Yet over teacups and fences, they'd say that, in truth, they'd expected nothing less from me: hadn't I always seemed too bold, too strange, unladylike? As for Kit, this was wholly in keeping with the man they knew, or thought they knew. He wouldn't have cared for malformities. He'd have disregarded my bones entirely, laid me on the bed without words or courtesy and taken what he'd come for; or perhaps he'd have taken his time in his exploration of scars and mended places, for curiosity's sake, no more. I wasn't sure which tale they'd tell. But they'd tell one, at least.

I waited. I knew Kit was thinking the same. He was recognising the perfection in this lie. We unclothed the other, pressed ourselves together until it grew light; we could vouch for the other from dusk till morning. There were no flaws in it.

'Do you understand,' he said, looking up, 'that this rumour would never leave you? You'd always be known for it – before anything else.'

I understood. But what did it matter if they knew me for this one nocturnal act? It didn't matter. I only wanted safety. To ensure that there were not enough doubts or loose threads to make a noose for this man who couldn't quite believe what I was holding out to him, gift-like. I told him that yes, I understood. And he nodded once, consenting to it.

Kit, therefore, stayed. He'd need to be seen leaving Shadowbrook at first light, walking back through his fields in the same blue shirt he'd worn at the fair. Whistling and satisfied. He hoped to be seen by the garden boys so that, later, they'd confirm the tale. *Yes, we saw him.*

Until then, we barely spoke. We sat, adjusting. We listened to the distant music as it finally ended; applause came over the fields to us, and the grandfather clock chimed twelve times in the hall. We would not look directly at each other so that when Kit offered brandy to me, it was his wrist that I stared at – a wrist that could withstand any weight or gesture.

At one in the morning, he stood. Struck a match and lit a lamp.

'Where are you going?'

'The bathing pool,' he said, and I knew why. In his absence, I imagined it: how he'd set the lantern down as he crouched beside George, lifted him over his shoulder. How he'd carry him – a man of timber, stiffening – down to the flooded stream and lay him down as if he were sleeping. He'd rest George's head near a prominent stone. But I imagined this, too: how it would be if it did in fact happen. If – despite the circumstance and the hour and my wrist and my appearance and stubborn nature – Kit returned through the French windows with purpose and kneeled beside me; if he placed his hand under my hair, cupping the uppermost part of my neck as he might cup a bird. If, later, I might undo the handful of buttons which remained on his shirt, revealing him. It was all I could think of, at that moment – not George, not my mother. For what difference would it make now? What harm could it bring? *You'd always be known for it.*

Kit returned, drained his brandy. 'It's done.'

The clock's sound. In the far woods, an owl. He dropped down into the chair; he grasped his hair with both hands, released it, and I thought of him following in his father's wake. Whistling for his childhood dog. I thought of the lichen that had been cleared from the gravestones of other Preedys, and I knew this had been his work – that he'd done it privately at the end of a farming day – and yet he would not admit to it. I said, 'Our story. We could make it true.'

'It will be true for them. You're right – they'll believe it.'

'Not for them. For us. We could make it true for us.'

My heart was drum-like. My pulse was pronounced in my wrist – I could see it there, against my skin – but I felt it, too, beneath my collarbone and ribs and in my throat so that speaking was, suddenly, harder. Kit looked up, amazed.

He studied me in a brand-new way: open-mouthed, and breathless. A deep vertical line between his brows. 'No, Clara. I can't do that.'

'Why not?'

'Why not?' He rose and walked away from me – towards the French windows so that I thought he might leave – appalled, incredulous. But he stopped by the curtains, turned back. His eyes were at their brightest. 'You and your questions. My God.'

'Where is the crime? you said. *They* come to *me*, you said – and did you turn them away? Any of those women? Am I so very dreadful to you that you won't entertain the thought of it?'

'You,' he said, 'know nothing. You know nothing, Clara.'

'I know enough. And have all the others been so wise? Have they? Am I so different to them?'

Kit took four steps towards me, and if he'd ever been walled or defensive or contained, he wasn't now. 'Different? Yes. Yes, you are different, Clara. You're not like the rest, I'll give you that. There's been more talk of you in The Bull than of anyone else; you stand out. People look for you – and no, in truth, you are far from dreadful to me. But do you think that's enough? You think you can ask whatever you want? Like the answers do not matter to you? Or the feelings of others?'

This silenced me.

'How old are you, Clara? Nineteen? Twenty? All your books and interrogations and yet you're still so ...' he shrugged, '*new*. So undamaged. And this house ... I vowed I'd never enter it in my lifetime and there's no way – none – that I'd touch someone in it, even in passing. Jesus Christ.'

I faltered. *Undamaged* made no sense at all. I had been damaged since birth and here was my wrist, blood-coloured.

But the house? This too was strange to me. How did the house matter? Shadowbrook was imperfect – it was damp in places and still had mice – but it had known physical love. It was, surely, the perfect place for touching somebody; a place whose previous owner had lived without regard to social niceties. Where she'd been unmarried by choice, untethered by rules and had paid no heed to the word *reputation*. And hadn't she been beautiful to Kit? More so than any other? The woman who slept under apple trees.

'I don't understand,' I said.

He exhaled, did not speak unkindly. 'Of course you don't. Why would you? You've no idea what happened here.'

'I do. She lived as she wished to.'

'Veronique? Did she? Really?'

Kit held my gaze and for a time, he saw me. But then his stare clouded, so that I felt he was no longer seeing me; rather, he was making a choice. He was moving between the two possibilities – of saying either nothing or saying far more. He considered these two choices as he looked at me, shifting his jaw.

He turned away. He poured himself a further brandy, drank it quickly; on swallowing, he pressed the arm which held the glass against his mouth and closed his eyes, and I knew he'd decided. 'Damn it,' he said. 'All those questions you've asked . . . One after the other, yet you're no further to knowing. Clara? Listen.'

Kit did not sit to tell me. Instead, he crouched on the balls of his feet – as he had when mending his wall. A balanced, ready position. He stayed like this for a long time before speaking, calming himself. Choosing the way to tell me.

'The farm is barley now. But my family had cows, once.

It's poor pasture for cattle – thin soil, and dry – but we had them. And in late summer, my uncle would take the breeding cows to the bull near Yabberton. Five miles each way. I was ten, maybe, no older. The cows were pushed into the bull's stall for the purpose and often the cows weren't wanting it. They'd fight, refuse to enter the stall, so we'd use sticks against them, force them inside. That's the farming way. That's how it's done. I was nine or ten. Do you understand?'

No. There were shafts of understanding in this but not enough to see by. And I felt full, suddenly. I was full of what made no sense to me. V was for Violet. The fox had been sly.

'The cows,' he said, 'had no choice. The bull was stronger. We were stronger, with sticks and rope. Christ, I shouldn't be telling you this.'

'She was the cow? Is that what you're saying?'

'Veronique. Yes.'

'How? And who were the bulls?'

'Guests. Her brothers' friends. Those Pettigrew parties? Yes, they were all men, and they set creatures against each other for money – dogs against badgers, dogs against dogs. They wrestled, broke furniture. Rich, spoilt men who'd drink until they fought their own shadows and who'd never allowed no to be said to them. That was why my grandmother left so quickly; she said she'd find blood on the floor in the mornings. She feared for herself. Then Mortimer died. His sons became masters of the house; the violence and drinking got far worse – and Veronique was fifteen, that year. Fifteen – in a house like that. I doubt it took long for the men to climb the stairs. What could she do? Where might she run to? Who would help a Pettigrew?'

This was not possible. 'She lived as she chose to. As she wished.'

'No. The rumours are wrong – I told you this. They were wrong in her lifetime and they won't change now.'

Kit stood. He moved to the window, looked out. And this new, dark knowledge rose in me. It filled me as water will fill a vessel, changing pitch in the process, so that I made a sound as I understood it fully; a rush of air. 'How long?'

'Did it last? Years. Until her brothers died.'

'And how do you know this?'

'Reverend Stout. He heard a confession, once. One of the men – a Pettigrew guest – came to church, begged for forgiveness. Said that other men had done precisely the same at these parties, many times – as if that excused it. He said the brothers took money for it too sometimes. Money ... But Jack Stout was more of a drinking man than a priest. Couldn't keep secrets. He told my father in The Bull one night.' Kit glanced back, saw my expression. 'A confession, Clara. By its nature, it's the truth.'

'What then?'

'Stout did nothing. But my father ... '

And I knew. I understood why Hugo Pettigrew had died in a brawl in a tavern. One punch from Bill Preedy, who knew what happened at Shadowbrook parties, in an upper, north-facing room.

Kit returned to the chair. He closed his eyes and rested his head back as if these words had exhausted him, or as if, perhaps, he was relieved that a weight had been set down at last. I imagined him leaning over a glass in The Bull, as if protecting it – hunched against rumour, hearing such words as *slattern* and shifting his jaw or clenching his hand before rising and walking towards the ones who were saying it. Bad blood. For what? Protecting her. Knowing and hating the proper truth.

I tasted sourness again. Inhaled sharply. 'Who else knows?'

'Hollis. My father told him all of it. They'd always been friends. And Hollis did his best; he told the police over and over, but their pockets clinked with Pettigrew coins and they did nothing. Later, Veronique inherited the house; she kept the truth to herself, saw no one. And what might we do then? It was over. It was not our news to tell.'

'We could tell it now. Tell the truth.'

'No point. You think they'd listen? They have the rumour they wanted; it entertains them, even now. That she made all her choices. Wore nothing but pearls at these parties of hers. After her death, we decided – Hollis and I – that Veronique had been manhandled enough in her life so that we'd let her find peace at last. We vowed we'd never talk of it.'

Kit quietened at that. He adjusted himself in his chair, knuckled his eyes as a boy might do, yet I knew no single part of him was resting. He knew the time precisely, knew the objects in this room; if I made any sound – my heel against the rug or an exhalation – he'd rise instantly. I wondered if he always slept like this – lightly, so that only an owl's sound or a scurry in the lane or roof would be enough for him to wake and dress – and I had these thoughts because I could not think of others. Could not say Veronique's name.

Two o'clock chimed. I did not think I'd sleep. But the brandy, the many truths of the night and the exhaustion of my physical pain meant that my chin dropped forwards. I tried to stop sleep, but sleep came. Later, I woke to find Kit had gone. A quadrant of the drawing room was lit with morning sun; the blanket had been unfolded and laid across me – over my legs, tucked by my sides – and I looked at the room without him in it. His chair was empty. The French doors were partly open. There was no evidence that he'd been here except for his brandy glass, the blanket and the scent of him.

At five, I went upstairs. It was a stiff, painful enterprise that I could not do silently. I murmured to myself, *Be careful*, as if I were my own friend. In my father's museum of trophies and skins and sandalwood and books with mildew upon them, I found my cane. It seemed to belong there but I took it, made my way downstairs.

A blackbird sang as I made my way to the lower garden, where George lay. I thought, momentarily, that he might rise if I called his name but he was too pale; the pose was too awkward, and I knew he would not.

I positioned myself in the mossiest place. It was Albert who found me. It was Albert who crouched beside me as I wailed in pain, who murmured reassurances before running back into the garden in search of his father. He shouted for him. Hollis, in turn, shouted for the doctor. And the doctor, still in his nightclothes, rang the police in Stow.

Kit was right: in the weeks to come, this rumour was feasted on. It was passed over shop counters; it was murmured through the frothy mouths of drinkers in taverns so that even now they speak of it. They didn't talk of George's death as such. That was, after all, an accident, and how many rumours could spring from such things? All they could do was shake their heads. *A shame.* But there was far more to speak of regarding the farmer and the crippled girl. How they clutched each other like insects, grasping one another's hair as they moved together without words or sentiment. A perfunctory act.

They'd talk of me specifically. After all, they'd heard such tales of Kit before; his physical, intimate life was not new to them. But I was an unwomanly woman, in every conceivable way. A disgrace, said the men, to my sex. They'd muse on my strange, insubstantial body: how could it have borne Kit Preedy's weight? How did my ribs not give way beneath him? At first, they credited Kit's knowledge of the female form for this, his expert's eye. But these days, there is a different version which I still hear, in passing. That I saved my bones by being the upper, working one. That, like an imperious queen, I gave the commands; I looked down at his face.

XV

By eleven in the morning, they all knew. Dr Warrimer tended to my wrist. He wondered how long it had been broken for, and I said I could not remember the hour; this was his only question to me. He set my arm in a sling. 'I'd advise a hospital visit, in most cases. But I rather think you are used to fractures.' Then he snapped the lock of his leather bag and left without offering relief for the pain which told me he'd already heard how I'd spent my night, and with whom.

The police were more cautious, kind. They took their time in the lower garden. Hollis warned them of its treachery as they entered; he apologised for it, as if the slick nature of moss was his own personal fault. He did, partly, blame himself. 'If I'd tended to that part of the garden more often ... if I'd roped it off, placed a sign ... ' But I told him what was true: that streams overflow. That George had been drinking all day. He'd known about the effects of water on rocks and vegetation. Hollis, I urged, was not to blame.

George was carried away by four policemen late on Tuesday afternoon. They used a stretcher. The proof of the lower garden's nature was found in how they struggled themselves: a slipped foot, a tilting of the stretcher, so that there was a shouting of warnings and a scrambling of limbs. This also helped Hollis, I think. He watched, understanding that no gardener can alter the wishes of running water. That even four strong policemen can be overcome by it, and so what could he have done differently?

The inspector smelled of soap, I remember that. He sat at the kitchen table with me, asked what he was required to: when had I last seen George Lowe? Had I been at home last night? Had I been alone? He did not inspect the house itself. He never found or questioned the splintered, shouldered door.

No strangeness, he concluded, in George's death. It was a mistrusted, treacherous part of the garden. Also, a dozen people or more came forwards to say that yes, they'd seen George drinking that day. There'd been a dispute in The King's Arms in which he'd upturned a table; he'd ordered a drink for which he wouldn't pay and later, he'd thrown glasses. And yes, it was true that the man called Preedy disliked him – *had it in for him* was the inspector's phrase. But Kit's movements could be verified that night. I could place him in a single, precise location between eight in the evening and first light; Kit could verify my own movements in turn. So what was left to presume? Or know?

The inspector seemed unabashed. Perhaps he'd seen or done far more in his life. He wrote a word in his notebook, underlined it twice. 'It happens, Miss Waterfield. Drink and bravado. Stupidity. I've fished them out of rivers before. Or they've fallen from greater heights than this, so that we've had to scoop them up. There'll be more to come, too.'

'More? Why more?'

'Haven't you heard?' He rose from his chair, reached for his hat. 'We're at war. It's been declared. How's that for news? We'll show the bloody lot how it's done. So there'll be plenty more drinking and toasting of the King and foolishness in the days to come.'

This was how I heard the confirmation of war: from a police inspector whose name I never knew. No one else had mentioned it to me, as if the news would be a further weight on my wrist and I wouldn't bear it. As I followed him down the corridor, he remarked on the house's faded sense, on its dust and trapped light, and he asked why he might know the name of this place. 'Shadowbrook ... it's familiar to me. Was there trouble here once? A robbery?'

'It's haunted,' I told him. 'The upper floor.'

'A ghost? Ah, that's right. A woman, I think.'

So Veronique remained, despite it all.

Those were unprecedented days. And within them, Maud did not return. She'd left for the summer fair, heard of George's death and refused to come back. She believed it was Veronique's work and feared her more than ever. But I sensed, too, the sore heart in Maud; we knew what she'd thought of and felt for the man like a tree, with his curls. Maud's mother came for her daughter's clothes. She had the same tight, suspicious expression. She sniffed as she considered the high ceilings and the dust, and yet she retained her hardest stare for me: a gradual assessment from head to toe. The hair and the sling. The blue-coloured whites of the eyes. And I knew she'd come, in fact, for these things, not the clothes.

Harriet, in contrast, did not leave. She was sorry for George's death, and shocked; she spent an afternoon on the edge of the lower garden on her own and came back tired. But soon she altered. She seemed stronger, unafraid. In one single day, she emptied the billiards room of George's belongings, washed and wrung his bedlinen and pinned it on the line, and gathered his written documents and arranged their postage to London. I watched this and thought to ask why. Why was she at Shadowbrook still? And strangely radiant? But I knew and did not have to ask. Her reason for staying was six feet in height, and he dug the earth as his father did – with the ball of his foot on the uppermost part of the spade, pausing at times to admire a bird's call.

It was the announcement of war that altered her. The realisation of life's brevity had ignited her, so that within three days of war's declaration, she kissed Albert unashamedly in the courtyard, in front of his father and the garden boys. She began to lie with him on the croquet lawn at the end of their working day, laugh at the whistles that came, and I knew too that one night – a Friday – Albert crept back to Shadowbrook, climbed through her window and slid into bed beside her. I knew this because I heard the window being drawn up in its casement; at breakfast, I saw her new appetite. I did not know all parts or gestures of love, but I knew enough.

This was why Harriet stayed. We had become tentative friends in two months, yes. But also, in the face of war, she understood what mattered to her, and it was not good manners or polishing silver. She knew what she wanted to do and say. And according to rumour, both I and Veronique Pettigrew had said and done these things too, in our own ways.

But for me, I wanted solitude. It was all I wanted – to hibernate, as creatures do. To withdraw from the world and not be found. I could not walk very far; the sling meant that I could not use my cane, and I limped with my unbroken arm held out in poor compensation. So I looked for near, abandoned places where I could hide myself. I'd fold myself down onto the potting shed floor. I'd rest against the weathered board that had once kept tennis scores, or I'd lower myself in the beechwoods and try not to think of what I'd discovered in this past handful of days: Rex and poppies. The words *half-brother*. A yellow patterned skirt in the mechanics of a train.

I thought of Patrick instead. In the potting shed, he came to me: the spectacles, the pristine moustache and how he'd presented that rocking horse to me one Christmas with a flourish that was so unlike him; he'd held his arms out – *ta-da!* He'd never been *Papa* to me. Yet he'd hovered outside my bedroom door with each fracture; he'd carried books back through the rain and had spent more than I could imagine on my silver-tipped walking cane. One day he'd taught me the rules of chess. Allowed me to beat him.

I wrote to him that night. I did not mention Rex Emerson to him: such news, I felt, deserved to be spoken face to face and not given in ink, if it had to be given at all. Instead, I thanked him. It was all I wanted to do: to write thank you in various guises. It was, therefore, a short letter. But I knew my heart was in it – I underlined words, wrote carefully – and I knew that he'd detect this. *From your loving Clara.*

I wrote to Forbes, too. A shorter note still, but not without its tenderness. He'd tricked me, as others had. Yet he'd written such labels for those plants – *handle with care, dead-head frequently* – that I knew he'd walked with guilt in Kew. He'd acted with love, or a smaller version of it, but he'd doubted his act in the weeks that followed, I was certain of that. This man who'd missed his own daughter. Who'd spoken to plants as if they could hear him and who'd raised his hat to passers-by. He'd have worried all summer, privately. Found Gloucestershire on his nearest map.

*

I thought of Charlotte, too. At first, I did not want to. I felt too tired, too shaken; I felt confused by her. For she'd been the spinner of globes to me; she'd told tales of mangoes and wide brown rivers in which people cast nets, and I'd never imagined deceit from her. But there must have been deceit. Rex Emerson had had his knowledge of poppies, and a wedding ring.

Rage, for a time. But this rage promptly turned to further grief. I reasoned that her Indian days – their truths and secrets – did not change her London ones; as my mother, she stayed the same. I'd stare at the broken furniture in the tennis pavilion whilst remembering how she'd remove her gloves, finger by finger. How in hospital she developed such a fierce, protective love for me – *get me a different doctor* – that I thought of bears or wolves. Her poor sewing skills. Rose water. How she'd sometimes become entangled when disrobing in the hallway – her coat, her bags, her suffragist sash, her hat, her half-pinned hair – so that Millicent would hurry forth with instructions: *Give me your left arm, Mrs Waterfield*. These things were of the same value to me. I missed them with the same deep ache; a lasting internal bruise.

Sometimes I'd hear the wheelbarrow's squeak as Hollis passed the potting shed, so that I'd hold my breath until he'd moved away. Also, I'd hear Harriet calling for me, or Matthew, returning from the beechwoods or red borders, saying that no, he couldn't find me and might Harriet tell me that he'd come to see me? To see how I was? And Harriet would assure him that yes, she would.

As for Kit, he stayed away. I expected this – he had a harvest to salvage, after all – yet it was hard not to lift my head at any purposeful male tread in the yard. I'd been left with fragments of that night, that was all. Gestures.

How he'd said my name on the lawn with such urgency. Also, *undamaged*, which was the strangest adjective I'd been given; who had ever called me that? Me, with my peculiarities? My plundered ribs and embarrassing gait? Once, I slept all afternoon in the potting shed, woke to find the sun's angle had changed – and, briefly, I thought he was with me.

This was how I spent the first days of war: crouched over my wrist, very small. But what use was this? It wasn't in my nature to tuck myself up, pitiful. So on the fifth day, I brushed myself down, inhaled. Carried on.

He came to Shadowbrook on the second Friday of the month. I did not hear the car, nor his footstep in the garden, but I heard a single, rattling cough. Smelled his tobacco.

He looked precisely the same. The same nonchalant stance. The same faint yellowing on his fingertips and moustache, and I knew that in his pocket he'd have butterscotch.

I was standing near the gold roses. 'You never told me your name,' I said.

'You never asked. I'm Coghlan. Do you know why I'm here, Miss Waterfield?'

'You have news. Or you're taking me to him.'

'His sanatorium is less than an hour away by car.'

'Now?'

'Yes, now. It can't wait.' This flat, simple emphasis on time.

The same car. Within it, the same smell of leather, and I thought of the last time I'd sat here. *Trouble* had been set down before me like bait, neatly done.

'You're not his driver, are you?'

'No. Who do you think I am?'

His profile, too, had not changed in seven weeks. I did not look away from it. 'I think you're a hunter of people. A private detective.'

'Yes. He wrote to me last autumn. He asked me to find two people – his children. Offered good money. His son was easy to find. We had his name, date of birth, hair and eye colour, but even so, I'd have found him quickly. The boy hadn't lived a quiet life; he'd been charged with affray four times in different places. Once, he pushed a fork into the neck of a friend – some friend! – and it made the national papers. He'd written in journals, too, about poltergeists, seances. Something called discarnate entities. God knows. That's how I found him. Wrote to the society he worked for.'

'How did you find me?'

He glanced across. 'You? You were harder. I demanded more money to find you. He only had your gender and year of birth. Your mother's name, too, but she'd have married. Pugh wouldn't have been your own name, I knew that. So I started to look at marriages. And guess what? My lucky day. I saw her name in the paper by chance – her death notice. *Waterfield, née Pugh. Mother of Clara.* So I came to London, followed you. All those buses you took . . . I watched you at Kew.'

He said this so simply, as if it was neither predatory nor strange. And once, I might have been angry at him. I felt it a little, perhaps. But it was done now. 'How did you know? For certain?'

'I told Mr Emerson what you were like – crippled, I mean, and very small – and he said, That's her.'

The sanatorium was on the border with Oxfordshire. It was a long white rectangular building of two storeys, with pitched roofs and balconies and a view over parkland. It looked, at first, like a hotel, or a classical structure or a place of worship. Its front door was between two columns. A glass-covered veranda wound its way round the ground floor, on which I could see beds and wheeled chairs, immaculate nurses with tapping shoes. The windows were all wide open. A lawn as green as a jewel.

'Nothing but the best for him. Even in death.'

Coghlan did not enter with me. Rather, he retrieved a newspaper from the car, found a bench in sunlight and sat down. He took out his cigarette holder, placed a cigarette in his mouth, struck a match – and seemed surprised to find me there, watching. 'Off you go. I'll wait here.'

It echoed inside. Its walls were pale green; its staircase spoke of formal Georgian houses, winding up on three sides of the hallway. Watercolours and portraits hung on its walls. Polished floors. I found a nurse, named him – Emerson, which still seemed an unfamiliar name, so that I said it slowly – and she looked so sorry on hearing it. 'Of course. Can you manage the stairs?' She had seen my sling and rotational gait.

'Yes,' I replied. 'I can manage the stairs.'

Down corridors. Past doorways. Through them, I could see beds, open windows, metallic equipment. A building of glass and air. The nurse spoke as she went: of the age of the building, the benefactor, how they prided themselves on being a very genteel place. And I thought of Mrs Bale's bright, rushing language, which had been to distract me in the early days; I thought of the preparation it took. The planning and forethought.

'How long does he have?' I asked.

At this, the nurse slowed. She seemed surprised, as if everyone knew the answer to this; how did I not know? 'I'm afraid he doesn't have long at all.'

'Days? Weeks?'
'No, not days.'

His room was the last on the second floor. Its door was open, and she entered it without me. I stared at the pale-green walls and heard her soft voice, the movement of a chair. The adjustment of bedding. A single watery cough.

What did I remember of him? That lifetime ago, when I went to his room? His colouring of faded fox. His hands clasped behind him. He'd stood with the desk between us, defensively, and now I knew why. I remembered, too, how he'd observed me, an owl's assessment, as I'd studied the books and tapestries. Had he thought, this is my daughter? Suddenly, I felt I had a choice: I could either back away from this room, return down the corridor and demand to be taken back to Shadowbrook, learning nothing more from him; or I could enter this room as I'd entered others. Defiantly, with a lifted jaw. Thinking, I am not afraid. And I could learn more.

It was, perhaps, no choice at all. I knew myself fully.

The nurse returned. 'He's ready, Miss Waterfield. He's on the balcony. There's a chair for you beside him – near, but not too near.' I thanked her, smoothed my skirts and hair.

In my first week at Shadowbrook, Hollis had spoken of how little time it takes for nature to enter an empty house or a potting shed. Vines will push through broken glass. Leave a pail for a week and it will be inhabited – by rust or beetles, or a greenish bloom.

I remembered this when I saw Mr Fox again. Five weeks since we'd met. This was no time, I knew that, yet he had changed immeasurably. He looked older. He sat in an elongated chair – bed-like, the home of an invalid – and a blanket did not disguise how much he'd reduced in size. He was impossibly thin. His shoulders had narrowed; his scalp showed prominently through his hair. He was so skeletal and translucent that I felt I could see the bones in his forearm. It seemed a skinless wrist.

There has been a mistake. But it was him. Tuberculosis had hollowed him.

'There is,' he said, 'a chair.'

I lowered myself, still watching him.

'I was not sure you would come. But then' – he swallowed – 'I told myself, she is curious. Bold. A reader of books. She will come.'

His voice, too, had changed. I could not recall how he had spoken before but this was a form of wheeze. This was a voice that moved between a clotted dampness and a parched, dry, crackling voice that craved water. His eyes moved in their sockets – he could not, it seemed, move his head – until they found me. 'Clara,' he said. 'Latin, I think? For light? For clarity?'

I wondered what to say. What to offer. He already knew it all, I was sure of that. He knew that George had fallen and died; knew that I'd broken my wrist in my discovery of him at first light. Coghlan or Mrs Bale would have told him this, by letter, or face to face.

'Was he my half-brother?'

A sharp bodily response. He shuddered, leaned forwards. He reached for water, opened his mouth as if already tasting it, and I held the glass against his lips. A childish way of drinking – rhythmically, with half-closed eyes. A droplet ran down his chin.

'She was also,' he said, 'direct. And demanding.'

'Who?'

'Your mother. Forthright. She asked if I had been

admiring her that evening – which I had been, of course. I think the whole room had been. But who might have asked that? Impertinence. Even so, I was quite taken. Would you like to know how we met?'

I might have said no and left. But I said, 'What did you tell her? You were married.'

He frowned. 'You think I lied? Made promises? No. I spoke of my wife and son. She knew.'

'I don't believe you.'

'She knew, Clara. She wasn't innocent. She wasn't ... ' he paused, licked his lips with a textured, colourless tongue, 'led astray by me. She was bored, trapped. She was a bird in a cage in that place – oh, she was restless – and ... ' His eyes returned to me. 'Are you sure you want to know more? I won't waste my last breath on telling you if you don't care. If you won't believe me.'

I looked out at the view. The immaculate gardens rolled down to a fountain – a nymph, holding the water aloft. Beyond this, a wall. And beyond the wall, there was woodland, in which most trees were still verdant but I could make out, too, the first signs of autumn. The quiet browning of leaves. He would not see the autumn. He would not see another August's end or September. And I knew that any anger or frustration I had, or dislike, must be tempered by this knowledge. He might not see nightfall. And I would never sit by his side again. 'Yes.'

He opened his hand. In it, there was a handkerchief. He'd been gripping it for so long that it retained the shape of his grasp – a well; a damp, hollow finger of cloth into which he'd been coughing blood, so that it had soaked through the fabric and reddened his left hand. Money means nothing, I thought. Wealth and investment and gold-headed notepaper and tiger-skin rugs and freshly pressed linen cannot stop

'The locket. Did you leave it for me deliberately? As part of the game?'

'Leave it?'

'Veronique. The V upon it.'

'No. I dropped it, that's all. After Ellie's fall, I couldn't find it. I looked on the stairs. Emptied pockets, felt along the skirting boards ... You found it, didn't you? Gave it to George? My Violet. She posted it to me with her last letter.'

'On the day she died?'

At this moment, it happened. He discarded his indignance and self-protection. His anger, strength and justifications all sank away, as tides do, to reveal the wreck of him. The rusting hulk of his life. The old, heavy chains of regret that he'd carried since her death – or since the girl with the bright green dress had walked barefoot – were here to see. He wheezed into his chest, folded over. He lifted a hand, laid it on his forehead. 'She'd known for a time, I think. She'd guessed, at least, but I told her the truth, one night. And afterwards I travelled north, into China; I was away for weeks, and a letter found me there, in Gansu, telling me what she'd done to herself. Or what she'd intended to do. *By the time you read this* ... I'd given that locket to her. I bought it after our second meeting.'

'What of George?'

'Taken to England. I thought to follow him, but ... I had work. I sent money.'

'You sent money. How kind.'

It made more sense to me now. How, on the night of the thunderstorm, George must have stood on the upper floor and seen the face of the man who for twenty years or more had only sent money. No birthday cards. No arrival in England, begging on his knees.

'And me? How did you know about me?'

'Violet was dead. I'd not returned to Simla for eight months, or nine; I'd had no wish to. But work demanded it, in the end. I looked for your mother – I did – but I heard she'd been sent to England. Had left in disgrace, or so the gossipers said. She'd borne a daughter. I worked out the dates.'

I might have hated that face. I might have thrown water at him or sworn, for what life had this been? So self-involved and dismissive of others? No empathy, George had said. But Mr Emerson coughed then – a thick, convulsive, fibrous expulsion into the cloth. The handkerchief darkened; his body strained and I saw the blood on his chin and under his nostrils, so that I rose to summon a nurse because I thought he was dying – that this was his death – but he gestured at me. Ordered me wordlessly to sit back down. I lowered; I watched the slow, clumsy rearrangement of himself. Saw the swallowing. And I thought that here, too, was an example of a book's limitations, for it might give the technical name for such a projection of blood or for this stage in dying but it couldn't give the disbelief that came with seeing it or the pity that rushed into me, despite it all. Nor could it describe the childlike demeanour to be found in a man who was trying to remove his blood from a blanket in a weak, ineffectual way. His hands were too frail for the task.

'The nurses can't help me now.'

I thought he would rest. But he tried to say more.

'I know how it must seem. Selfish? Yes. Yes, I have been. All I wanted before I died was to' – he swallowed – 'see him again. See the man he'd grown into. And you, too. To see your face. To see my son once more and to meet Charlotte's daughter.'

I could not curse him. These were the last few words of his life. 'Why the deceit? Kew, and Veronique?'

'Why didn't I simply write to you? Tell the truth? You wouldn't have come. Or George would have rushed up with armies or knives, and why not? He had a right to. Also, I wanted to see you as you are, without anger or resentment. Without sniffing the air for inheritance.' His eyes found me, stayed. 'I watched you from my room as you walked through the gardens. And Ellie gave me her thoughts on you. She saw through your armour to your recent loss. Called you sorrowful.'

This old, frail man. He seemed so insubstantial that if I had lifted him up, he'd have powdered; if I'd dared to blow across him, I'd have heard a deep, mourning sound, as a wind draws over a bottle. A well of guilt. Of loneliness and waste. Too late, he'd become wise; there was nothing here to hate.

'I'd hoped to share it all between you – my daughter and my son. But George is ... ' His voice faded. He closed his eyes to see him, the boy who'd been so fair in his youth that locals had wished to touch his hair in case it brought good luck to them. When he looked back at me, his expression was tender. 'Shadowbrook is yours.'

Mr Emerson rested after this. He did not sleep, as such; his eyelids fluttered and he talked to himself – words that were not meant for me. He mentioned a river. Spoke of closing a door, and nodded as if it had been done.

I watched. And I wondered what I was feeling. No contempt or deep anger. No real sadness, although later this would come. I only pitied him. And I told myself to remember this face if I could, for my mother had liked it, briefly.

'*Osteogenesis imperfecta.*'

He opened his eyes, understood. His lungs rattled; his breath moved up to his mouth and he used this short, damp fragment of breath to answer me. 'My uncle. His spine was ...' He tried to hook his forefinger. A wordless form of *like that.*

There was nothing else to say.

Nurses came and went. I was asked if I wished to stay. I'd expected to say no, to rise and leave. But I surprised myself by feeling a need to stay, to watch a second death. It felt a proper courtesy. For if I left him, who would sit with him? Note his last breath?

He stopped breathing at the day's end. He died with his mouth open, with his hands retaining the shape they had had in life, holding the blanket's edge. A small, feeble demise.

Downstairs, I found Coghlan. He rose from his bench, walked over to me.

'Dead?'

'Yes.'

We stood for a moment in silence, acknowledging this. I looked up, saw the undersides of birds. Also, I saw how we'd opened the window one winter, my mother and I, reached out for snow, and I remembered how happy I had felt in that moment; I could not have been happier. We'd called for Patrick and Millicent, and they had joined us in reaching out. And I thought, looking up, of my fortune. Of how lucky I'd been.

Coghlan lit a cigarette, inhaled. 'Ready?' he asked. Blew the smoke out.

I nodded. 'Yes.' We walked towards the car, drove away.

XVI

I did not speak to others of the death of Rex Emerson. It felt too intimate, too frail, as if sharing it would break it further. To talk of his last expression or words would seem a betrayal, although no loyalties had been spoken of. Yet they all knew, soon enough. His obituary – paid for in advance and written by him – was placed in *The Times* in early September; in it, he had named Shadowbrook House, and this was enough for the surrounding villages to decipher the truth of this lying fox. I read the obituary in the kitchen, one afternoon, as I ate the last of the summer plums. *His Gloucestershire estate will be inherited by his daughter.* I slowed in my eating. Here it was. The truth in newspaper print.

I was no longer the girl from Kew. I was the heiress who undressed for Kit Preedy. Who had lived as the reckless Pettigrew woman had done, in her ermine and pearls. I sought sympathy, they said, by wearing my sling for over two months and not using my cane when in truth the fractures proved slow to heal; they were intricate, severe. George had used all his force, after all. And I didn't care that they spoke of me like this. I didn't care that conversation stopped when I entered the shop, for I knew the real, proper truth; I thought, I know more than you. But there was, too, a third rumour, and I minded that. My father, they said, had

333

secreted himself on the upper floor because his bones had been like mine, or worse. He'd been a hunchback. Or he'd been so entirely disfigured that he'd lived in half-darkness, turned mirrors to the wall. Harriet shared these whispers with me, and they angered me, felt unfair. When I heard them directly in the market at Stow, I answered back.

Yet even these rumours were laid aside, in time. As the summer grew old, the talk of war grew stronger. The men shook hands with each other, clapped one another on the shoulder. They'd emerge from The Bull, climb onto the ancient oak and call through cupped hands: *To war!* A promised land. But they could not leave yet. It was a fine, sun-bright September: there was fruit to pick and hay to bale; the garden boys had to cut the beech hedges for the last time that year, and I'd watch them from the veranda and hear their talk of battalions and rank. The function of the bayonet. They'd try French words between them, laughing: *Albert, avez-vous?*

This seasonal work felt safe and expected. Blackberries and the raking of leaves was far removed from any trouble, old or new. And as the days began to shorten, I'd look to the south-east corner of Shadowbrook and the barley fields and the long stone walls. I did not think Kit would come. But I thought I might see him walking his boundaries, examining the barley's condition. Leading his horses between pastures or mending sections of wall. I thought stories might come from The Bull – of an exchange of words, or fight – but no stories reached me. The lichen grew back on the Preedy graves and Kit, it seemed, stayed out of sight.

I finally returned to the orchard in the first days of September, and found others there. Stepladders were propped under branches; fruit was passed down from hand to hand. The orchard was, on those days, apple-scented. And after the boys had gone, blackbirds and thrushes came for the fruit that had been discarded – too soft, too old.

Veronique. I knew I had stowed her away for a time. Since the night of George's death, I'd felt unable to think of her; I'd had too many other thoughts and had chosen them – they had come first. But now, I felt able to say her name. And in doing so, I felt she was no less present or observant than she'd been before I knew the proper truth. There was, of course, no proof of her. The locket had been another's; the marked door had been admitted to. But the sense of being watched in the orchard, at that moment, was as strong as it had been in her room of dust or the upper corridor or the gardens at dusk. No, she hadn't been who I'd imagined her to be. But nor had my mother. Nor had any of us.

The birds pecked at the windfall fruit. And slowly, I imagined the Veronique who in her teens had read books behind curtains or under tables. She'd been quick to leave rooms, and now I knew why. This black, abominable truth. These unconscionable acts. Her younger life had not been her own, and whilst I had no wish to think of this, I also knew I could not turn from her years of endurance as if they hadn't happened to her, as if she hadn't feared the slow, deliberate, nocturnal approach to her bedroom door. Whilst I wanted to think that she'd hardened herself against it – sealed herself, protected her soul and her woman's heart, so that she'd looked over the fields thinking defiantly, *one day I will* . . . – I did not doubt that she'd also cried into darkness. Had pushed what she could against her door.

This truth must be stared at, I knew that much. But also, it wasn't all she'd been. Kit was not only a murderer's son.

I was more than substandard bones. And Veronique would not be defined by the acts of others, or by her last name. So I remembered what I'd been told by those I trusted: that she'd played the piano. That she'd stand in windows and watch the ploughing. That she loved novels, so that I imagined her running a forefinger over their spines in the library before thinking, this one, and taking it down. Resolve in her. A real, lasting pleasure in flowers. Later, how she'd write notes of gratitude to Hollis and place them beside his week's wages, wrapped in brown paper. I'd think of her lying in woodland at dusk, a guest of the owl.

Yes, this was Veronique. Resolute. Wise and surviving and inheriting, and still able to see beauty, so that Kit's words to me – *I've never seen anything more beautiful than her* – had a far deeper meaning now. She rose, star-like. She marvelled at gifts like a chestnut leaf. And I supposed that maybe Rex Emerson's prediction would come true: that a time would come, in the future, when the soul would be identified in a theatre or laboratory; it would be held in the cupped hands of surgeons or mathematicians or philosophers or priests, and they'd wonder at the fact that, for millennia, this part of a human had only been hoped for. How strange, they might say, that nobody knew! Yes, one day there might be proof. Until then, I did not need it. We can think with our hearts as much as our heads – and souls, for me, were the truth.

Sometimes I met Hollis there. He'd be standing in the same manner each time, with a fork or spade planted before him and his forearms resting on its handle. A contemplative pose. He might look up at the empty boughs and changing leaves or consider the grass, but mostly he'd gaze at her grave.

'I've always come here, that's the truth,' he said. 'In those thirteen years in which Shadowbrook was empty, I'd bring my flask here and talk to her. I never told you that. I've not tended to the orchard in years, but it's my favourite part.'

Guilt in him. I asked very little – I'd lost, perhaps, my wish to learn more after so much hard education – but I let him talk, if he chose to. Only if he chose. And gradually, he opened up. He'd talk of how he wished, even now, he'd done more. How he could have gone to other constabularies – in Warwickshire or Oxfordshire – who weren't friends with the Pettigrews and who might have come forwards, entered the house. 'I should have done this. I should have done. Instead I planted and grew any flowers that might suit vases. Sweet peas or dahlia. I'd leave them by the kitchen door for her and I'd see them later, on windowsills. And the rose? The yellow rose? I planted it so that it might reach the upper floor for her. Was that enough, do you think?'

No, I thought. It wasn't enough. But it was something, at least. And what else might he have managed, with his gentle nature? It was Bill Preedy who'd ended it; he'd provided the greatest peace for Veronique at his own greatest cost – and I understood why the Preedy farm was Kit's, now; why it was no longer rented land. She'd left it to him in her will, just as she'd made sure that Hollis would always remain here, trimming the topiary trees and digging the plots for as long as the house remained standing. Her acknowledgement. Her gifts of gratitude.

'There was no chance,' Hollis said, 'of her being buried with those men, in the same grave. Never. We chose here for her – Kit and I. Here was the right resting place for her.' And it was, with its leaf fall and its silences. With the four distinct seasons showing themselves in the trees.

*

I came to know Hollis better that autumn. We talked of what we knew: the real name of Mr Fox, his tuberculosis, how the glasshouse had been a trick to bring me here from Kew. War, and preparations for winter. But Hollis – like everyone else – did not know that the ghost had been a lie. Did not know that the lower garden had not, in fact, been where George had died. Nor did he know of George's history, or his true identity; these truths were never spoken of between us, or elsewhere. They stayed hidden, somehow – bone-like – and it suited me that they did.

As we left the orchard together one afternoon, with rain in the air, the gardener said, 'I never cared for him very much. Charming, of course. And the garden boys followed him and spoke of him, and he was good to them, I know. But I heard what he said in The Bull. Those weren't the words of a man to be trusted.'

'About Veronique?'

'Veronique?' He wrinkled his nose, not understanding. 'No, Clara. George talked of you – didn't you know this? I won't repeat the words but they were ungentlemanly, I'll say that much. Unsavoury. Kit was never the kind to endure such talk about women, as his father was not. That's why they had their exchange that night ... I think there's rain coming; don't you agree?'

I stared at this knowledge for days: that Kit had protested. That he'd lifted himself from his stool, crossed the room with the single intention of stopping the mouth of this tall, strong man for my sake. Mine. And hadn't he moved George's body for me? At his own suggestion? Called me undamaged, as if my bones were well-made? I gathered these fragments, one by one.

Here is a confession: that as I peeled vegetables with Harriet or washed my hair or ventured into the beeches as the leaves were coming down, I daydreamed. In doing so, I formed a quiet truth of my own. *Yes, you are different*: had there been, in fact, a compliment in that? Had *different* been a good adjective, for the first and only time? I decided so. For this was, very simply, what I wished the truth to be: that in the drawing room, Kit had not refused me easily. That a part of him had, in fact, whispered yes without hesitation – and he'd wanted to cross the room to me. But he was not without his principles; undamaged had not meant unbroken to him, but undimmed by life, untouched. *New*, he'd said. And wouldn't a thousand other men have answered differently? Taken advantage of this request? An Emerson? Or a Pettigrew guest? Explorers who found an unclaimed land?

I liked believing this. It helped to think that yes, Kit had also imagined us coupling, as the rest of Barcombe had done. That he was, in fact, imagining it now, at this moment. For I thought of it all the time. I thought of him pulling his shirt over his head in a swift, practised movement and dropping it on the nearest chair. Of how he might lift my hair away from my face with his forearm, as if shielding his eyes. Did he also think of our bodies? Or of my body, on its own? Of where it might need the most care? At night, I told myself: yes, he dreams of this and remembers these dreams on waking.

Kit's barley was harvested, at last, by the travelling gangs of men who carried the same shape as him, whose shirts, like his, were discoloured. They scythed through the fields in lines; when they drank water, they poured the flask over themselves.

I saw this from my land. I stood at my boundary deliberately, moved my eyes over the men with the hope of seeing him. For a while, he wasn't there. But later in the day, I did see him. He came into sight with his shirt untucked and stained from work; he stopped by the cart, talked with the others as they passed a flask between them and he pointed towards the farthest corner to show his meaning to them. He saw me, then. He lowered his arm, looked for a second or two. And he might have looked for longer – motionless, caught by this – but the conversation carried on and needed him so he returned his attention to the gathered men, and I stayed, watching. A breeze found my hair; I held it back from my face to see him better as he clapped his hand on the flank of a horse, seized an armful of fastened crop and hauled it into the waiting cart. He did this several times before walking away.

I willed him to look back. I thought he would not. But at the last moment, as his field began to roll downhill so that I lost his lower half, Kit glanced over his shoulder casually, as if at nothing. But he stilled, on finding me watching him.

I was always the one for facts and words. But we gazed at each other momentarily – with horses between us, and scythes and noise and other men calling – and I decided that this was enough. It was not definite proof, as such. But I knew what I longed for, and thought of. So I chose to believe it was.

'Albert,' Harriet told me, 'is packing his bag to go. He says everyone is doing it.'

So it was, as September grew old. I'd venture down to Jarvis's – how he hated that I owned Shadowbrook now; how, in truth, I enjoyed that he did – and buy a newspaper in which I read such words as *expeditionary* for the first time. And in the village, I saw how unafraid they were, these men and boys lifting bags onto shoulders. War had no dark meaning for them. It was, rather, their mothers and wives and sweethearts who had the pale faces, who touched

quick, brief smile. 'It's a curious thing. How often have we spoken, you and I? Not often, I know. But it's been enough for me to note your inquisitiveness. Your directness. Clara, you understand that most women do not travel alone, or question their faith so openly, or have the knowledge to establish a tropical garden under glass.'

'They could, if allowed. If encouraged to.'

'Even so, I have stared at the same page of the Bible for hours and not read a word because I've been thinking of you. You think the cane is all people see as they pass you? No. They see other qualities. Boldness and curiosity. There is a naturalness, too – no ornamentation or care for it – so that you walk through fields and wear your hair as you do. And what you've endured ... In short, I've been ... ' He paused, unsure of the words. 'Distracted. Lost. Clara, I may not be the smartest of men. But I know – and accept, I do – that your feelings for me are not the same. And I do not tell you of my feelings now to persuade you; I can't believe you're the kind who can be persuaded, and why might I do that anyway? One wants sentiment to be offered freely, not coaxed. I simply tell you this because I want to. Because how can I stand in that pulpit and speak of honesty without being honest myself? With you? This, too, has been weighing upon me.'

He searched my expression. He saw in it that I had not guessed this.

'No, I don't suppose you knew. You've carried *cripple* for so long – since that wretched vicar of your childhood, who's angered me so much that I've had trouble sleeping. And if I may say so, I sensed you were circling your grief and not entering it. Sometimes, I've imagined stepping into church and finding you in a pew, as I have done this morning. But other times, I've been glad of your absence, because what might I have done if you'd come to me, Clara? Seeking comfort in the word of God, or in me? I'd have stuttered the words. I'd have wanted to set the word of God down to one side and tell you about Mrs Bale's lie. Read the Song of Solomon.'

I could not take my eyes from him. The arms of his spectacles. His throat's movement as he spoke. I felt, suddenly, terribly sad. I wanted to cry. Felt a pain in my chest.

Matthew gave a soft, reassuring smile. 'There's no need to be sorry for this. It's life, Clara. There are worse hardships. And I am wiser for it all; I'm a better man and vicar – both. So don't be sad for me, please. Take heart in it. I only told you for the best reasons.'

This seemed to be where he wished to end it. For he rose, talked of the light through the window at that precise moment; how the sun, at this time of year, lit different parts of the coloured glass. I walked with him down the aisle, heard his words on the imminent departures for war, but in my head, I only heard his talk of my inquisitiveness and how this, for him, had been an attractive quality. I wondered if I should ask more or thank him. Touch his forearm. But in the porch, he stopped. It was abrupt, as if something within the porch had startled him, but I only saw the boot-scraper and the bowl for the dogs in which there were leaves.

He addressed this bowl. 'I have no right to ask you what I'm going to. And you have, therefore, every right not to answer. But for honesty's sake – and for my sake, perhaps – will you consider giving an answer? The rumours, Clara. Of you and the farmer. Are they true?'

All I wanted, in that moment, was to tell the proper truth. Matthew stood before me. Kind. Honest, now. As tense as a wire. With eyes that seemed to implore through their lenses. I knew that he had his own preferred answer; that as he stood in the porch, he wished me to say no, the rumours of Kit and me were not true. That the farmer had never even touched me – either intentionally or in passing – and I had no desire for him to. Matthew wished to hear this; I, in turn, wished to offer it. I noticed the pulse at the base of his throat, near his collarbone. This rhythm of him.

But how could I tell him? Our lie – Kit's and mine – had not been created casually. And Kit's throat, too, had its own pulse, which I wished to keep beating and strong. If I confessed our lie to the vicar – at this very moment, in the porch – what might he do with the news? Keep it safe? He might. But also, he might be unable to. For a man had died of a single, hard injury and we had lied about how that death took place.

I could not confess to him.

I nodded once. 'They're all true.'

Instinctively, he smiled. Held up his hands as if the apology was his, for having intruded, for having asked at all. 'Of course. Forgive me.' He walked on and I followed, looking for his expression, wanting to check his words for signs of injury. But he spoke of the war, not Kit: the enlistment queues, the songs he'd heard, the expected duration. 'They say it will be short-lived. I hope so.' And then he remarked, brightly – too brightly – on the oak tree's gradual change in colour, how there would be many acorns this year, so that I wondered if I might have imagined the conversation in which he'd mentioned my unexplored grief and sentiment and the Song of Solomon.

Within the week, Matthew had enlisted for the war. He did not have to; it was understood that the clergy were needed at home. The parents and wives would look to him in the coming months; his sermons and companionship were required. Many of the parishioners reminded him of this, pleaded. I heard that Mrs Collier – against the war from the start, distrustful of laws and government orders – seized his cuff in communion, pulled him closer and urged him to stay. But Matthew reasoned with her – and, later, from his pulpit – that perhaps their sons and brothers and husbands needed him a little more. The Lord's comfort, whilst fighting. A known face.

He was, therefore, like a swallow himself. He'd spent time here, in the church; he'd formed a temporary home and moved through English fields in their finest weather. But now, he would fly south.

He took the train to London, the boat to Calais – and in 1916, Matthew died at the Somme in an unnamed, unspecified way: *died in action*, which said nothing to us except that his body was broken somehow. A lingering death, or an instant one? In a hospital tent or in mud or on wire? It mattered to us. For we had believed, somehow, that he'd be spared at least – that the bullets could not enter clergymen, that he'd be able to pass through shelling or gas – so that his death felt symbolic as well as true. But there was no more news to find on him. On a rainy day, the notice with its bland, shallow words was pinned to the church door; we gathered around it. And long after the others had walked away, I remained.

We'd never know how he died, so I formed a truth, as we tend to. And the truth became that, one night, Matthew saw a star. Or it seemed to be a star, at least – to have a star's beauty. He took off his helmet in reverence of it, this extraordinary brightness above a devastated place. But it was not a star: the enemy had flung it high, and in falling, it killed Matthew instantly along with other men, and whilst there was no comfort in this bodily loss of him, I found comfort in believing it had been a radiant death. That he